Praise for *Awakened by a Kiss*

"Lila DiPasqua's lushly erotic writing is sophisticated, sensuous, and deeply romantic. If you love historical romance, this is an author to watch!" —Elizabeth Hoyt, *New York Times* bestselling author

"The most luscious, sexy take on classic fairy tales I've ever read! The three heroes are delicious!"
—Cheryl Holt, *New York Times* bestselling author

"An erotically charged retelling of classic stories. Steamy yet sweet, DiPasqua expertly melds emotionally charged erotica with fantasy, love, and hope, leaving no doubt as to the happily ever after. These are not your mother's fairy tales!"

—Kathryn Smith, *USA Today* bestselling author

"Lila DiPasqua brilliantly pens three unique stories filled with mirth, passion, and sinfully charming heroes." —*Romance Junkies*

"*Awakened by a Kiss* is a sinfully erotic collection of multilayered plots and characters that's sure to please."
—*Lovin' Me Some Romance*

"I would highly recommend this book to anyone who loves HOT romance filled with sumptuous fantasy." —*Bookaholics*

"Three fantastic stories that will take you away into a world of fairy tale romance, capturing your heart as well as your emotions . . . Love scenes that will light the pages on [fire] . . ." —[Ju]zie

Berkley Sensation titles by Lila DiPasqua

Awakened by a Kiss
The Princess in His Bed

The Princess
in His Bed

Lila DiPasqua

BERKLEY SENSATION, NEW YORK

THE BERKLEY PUBLISHING GROUP
Published by the Penguin Group
Penguin Group (USA) Inc.
375 Hudson Street, New York, New York 10014, USA

Penguin Group (Canada), 90 Eglinton Avenue East, Suite 700, Toronto, Ontario M4P 2Y3, Canada
(a division of Pearson Penguin Canada Inc.)
Penguin Books Ltd., 80 Strand, London WC2R 0RL, England
Penguin Group Ireland, 25 St. Stephen's Green, Dublin 2, Ireland (a division of Penguin Books Ltd.)
Penguin Group (Australia), 250 Camberwell Road, Camberwell, Victoria 3124, Australia
(a division of Pearson Australia Group Pty. Ltd.)
Penguin Books India Pvt. Ltd., 11 Community Centre, Panchsheel Park, New Delhi—110 017, India
Penguin Group (NZ), 67 Apollo Drive, Rosedale, North Shore 0632, New Zealand
(a division of Pearson New Zealand Ltd.)
Penguin Books (South Africa) (Pty.) Ltd., 24 Sturdee Avenue, Rosebank, Johannesburg 2196,
South Africa

Penguin Books Ltd., Registered Offices: 80 Strand, London WC2R 0RL, England

This book is an original publication of The Berkley Publishing Group.

This is a work of fiction. Names, characters, places, and incidents either are the product of the author's imagination or are used fictitiously, and any resemblance to actual persons, living or dead, business establishments, events, or locales is entirely coincidental. The publisher does not have any control over and does not assume any responsibility for author or third-party websites or their content.

Copyright © 2010 by Lila DiPasqua.
Cover illustration by Sam Montasano.
Cover design by George Long.
Interior text design by Laura K. Corless.

PRINTING HISTORY
Berkley Sensation trade paperback edition / November 2010

Library of Congress Cataloging-in-Publication Data

DiPasqua, Lila.
    The princess in his bed / Lila DiPasqua.—Berkley Sensation trade pbk. ed.
        p. cm.
    ISBN 978-0-425-23700-7 (trade pbk.)
    I. Title.
    PS3604.I625P75 2010
    813'.6—dc22

                                                2010031426

PRINTED IN THE UNITED STATES OF AMERICA

10 9 8 7 6 5 4 3 2 1

To my children and my very own Prince Charming, Carm.
To my editor, Kate Seaver; editorial assistant, Katherine Pelz;
and my agent, Caren Johnson Estesen, all of whom work magic
every day in their own special ways. To Carolyn Williams,
Donna Jeffery, Franca Pelaccia, Vickie Marise, and
Mary Barone, who are the best critique partners
anyone can wish for.

And to my readers who share my love of fairy tales
and a happily ever after.

A Historical Tidbit

The court of Louis XIV was as decadent as it was opulent. It was a time of high culture, elegance, and excesses. The pursuit of sinful pleasures was a pastime. Sex, an art form. Louis was a lusty king. He and his courtiers were connoisseurs of the carnal arts.

It was during this wicked time period that authors first began writing down fairy tales—the folklore that had been passed on verbally for generations. It wasn't long before fairy tales became a highly fashionable topic of discussion in the renowned salons of Paris. Though the fairy tales in this collection were made famous by Hans Christian Andersen, a Danish poet and author, perhaps his muse was stirred by hearing stories about characters such as these . . .

Happy Reading!

Lila

Contents

The Marquis'
New Clothes

1

[faintly visible text bleeding through from reverse side of page]

"My life is over!" Louise d'Arcy exclaimed the moment after she'd yanked Aimee inside her elegant private apartments and slammed the door shut.

Aimee de Miran sighed. She'd just arrived at Versailles. Her sojourn at the palace was only ten minutes long and already she was rethinking her plan to attend court and visit with her cousin.

Dear Louise was always in the midst of chaos. It seemed now was no different.

Parched from the long carriage ride, Aimee walked over to the pitcher of water and orange slices on the ebony side table and promptly filled two crystal goblets. "Louise, darling, I'm certain your life isn't over." She held a goblet out to her cousin. "Now why don't you tell me what's wrong."

"What's wrong? Renault is what's wrong. He's cast me aside!"

Wringing her hands, Louise began to pace, completely oblivious to Aimee's extended arm and the goblet of fresh water being offered.

Aimee availed herself of the refreshment instead and set the goblet down.

A lovers' spat. Nothing new.

"I see." That would be all she'd need to say for the next hour while Louise ranted. When she was done, her cousin would collapse in a chair, quite theatrically, and weep for at least twenty more minutes.

Aimee had been through this before. Many times. Louise was always having spats with her longtime lover, Renault de Sard.

Louise stopped dead in her tracks. "No, you don't see. You've no idea what has occurred. Everything is a mess. And it's over this time! Truly over!" Her hazel eyes filled with tears. "He'll not have anything more to do with me. He's said so!" She dropped her face into her palms and sobbed.

Aimee approached and put a consoling arm around her cousin. Of similar age, they'd always been close. She did adore Louise, despite her histrionics. "Louise, it will work out. You'll see. He always comes back."

"Not this time," she said without lifting her head, the words muffled by her hands.

"You say that every time."

Her cousin's head shot up. "This time it's true!"

"You say *that* every time, too."

Louise let out a sharp breath. "Aimee, he favors another! I have been replaced. He's with Diane de Millon. I'm no longer his mistress at all! I tell you, he is a horrible, *horrible* cad! He purposely misled me."

"Oh? Misled you how?"

"I was positively thrilled when he asked me to accompany

him to the palace for his regular official visit with the King. He'd been so cold and distant lately that I didn't think he'd permit me to attend this time. In truth, his plan was to bring me here to end our affair. He thought I wouldn't pitch a fit at the palace. And do you know what I did?'

"You pitched a fit at the palace."

"No. Well . . . yes." Louise waved her hand dismissively. "But that was in private. And that's not what I'm talking about." Her cousin began to pace and wring her hands again. "I did something. Something terrible. Something I regret."

Trepidation was mounting in Aimee. Louise always had a flare for the dramatic, but . . . Aimee couldn't shake the disquieting feeling tightening in her stomach. There was a certain look in Louise's eyes that made her a little anxious.

"What did you do?"

Her cousin smoothed her hands down her gown. A habit. Something Louise always did when she was nervous. Or uneasy. Or terribly guilty.

"Well, you see . . ." Louise began and smoothed her hands down her gown again. "You must understand, I was quite angry with Renault at the time, and very hurt by his cutting coldness toward me. So I . . ."

Aimee braced herself. Having no idea what she was about to hear, her instincts told her it was going to be bad. Quite bad. "You *what*?"

"I took something of his."

"Took?"

"All right, I *stole*. There, I said it. Is that better? I *stole* something he holds dear."

Good Lord. This was a new low, even for Louise. "What on earth did you steal?"

Louise threw up her hands. "The man has never given me *any-thing*, Aimee. In all these years, no lover's trinket. No jewelry at all! I felt he owed me at least that much."

Aimee struggled with her patience. "Louise . . . What. Did. You. Take?"

"His jeweled ring. One of the ones given to him by the King."

"Oh, Louise, you didn't."

"I did!" Louise flopped down onto the nearby chair, dropped her face into her palms again, and wept audibly.

Aimee shook her head, dismayed. Of all the predicaments Louise had landed herself in, this one was by far the most shocking. "Didn't it occur to you that Renault is the King's Lieutenant General of Police? A man who is overzealous when it comes to the duties of his post and would arrest his own mother for the most minor infraction?"

Louise looked up. "Well, not at the time, but it certainly has over the last few hours . . ." She choked on a sob. "What am I going to do? My life is over! He'll throw me in one of those horrible cells without batting an eye. If he's angry enough, he could have orders drawn up against me, and I'll be held without trial— for who knows how long."

Aimee took in a fortifying breath and let it out slowly. She walked over to her distressed kin and placed a hand on her shoulder. "Everything is going to be fine. We can remedy this problem. This really isn't as great a dilemma as you think it is."

Her cousin swiped away the tears on her cheek. "Oh, but it is."

"No it isn't. You will return the ring with a sincere apology—"

"I can't."

"You're right. The man is so rigid and uncompromising, he won't understand. I have it," Aimee said as an idea occurred to her. "You'll sneak into his rooms and put the ring back, without him being the wiser."

"I can't do that either."

Aimee frowned. "What do you mean, you can't?"

"I lost the ring."

"You *what*?"

Louise rose from the chair. "Well, it's not entirely lost. I know where it is. Sort of."

"Where in the name of God is it—*sort of*?"

"When I was in the Hall of Mirrors yesterday, it was very crowded, as usual. I was bumped from behind, and it fell out of my hand and into the pocket of one of the courtiers."

"Do you know who?"

"I do. The Marquis de Nattes."

Aimee's heart missed a beat. "Adam de Vey, Marquis de Nattes?" she questioned, hoping she'd heard wrong.

"Yes. Exactly." Her cousin grasped Aimee's hands and squeezed them. "Aimee, I can't let Renault learn what I did. If the ring is found on the Marquis de Nattes's person, Renault would never believe he stole the ring. He has one of his own from the King. You must help me get the ring back before Renault discovers it missing. He'll not stop until he uncovers the thief. Me!"

This was only getting worse. She didn't like the direction this conversation was taking. "What exactly are you suggesting I do?"

For the first time since Aimee entered the room, her cousin smiled. "You know as well as I do the Marquis de Nattes would be receptive to any attention you would give him. Since Marc died, he looks at you 'that' way. You could easily get close enough to him to search his clothes."

Aimee's brows shot up. "Have you gone mad? You want me to encourage that libertine just so I can dip my hands in his pockets in search of your ring?"

"Precisely. And perhaps you can search his armoire in his

private apartments, too. The man does have a rather extensive wardrobe . . ."

"No. Absolutely not." Adam de Vey was the worst sort of man. The very type she detested. He was no different from her late husband. Beautiful as sin. A master at seduction.

And completely faithless.

A man who believed women were interchangeable. Who cared nothing of what he did to a woman's heart. Only what he did with her body.

It was no wonder that the Marquis de Nattes and her late husband, Marc, Comte de Gremont, had been friends. They were of like mind and poor character. Since Marc's death on the dueling field three years ago—a duel over his favorite paramour at the time—Aimee thankfully had had nothing more to do with her late husband's licentious friends.

Louise's bottom lip began to tremble, her eyes welling with fresh tears. "Renault will show me no mercy. He cares nothing for me at all now. If—If you don't help me . . . then I will surely be arrested, Aimee. You won't let that happen, will you? You'll help me, won't you?"

The pitiful look on her cousin's face tugged at Aimee's heart fiercely. She wanted to help her, but . . . she'd noticed the lingering looks Adam had given her since Marc's death, too. The last thing she wanted to do was to make him believe she'd be receptive to him.

"Louise . . . There's got to be another way . . ."

"There isn't! Oh, please, Aimee. I haven't anyone else who can help . . . I know you don't care for Adam de Vey, but think of it this way: You can do something most women cannot. You can easily flirt with Adam, yet resist him, and in the end do what no female has done—rebuff him."

Now, that did have a certain appeal. Men like the Marquis de Nattes toyed with so many women, luring them with their polished manner, potent sensuality, their false affections. She would definitely love to play him. Lure him. She could flirt a little. Draw close enough to locate the ring and save Louise.

She was likely one of the few women in the realm who'd resist his allure.

After giving herself over to her husband—heart, body, and soul—leaving herself open to the humiliation and heartbreak she'd ultimately endured, Aimee knew she'd never fall into the arms of another rake like Marc again.

"All right," tumbled from her mouth.

Louise squeaked with joy and threw her arms around Aimee. "Thank you! I knew I could count on your help."

Aimee sighed. "I don't suppose you have any idea what he was wearing when you dropped the ring?"

"I do!" Louise was finally smiling again. "He was wearing a blue justacorps."

"Blue? That's it?"

"I know how much the man adores fine clothing, and I did hear he had a new wardrobe delivered two days ago, but really, how many blue justacorps could he have in all?"

True. But given the number of knee-length coats he owned, what were the chances he'd wear the same blue justacorps again anytime soon? Just how mindful was he of such things?

"Between the two of us, we'll be able to locate the ring quickly and easily," Louise said confidently.

Aimee couldn't believe she'd become embroiled in this mad plan. Outfoxing a seasoned roué; locating and lifting a ring out from under the nose of a man who, by his very womanizing nature, was highly attuned to the opposite sex. Reading women was his forte. He knew how to detect signs of amorous interest and sexual desire. Her performance would have to be believable and flawless, despite her limited skills at being a coquette.

Success hinged on her ability to stay focused. The problem was, she hadn't been touched by a man in over three long empty years. Though she'd never admit it to anyone, she yearned to have a man's arms around her. The press of his hard body against hers. His body inside her. Her marriage bed had been most satisfying. Too satisfying. There had been many nights she wished her late husband had never introduced her to the pleasures of sex. That his conjugal visits had been more typical of his peers—brief. Obligatory. For the purposes of procreation only.

Awakening her to physical delights had caused her nothing but suffering.

For many reasons.

But no matter how much she desired a lover, she *wouldn't* take a man like the Marquis de Nattes to satisfy her carnal cravings.

For Louise's sake, Aimee had to succeed. She couldn't fail. She *would* best Adam in this cat-and-mouse game they were about to play.

And she was going to use his libertine nature to her advantage.

* * *

Adam de Vey, Marquis de Nattes, surveyed the various justacorps— fitted knee-length coats of various fabrics and colors. He'd had a second armoire placed in his private apartments to hold his recently arrived new clothes.

Doors to both armoires were open wide as he decided on his attire for the afternoon. The news of Aimee's arrival made his selection a little more important. Made his heart beat faster, and his blood course hotter just knowing she was close by.

Adam couldn't believe his luck. Just when he'd reached his

breaking point. Just when he'd been racking his mind, trying to orchestrate an opportunity to spend time under the same roof with the dark-haired beauty, she fortuitously showed up at the palace. He'd no idea when he'd been summoned by the King for an official meeting that she'd be in attendance at Versailles as well.

It was a good sign. A great sign. Somehow the stars had aligned and he was getting what he'd been wishing for for years. Access to Aimee. She wouldn't be able to leave anytime soon either. The King took personal offense to brief visits at the palace.

Her stay would have to be no less than half a month. Plenty of time for him to do something that he should have done long ago.

Bed her.

It was going to be a challenge—his very first when it came to seducing a woman.

Dressed in black breeches and a white linen shirt, he watched as his loyal servant pulled out yet another justacorps, this one gold-colored, and brought it to him.

Adam touched the silk sleeve. "Not this one, Laurent," he said. Too bold.

The man, ten years his senior, returned the gold overcoat to the armoire.

"Really, Adam, I don't understand your interest in all these clothes." Reclining in a plush chair, his fingers laced behind his head, his friend Robert, Comte de Senville, smiled.

"I like the finer things in life. Fine clothes. A fine château. Fine women." Aimee de Miran was by far the finest he'd ever laid eyes on.

"How is this, my lord?" Laurent held before him a red justacorps. Also bold. "I don't think so."

He was looking for something more understated. A quiet elegance. Just like Aimee.

"All this trouble for a tumble. Don't think I don't know you're

planning on seducing Aimee de Miran. And it's about time, I say."
Chuckling, Robert crossed his arms over his chest and shook his
head. "Six years . . . *Dieu!*"

Adam placed his hands on his hips, cursing the night he'd gotten drunk last month and let it slip to Robert about his longtime
fascination with their dead friend's wife.

Ignoring Robert's irksome remarks was easier than ignoring
his own hardened cock—his body's natural reaction to the mere
thought of the lovely Comtesse de Gremont.

From the moment he'd met her, during her betrothal to Marc,
she'd incited his libido. He'd spent a ridiculous amount of time
famished for this woman.

Merde. He could make no sense of this incessant, unbreakable
pull to her. His desire for her plagued him. Haunted him. The
longer it went on, the more it tormented him.

The stronger it got.

So she was beautiful, elegant, graceful, and intelligent. There
were others who shared those qualities. So Marc had boasted
that his wife was passionate and sensual and highly receptive
to his husbandly rights—a woman who saw her marriage bed
as enjoyable rather than as a duty. So what? There were other
women who enjoyed sex.

He'd fucked scores of them.

Nothing he did got golden-eyed Aimee de Miran out of his
head. Out of his system. Not time. Or women. He was tired
of wanting her—and worse, comparing other women to her. It
drove him to distraction.

Jésus-Christ. He couldn't recall the last time he'd bedded a
woman when Aimee hadn't intruded into his mind, where he
didn't fantasize it was her he was buried inside.

For the last six years, Adam had kept his distance from Marc's
beautiful wife for two reasons. First and foremost, Aimee was in

love with her husband, and he never poached where real feelings were involved. Second, Marc was a friend—one who was completely undeserving of his wife's affections. Marc knew full well he'd stirred her heart. He'd laughed about it and found it "adorable," and without discretion of any kind, bedded every woman who crossed his path.

"What about the blue, my lord?"

Adam scrutinized the blue-gray justacorps held out before him.

It was of the finest cloth, yet not boastful. And a fine cut, too. "Perfect."

"I think the lady will be most impressed, my lord." Laurent smiled as he handed him the matching vest—Laurent's usual statement whenever he sensed Adam had a new conquest in mind.

Adam slipped on his vest. "Do you now, Laurent?"

"I think you overestimate your charm." Adam could hear the humor in Robert's tone.

He glanced at Robert. "I think you should leave the lady to me and concern yourself with the King, and whether or not he'll approve of our drawings and ideas." Adam slipped on the justacorps with Laurent's assistance.

A member of the Royal Academy of Sciences, he was recognized for his engineering expertise. Over the years, Adam had worked on a number of projects for the crown—the fortification of strongholds in case of attack. Now with the country at peace, at least for the time being, Louis had turned his attention to his prized palace. Versailles. Unhappy with the water pressure of his fountains, His Majesty had asked Adam to offer a solution to rectify the deficiency the original engineers had produced.

Robert stood and walked over to him, grinning. "It's far more fun watching Adam de Vey fail for the first time with a woman." He placed his hand on Adam's shoulder. "In all seriousness, the lady doesn't much care for either of us. Marc broke her heart. She sees us as being no different from her late husband."

That much he knew.

But Adam wasn't looking for her love. Or to replace Marc in her heart, if he was still there. He was looking for a few hours of shared carnal pleasure. He simply wanted to, no—had to—put an end to this inexplicable mental and physical torment. And there was only one way to kill the longing—and that was to have Aimee every which way he could to sate his lust for her.

Success hinged on his ability to stay focused. Patient. Unfortunately, just as Robert stated, she disliked him.

"I'll succeed," Adam said.

Robert lifted a dark brow. "You're that confident?"

"I am."

A slight smile lifted the corner of Robert's mouth. "Oh, I can't wait to see this. I predict she'll run the other way each time you draw near."

A realistic prediction.

For his sanity's sake, he had to succeed. He couldn't fail. He *would* best her in this cat-and-mouse game they were about to play. Beautiful, passionate Aimee hadn't had a lover since her Marc's death. He'd left his wife at their country château while he'd carried on with his favorite mistress in the city, and hadn't been anywhere near her for months prior to his fatal duel. In short, she hadn't been touched in a very long time.

And she was ripe for the taking.

Adam was going to use her passionate nature to his advantage.

2

"Well? Is that the blue justacorps he wore when you dropped the ring?" Aimee asked, her eyes fixed on Adam's tall sculpted form.

In the gardens of Versailles, scores of courtiers stood about, lords and ladies murmuring among themselves. The violinists that followed the King around the gardens all day stood still, but continued to play. Having motioned everyone back, His Majesty had wanted only Adam de Vey and Robert de Senville near. The three men were at the Dragon Fountain in deep discussion, His Majesty listening intently to Adam's comments.

Unable to stop herself, she took in his broad shoulders, his handsome profile. As the King demanded of all men at court, Adam wore his periwig, but underneath, Aimee knew he had dark hair that matched his dark velvety eyes. Away from court, the periwig was nowhere to be found. His hair was always long, loose, and as appealing as the rest of him. Despite the man's lascivious character, he was beautiful beyond belief.

Highly attractive men with disarming charm were the very bane of a woman's existence. A wicked promise always shone in their eyes. It drew women, despite their better judgment. Aimee understood the allure well. She'd been one of those women. She'd allowed herself to be drawn in by Marc in the same helpless, pathetic way. She should have limited her husband to her body, yet she'd foolishly relinquished her heart as well.

Louise had her head tilted to one side studying Adam when Aimee finally dragged her gaze away from him.

"Well?" Aimee prompted.

"I'm not sure . . ." her cousin said. "It could be."

"Louise, that answer is no help at all."

"I'm sorry. It's difficult to remember!" Louise looked about. "Do you see Renault? Is he here? Is he with his mistress?"

"Stop looking for him," Aimee cautioned and added sotto voce, "Until we locate the ring, you're to keep your distance." Hopefully, Renault would keep his. For his years of loyal service, the man thankfully had two rings from the King. According to Louise, his finger was always adorned with one. Aimee was fairly confident he hadn't noticed his other was missing—yet.

Just then, the King began to walk, a signal for others to follow. He moved away from Adam, Robert, and the fountain, out toward the east side of the vast gardens.

Adam, who had been speaking to Robert, looked past his shoulder, his gaze meeting hers. A slight smile raised the corner of his sensuous mouth, and he gave her a nod.

Aimee's stomach fluttered. A ludicrous reaction that took her by surprise. A reaction that dismayed her. One she wasn't going to repeat.

"Oh, my . . . Adam is looking this way." Louise pointed out the obvious.

"Yes, I know."

"Well, what should we do?"

Aimee returned his smile and nod. She thought something akin to surprise flashed in his eyes, but it was so quick, she couldn't be certain. "If I'm going to do this, I might as well start now."

Feed into his conceit—that every woman is interested in him. Be bold. And if luck was on her side, locate the ring in the pocket of the very justacorps he was wearing. Out of mourning, she'd make him believe she was a lonely widow, looking for a lover. The fact that she really was a lonely widow who could truly use a lover should only make her performance easier. No?

As the crowd thinned down to a few stragglers, Aimee marched straight up to her late husband's notoriously rakish friends, Louise quickly on her heels.

Stopping before them, Aimee heard Robert saying, "She's not going to come over—" He choked back his words when he noticed her.

"Good day, Madame de Gremont." Robert quickly stepped forward with an instant smile and, taking her hand, pressed a kiss to her knuckle. Aimee returned his greeting, then turned to Adam.

He stepped into Robert's spot and took her hand. "Good day, Aimee." His familiarity momentarily unbalanced her. He'd never addressed her so informally. The way he'd said her name—a low sensual sound—caused yet another flutter in her belly.

Adam took her hand, but didn't kiss it immediately, like Robert. Instead, holding her gaze, he grazed his thumb across the back of her hand so lightly, it sent tiny tingles up her arm.

With his eyes locked to hers, he bent and pressed his warm mouth to her hand, sending her pulse racing, her thoughts scattering. His lips lingered for a moment longer than was necessary before he stepped back and released her hand.

Realizing it had fallen agape, she clamped her mouth shut.

Good God, there's no doubt about it; he is trying to seduce you. And heaven help her, he was far too good at this. Even better at unraveling a woman than Marc had been. A mere touch had had the most unsettling effect. Worse, the look in his eyes told her he knew exactly what he'd done to her insides.

Aimee managed to force out a greeting, mentally cringing over how awkward she sounded.

Adam moved to Louise, who had been greeted already by Robert, and offered his own greeting. One that was completely proper and entirely different from the one he'd offered her.

Chastising herself for her responses to him, Aimee took a deep breath and returned her smile to her face.

"It is good to see you, gentlemen," she said, her voice thankfully belying her disquiet. "I wondered if you would be so kind as to be our escorts through the gardens?" She looked pointedly at Adam. "My cousin and I would be most appreciative." The crowd of courtiers was well ahead.

He smiled and offered his arm. "It would be my pleasure."

Taking Adam's arm, she walked along, trying not to notice the muscle and sinew under her hand that was entirely too easy to detect, even through his clothing. Or how his strong hard body moved with the most beguiling masculine grace.

Her traitorous body began to warm.

With her cousin and Robert walking behind, Aimee tried to think of something to say. A topic of conversation, any distraction at all that would take her mind off the mounting heat rushing through her system.

"You look lovely, Aimee. Blue is most becoming on you," he said, his dark gaze dropping ever so briefly to her décolletage. Her nipples hardened.

Oh God. Much to her mortification, Aimee felt a blush coming on. She hadn't blushed in years.

You haven't had a man in years either. Compose yourself!

"Thank you. It's my favorite color," she lied. "I love to wear it. I love to see others wear it, too. Any shade, really. It draws my eyes to them immediately." Excellent recovery. Since he was trying to bed her, he'd definitely wear what pleased her.

What would please her immensely would be to locate the ring and end this quickly.

His smile broadened. "Really. I'll keep that in mind."

He had an incredible smile. Quite perfect, actually.

"I must say it was a pleasant surprise to see you approach," he continued. "I didn't think you cared much for me or Robert."

Perhaps she'd been too bold in approaching him. Perhaps she should have waited for him to approach her. The last thing she wanted was to raise his suspicions—that she was up to something.

"I'm sorry to hear that." Gravel crunched under her feet as they moved along the path. "I didn't realize I gave you that impression. It was not my intention, Monsieur de—"

"Adam," he interjected. "Simply Adam. No need for titles, Aimee. We've known each other a long time."

Mostly from afar—and by reputation. She'd heard more than one woman atwitter about gorgeous Adam de Vey and his wickedly delicious carnal talents. Her husband's friends didn't visit the château. She only saw them when she was in the city, and since Marc's death, she'd tried to avoid them whenever possible.

"All right. Adam it is, then." She smiled, though her heart thudded in her chest. "You certainly had the attention of the King just now." That's right. Make idle conversation and come up with a way to check those pockets.

"Yes. His Majesty has summoned me for a meeting. He's displeased," he said, still smiling.

Her brows furrowed. "With you?"

"With his fountains. He wants me to fix them."

She glanced back at the fountain that was now silent and no longer spraying water. "You know how?"

"To fix them? Yes. It's going to be costly and require work, but it can be done."

She was intrigued. She thought he—like Marc—didn't know how to do anything other than indulge in vice.

"What's wrong with the fountains?" she asked, genuinely curious.

He lifted a brow. "You really wish to know?"

"Yes," she responded without hesitation.

This was novel for Adam. It was the first time she was actually talking to him, touching him. And for the first time in his life, he was going to discuss science with a stiff prick. In fact, she had him stiff as stone from the moment he caught her looking at him. There was no doubt about it; she'd reacted to his touch and the kiss on her hand.

And that delectable thought tightened his sac.

He didn't know why, but her interest in the fountains pleased him immensely. Most women wouldn't have cared to ask more questions, the subject too dull for their taste. He was as delighted about her curiosity as he was by her bold approach and request for an escort. Especially since he'd been sure he was going to have to corner her for any sort of conversation.

Celebrating in the turn of events, he silenced any questions he had regarding her uncharacteristic behavior.

"There are a number of fountains throughout the gardens," he explained. "There isn't enough water pressure to have them spout water at the same time and with the majestic height the King desires, so the fountains are turned on and off one at a time as the King approaches and leaves during his strolls around the gardens. But he wants them working all at the same time, in the same way."

"Really? I hadn't noticed until now . . . How will you fix them?"

"Since the water is presently being rerouted from the Seine—"

"All the way from Paris?" she injected, her eyes widened.

"Yes, all the way from Paris. The distance is significant, and the elevation of the land where the palace is located is high, both factors contributing to the problem. We are going to use a special machine, a pump to draw the water."

"Will that work, your 'pump' machine?"

"It should. Robert and I have made a number of calculations. I've done up detailed drawings. We'll be showing them to the King later. I think he'll be pleased."

"And how is it you know so much about such things?"

Still she hadn't lost interest or become bored. Those beautiful golden-colored eyes were fixed on him the entire time, giving him her rapt attention.

He stopped walking and turned to face her, a smile tugging at the corners of his mouth. Yet another first. When all he'd ever done was fantasize about bedding her, he never would have guessed he'd derive such pleasure from a simple conversation with her.

Robert and Louise d'Arcy walked on past, involved in their own conversation.

"Science is a passion of mine," he said, without boasting about his reputation in the area or his achievements that had earned him the esteem of the King.

Mirth entered her eyes. She lifted her chin a notch. "Really? I thought women were a passion of yours."

One particular woman had become an obsession of his, truth be told.

Adam slipped his hand under her chin and brought it up a notch more, their lips so very close together. She drew in a sharp breath, surprised by his unexpected action. "You hardly know me, Aimee . . . so I will tell you, I am a man of many passions."

He saw something flash in her eyes before her gaze briefly

dropped to his mouth. An excellent sign. Her breathing had increased. Her skin was flushed. Drawing from his experience with women, he knew he was right about Aimee. She *was* hungry. *She wants a lover.* It wouldn't take much to coax her into sex.

As he stared down at her upturned face, her perfect lush mouth, he wondered what she would do if he kissed her here and now. His every instinct told him she'd succumb to it, to him, in a sweet surrender, unable to stop herself. The notion was delicious. As delicious as she was going to be in bed. Still holding her chin, Adam brushed his thumb across her soft cheek with a light caress.

She jumped back, startling him. "It's cold!" she blurted out. Now a few feet away, she was rubbing her arms vigorously. "Don't you feel it? It's become quite chilly all of a sudden."

"Chilly?" Adam glanced up at the late afternoon sun. Did she jest? It was a warm summer's day.

"Yes . . ." She was still rubbing her arms, though her cheeks were pink, indicating inner heat rather than a chilled form. "I could really use your justacorps. Would you mind?"

"No, of course not." Adam removed his overcoat, walked up to her, and placed it on her shoulders.

She shot her arms into the sleeves. On him the coat was knee-length. On her it was much lower. She wrapped her arms around herself, the sleeves too long for her. He could barely see her fingertips.

"Are you all right?" he asked. Her behavior was bizarre.

"Yes . . . No. No, actually, I'm not feeling quite myself. I'm going to lie down until supper. If you'll excuse me . . ." She gave a quick curtsy. "Good-bye," she said as she turned on a heel and stalked away, calling out to her cousin.

Louise d'Arcy abruptly ended her conversation with Robert and raced to Aimee's side, casting a nervous glance Adam's way.

Aimee turned around quickly and tossed out, "I'll return your justacorps later . . . and thank you," then picked up her pace, both women rushing away.

Adam placed his hands on his hips as he watched the hasty retreat.

Robert sauntered over to him, frowning. "What on earth just happened?" he asked.

"I've no idea."

Robert rubbed the back of his neck. "Any reason why she is wearing your justacorps, Adam?"

"She's cold."

Robert lifted a brow. "Cold?"

"That is what I said. Cold."

"*Dieu*, it's about as hot as Hades out here."

Adam watched as the two women entered the palace through one of the garden doors. "Yes. I'm quite aware of that."

Robert shook his head. "It's baffling . . . First there was interest— which is rather astonishing in itself—and then a fast strange exit. What do you suppose is going on?"

"Don't know." It could be that he simply overwhelmed her and she lost her courage. After all, she hadn't been with any other man besides Marc. Or there could be more to this than he knew. "But I do intend to find out." Now that he saw just how responsive she was to him, he was going to continue his pursuit. Adam had a slow seduction in mind for Aimee de Miran.

He wouldn't let her run off the next time. Not until he had her willing and wet and had rocked her beautiful body with a powerful release.

* * *

"Nothing!" Aimee tossed the blue justacorps onto her bed. "There is absolutely nothing in the pockets." She was so frustrated she wanted to scream. Her body was burning from the inside out, thanks to Adam de Vey—the last man on earth who should stir her. Her husband's friend. A womanizer who had used the very same tactics on countless women.

Those tactics weren't supposed to affect her. But they did. Dear God, had she learned nothing from her experience with Marc? Instead of being the one doing the playing, Aimee was the one being played—by Adam. It unnerved her that he'd incited her senses.

And that he knew it.

"Are you certain?" Louise picked up the coat and ran her hands through the pockets. A sound of exasperation erupted from her as her cousin tossed the justacorps back onto the bed. "We're going to have to search again."

"Oh, no. I'll not go through that again, Louise. We've got to think of something else. Perhaps we can have a jeweler make an identical ring . . . or . . ."

"But that will take too long!" Louise's eyes filled with tears. "Time is of the essence. Renault could realize his ring is missing at any moment."

She knew Louise was right. She was grasping for ideas.

Louise flopped onto the bed. "I'm going to prison." She slapped her palms over her face and wept.

Aimee sighed. Clearly, she was no coquette. Or seductress. She wasn't good at playing the siren. Or the games men like Marc and Adam played. And after her irrational behavior in the gardens, it was almost certain Adam thought she was a lunatic.

But for Louise's sake, she'd have to do better. She knew her cousin would move mountains for her if Aimee were in need. In fact, Louise had been the only one who had been there for her during all the pain Marc had caused her.

"Louise." She walked over to the bed. "You are not going to

prison. I'll search his justacorps this evening, providing he wears a blue one, and if that proves fruitless, I'll figure out a way to sneak into his rooms and check all his blue justacorps."

Louise's hands dropped from her face. She sat up immediately. "You will?"

"I will."

She squealed with happiness and leapt off the mattress to give Aimee a tight hug. "Thank you, thank you, thank you."

Despite herself, Aimee smiled. "You're welcome."

Louise pulled away and wiped her tears from her cheeks. "You might want to check his justacorps tonight if he's wearing yellow."

Aimee's smile died. "Yellow?"

Louise forced a smile, and taking a step back smoothed her skirts. A bad sign. "Yes, you see . . . I was thinking about when I dropped the ring . . . the Hall of Mirrors was very crowded. I was bumped . . . and well . . . he might have been wearing a yellow justacorps."

Aimee simply blinked. Astounded. "How, by all that is holy, can you confuse *blue* with *yellow*?"

"Well . . . It all happened so fast and with the crush of people . . . the truth be told"—she smoothed her skirts again—"I don't recall *exactly* what color he wore."

Aimee strived for patience. For the first time in her life she wanted to throttle her cousin. "Are you even certain that it was Adam de Vey's pocket you dropped the ring in?"

"Oh, yes! Of that I'm certain. The man does stand out in a crowd—with his good looks and tall form, although I did find Robert de Senville quite appealing. He's very handsome, and he isn't married. Did you know that?"

"Louise! Focus!"

"Oh, yes, of course. It was *definitely* Adam de Vey. I'm positive.

In one of the pockets in one of his justacorps sits Renault's ring. We just have to find out which."

It was like looking for a needle in a haystack given the man's penchant for clothing.

Aimee's every instinct warned her to stay away from the Marquis de Nattes. But she was about to approach . . . and get very close to him, indeed.

A rake who sets your body on fire with the slightest effort . . . Good Lord.

She was going to give this another try.

3

Music from violins and harpsichords filled the Hall of Mirrors.

By the time Adam arrived, His Majesty's fete was well under way. Seated on his silver throne at the opposite end of the majestic hall, several carpeted steps high, the King observed those who danced the allemande before him in perfect unison. Onlookers not part of the dancing lined the great mirrored hall.

Adam spotted Aimee immediately. In a royal blue gown, with a radiant smile on her sweet lips, she danced with grace. He'd looked to the dance floor first, knowing he'd likely find her there. Riveted, he watched with pleasure each elegant turn and movement she made. She'd attended many balls with Marc where Adam had caught himself watching her dance. She danced so well, always with that captivating smile that bedazzled him every time.

There was no doubt in his mind—Aimee de Miran was the most beautiful woman in the realm.

Clearly enjoying herself, she made him smile.

He liked seeing her face aglow. Flushed with pleasure. Mental images of her naked form in his bed, her soft skin just as pink, just as warm, as he rode her to ecstasy and back, burned through his mind.

His groin tightened.

Unwittingly, Marc had tortured him for years with countless details of his wife's beautiful body. He hated it that Marc had discussed his wife with the same level of disregard he had for his paramours—more than he could ever express. Though Adam couldn't remember any of the particulars of his friend's many mistresses, he recalled every single detail Marc had mentioned regarding Aimee's sweet form—when he hadn't wanted to. When he'd wanted nothing more than to forget them. Forget her. Adam knew Aimee had a beauty mark on her inner right thigh and another on her left hip. And he didn't need Marc to tell him just how beautiful her tits were. He could see that for himself. The top curves of her breasts were presently visible above her décolletage.

And tantalizing in the extreme.

Aimee pressed her palm to her partner's raised hand, and turned in a circle in time with the music and dancers around her. Her dark curls were swept up and adorned with tiny blue ribbons; the few cascading down flounced about her as she moved. He drank in the sight of her. She was breathtaking to behold.

The only woman he knew who could render him awestruck again and again.

As the last notes were played, she made a final turn and a deep curtsy to her partner, the Baron de Ranvier. He immediately offered his arm and escorted her off the dance floor.

Intent on intercepting Aimee before she disappeared into the crowd, Adam began to make his way through the throng, just as the King rose, descended the steps, and exited the Hall of Mirrors to enter his gardens.

The crush immediately followed him out, the mass moving

across Adam's path making it impossible to do anything but move with the flow.

He lost sight of Aimee.

Moments later, he found himself outside in the gardens. A hush fell over the crowd. Anticipation infused the silence as the mass gazed up at the night sky, everyone aware of what was about to happen. Suddenly, the heavens filled with explosions of lights and sounds, spectacular fireworks dazzling and delighting His Majesty's court. The King did everything on a grand scale, to demonstrate to all that he was the head of the most powerful realm in all of Christendom. Adam scanned the crowds but couldn't find his golden-eyed beauty.

A hand touched his sleeve and grabbed his attention. To his astonishment, Aimee was standing beside him smiling. His heart quickened, sending blood rushing to his already hardened cock. *Dieu*, this woman had him unbalanced. Each time he thought he'd have to do the chasing, she appeared before him.

Because of the crush around them, she stood so close to him, her soft breasts lightly pressed against his arm, wreaking havoc on his senses.

"Good evening, Adam." Her voice was elevated due to the noise of the fireworks. "Are you enjoying the fireworks?" she asked. He barely noticed them with her so near.

"Yes. Are you?"

Her beautiful golden eyes swept heavenward. "Yes. They're lovely." She returned her gaze to him.

Adam leaned in, using the loudness of the exploding fireworks as his excuse to move closer to her. "I trust you're feeling better?"

"Much better, thank you. How goes the work on the fountains and your machine?"

He smiled, once again pleased by her interest. "It goes well. I'll be giving the King a demonstration tomorrow afternoon."

"Tomorrow? With the keen interest he showed today, I would have thought he'd want to see your demonstration immediately."

"The King has other officials here to meet with. I understand that he was occupied the better part of the day with his Lieutenant General of Police."

Her smile faded slightly. "Oh . . . really? The Lieutenant General of Police . . ." She looked away, gazing up at the skies.

All the telltale signs of her desire were there. Her heart raced; he could see the rapid pulse on her slender neck. And her breathing was a little faster than normal. Someone bumped her from behind, pushing her soft form up against him harder.

A bolt of lust rocked him.

Merde. He had to fuck her. Soon. He couldn't take much more.

She placed a hand against his chest and gently pushed herself away as best she could. "I'm sorry," she said.

"Don't be. I'm not."

To his delight, she didn't shy away. In fact, she hadn't looked all that sorry she'd bumped into him. Her smile was unwavering, bordering on sultry, as she moved to stand in front of him, her skirts deliciously caressing his leg, the space between their bodies so provocatively minimal.

"You're wearing blue," she said, looking pleased.

His gaze drifted down over what he could see of her appealing form. "So are you. Quite magnificently, if the truth be told." He liked the awareness between them.

"I'd say just about any color suits you, Adam. You truly have the finest justacorps."

"Thank you." He'd no idea why they were talking about his clothes except to guess that she was nervous. He could sense it. She wanted to touch him. That much was obvious. As was the heat mounting between them the longer their bodies remained this close.

He definitely approved of the direction this was going . . .

Aimee had stirred his hunger. She could see it in his dark eyes. It was so raw and real, it made her head spin. Clearly, her skill at seduction was improving, for she was the one in command of the game at the moment. All she had to do was remain in control of her desire. And his. *That's how this game is played, no?*

The seducer had command over the seduced.

Adam had used women for his own purposes. For his pleasure. She'd use him for hers.

It would give her great pleasure to search his pockets, find the ring, and leave him burning.

Fool. You'll leave yourself burning, too.

She ignored the errant thought, and her slick, aching sex that conspired against her. Knowing her own limitations, not wanting to push him or herself too far, lest she got ensnared in her own game, she decided this was a good time to change tactics, demeanor, and tone. She abruptly clamped her hands on his shoulders.

"Yes, this is quite a lovely justacorps." She stroked the fabric down his chest, stopping to tap over his breast pockets. No ring in there.

"Wonderful fabric . . . Silk, is it?" She moved her hands farther down the coat, using short strokes in much the way one would pet a horse. His brow furrowed as he glanced down and watched the odd motions of her hands. *What the bloody hell . . . ?* clearly shone in his eyes. She fought to keep a straight face. His expression was priceless. It was obvious he was expecting to be touched in a more amorous way. In perhaps more intimate places on his muscled body.

Aimee refused to dwell on how deliciously solid his chiseled chest felt.

"I just adore silk," she said, then purposely steering well away from his sex, she shot her hands out toward his hips and the pockets there.

He caught her wrists, her hands only inches away from her goal.

"*Chère*, perhaps it's been a long time since you touched a man. Why don't we try something like this?" Before she could react, he pulled her hand inside his justacorps and pressed her palm to the bulge in his breeches and stroked it down his length and back up the crest of his cock.

Her knees weakened. He was much thicker and bigger than Marc. And so delectably hard and hot. Heat emanated from his body through the fine cloth of his breeches.

The bud between her legs pulsed with need.

With the crowd so gripped by the entertainment in the skies, Aimee and Adam were cocooned in their small spot, their bodies too close together for anyone to see the wicked motions of their hands over his shaft. Her gaze was locked with his. She couldn't break away, mesmerized by the passion in his eyes, his fever for her inciting a voracious sense of urgency.

"That's much better . . ." he murmured, yet somehow she still heard him over the noise.

Her breathing was shallow and sharp. Aimee curled her fingers tightly around his straining sex inside his tented breeches.

He released her wrist. "Perfect . . ." he said, and she realized she was still stroking his glorious cock. As much as it shocked her, she didn't want to let go. Adam slipped his hand behind her neck. He was going to kiss her.

You can't let him! She was teetering on the edge of a complete surrender. Right here. Right now. She'd never been so brazen.

Adam de Vey had masterfully turned the tables on her.

Aimee had wits enough to know when to cede defeat and run. She yanked her hand away from his alluring shaft. "I am feeling a bit chilled." *Get the justacorps and go! Hurry!*

"Chilled?" Amusement flicked in his dark eyes. To her relief, he removed his hand from the nape of her neck. "We can't have that. Allow me to be of assistance." He caught her arm and pulled her to the right until his shoulder met the tall palace wall. Within the tightly packed throng, their new spot was no less dense with spectators of the King's show of fireworks.

He pulled off his light blue coat. "Turn around, Aimee," he said, slipping the justacorps onto her shoulders the moment she complied.

She slipped her arms into the sleeves and gave him a semblance of a smile over her shoulder as the explosions continued overhead.

He slid his arm inside the justacorps and pulled her up against him. Aimee stiffened. The bulge in his breeches was pressed against her bottom. Surely, he wasn't going to do anything more with this crowd around them? Her answer came when she felt her skirts being raised from behind. She sucked in a breath. He was using his hand closest to the wall, using their bodies to hide what he was doing from view. She reeled, stunned by his actions.

"Adam . . ." His name rushed out of her lungs, but the rest of her words were choked off when she felt his hot hand graze over the front of her thigh and cup her sex through the cloth of her drawers. She jumped on contact.

He tightened his arm around her. "Easy . . ." His mouth was against her ear. "Spread your legs for me, Aimee. Let me warm you."

Her heart was hammering. Warm her? If she got any hotter, she'd burst into flames. Aimee looked at those closest to them. Did no one notice his hand up her skirts? Heads tilted back and eyes skyward told her definitely "No."

"Your caleçons are wet with your juices. I like that." He rubbed her lightly over her drawers.

Her breathing hitched, and she grabbed the wall, digging her fingers into the stone. The heat from his hand was spine-melting. Her clit throbbed in time with the hard thuds of her heart.

"Excellent . . ." His hand had slipped inside the slit of her drawers and he was gently caressing her slick folds, strokes that were all too perfect, inundating her with voluptuous sensations. She whimpered. She'd no recollection of widening her stance, but clearly she had, giving him easy access to her needy sex. She'd never done anything like this. So outrageous. So unbridled.

He slid his fingers inside her core. She lurched but his strong arm around her waist kept her in place, not allowing her to escape his delicious invasion. Adam pumped his hand, the heel of his palm tantalizing her clit. She'd no idea how many of his long wonderful fingers were sliding in and out of her. She knew only a sublime pressure and exquisite friction as he filled her and withdrew. Filled her and withdrew.

"You have the sweetest cunt, Aimee. So wet and silky soft . . . I love how you're squeezing around my fingers. You like being possessed this way, don't you?"

Yes! Shaking, her breaths ragged, she turned her head and pressed her forehead against the back of her hand still clutching the wall, refusing to answer him. Her mind screamed, "End this now!" but she'd no will in her body to stop him. She couldn't even muster a protest when his other hand opened the front of her gown, and pulled down her chemise. The cool night air whispered through the opening of the justacorps and blew gently across her hardened nipple. A soft cry slipped past her lips.

He captured the distended tip of her breast and masterfully rolled and pinched it, sending sensations streaking through her breast down to the bud between her legs, which he expertly teased with his palm. She could barely hold in the sounds surging up her throat.

"Have you ever been fingered like this in public, Aimee?"

She shook her head. Her husband had never done anything like this to her. Had never incited her to this magnitude. Her muscles were taut. Her body tensed as she fought against the waves of hot lust crashing through her, wrestling for a modicum of control.

"*Chère*, don't fight me. Let me give you the pleasure your body is hungry for . . . You want to come, don't you, beautiful Aimee?"

She was panting now, yet she managed to nod her head. What was the point in denying it? He was purposely holding her on the edge with his skillful hands and measured strokes. He could send her over the edge anytime he wanted.

"Let me hear you say—"

"I want to come!" she quickly injected before he could finish his sentence. "Now! Right now . . ." She didn't care if someone heard her. Or where she was. She needed this. Needed him. Wanted what he was offering. Had to have it or die.

"I want to come for you, Adam." She heard the smile in his tone as he fed her the line in her ear, his experienced hands holding her gripped in a flood of erotic sensations.

"Yes . . . I want to come . . ." Squeezing her eyes shut, she was practically delirious with desire.

". . . for you, Adam," he supplied.

". . . I want to come for you . . . Adam."

He kissed her neck, trailing his way to the sensitive spot below her ear. "It would be an honor to pleasure you, Aimee . . ." Curling his buried fingers, he brushed over the ultrasensitive spot inside her vaginal wall.

A cry burst from her lips, her knees almost giving way as he stroked that sweet spot with stunning finesse, milking more juices from her sex. Her hips jerked forward. Her sex contracted, and she knew she was going to go over soon. Very soon. The pleasure and tension inundating her became entwined into one exquisite sensation, mountaining inside her. Surging fast. And furious.

His name escaped from her mouth. Rapture exploded through her senses, her body stiffening. She pushed up against him hard, her scream eclipsed by the final firecrackers in the sky, her sheath contracting wildly around his fingers.

"That's perfect, Aimee. Ride it out. I've got you." He held her, his strokes slowing down only when the delicious spasms ebbed.

Applause burst around her, signaling the end of the fireworks display.

Adam slid his fingers out, the luscious sense of fullness slipping away. She shivered. Her skirts fell back in place while he busied his other hand with her bodice. Knowing people were about to leave, she tried to help, her trembling fingers fumbling, hindering his progress.

"Let me," he said softly in her ear. In short order, he had the front of her gown closed without anyone around them being the wiser.

She turned and slumped against the wall, still wearing his justacorps as the crowd disbursed toward the tables set out in the gardens for the feast about to be served. Her breathing and heart calmed. Aimee felt euphoric, her muscles deliciously lax.

She felt light enough to fly.

Her marital relations with Marc had been the best part of their marriage, and as good as they were, they had never been like this. She'd never been left feeling this incredible. There was a wonderful warmth in her belly that was slowly seeping through her entire being. A calm sated feeling. A feeling of well-being. A peace.

She met his gaze. The night's light shone on one side of his handsome face, making him look even more devilishly beautiful.

He was beyond potent. Dangerously irresistible. Women throughout the realm should be warned—the Marquis de Nattes had devastating allure and sexual talents no mortal man should possess.

He ran a knuckle lightly down her cheek. It was then she
realized it was wet. Oh God . . . He'd moved her to tears during
sex. She swiped her other cheek dry, embarrassed by the unprecedented occurrence. She'd made it a habit of hiding her tears during her marriage. Never once had she shown them to Marc.

"You come beautifully, Aimee."

How did one answer that? "Thank you"?

Most of the crowd was gone. They were all but alone. Did
he expect pleasure in return? Of course he did. Marc demanded
pleasure for pleasure. Didn't all men?

A sudden urge to taste him swelled inside her. She quashed it.
"I . . . should go." She expected his ire to hit at any moment. Yet
it was the only response she could offer. She desperately needed
some distance to collect herself. To snap this unsettling spell he'd
cast on her.

The corner of his perfect mouth lifted in the most sensual
smile. "If you must."

No anger?

"My cousin awaits me," she told him, completely unsure why.

He took a step back. "Then you shouldn't keep her waiting."

She shouldn't? No argument? He was simply letting her go
after giving her the strongest orgasm of her life?

She held his gaze, unsure what more to say. His expression
was unreadable, and she wished she knew what he was thinking.

She pushed herself off the wall. "All right then." She managed
a smile, feeling out of sorts, unable to shake the wish that he'd
demand more of her. A kiss. Or simply to give that delectable part
of his male anatomy that was still solid and erect some carnal
attention.

If he's this talented with his hands, imagine what he can do with that beautiful cock.

She immediately chastised herself. *Those sorts of thoughts will get you into the kind of trouble you don't need.*

"Are you sufficiently warmed now?" he asked.

"Pardon? Oh, yes, I . . . I'm warm now." *Warm me some more . . .*

"Then may I have my justacorps?"

Her brows shot up. "Oh, of course . . ." It suddenly occurred to her she'd never checked the lower pockets. She'd completely forgotten to search for the ring. Aimee drove her hands into the pockets and brightened her smile. "This really is a very nice justacorps." She slid her fingers around the pockets, hoping to touch upon the ring. "You do have exquisite taste in clothing."

"Thank you." He looked amused. "The justacorps, if you please?"

Nothing. The pockets were empty. "Yes . . . Here." She removed the coat and handed it to him.

He leisurely put it on. She watched with fascination as one strong shoulder and then the other slipped inside the blue knee-length coat. In the distance she could hear the chatter of the courtiers and strains from the violins.

His dark eyes gazed back at her, but he said nothing more. *Why are you still standing here, Aimee? Leave!* "Good evening, Adam."

"Good evening, Aimee."

She took a step, then stopped and said, "Thank you." *Thank you? Good God. Did you just thank him for giving you a climax?* She felt her face turn red. One release and she was behaving like an unsophisticated fool.

His lips twitched, and she could tell he was holding back a smile. "For what?"

The devil. He knew full well what she'd just thanked him for. He was going to make her spell it out. "For the . . . uhm . . . the . . ."

"Orgasm?" he supplied.

She was grateful it was night and he couldn't see just how red her cheeks were. "Yes, for . . . that."

A slow steady smile graced his mouth, one of pure male pride. "It was my pleasure."

Oh, he was good. Much better than Marc on too many disquieting levels.

She gave a nod and, feeling completely awkward, forced one foot in front of the other, walking away from Adam, only to stop dead in her tracks when she saw Renault de Sard, Louise's former lover, marching toward her.

"I want a word with you," he said the moment he reached her.

"Really? I don't much care to have one with you, sir," Aimee bit back. The wonderful lassitude that had been humming in her veins dissipated instantly by Renault's presence.

"Have you seen your cousin?" He was unfazed by her curtness.

"Of course I've seen her. I see her quite regularly." She stepped around him.

"Halt right there," Renault ordered.

Aimee turned around to see Adam approaching, a frown furrowing his handsome brow.

"I've not dismissed you," Renault added.

Aimee set her jaw. "I don't need your dismissal to leave your presence, sir."

Renault walked up to her. "I am the King's Lieutenant General of Police."

"So?"

"So I am permitted to detain anyone I choose and ask them questions."

Aimee's ire heated her blood. "Do you dare speak to me as if I were a criminal? Have you forgotten your place?" She never threw her title or social standing around for clout, but he'd been made noble because of his political office.

She was a noble by blood.

"What is the problem, Renault?" Adam placed his hand on the vermin's shoulder.

She disliked everything about the man. His arrogance. His ill-treatment of Louise and her affections. She never understood what her dear cousin saw in the man.

Upon seeing Adam, Renault changed his demeanor. "Oh, it's you, Nattes. It's nothing . . . Just a matter between a former mistress and me."

Adam looked at Aimee and lifted a brow.

She immediately added, "He's referring to my cousin. A lovely woman with terrible taste in men." She looked pointedly at Renault. The last thing she wanted was for Adam—or anyone—to think she'd take a lover as unappealing as Renault.

"Your 'lovely' cousin has never behaved herself a single day I've known her, yet she has stayed away as requested and not a peep has been heard from her," Renault said. "A most uncharacteristic behavior. I want to know why. What is she up to? It's usually no good."

"Perhaps she's finally come to the conclusion that you are a waste of her time."

With that, Aimee picked up her skirts, turned on her heel, and stalked away on weak and wobbly legs, her heart pounding. That was all she needed—for Renault to be keeping Louise under close scrutiny.

Reaching the long elegant tables with gold service, surrounded by torchères, Aimee scanned the area and quickly located Louise. She was by her side in an instant and sat down.

"Where have you been, Aimee?" Louise whispered. "I've been looking for you everywhere."

"I got caught up in the crowd," she responded vaguely.

"Did you find Adam de Vey?"

Just as Aimee was about to respond, she glanced down the lengthy table and caught Adam's gaze. He was seated at the same table at the opposite end. He smiled at her and lightly ran the length of his finger along his upper lip, just under his nose.

Heat rushed to her cheeks as the impact of what he was doing hit her. Her scent was on his fingers, and he was clearly enjoying it. She felt a quickening low in her belly. Her sex clenched, hungrily.

She tore her gaze away and forced her focus onto Louise.

"Oh, look, Aimee. Adam de Vey is at our table." Once again, Louise pointed out the obvious. "Do you want to check his justacorps?"

"No!" she cringed at how strongly that came out. "I mean, I already did, darling. There was no ring."

Louise's disappointment was etched across her features.

"That's not all, Louise." Aimee covered her hand affectionately. "Renault is suspicious of you and thinks you're up to something."

Louise flinched. "Oh God! He does?"

"Yes, I think I defused it some, but we must be careful. And we must act quickly." Aimee glanced down the table, but found the beautiful Marquis de Nattes gone. His seat had been vacated and another sat in his place.

Disappointment over his disappearance stabbed into her. And irked her.

Her unusual behavior toward him was completely explainable. Her lengthy celibacy was to blame, motivating her wanton reactions to him. Nothing more.

"Tomorrow afternoon the Marquis de Nattes has a meeting with the King."

Louise's eyes widened. "And?"

"And I intend to go to his personal apartments and check in each and every justacorps he owns until I find the ring."

All this madness was going to end tomorrow.

4

"You can stop grinning like a fool, Robert," Adam said dryly. Palms pressed against the large desk in the King's private apartments, studying his drawings while waiting for His Majesty to arrive, Adam could see his friend out of the corner of his eye.

"You're being very quiet about your whereabouts last night." Robert was smirking. "And as coincidence would have it, last night Louise d'Arcy couldn't locate her cousin anywhere. She came to me and asked if I'd seen her. Any idea where the fair Aimee de Miran was last eve?"

Adam felt his cock harden at the mere mention of Aimee and last night. *Merde.* A stiff prick was the last thing he needed just before he met with the King. Damn Robert.

The memory of Aimee in his arms, of her honeyed sex squeezing around his fingers while she came, rushed through his mind. That very same memory had kept him up most of the night—keeping both him and his cock fully awake.

Adam had always enjoyed a chase—especially since he didn't usually get much resistance to his advances—but his pursuit of Aimee was far more than mere entertainment. Having her meant too much to him.

More than it should.

More than he was comfortable with. His desire for her had spanned an eternity. Nothing had been so difficult as to watch her walk away last eve and not pull her back and claim what she so obviously wanted him to take. Every inch of his body clamored for her.

But he refused to do it and resisted by sheer iron will.

If she wanted to be taken, she was going to have to come to him and ask with her very own sweet lips—without reservation or inhibitions. To that end, he'd made great strides last eve, despite being left with a painful prick. She'd lingered afterward, waiting for him to demand more, and the disappointment in her golden eyes when he hadn't had been difficult to miss.

Adam sensed it wasn't going to take much longer. Then she'd be all his.

And he had six years of pent-up fantasies to indulge in with her.

Robert walked over smiling, and stopping on the opposite side of the desk, pressed his palms down onto the surface. "Please tell me you fucked her. Any man who's been walking around with a stiff cock for another man's wife for six years deserves some relief."

Adam looked him square in the eye, grasping for patience with his irksome friend. "Remind me again why I tolerate you?"

Robert laughed and straightened. "You've got that wrong. I tolerate you," he teased. "What happened with Aimee? Out with it."

Adam pushed himself off the desk and blew out a breath. "Robert, she's never had a lover." Of that he was certain. Since Marc's death, he'd kept his ears open, always listening for news about her.

While in mourning she'd kept mostly to herself at her country château, her main company, her cousin Louise. But once the mourning was over, she'd returned to Paris. Adam knew whenever she was in the city and he'd made it a point of attending those salons and fetes she'd be at. He'd kept his distance, sensing the timing wasn't right, sensing she wasn't ready to take a lover, though controlling his gaze whenever she was in the room was a different challenge altogether.

"If I push for too much too soon, she'll bolt." He was approaching this the way he'd approach any challenge, methodically, carefully, with well-thought-out steps.

"So you didn't bed her."

"Not exactly."

"Not exactly?"

"It was more of a sampling."

"You *sampled* her?" Robert burst out laughing.

Adam rested his hands on his hips. "What about that amuses you?"

Robert shook his head, still chuckling. "Nattes, you are either losing your touch, or you have the worst *tendre* for this woman. Which is it, my friend? I'm starting to strongly suspect it's the latter."

"Don't be ridiculous. Once I have her, the fascination will be over." Adam instantly quashed the doubts that assailed him. He had this under control.

Last night was a perfect example of how he had mastery over himself.

"Well, it's fortuitous that the King has moved our meeting up. By the time we're done here, it should be midday. You'll have the entire afternoon and evening free to find the lovely Comtesse de Gremont and break your 'fascination' with her."

True enough. The moment his morning meeting with His

Majesty was over, he planned to return to his rooms, refresh himself, and seek Aimee out.

She didn't know about his change of plans and thought he'd be occupied most of the afternoon with the King.

He couldn't wait to surprise her.

*   *   *

Aimee's heart pounded as she approached the doors to Adam's apartments. She couldn't believe she was doing something like this. For the last three years her life had been a staid, quiet existence. Stealing into a man's rooms was much more adventure than she'd ever known.

Or ever wanted to know.

In truth, her entire visit to the palace had been one unprecedented experience after another.

There were so many apartments at the palace—housed in the various outbuildings—that it had been quite the chore simply learning where Adam's rooms were located. She'd been forced to make careful, discreet inquiries.

Fearing she'd be seen in the corridor by someone she knew, Aimee picked up her pace and rushed to the door. The last thing she wanted was to be questioned about being in an outbuilding that was not where her apartments were located. Or even close to it.

Standing before Adam's door, she paused, her left hand clutching his justacorps in a white-knuckle grip. If caught by a servant, she'd simply say she was returning the Marquis's overcoat that she'd borrowed the other day—because she was cold.

In the middle of a hot summer's day.

Most definitely a weak and sorry excuse, Aimee.

Sadly, it was the best she could come up with.

Taking a deep breath, she exhaled slowly. She was doing this alone. Louise was so nervous, she'd trembled and babbled uncontrollably, leaving no doubt in Aimee's mind that her cousin would have foiled the plan.

Get on with it. You can't stand here staring at the door all afternoon.

Aimee raised a shaky hand and lightly rapped at the door.

Silence. An excellent sign!

Placing a hand on the door handle, she turned it and opened the portal, her heart galloping wildly. A quick peek told her no one was in the antechamber. She slipped inside and closed the door softly.

Aimee looked around the elegant room. White and gilded walls. Tall windows overlooking the gardens, and two doors. One ajar. The other closed. Approaching the open door, she could see it led to the bedchambers, the floral-patterned carpets on the floor muting her footsteps.

However, nothing quieted the thundering of her heart. It was so loud in her ears next to the stillness surrounding her.

Entering Adam's bedchamber, she couldn't miss the massive four-poster bed with its blue counterpane and matching bed curtains. Seeing it made her insides dance and conjured up heated images of last night in her mind. This was not the time to think about *that*.

Pulling her gaze away from Adam's bed, she glanced to the right and spotted exactly what she was looking for.

Two large ornately carved armoires.

This would be so much easier if the man hadn't had the amount of clothing that required a second armoire.

She walked to the closest one and opened its doors. Numerous suits of clothing, in various colors, were folded and stacked high in neat piles. Throwing open the doors to the second armoire, she found it just as overflowing with clothing. My God. It was going

to take hours to unfold, search, and refold each justacorps and
return it to its spot.

Frustrated, Aimee cast a glance heavenward, needing a miracle. *Why couldn't it be as simple as reaching in*—she shoved a
hand in to one of the piles—*and pulling out the ring?* As she was
sliding her hand back out, her fingers stroked over something
small and hard inside a pocket.

The ring!

"May I help you?" A male voice made her jump, tear her hand
out of the pile, and spin around.

Her knees almost buckled when she saw Adam leaning against
the doorframe wearing nothing but a bath linen around his waist.
Riveted, she moved her gaze over his magnificent sculpted chest,
each beautiful dip and ripple. He was nothing short of breathtaking. Pure masculine perfection. Mesmerized, she watched as he
ran a hand through his wet dark hair, then crossed his muscled
arms over that powerful chest.

Gracious God . . . As handsome as her husband had been,
he'd never looked like *that*.

"What are you doing here, Aimee?"

Stop ogling him.

She tore her eyes away and glanced back at the armoire. Her
heart plummeted the moment she realized she couldn't remember
which pile she'd stuck her hand in, or the color of the justacorps
she'd been touching in the stack.

"Aimee, I asked you a question."

Her gaze shot back to him. She quickly averted it when she got
another eyeful of his glorious—mostly naked—physique.

"I came to return this." She held her arm out, the justacorps
she was holding now dangling from her grip, purposely blocking
the sight of him. "I was . . . going to place it back in your armoire.

I didn't know you were here. I am sorry to have interrupted you. You're clearly busy. I'll go."

She placed the justacorps down on his bed and, with her heart pounding in her throat, turned to leave.

"Come here, Aimee."

That arrested her steps. His voice was low and so wickedly sensual. She had to swallow hard before she could speak, her insides frenzied—a dizzying combination of dread and something else she didn't want to name.

"That's probably not a good idea," she said without turning around. Waving her hand in his direction behind her, she added, "You'll want to get dressed, lest you catch a chill."

"It's a warm summer's day outside and it's quite pleasant in here. I'm not in the least bit cold. Are you chilled, Aimee? Do you need warming—"

"*No!*" She winced, not intending the word to come out quite so forcefully. "No . . . I'm fine . . . Warm enough, thank you." *Get out now or you'll end up being warmed in ways best avoided.* As it was, the sight of him was already heating her blood.

"Aimee, come here," he repeated. By his tone, it was clear he was insisting.

Did she have a choice? Adam and Renault were friends, and they were both in the King's inner circle. She had to get out of this situation as smoothly as she could.

Which meant she couldn't bolt out the door as she wanted.

Keeping her eyes averted, she turned around and approached him, praying he couldn't tell just how discomposed she was.

Aimee stood before him and purposely kept her gaze fixed to the wall past his shoulder. She clasped her hands in front of her, then quickly unclasped them, realizing that she'd brought her hands near that particular part of his male anatomy. The one covered by the bath linen she was trying not to think about. Or peek at.

He slipped his fingers under her chin and tilted her face, forcing her to meet his gaze. "What are you doing in my bedchambers, Aimee?"

"I told you. I wanted to return the justacorps . . ."

He gripped her shoulders and pressed her back against the wall, surprising her with his actions. He braced his hands on either side of her head, his body hemming her in.

Adam dipped his head, bringing his handsome face closer. "Why don't you try again."

"Try again?" she asked.

"With a better answer. One that's honest."

Her heart lurched. Aimee forced herself to look him firmly in the eye.

"I was returning the justacorps," she insisted. Could he hear her pounding heart? How she wished he had on clothes. The lack of which was making this entire episode even more distressing. His skin was driving her to distraction. It looked warm and inviting as it covered all that impressive muscle and sinew.

"Aimee, you have servants. There is no need for you to come here, unless you had a reason for wanting to be in my bedchambers yourself."

She didn't like the direction this conversation was taking. Unsettled, she wanted out of his chambers. Right now.

"You have my answer. Please step back. *Now.*" Her response was sharp.

He blew out a breath. "I'm not trying to upset you. I simply want to hear the truth from your beautiful mouth." He pulled a hand away from the wall and lightly brushed his fingertips across her bottom lip. Leaving a tingling in its wake. "*Dieu*, I have fantasized about this mouth, your sweet form . . . you . . . for a very long time."

That, too, took her by surprise.

He ran the back of his fingers gently down her cheek, the side of her neck, and onto the swells of her breasts. Her breathing quickened. Ever so slowly, his fingers grazed her skin, following the contour of her décolletage, his soft touch sending her nerve endings into a frenzy, making her nipples harden and her sex slick. "I enjoyed making you come last night. I only wish I'd seen your face when you came . . . And as for these lovely breasts, I still don't know the exact shade of your nipples."

He stroked the tip of his finger down the front of her gown, directly over one distended tip. She gasped, the sensation intense despite the clothing. "I've lost count how many times I imagined touching you. Tasting you. In my mind, I have fucked you a thousand times." He cupped her breast and caressed her nipple with his thumb, the rhythmic strokes making her shiver in delight. "That is honest. That is the truth. Now I want the truth from you. Why did you come into my chambers? I know you feel the heat between us. Admit that you want me as much as I want you."

Oh God. And here she thought she'd stirred his suspicions. She'd no idea that *desire* was the truth he wanted to hear—to admit to the hunger he incited in her. Nor did she have any idea he'd desired her "for a very long time."

"I didn't know that you have—"

"Wanted you for years?" He shrugged. "You were married to Marc and he had your affections. Why let it be known?"

Years? "How many years?"

"From the moment I first saw you."

Six years? She wanted to discount what he was saying, to believe it was just the kind of lie a libertine would tell a woman he wanted to bed, but there was such touching sincerity in his dark eyes, she couldn't dismiss it, no matter how much she wished to.

When Marc had stopped wanting her, stopped touching her, and left her feeling undesirable and empty, Adam de Vey had wanted her. From a distance he'd craved her—*for six years . . .* It was stunning. *Incredible . . .* Unbelievably stirring.

"This is our time, Aimee. I want to share more carnal pleasures with you, but first I'm going to need to hear from your lips that you want it. That the reason you came to my rooms is because you're hungry for what I can give you."

With his thumb lightly tormenting her nipple, she could barely think. He had her cornered into quite a predicament. If she denied her desire for him, then she'd have to convince him that her original excuse for being in his rooms was the truth.

The problem was, she didn't want to deny her desire. Every fiber of her being wanted him with shocking desperation. Wanted to tell him the truth on that score.

He dipped his dark head and brushed his mouth over the sensitive spot below her ear; a frisson of excitement quivered through her. "Last night, while you were lying in bed, did you think of me?" His warm breath caressed her ear.

She licked her lips, starved for his taste. "Yes . . ." she whispered.

"Did you imagine me in your bed with you?"

Her core clenched. "Yes."

He nuzzled her neck. "Did you imagine my cock inside you, Aimee? Did you imagine me fucking you?"

He was trailing knee-weakening kisses down her neck. Briefly she closed her eyes, the sensations so decadent. She'd never had a conversation like this in her life. She would have been too embarrassed to tell Marc about any sexual thoughts she'd had, but with Adam the words slipped past her lips with ease. "*Yes . . .*"

"I'm pleased to hear that." She could hear the smile in his

tone. "Last night, I thought about you, too. I thought about that perfect sweet sex of yours and how delicious that slick, snug heat would feel around my cock." He pulled back, looked into her eyes, and slipped his fingers under her chin. He tilted it up, bringing her lips so temptingly close to his seductive mouth. "It seems we are of like mind," he murmured, then swooped in for a kiss, his tongue possessing her mouth immediately. She all but swooned. The intensity of his kiss was inebriating.

She wanted to touch him so strongly—but hesitated. This man was far too devastating on her famished senses. He had the uncanny ability to arouse her to a feverish pitch and had her saying and doing things she'd never said or done before. Last eve he'd driven her so wild, she'd allowed him to have shocking liberties and in a public place—the palace gardens surrounded by the King's court. Everyone knew her as a dutiful wife and at present a respectable widow. Yet in *his* arms, she was uninhibited and undone.

Aimee pressed her palms to the wall behind her back, but let the delicious fire emanating from Adam burn through her, unable to help herself.

By the time he broke the kiss, she was utterly breathless.

Desperate for more.

"Tell me, Aimee, are you here to give yourself to me?"

5

All right, perhaps it wasn't the real reason Aimee had entered Adam's chambers. But Lord knows she wanted to give herself to him. Again. The bud between her legs pulsed fiercely and her sex, soaked with her juices, ached to be filled. By Adam de Vey. She never thought she'd ever desire another man as much as she'd desired Marc.

She desired Adam more. With a reckless abandon she didn't know she was capable of.

Why couldn't she help her cousin *and* enjoy Adam's sexual skills? The last few years had been devoid of joy, why deny herself some pleasure? This man knew how to give it in wicked abundance.

"Answer me, *chère*. Did you come here to give yourself to me?" His sinfully seductive eyes were locked with hers, waiting for her response.

"Yes" tripped off her tongue.

He smiled, clearly pleased by her response. "Open the front of your gown and offer me your nipples."

Hot excitement melted down her spine. Everything he said to her was so deliciously carnal. It amazed her how much she liked it. Marc had never spoken to her like this in or out of the bedchamber.

Without another thought, her fingers flew to her bodice, opening the fastenings. Her nipples were so hard, she couldn't stand having them confined any longer. Bracing his palms against the wall, he watched, patient yet hungry. She yanked at her clothing, pulled at her stays, her fingers fumbling a bit, until she reached her chemise. Grabbing its lace neckline, she pulled it down, revealing herself, and tucked the neckline under her breasts.

Her breathing sharp and shallow, she watched as he took her in. Her body so eager, it trembled with anticipation.

"You're even more beautiful than I imagined," he breathed. She felt a quickening in her belly. His palms were still pressed to the wall. How she wanted his hands to be on her. "Tell me, Aimee, what is it you want me to do to these pretty pink nipples?"

Her head fell back against the wall. It was getting more and more difficult not to squirm and beg. "Whatever you want."

The look in his eyes darkened immediately, almost as though a feral need rolled through him. Softly he swore. "I like your answer . . . very much." He lowered his head. She braced herself for the thrill of his mouth.

He swirled his tongue around the sensitive tip of her breast. She squeezed her eyes shut, mentally willing him to take her into his mouth. He then sucked her nipple in, wet heat closing around her, tearing a cry from her throat. Her hips jerked forward, her fingers tangling in his hair, pulling him tightly against her.

He released her nipple in an instant. Gently grasping her wrists, he lowered her arms to her sides, the corner of his mouth lifting, giving her his usual seductive smile. "Your responses are delicious, Aimee. But I want you to stay just like that. Arms down. For now, the only touching I want is my mouth to your breast. I've waited so damned long to have you. I'm going to savor you."

He dipped his head and sucked the sensitized nipple back into his hot mouth. A whimper shot up her throat. If she thought he was extraordinarily talented with his hands, he was even more so with his mouth. He had her digging her fingers into the wall, practically clawing at it as he lightly bit and laved and suckled her. Each perfect pull of his mouth made her clit throb.

Adam turned to her other breast and assailed it with the same sweet torment.

He loved it that she couldn't stop the erotic rocking of her hips. That she couldn't take her eyes off him, utterly enthralled as she watched his mouth on her breast. Her reactions were unrestrained and so sensual. She was even more luscious than he'd imagined.

This was far better than anything he'd imagined in his wildest dreams. Nothing compared to actually tasting and touching this woman. The very woman who'd invaded too many of his dreams and waking thoughts.

His heart pounded against his ribs.

He was really going to have Aimee de Miran. This was no dream. It was real.

His golden-eyed siren was before him and his for the taking.

The mere notion made his cock thicker and harder. Made the tip of his prick ooze. His sac was so full, it ached.

"Please . . . Adam . . ."

Jésus-Christ. Every time she said his name, a jolt of lust shot through him.

Releasing her pebbled teat from his mouth, he pulled back to admire the pretty bud.

"Please what, Aimee?" He pinched her nipple, enjoying the sensuous mewl she made.

"I can't . . . take any more." She was visibly trembling against the wall.

"Tell me what you want. Let me hear it." He'd waited forever for the words. For this moment. For her.

"I want . . . to kiss you . . . and . . . to touch you, Adam."

That wasn't exactly what he expected to hear, but then just about anything from her mouth sent him up in flames. *Dieu*, she was as endearing as she was arousing.

"Come here and do it, then," he said, his voice rough with desire.

She pushed herself off the wall and stepped close. Her soft hands cupped his face and she pressed her warm mouth to his.

Adam parted his lips, a silent demand for her to slip her tongue inside his mouth. She complied in an instant, lavishing his tongue with soft swirling caresses, a kiss that was so tender it leveled him. At the height of passion, when the fire burned this hot, he hadn't anticipated being at the receiving end of anything this gentle.

His groin tightened as did his heart.

He was suddenly flooded with soft emotions he didn't ordinarily experience during sex.

Unsettled, he pulled her to him, her soft breasts colliding against his chest, intent on keeping this on familiar ground. The way he preferred it—sex that was raw and recreational. Without emotions involved. Love was for poets. He was a man of science. He was governed by logic. Reason. He wasn't ruled by emotion. He didn't fall in love. He fell in and out of lust.

A sultry sound escaped her. She slipped an arm around his neck while her other hand still cupped his cheek, and she began caressing the side of his face with the softest strokes.

He pushed her up against the wall and took charge of the kiss, his tongue possessing her mouth as his hands busied themselves with the fastenings on her clothing. Forget savoring. He was moving straight to fucking. He had to sate this unfed hunger—once and for all. To silence the maddening ways she made him feel.

His practiced hands discarded her clothing and had her quickly down to her chemise.

Removing the knee-length garment off her, he swept her up in his arms and, walking up to the bed, dropped her in the middle of it. She landed with her legs sprawled. Her breasts gave a luscious little jiggle.

Having stripped off her garments, all he'd left on her were her drawers. On her back, her pretty tits rising and falling with her rapid breaths, she watched him intently. Adam grabbed the ties at her waist, pulled them loose, and yanked the drawers off. His breath lodged in his throat.

She had mouthwatering curves, the softest-looking skin, and the most adorable belly he'd ever seen. She was beyond beautiful. She was perfection.

Better than any man had a right to.

"Spread your legs wider." His impatience to have her showing in his tone. His words came out sharper than he intended.

His breaths dragging in and out of his lungs, he watched as she did what he asked. There, on the inside of her right thigh and on her left hip were the beauty marks he'd heard about.

They were even prettier than he'd pictured.

Adam tossed off his bath linen and sank his knees into the mattress between her opened thighs, his cock throbbing and eager. Her glistening sex now had his rapt attention. He'd intended on savoring that sweet sex until she came against his mouth, but he had to bury his cock inside her. Or lose his mind.

And yet, with urgency pounding in his veins, with his cock

hard and heavy, he couldn't resist a small sampling of her sex. Especially that edible little clit, so swollen with need. A delectable offering he simply couldn't deny himself. He lowered his mouth onto the sensitive bud and gave it a light suck, sending her arching off the bed with a cry. With a soft teasing lick along her folds and over her clit, he straightened and was back to kneeling between those gorgeous legs. Her taste on his tongue spiked his hunger.

Heavily panting, she held his gaze.

"You're delicious, Aimee. There will be more of that next time. Right now, I'm going to fuck you," he said.

She sat up. Before he knew what she was about, her hand was clasped around the base of his shaft and she'd sucked the head of his cock into her hot wet mouth. A growl shot out of him, his eyes practically rolling back in his head as she milked a dollop of pre-come out of his prick and into her mouth. Slowly, she drew him back out, licked the tip and then her lips, leaving his cock throbbing harder, rioting for more.

Rising up onto her knees, she wrapped her arms around his neck. "You're delicious," she whispered near his mouth. "There will be more of that next time. Right now, I want you to . . . to . . . fuck me, Adam."

Merde. If he could smile, he would. There weren't a lot of women who could turn the tables on him. And in such a delicious way.

He should have known bright and beautiful Aimee would be different.

One simple suck from her mouth left him shaky.

She leaned in and Adam knew she was about to deliver another of her heart-stirring, mind-bending kisses.

He had her down on her back on the bed in an instant, his body covering hers, making her squeak in surprise. Staring into her eyes, he took her wrists and slowly raised her arms above her head, pinning them there. Her eyes widened, but she did not fight him.

"I'm not going to be gentle," he warned, his knees spreading her legs wide. He had six years of pent-up hunger to purge.

She shivered. "I don't care."

"I'm going to take you fast and hard. Then, I'm going to have you again and ride you slow and deep." He brushed his mouth along her jaw and down her throat. She was so silky soft everywhere. Having her naked and against him was indescribable bliss. Still holding her wrists pinned to the mattress, he said. "You're going to come for me all afternoon and night."

She was panting and squirming, impatient, but his body held her relatively still. "Yes. I want that . . . I want . . .*Oh!*"

He firmly jabbed his engorged prick against her opening, intentionally making her gasp. "What do you want, Aimee?" The urge to drive his cock into her wet heat was near overwhelming.

"I want your beautiful . . . c-cock." It was adorable how she stumbled over the more indelicate words each time, telling him this wasn't normal bedroom talk for her. Clearly, she hadn't done this with Marc, and that pleased him, more than he'd ever admit.

Adam thrust the crest of his cock inside her and froze, a guttural groan rumbling out of him. Hot silk was clenched around him. She was tight. So gloriously tight. His heart hammered wildly against his ribs. He had to bury his entire length in her. *Right now!* Retreating slightly, he drove into the most heavenly cunt he'd ever known. She cried out and arched, sucking him in a fraction deeper.

Adam wanted to howl with bliss.

He had his siren nailed to the mattress, his shaft buried to the hilt. His mind, body, and soul reveled. At last . . . she was his. And she felt incredible; her snug grip on him was nothing short of spine-melting pleasure.

All the years he'd hungered for her was worth *this*. She was worth the wait.

Their chests heaved as he stared down at her lovely face. Her eyes were shut. Her head was turned, her quickened breaths warming his arm. A single tear slipped out the corner of her eye.

"Are you all right?" he croaked out.

She met his gaze. "Yes . . . You feel so good inside me." Those words and the sweet way she'd uttered them constricted his heart. "Please, Adam, let me touch you . . ."

Her kiss and touch had a potent effect on him. His every instinct warned him not to release his hold on her wrists, to maintain a level of distance, to keep this more sexual than personal, but the next thing he knew, he'd let go and she was drawing her arms around him, then her legs, her heels digging deliciously into the small of his back.

And nothing, *nothing* in his life had ever felt better than having Aimee wrapped around him, her warm soft hands moving over his shoulders. Caressing his back. Pressing hot kisses along his neck. He closed his eyes, basking in the sensations. In her.

"I want to come for you, Adam," she whispered against his skin, sending a fresh wave of lust slamming into him.

He swore. Then reared and plunged, reared and plunged, quickly picking up the pace, driving his cock into the softness of her sex, deep and hard, fucking her with all his strength. She was going to come for him, all right. She was going to come on his cock. Harder than she'd ever come in her life. For every plunge and drag, the friction stunning. It seemed every sensation was intensified with her. He knew he was headed toward his own powerful release.

Adam caught her face between his hands and claimed her mouth in a ravenous kiss as he continued ramming her, enjoying the mews she made against his mouth with each deep thrust. His mind no longer ruled his body. He was completely engulfed in the unsated desire he had for her. She tried rocking her hips, but she was pinned under him, unable to do more than take his solid thrusts.

A bead of sweat rolled down his back. He was reeling in the moment. He wasn't just fucking a woman. This was *the* woman. His golden-eyed temptress. His angel and tormentor. Possessing her. Claiming her. Her body surrendering to him.

Her slick walls clenched down around him, sending a wicked jolt through him. Stealing his breath away. She was about to fly over the edge. His semen surged in his sac.

The urge to spend was almost more than he could take. He'd never had to fight so hard to control his climax the way he had to with her. "Give me what I want, *chère*. Come for me."

Her body stiffened. Her slick walls tightened. Then she screamed, her feminine muscles contracting along his plunging length, snatching a groan from his throat.

He was shaking, thrusting, holding on to the load of come he was dying to discharge, just so he could ride her longer. Not wanting to leave her sweet form. Not wanting it to end.

His control frayed until it finally snapped. Hot come came barreling down his cock. He reared just as semen spewed out of him and onto her belly. He threw back his head and roared her name, gripped by the paralyzing pleasure flooding through him. Come drained from his prick in forceful blasts until at last he'd emptied his cock, leaving his muscles weak and his blood humming in ecstasy.

He met her gaze, his breathing as labored as hers. She looked just as shaken by the intensity of their release as he was. Adam collapsed onto his side, beside his golden-eyed beauty, and snagging the first article of clothing he touched, her drawers, he swiped her belly and then his cock clean. And tossed it. The languor and tranquility pervading his body were sublime.

Quickly she turned her face away from him and swiped her cheek.

His brow furrowed, he propped himself on his elbow, slipped his fingers beneath her chin, and turned her face toward him. Tears glistened in her golden eyes.

Clearly, she noted the questioning look on his face. She smiled and said, "I'm sorry," looking embarrassed. "I'm not usually like this—emotional, that is, after . . . after—"

"Sex?"

"Yes. I seem to keep doing this with you. Not very sophisticated of me, is it?" Her cheeks pink, she was adorably flustered. "I've never done this sort of thing—had a lover—and I've never done what we did last night ever before . . ."

Adam smiled, leaned in, and gave her a long slow kiss.

"There's no need to apologize." He knew she wasn't the sort of woman who wept easily. In fact, Marc had once stated that he'd never seen his wife cry. And he gave her plenty to cry about. Tears were something she'd obviously hidden from her husband and yet, last night and again today in Adam's arms, her social mask had fallen away. This was the third time he'd moved her to tears.

There was something about seeing them in her eyes, on her cheeks, that he found deeply touching.

"You are . . . you're a tad overwhelming . . ." Her sweet smile returned. "You're no doubt used to women who are more urbane in the boudoir."

Under no circumstances was he going to venture there. Knowing Aimee considered him no less a womanizer than Marc had been, the subject of Adam's former paramours was the very last thing he'd discuss with her. He wasn't about to make any apologies or excuses for his past.

Unlike Marc, he'd never had a wife.

"Now that we're done . . . I—I suppose I should go." She sat up.

Adam caught her around the waist before she could get any farther and pulled her back down beside him.

"We are not done, and no, you should not go. Are you forgetting the part about coming for me the rest of the afternoon and night?" he gently reminded.

Her delicate brows lifted. "I didn't think you meant it."

Adam slid his body on top of hers, his cock already stiffening against her belly. "Does it feel as though I don't mean it?" He saw a fresh flare of arousal in her eyes. *Dieu*, he loved how responsive she was. His beautiful passionate Aimee. "I haven't said anything to you that I haven't meant."

He didn't lie to women. Never made promises he didn't intend to keep. Or false declarations of affection just to entice a woman into bed.

He liked sex to be uncomplicated.

For him sex was about mutual pleasure in the moment—without emotional entanglement or the expectation of exclusivity for either party. That's how it had been with every woman he'd ever bedded.

And then there was Aimee. His fantasy come to life.

Adam kissed her again, slipping his tongue inside her mouth the moment she parted her lips. He delighted in her soft sighs and in the mounting heat sweeping through them.

Having taken the edge off his lust, he was now in better control of himself.

Just as he preferred it.

Adam rolled with her onto his back, pulling her soft form on top of him. He pressed his palm to the nape of her elegant neck and splayed his other hand on her lower back. Holding her, he luxuriated in the feel of her body against him, her taste, the warmth of her skin, letting his fingers graze along the seam of her derrière. A soft moan escaped her, and with a little wiggle, she spread her legs, allowing him to dip his fingers into the wet folds of her sex. Lightly he petted her, gently working the sensitive flesh, making her moan louder.

Though his cock was hard and desire burned in his blood, he felt as though someone had poured warm nectar over his insides. Maddeningly, lust and soft sentiment had melded. Unable to separate the two. Of all the times he'd imagined what he'd feel like after having had her, he never imagined this. Never counted on *this*.

He wanted—needed—exclusivity with Aimee. At least until this spell he was under was broken. And the novelty wore off.

6

Aimee rushed toward the gardens the next morning.

Louise was frantically looking for her.

When last they parted, it was yesterday afternoon and Aimee was on her way to search Adam's private apartments. Almost a day later, Louise hadn't seen or heard from Aimee. She didn't blame her for being concerned, but she couldn't send any sort of message while she'd been with Adam. Upon entering her rooms not thirty minutes ago, one of her maids had notified her that Louise had spent the night waiting for Aimee in her bedchamber. By morning, Louise had left in search of her.

Entering the Hall of Mirrors, Aimee moved along the long empty corridor and slipped out the doors leading to the vast palace gardens. Standing outside, she scanned the immediate crowd milling about and then beyond, courtiers stretching past the Petit Parc and into the Grand Parc. There was no music in the air, indicating that the King was elsewhere, his court left to amuse itself.

The massive size of the gardens—manicured lawns, groves, and avenues as far as the eye could see—was going to make locating Louise a challenge, if she was here at all.

Aimee prayed Louise hadn't done anything so foolish as to venture toward Adam's apartments in search of her.

Stepping down the stone steps, she caught a glimpse of her cousin in the distance the moment the crowd to her right shifted. Relief flooded through her. Fisting her skirts, she moved briskly in Louise's direction. It was obvious she was speaking to someone, but there were too many people in between them for Aimee to tell whom.

It was only when she neared did fear slam into her chest. Louise had her head bowed, her shoulders slumped as Renault was clearly giving her a dressing-down.

Aimee all but ran the remaining distance. "Ah, there you are, Louise." She smiled and slipped a reassuring arm around her cousin's shoulders. Louise's head jerked up and surprise then relief crossed her features.

Aimee turned to Renault. The man was scowling at them. "Have you no manners, sir? Do you not offer a greeting when a lady approaches?" She got perverse joy out of reprimanding him. The man needed to be taken down a notch or two.

Renault's lips thinned. He glanced around then gave her a stiff begrudging bow. "Good day, *Madame la Comtesse*," he offered in a surly voice.

Yet again, Aimee found herself wondering what on earth Louise ever saw in this man. She supposed he could be considered physically attractive. Yet his appeal was soon vanquished upon his first utterance.

"Good day, sir." Her response was curt and dismissive. "Come along, darling," Aimee said to her cousin, her arm still securely—protectively—around Louise. She could feel the tension in her cousin's body. And her fear. She knew they were of like mind; they both wanted out of Renault's presence. The quicker the better.

"Not just yet. I asked Louise a question and she has yet to answer me," Renault interjected, arresting their steps.

Aimee let out a sharp sigh. "The answer is yes."

Renault cocked a dark brow. "Your pardon?"

"I said the answer is yes. In answer to your question: *Yes*, she does think you are a boor. Now that you are fully aware of her feelings toward you, we are leaving."

Renault stepped in front of them. "Most amusing, madame." He didn't look amused by her cut at all. She wasn't usually impertinent, but the man brought out the worst in her. "I'll need you to kindly step aside. This is a matter between your cousin and me, and none of your concern."

"I'll do no such thing. Anything concerning my cousin, concerns me," Aimee countered. "If you don't cease your harassment, I'll be forced to bring the matter to the attention of the King. He has a rather soft spot for the finer sex. He'll not take kindly to your deplorable comportment toward my cousin."

At that Renault laughed. "Madame, do you really think His Majesty would take the side of my former paramour over me, one of the most trusted men in his realm?"

Aimee narrowed her eyes and held his gaze firmly, praying he couldn't hear her heart slamming against her ribs. She hated it that he was right. Men in His Majesty's inner circle—men like Adam and Renault—had the confidence of the King. Anyone given the prestigious royal ring had the King's regard—whether they deserved it or not. Renault did not.

"Now then." Renault grasped Louise's lowered chin and jerked it up, making her gasp and Aimee stiffen. "We both know that you didn't simply accept our parting as well as you pretend. That isn't like you, Louise. You are up to something, aren't you? Why don't you tell me what it is and I may be lenient on you."

"I've nothing to say to you, Renault. Leave me alone." Louise yanked her chin from her former lover's grasp.

"Ah, now there is that temper of yours." His smile was mirthless. "The one that gets you into trouble. Again and again."

"You brought me here so I wouldn't carry on. I haven't," Louise bit back.

"No, you haven't carried on. Your behavior has been exemplary. A little too exemplary—for you. Which is why I'm suspicious. I expected at the very least badgering and begging."

It was Aimee's turn to speak up. "Clearly your conceit has made you blind to the fact that Louise has simply tired of you. My cousin does not badger or beg any man."

Renault didn't so much as glance Aimee's way. His glare remained fixed on Louise the entire time, the weight of his regard intent on intimidating her.

To Aimee's dismay, Louise lowered her gaze.

"I'm watching you, Louise. Whatever scheme you are hatching or already embroiled in," Renault said, "I can assure you that once I find out—and find out I will—I'll use the full authority of my post to see you punished for your unruly behavior. I put up with far more than I should have from you, for far too long. A *Lettre de Cachet* I think would definitely be in order. For you and"—he glanced at Aimee—"anyone aiding you."

A cold shiver raced down Aimee's spine. She felt Louise flinch. A *Lettre de Cachet* was an order signed by the King, authorizing the arrest and confinement of an individual or individuals, without trial. For an indefinite period of time. A person could be held in a prison or confined to a convent, among other places. As an abuse of their power, some men of wealth had obtained the order against their ungovernable wives. Certainly if there was anyone who could obtain a *Lettre de Cachet* from His Majesty with little trouble, it was his Lieutenant General of Police.

The very man whose responsibility it was to enforce them.

"Marvelous." Aimee forced herself to smile in the vermin's face. "Should she hatch up a 'scheme' or become embroiled in one, I'm certain she'll keep that in mind. Do find someone else to annoy, Renault." She maneuvered Louise to her side and, keeping her arm around her cousin, escorted her away. Aimee kept to a leisurely pace, despite the suffocating urge to run.

"Thank you, Aimee," Louise said sotto voce. She was about to cast a worried glance at Renault when Aimee squeezed her shoulders, halting her.

"Don't you dare turn around. Keep walking. Smile. That's right. Just like that, as though you haven't a care in the world." Aimee did the same, nodding greetings and exchanging brief pleasantries with other courtiers as they made their way across the Petit Parc of the gardens of Versailles.

With her smile fixed to her face, Louise asked, "Where on earth have you been?"

"Not now. We'll act as though we are enjoying a walk. Once we reach the far end of the gardens, we'll use the avenue along the side of the palace to make our way to my apartments. We'll talk there."

* * *

"I've been worried sick!" Louise exclaimed in Aimee's antechambers and began to pace, wringing her hands. "I was beside myself, Aimee! I imagined all sorts of terrible things. I thought perhaps Renault had somehow caught you in Adam's rooms. That you were under arrest."

"Well, he didn't. And I'm not."

"Yes, and I'm enormously relieved. What happened, Aimee? All night I waited here for you. Did you make it into Adam's private apartments?"

"Yes."

"Did you find the ring?"

"Yes. I believe I did."

Louise let out an exuberant squeal and clapped her hands. "That's marvelous! Oh, thank heavens! Our worries are over. May I see it?"

"No. I don't have it. It's still in one of the pockets of Adam's justacorps. And before you ask, no, I don't know which one. I found it and lost it just as quickly." Aimee sighed and shook her head. "Louise, I went into Adam's rooms for your ring . . . and I came out with a lover instead."

Slowly, Louise's eyes widened and her mouth fell agape. She clamped it shut. It fell agape yet again. "A-A lover?"

"Yes. A lover. You asked me where I was all night. I was with the Marquis de Nattes. He caught me in his rooms and . . ."

"And?" Louise pressed.

Aimee walked over to the window and rested her forehead against the glass, blindly staring down at the gardens. "I gave myself to Adam de Vey . . . Repeatedly, actually."

"Re-Repeatedly?"

"Yes. Repeatedly . . . as in over and over again throughout afternoon and night." The heated image of Adam, resting on his elbows, gazing down at her, his handsome face etched with passion as he slid inside her flashed in her mind. Aimee's body warmed.

Louise burst into a fit of giggles, her joviality yanking Aimee out of her thoughts.

"What, pray tell, is amusing you?"

Louise approached, smiling, and looped arms with Aimee.

"If you gave yourself 'repeatedly,' then I'd say the Marquis de Nattes's skills in the boudoir were quite good indeed."

Aimee glanced back at the gardens. "That's the crux. He wasn't good at all."

Louise's smile dissolved into a frown and she placed her hand on Aimee's shoulder. "Was it . . . terrible?"

"No." Aimee turned around, pressed her back to the window, and leaned her head back against the glass. "It was the most incredible experience I've ever had. There is a good reason women are drawn to the Marquis de Nattes, Louise. He is far, far better than good."

"He's *that* good?"

"He is beyond compare."

True to his word, he made her come so many times, she lost count, taking her in various positions, most of which she'd never tried. All of which brought her to new heights of pleasure as the clever man found different hot spots on her body that drove up her fever. So unlike Marc, who had left soon after sex, Adam had had no interest in parting company. They'd spent hours together and he never tired of her.

Even now, away from him and his touch, his kiss, she craved him and the voluptuous sensation of his generous sex filling her so completely.

And if that weren't amazing enough, between decadent delights, he pulled her near, and lying naked with him, skin against skin, they talked. Teased. Even laughed.

Of course, she knew that being with a husband and being with a lover were different. But she also saw the glaring differences in how she responded to Adam. And how he made her feel in the aftermath.

Marc had always left her feeling sad. Inadequate. As though there was something about her he found lacking.

With Adam, she simply felt wonderful.

She was still reeling from her experience with him.

"The man is altogether too perfect," Aimee said.

A squeak of joy erupted from her cousin. "I'm so delighted. You deserved to enjoy a man—especially after *Marc*," Louise said with a slight sneer. "You've got to tell me more." She grabbed Aimee's hands and pulled her down onto a nearby settee. Aimee winced when her private area came in quick contact with the upholstered furniture. Sexual excess wasn't something she was used to, but she didn't mind the twinge of tenderness. It was a reminder of her experience with Adam.

"Details," Louise demanded. "What sorts of things did he do that made him 'beyond compare'?"

"Louise, we've got to talk about the ring."

"Yes, yes. But first answer the question. Better yet, do you think Robert is likely to be 'beyond compare,' too?"

"Louise," Aimee said firmly. "The ring. Please focus."

Louise let out a sharp breath. "I hate talking about the ring. Talking about the ring unsettles me. Especially with Renault behaving the way he is, but on the bright side, Adam de Vey is your lover. A lover who is 'beyond compare.' A definite benefit. You can access his rooms and search with ease now. Another benefit."

"It will not be with ease at all. The man is an extremely light sleeper. I tried to leave the bed, but he stirred, and well . . ."

Her cousin gave her a knowing smile. "He distracted you?"

Aimee felt a blush coming on. It was embarrassing, really, for she wasn't the blushing type. Ever since she'd crossed paths with Adam at the palace, she wasn't behaving like herself at all.

"Yes, he distracted me." She admitted. "For about another hour." He'd flipped her onto her stomach, taken her from behind, and had her screaming with rapture into the mattress.

She didn't get an opportunity to search first thing in the

morning either. He'd awakened her from her slumber with stirring kisses, brought her to ecstasy and back, then carried her to
his *salle de bain*, where he had a warm bath prepared for both of
them. Never had she shared a bath with a man.

Never had she enjoyed a bath more.

"This is all so excellent. Really," Louise stated with a grin.

"How is this excellent? We still don't have the ring and . . ."
She paused.

"And?" Louise prompted yet again.

Aimee let out a sharp sigh. "And . . . it appears I am hopelessly
drawn to charming roués. Like Marc. Like Adam. Men who are
sure to break a woman's heart each and every time." Adam was
the last sort of man she should find appealing. And yet, she found
herself enormously attracted to him. If she were wise, if the ring
didn't need to be found, she'd flee from the Marquis de Nattes.

But she wasn't wise. She was too captivated by Adam.

And she'd no choice but to draw near. She was going to locate
that ring. In no way would she allow Louise to be at Renault's
mercy.

Last night, she'd considered telling Adam about the ring, but
immediately silenced the urge. He wouldn't be pleased to learn
she'd lied to him, that she hadn't come to his rooms to be with
him at all. It was sure to put him in a less than generous mood.
And given his relationship with the King and his friendship with
Renault, it was too great a risk to take.

"You don't know Adam will break your heart," Louise said.

"He will if I give it to him. And that is something I will not do."

This was merely a physical allure. Nothing more.

7

This was more than just a physical allure. No doubt about it.

Adam shook his head as he made his way toward his private apartments.

Merde. He couldn't believe it had happened to him. He'd tried to prevent it. Stop it. Damn it, even deny it. Now there was nothing more to do but acknowledge, and accept it.

He was in love with his golden-eyed beauty.

He'd been in love with her for years.

Priding himself on his acumen, on his analytical skills, he'd completely miscalculated, downright erred in his assumption that more of Aimee would diminish his feelings and kill his craving for her.

The very opposite occurred. The more he tasted, the more he hungered. The better he knew her, the more his heart engaged.

This was foreign ground for him.

What the bloody hell was he to do now? The attraction between them was intense. That was indisputable. Mutually acknowledged.

He knew what to do there.

Courtiers were expected to be in attendance each morning as the King strolled about in the gardens, until he retired to his private apartments for his midday meal. Adam had spent the last few days walking through the palace's avenues and groves with Aimee on his arm, immersed in their own conversation, as though they were completely alone, despite the hundreds of people around them.

The inability to steal kisses had steadily driven up the undercurrent of sexual heat between them. By the time they made it to his rooms, they had at each other before the meal awaiting them. Nothing gave Adam more joy than broadening her sexual repertoire. He was amazed at just how limited her sexual experience was. Marc had been a thousand times a fool for picking his paramours over his highly responsive, stunningly sensual wife.

Adam couldn't keep his hands off Aimee. He couldn't stay away from her.

He couldn't stop thinking about her. And for the first time ever, he was having a difficult time reading a woman. Her behavior and actions ranged from downright bizarre to touchingly tender.

She was constantly surprising him.

Since arriving at the palace, there had been a series of unexpected events where Aimee was concerned.

Starting on the very first day when she'd approached him in the gardens, to the following day when he'd found her in his chambers, wanting to be taken. Having her that day had been unbalancing on several scores, not the least of which had occurred as he was driving her into a third orgasm. Shyly she'd tried to urge him to come inside her. It was a stunning request, one no woman had ever made to him before.

The thought of spending himself inside Aimee held immense appeal.

So much so that the temptation grew stronger each time his climax rushed down his cock. But he'd steadfastly refused.

He wouldn't put her at risk.

He couldn't miss the sadness in her beautiful eyes when she'd told him there would be no risk involved. That she couldn't conceive. That after three years of marriage, it was clear the problem was with her because Marc had told her about the two bastards he'd sired in his youth, prior to marrying Aimee.

There had been times Adam was angry with Marc over his cavalier treatment of his wife.

Yet at that moment, he'd never hated Marc more.

There had been no bastards.

He and Marc had been friends since childhood. Marc never withheld a single detail of his sexual exploits. He loved to brag about whom he fucked. And how.

He'd lied to his wife. Because he didn't want to admit the truth.

After bedding more women than he could count, pouring his prick into every one of them without a single offspring resulting from the unions, it was Marc who'd had the problem.

Not Aimee.

And though Adam had objected to her statement, she didn't believe him. He was left holding his tongue, unsure whether revealing the extent of her husband's infidelity would sway her or simply hurt her.

The door to his private apartments was in sight and Adam felt a smile tug at the corners of his mouth.

His meeting with the King had been preempted. A more pressing matter required His Majesty's attention.

Adam intended to change his attire.

Then look for Aimee.

With his thoughts on an afternoon of decadent diversions, and a smile on his face he couldn't vanquish if he wanted to, Adam turned the door handle and stepped into his antechamber, closing the door behind him. The sound of rapid footsteps across the carpeted floor in his bedchamber greeted him. It wasn't loud, but in the dead quiet of his chambers, it grabbed his attention.

Laurent? The older man never moved that quickly.

Adam crossed the room and stopped dead in his tracks at the threshold of his bedchamber. Stunned by the sight that greeted him.

Aimee smiled and instantly set the justacorps she had in her hands down on his bed.

The doors to one of his armoires were opened wide. A pile of clothing had been removed and was presently covering the entire surface of his bed.

"Good afternoon, Adam." Her tone was cheery.

Frowning, he took in the room, so unaccustomed to seeing his personal space in disarray. "What are you doing?" he asked, baffled.

She approached, her smile still on her face. "Oh that?" She gestured behind her. "I was waiting for your return and . . . well, I was admiring your justacorps. You know how much I adore your clothing."

He adored women, each one unique, but this compulsion she had with his justacorps was . . . odd.

Aimee's heart pounded wildly, yet she managed to maintain her smile, belying the extent of her distress.

Oh God. She'd been caught checking his clothing.

Again.

It was bad enough having him wake up last eve in the middle of the night to find her ramming her hand into the piles, trying to repeat her actions of the other day that had successfully located the ring.

Now this.

His brow was still furrowed as he glanced at the justacorps strewn on the bed and then at her. Nervous, her smile slipped slightly. Then dissolved. "I'm sorry, Adam. I'll refold them and put them back for you." Aimee turned toward the bed, eager to appease him, cursing her bad luck.

"No. I don't think so." He walked up to her and caught her hand. "Come with me," he said and strode out of his apartments with her in tow.

Anxiety tightened her stomach. She couldn't decipher from his tone or his words if he was angry. Or worse, suspected what she was up to. *No. Impossible. How could he know?*

Because you've made so many ridiculous mistakes and have been caught too many times.

Adam led her out of the outbuildings and across the cobblestone courtyard straight into the palace, his grip on her hand firm. Distressing.

"Where are we going?" She tried keeping her tone light, genial, her pulse beating double time.

"You'll see soon enough."

Her heart plummeted when she saw they were headed to the State Rooms. Where His Majesty could be found in the afternoons attending to official business. *Heaven help her . . .*

"Perhaps you can give me a hint?" *Please!* Each day she felt more and more corrupt lying to him. Hiding the truth about the ring. Now she was simply terrified. Adam was an intelligent man. Had he indeed learned the truth on his own? Were the King and Renault waiting to see to her arrest? Had they already caught Louise?

She tried to swallow despite the knot in her throat as he marched her down the long corridor, then stopped at one of the State Room doors.

"After you," he said, then turned the door handle and swung open the door.

Taking a deep breath, she stepped inside.

Empty! Relief flooded through her. Adam gestured toward the long marble table in the middle of the room.

She drew near, noting the number of drawings covering it.

Closing the door, Adam then approached. "What do you think of my machine?"

Slowly, she walked around the table, taking in each drawing. One after another detailed a different angle of an intricate contraption. Stopping before the final drawing, she leaned over and studied it carefully. It was the most elaborate depiction. She'd never seen anything like it.

"Is this your 'pump' machine?" she asked, glancing up at him.

A small smile graced his mouth. "It is."

Aimee dropped her gaze down to the drawings again, marveling at them. "It's incredible, Adam," she remarked from the heart, moved that he would want to share these drawings with her.

She looked up and met his gaze. *You are an incredible man.* Aimee swallowed down the words. Holding back soft sentiments, hiding the tender feelings she had for him, was becoming more and more of a challenge. She'd never had a man who shared his interests with her. Who listened so attentively to what she had to say. Or who could melt her at a glance. One look from his dark seductive eyes, one touch, one kiss, and she was lost. In sheer heaven.

Face it, Aimee, you have failed at every turn. Failed to aid Louise. And failed to guard your heart. It was as lost as the ring. And Adam de Vey had both.

His smile grew. He moved closer to her. Her heart fluttered at his proximity, his tall sculpted body now beside hers. Touching hers.

Leaning a hand against the table, he placed the other on the small of her back. "Would you like to know how it works?" he asked.

Her nerve endings were already frenzied with delight at his touch. A wonderful warmth curled in her womb. "Yes, I would love to know how it works." She meant it. She'd had many long profound conversations with him. He had a brilliant, fascinating mind.

He impressed her at every turn, with everything he did, for everything he did he excelled in. His skills in mathematics and science. His mastery in the boudoir. And Adam had accomplished something Marc never had: Adam made her feel as though she mattered.

He pointed at the depiction before her. "These large wheels right here will turn with the current of the river and work these pumps over here, scooping up great volumes of water and sending it flowing toward the reservoirs at Versailles. This machine will be significantly larger and different from the one in use at the Seine now. Part of the problem is that the reservoirs are drying up. With this machine, we'll draw more water into them, and we'll have more water to work the fountains. To that end, there will be some modifications made here at Versailles as well."

She shook her head in awe. "It's remarkable." *You're remarkable*. "Has the King approved the machine?"

Adam slipped an arm around her waist and slid her in front of him. A wave of hot arousal instantly crested over her. The bulge in his breeches pressing against her bottom was difficult to miss.

"He's considering the cost first," he murmured and grazed his mouth along her neck up to her ear. Aimee closed her eyes and luxuriated in the sensations he inspired.

She rubbed against his delicious erection, unable to stop herself, loving the soft groan she elicited from him. "Is—Is it large?"

Splaying his hand against her belly, he rolled his hips and stroked the length of his hard cock along the seam of her derrière. Drawing a moan from her. "Is what large?" There was a smile in his tone. He nipped at her earlobe.

She gasped. "The . . . co . . . cost." Oh God . . . She braced her hands against the table as he swamped her senses with another roll of his hips.

"Substantial . . . It isn't going to be easily accomplished. In fact, it's going to be quite"—he jerked his hips forward, snatching her breath—"hard." His voice had taken on that low sensual quality she'd come to know so well, her body instantly recognizing it as the usual prelude to pleasure. Her sex moistened and ached for him.

"This is the first time I've discussed my drawings sporting a stiff cock, Aimee."

Her bodice suddenly felt too tight. Too hot. She wanted to peel away her clothing, his clothing, desperate for the press of his body against hers, without any barriers in the way. "You mean you're not this excited speaking to the King?"

He chuckled softly near her ear as he opened the front of her gown. "Hardly. His Majesty doesn't distract me with his physical appeal." He slipped his hand inside her chemise, grazing it over her skin. "Are you wet for me, Aimee?" He pinched her pebbled nipple. She shuddered with a whimper.

Her breathing was sharp and quick and the sensations from his every pinch and roll of distended nipple were melting her mind. "You know, for an intelligent man, that's rather a ridiculous question."

He released her nipple and slipped his hand out of her undergarment. Stepping away, he pushed his drawings to the end of the long marble table, then stalked up to her, picked her up off her feet, and placed her bottom down on the table. The suddenness of his actions surprised her and inflamed her further, especially when she saw 'that' look in his eyes.

The one that said, *I have to have you.*

"I don't think it's ridiculous at all. I like to hear the words from your mouth, Aimee. Are you wet for me?"

She cupped his cherished face and gave him long deep kisses, her blood rushing white-hot through her veins. He let her softly savor his mouth and she rejoiced in it, burned with it. Each stroke she gave his tongue stoking the fire. Higher and hotter. Willingly letting the flames engulf her, making the slick walls of her sex pulse with desire.

By the time he pulled away, his breathing was faster than before. "Answer me, Aimee."

"Yes . . . I'm wet for you."

"Lift up your gown. Show me."

She cast a glance at the door. They were really going to do this here? "In the State Room? What if the King—"

"The King is busy. I locked the door, and yes, here. *Now.* Lift the gown. Show me how wet you are for me." The hunger in his voice, in his eyes, was wicked and thrilling.

Grabbing handfuls of her gown, she yanked up the layers until her stocking-clad legs and caleçons were visible.

Adam pulled the ties to her drawers loose. "Spread your legs."

Holding the volume of fabrics against her belly, she spread her thighs as he requested.

"Show me," he said.

Aimee grasped the waistband of her drawers, intent on pulling off the caleçons, realizing it was going to be a bit of a struggle with her gown in her arms, if he didn't assist.

He caught her wrist, halting her actions. "Show me," he said again.

Her confusion must have shown on her face because he raised her arm and pressed a kiss to her palm, then he lowered her hand and slipped it inside her drawers, sliding her fingers down her slick folds, then slowly back up and over her clit.

She lost her breath.

Adam brought her wet fingers to his mouth. Holding her gaze, he sucked her essence off. The sweetest cream he'd ever tasted. The most potent aphrodisiac he'd ever known.

Aimee's taste.

Ravenous for more, he scooped up her legs, and placed them on the table, turning her in the process so that her side faced his front. Taking hold of her slender shoulders, he pressed her onto her back. She watched him intently as he slid her caleçons down her legs, her nervous excitement palpable. "I love the way you taste," he told her. He loved pushing her past her inhibitions. He loved the way she warmed and responded to it.

Dieu. He just plain loved her. He'd loved her forever.

He was never happier than when he was with her.

Leaning over her hip, he slid his hands beneath her thighs, spread them apart, and took in her pretty pink sex glistening with her juices.

His mouth watered.

He stroked his tongue down the slit of her sex. She gave a strangled cry. Her hips shot up off the table, securing her delicious sex firmly against his hungry mouth.

"*Adam . . .*" His name slipped past her lips on a pant, her fingers digging into his arm resting across her belly.

He plied her with steady licks and sucks, making his way to that sweet little bud sensitized and engorged with excitement. Adam drew it into his mouth. Her sultry moans made his cock thicken further. Throb harder. He wanted her wetter and utterly wild.

He sank two fingers into her wet heat. Locating that sweet spot inside her vaginal walls, he stroked it with expert finesse, instantly inducing the rocking of her hips and the moaning of his name.

Relishing her luscious taste, he groaned, enraptured, the sound reverberating onto her sensitive sex.

"Adam!" she called to him.

Unable to pull away, he continued to tenderly torment her clit with his lips, his tongue, his teeth, as his buried fingers worked her velvety sheath. Her feminine wall quivered and clenched around his fingers.

His cock railed inside its cramped confines, his sac tight and painfully full, and still he wouldn't pull away. This was Aimee. His Aimee. He couldn't get enough of her.

Only when she grasped his cock and squeezed it through the cloth of his tented breeches did she yank his attention away from her sex.

He jerked his head up from between her thighs and snapped it around, his lungs laboring.

"Adam . . ." She'd released her hold of him and was trying to open his breeches. "Let me taste you, too."

A request no hot-blooded man could deny.

Adam stripped off his justacorps, tossed it onto the table above her head, then opened his vest and breeches with the same impatient haste.

Freed, his cock strained out of his breeches toward her, greedy and eager.

She wrapped her slender fingers around the base of his shaft.

Brushing an errant lock from her cheek, he watched her lovely profile in heated fascination as she took him into her mouth. Wet heat engulfed him. Briefly, he closed his eyes and tightened his fingers in her hair. Her rhythm was slow and sublime.

He forced himself to hold still and not thrust despite the powerful urge, letting her dictate the depth, the pace. He was so hard. His prick was so full. And the sensations of her soft hot mouth advancing and retreating were stunning. Pre-come leaked from his cock.

She moaned with satisfaction, sending tiny vibrations racing up his prick, and then swirled her tongue around the engorged head, swiping the sensitive underside. He hissed out a breath from between clenched teeth. She had the perfect mouth. A natural talent for offering a man oral bliss. She made his sac ache. His knees weak. And because this was Aimee, his heart danced. *Jésus-Christ*, he had to decide what to do about his feelings for her. But not now.

Not when she had him completely ablaze.

Adam opened his eyes and met her gaze. His cock in her mouth as she gently worked it in and out, she was watching him intently, looking pleased with herself.

He swore. "You like arousing me to this fiery pitch, don't you, Aimee?"

She pulled him from her mouth. "I do."

"I like doing the very same to you. Would you like to come at the same time?"

"Yes!"

He smiled at her enthusiasm, despite the sexual agony he was in. "I'm going to come in your mouth," he warned, running a finger lightly over her bottom lip. "I'm not going to pull out."

"I don't want you to, pull out, that is." She squeezed his cock; a delicious jolt lanced through his sac.

Dieu, this woman was his soul mate in every way. His connection with her was so powerful—both physically and emotionally. He wanted to spend the rest of his days bringing her pleasure.

Adam leaned over her, spread her thighs wide, and lowered

his mouth straight down onto his intended target, her excited clit, enjoying her sharp gasp.

She responded in kind and sucked cock into her mouth, gliding him in and out, tearing groans from his throat. Spiking his need.

The double stimulation of his cock in her mouth and his mouth on her sex was almost more pleasure than he could bear. Driving two fingers into her snug sheath, he set a rhythm she instantly responded to. He had her trembling, her juices dripping from his fingers, her little mewls sending tingles along his cock, heightening the sensations of her sucking mouth, driving him to the edge of his control.

He yanked her up tightly against him and sucked her clit harder.

She cried out against his cock, arching hard. Her rapture rocked her, her sweet cunt contracting around his fingers.

And Adam finally let go.

He came with a blinding rush into the warm cavern of her mouth. She took everything he had, spurts of come draining from his prick went on and on until he'd emptied his cock.

Adam felt her slip him from her mouth, her breathing sharp pants.

But he didn't stop, intent on milking more pleasure from her body. Kissing her silky inner thigh, he kept a concentrated pressure and measured strokes over that ultra-sensitive spot inside her sheath, overwhelming her with erotic sensations until he hurled her into a second orgasm, enjoying her wail of ecstasy, relenting only when she'd finally quieted.

He pressed a kiss to each soft thigh before he straightened up and gently eased his fingers from her.

Aimee closed her eyes, dragging breaths up her throat.

Her muscles were lax. Her body was sated and still. She didn't want to move. She wanted to pull Adam near and slip into slumber in his arms.

Forcing her eyes open, she found herself captured in his gaze. He was smiling down at her looking so beautiful. Her heart swelled with a quiet joy, the likes of which she'd never known.

He tucked in his white linen shirt and closed his breeches, then held out his hand.

Placing her hand in his, she sat up. He helped her slip on her caleçons and pulled her off the table and back onto her feet. Leaning in, he kissed her, his tongue slipping past her lips, stroking the recess of her mouth.

She sighed with deep contentment.

"When I brought you in here, I didn't intend for that to happen," he said, breaking the kiss and nuzzling her neck. "Not that I'm complaining." The smile in his tone brought a smile to her lips.

She laced her arms around him and snuggled close, pressing her heart to his. Words of how happy he made her feel, how much joy she derived from the simple act of walking through the gardens with him, talking with him, or just being by his side welled up in her throat.

She wrestled them back.

She was going to miss his kiss. Him. Terribly.

But she wasn't going to embarrass herself—or him—by declaring her affections. The last time she'd declared her affections to a man, he'd all but rejected them. Marc had certainly never returned them. This was but a sexual dalliance for Adam. Not unlike many he'd had in the past, and would have in the future.

What was remarkable for her was commonplace for him.

Having removed his periwig upon entering the room, he had his dark hair tied neatly back. She threaded her fingers in it, enjoying its silky feel.

"I liked coming with you," she said softly in his ear. The only admission she'd allow herself to make.

He pressed his lips against the curve of her shoulder. "So did I."

"I want to come with you again, Adam . . . I want to come together with you inside me the next time."

He lifted his head and pressed his forehead to hers. "There is nothing in this world I'd love more, but I can't do that, Aimee. Marc had the problem. Not you. You're perfect. More than any man could want or hope for."

She felt a lump knot in her throat. His words slipped inside her heart. No man ever spoke to her the way he did. She doubted any other man would be as convincing to her.

"Let's go to your rooms," he said, a slight smile tilting his mouth. A simple sentence, but a handful of words that held the promise of decadent pleasures. Her stomach fluttered. "We cannot go to mine. It's a tad in disarray," he gently teased her.

His innocent comment stabbed into her conscience.

She was deceiving him, voiced so many lies—when he in turn had done nothing but conduct himself with sincerity and honesty.

But how could she tell him the truth?

What could she say? What words could she offer that wouldn't diminish what they'd had? Soil the memory. He hadn't spoken of a future beyond their palace stay. She wanted him at the very least to walk away with a fond memory of their affair.

She'd cherish it always.

Someone knocked at the door, startling Aimee. She jumped back out of his arms. Adam frowned.

Her hands flew to the front of her gown, quickly closing the fastenings with panicked haste.

"Who is it?" Adam called out, clearly irked by the interruption.

"Nattes?" Aimee recognized Robert's voice, her fingers working diligently on her gown. "I need the drawings." He tried to open the door, without success. "Why is the door locked?"

"Not now, Robert. Later."

"*Merde*, Nattes, open the door. The King wishes to proceed with the meeting. He is free now and has summoned us to his private apartments."

Adam swore under his breath. "All right. Just a moment." Turning to her, he cupped her cheek just as she finished with her bodice. "I'm sorry. I have to go."

She hid her disappointment behind her smile. "I understand. You must take your magnificent drawings to the King." She smoothed a hand over her hair then her bodice. "How do I look?"

He smiled. "Beautiful. Beautifully ravished."

She laughed. "So do you." Her comment drew a chuckle from him.

He began buttoning his vest. She scooped up his justacorps and draped it over her arm, holding it for him as his long lean fingers finished with the long row of buttons.

"Here," she said when he'd completed his task, running a quick hand down the knee-length coat to smooth out the wrinkles. Her fingers stroked over something hard and round that moved in the pocket. She froze.

The ring . . .

"Thank you." He pulled the justacorps out of her grasp and put it on.

Aimee watched helplessly as he snatched the periwig off the table, placed it back on, and strode to the door. Unlocking it, he opened it a crack. "I'll meet you there," she heard Adam say.

Robert pushed his way in. "What the bloody hell are you doing—" His words died on his tongue the moment he saw her standing near the table.

A smile appeared on his face immediately. "Madame de Gremont." He bowed.

"Please, Robert, Aimee will do just fine." She glanced at Adam's pocket and back at Robert who, still grinning, had a knowing look in his brown eyes.

"Of course, Aimee."

Her mind was awhirl as she tried to think of a way to get the ring out of Adam's pocket and deal with the delicate, rather compromising situation she found herself in. It was one thing to be seen walking about the palace gardens with the man among hundreds of courtiers, quite another to be caught alone in a locked room with him.

"I was showing Aimee the drawings for the machine," Adam offered, a frown still on his face. The look in his dark eyes gave a clear warning to Robert to choose his words carefully.

"Ah, yes, of course. And what did you think of them, Aimee?" Robert asked, being his cordial best.

"They're very impressive."

"Yes. I quite agree. It's been a pleasure assisting Adam on this project," Robert said, then to Adam, "We should gather them up and go?"

At Adam's nod, Robert collected the drawings.

Adam was about to leave. *Think!* This could end right now. End her lies to Adam. End Louise's torment. Every day that passed without the ring only raised Louise's anxieties. The strain over locating the ring was beginning to take its toll on her cousin.

Holding the drawings in his hands, Robert bowed to her. "Good day, Aimee."

"Good day." She watched Robert stride to the door.

At the threshold he tossed out, "I'll see you there, Nattes." And exited.

Adam turned to her. "I'm going to be a while. I'll see you tonight at the ball."

She smiled and nodded. "Of course." *Do something!* She rose up onto the balls of her feet and crushed her mouth to his in a kiss, and she slid her hands down his chest, moving over the brocade fabric of the justacorps, down past his waist, and lower still, fast approaching his lower pockets.

Adam caught her wrists at his hips and broke the kiss.

"Aimee, you keep that up, and I'm going to be hard," he gently admonished with a smile and placed her arms down at her sides. "I'd rather not walk into a meeting with the King with a stiff cock. Now, behave . . . until tonight." With a wink and a devilish grin on his handsome face, he turned on a heel and walked out the door.

Her heart plummeted. She was so close! She could have spared Louise another tortured night.

"Adam, wait!" He arrested his steps. She ran up to him.

His brow furrowed. "What is it, *chère?*"

Looking up at his beloved face, she wrestled with what to do. Perhaps she should tell him the truth. Perhaps it wouldn't raise his ire, after all. He was an even-tempered, reasonable man. Perhaps he'd understand about her duplicity and simply hand over the ring. And all this would be over. Dare she risk it? God knew she wanted it to be over. So badly. The ring was right there in his pocket.

"I wanted to tell you . . ." She swallowed and grappled with her words. "Well, you see . . . I . . . rather *you* . . ." Just say it!

"Aimee, the King awaits. What is it you're trying to say?"

"I'm trying to tell you that—"

"Nattes!" A male voice grabbed her attention. Her blood chilled when she saw Renault walking down the corridor toward them. Stopping beside them, the vermin met her gaze.

"Madame de Gremont," he offered stiffly.

Unlike Robert, she didn't give him permission to address her informally. Nor would she, ever. Aimee offered no more than a nod.

"Nattes," Renault said. "Where are you off to?"

"I've a meeting with the King in his chambers."

"Ah, so do I. He wants a brief word with me. I'll walk with you," Renault said with a smile and a pat on Adam's shoulder.

"Very well. Give me a moment, Sard," Adam said.

"Of course." Renault's smile faded considerably in his eyes, if not his mouth, when he turned to bid Aimee good day, then moved several feet up the hallway.

"What were you saying, Aimee?" Adam asked.

Aimee glanced over at Renault. He was leaning against the wall, the weight of his gaze squarely on her. He was too far to hear her conversation, but his presence unsettled her in the extreme.

She managed a smile. "I simply wanted to tell you how incredibly handsome you look in this justacorps." Reaching up, she smoothed the costly fabric across his broad shoulders.

His brows rose. "That's it? That is what you wanted to tell me?"

"Yes. Green is most becoming on you." *Green! Not blue or yellow. Green, Louise!* "You look exceptional in this justacorps. In fact, I believe it's my favorite of all the ones I've seen." She cringed at her prattle.

With a soft chuckle he shook his head. "You are delightfully different," he said and turned to leave.

She caught his hand. "I'd love it if you'd wear this justacorps tonight at the King's outdoor ball."

Smiling, he squeezed her hand. "I'll see." His hand slipping from her grasp, he walked away and joined Renault.

Aimee watched the two of them walk up the hallway engaged in conversation, until they turned the corner and were finally out of sight.

She stepped back into the State Room, closed the door, and slumped back against it.

Her gaze fell on the table in the middle of the room. Where Adam had given her so much pleasure.

It sank her spirits lower. She couldn't stand it any longer. She loathed the lies. He didn't deserve the deceit. He deserved the truth. Some truth. Any truth. Her heart ached just thinking about it.

Next thing she knew, she was racing up the hall toward the King's private apartments. Her heart thundered the entire way. Turning the final corner, she noted that a group of men were entering through a set of opened double doors. She spotted Adam at the back of the crowd.

"Adam!" She caught his arm the moment he was close enough to touch.

He turned around, clearly surprised by her presence. Her breathing was rapid and her heart raced, more from emotion than exertion.

"Aimee, are you all right?" His expression showed concern. "What's the matter?"

She glanced past his shoulder and saw the last man enter the King's rooms. They were alone. Fisting his justacorps, she rose up onto the balls of her feet and gave him a soft short kiss.

He looked baffled when she released his overcoat and dropped back down onto her heels.

"I just wanted to tell you . . . I love you." There, she'd said it. "That's the truth. I wanted you to know the truth." If nothing else, she was at least being honest with him, whatever his reaction.

And at the moment, that reaction was utter astonishment. He couldn't look more shocked. Uncomfortable with his silence, she began smoothing his justacorps where she'd grabbed and crinkled it. "You'd better go," she said, wanting to kick herself for the ridiculous, ineloquent way she'd just informed him of her deep affections.

"Aimee . . ." His voice was soft, but she couldn't bring herself to look him in the eye.

"Monsieur de Nattes," a tall, thin, older gentleman called to him from the doorway. "His Majesty is waiting."

"I'll speak to you later," she added with a shaky smile, turned, and walked away.

Behind her she heard the doors close. Casting a glance over her shoulder, she saw she was very much alone in the corridor.

He'd gone inside.

Excellent, Aimee. You handled that quite well. Before you had him wondering if you were mad. Now you've removed all doubt, and you've made yourself look like an unsophisticated ingénue. You certainly have a way with men.

She shook her head, her heart heavy. What a fiasco. She wanted to scream in frustration over the entire debacle. This would be so much easier if she hadn't fallen hopelessly in love with the man. And yet, despite it all, she wasn't sorry she'd told him how she felt. She only wished he'd responded in kind.

Between the lies and the love she had for Adam, this scheme was tearing her apart. The fabrications and falsehoods had to cease. This mad charade had to end. It was only getting more complicated and more convoluted by the day. One way or another, she was going to have the ring. Tonight.

She only wished she knew how.

Or what Adam was going to do next.

8

"Are you certain you wish to wear this one, my lord?" Laurent asked, holding up the green justacorps Adam had been wearing during the day.

Adam smiled. "Yes. That one." He knew Laurent thought it odd that he wasn't going to change into a new justacorps, as was his habit, but the golden-eyed woman of his dreams had requested to see him in it. And he was more than happy to please her.

In fact, he intended to please her the rest of their lives.

After her endearing declaration in the corridor, one that completely knocked the air from his lungs, taking him by surprise, he decided he, too, had a declaration to make.

What better place than under a starry sky with the King's finest musicians playing?

Smiling to himself, Adam slipped his arms into the sleeves. He'd chosen a different vest and black breeches to complete his attire.

"What do you think, Laurent?"

The older gentleman smiled and responded in his usual manner. "I think the lady will be most impressed, my lord."

"Ah, but this lady is very special, Laurent. She may very well become the Marquise de Nattes."

His servant's smile broadened. "She's a most fortunate woman if she does, my lord."

Adam looked at his reflection in the mirror and adjusted his sleeves. "I think I'm the lucky one."

Everything was going incredibly well. The King was most enthusiastic about Adam's machine and had given his approval to move forward on the project.

And Aimee . . . luscious, sweet Aimee was in love with him.

This night was going to be a night neither of them was ever going to forget.

"Have a good evening, my lord."

Adam couldn't seem to wipe the smile off his face. "Oh, I plan to." He turned on his heel to leave. His justacorps swung out and hit the table he passed with a *clunk*.

He stopped and glanced down, unsure what made the odd noise. Something small was bulging from his pocket.

Slipping a hand inside, his fingers touched upon a round, hard object. He pulled it out. A ring. One of the King's rings. Immediately, he checked his hand and found his ring securely on his finger.

This wasn't his.

Adam moved closer to the silver candelabra on the table and looked inside the ring for the inscription he knew each possessed.

R.S. were the letters inscribed. *R.S.?* One by one, he flitted in his mind through the men whom he knew had been given the prestigious royal ring.

Laurent's closing of the armoire's doors distracted his thoughts, yanking his gaze to his servant. Laurent had moved to the second armoire and was closing its doors as well. Suddenly, the image of Aimee standing in Laurent's place flashed in his head. Her hand moving over the justacorps . . . During the day. In the middle of the night. Aimee with his justacorps spread out over the bed.

Her hands moving oddly down his body—*to his pockets.*

Merde. She's been searching for this ring the whole time. R.S. Who was R . . . *Jésus-Christ,* he swore under his breath. Renault de Sard. Why was she seeking Sard's ring? Fool. Her cousin was the reason. Sard's former mistress. Sard had told him he'd ended the longtime affair while at the palace. That the woman was unbearable. Unruly. Ungovernable. And retaliatory.

He'd confided that he'd warned Louise she'd better not try anything. Had the woman taken his ring? There was no doubt in Adam's mind that Aimee was searching for it.

It became clear to Adam that she'd approached him for no other reason than to find the ring. Somehow she knew it was in one of his justacorps.

How it got into his pocket didn't matter. What mattered was that not once had he truly questioned her strange behavior; instead, he'd walked about in a haze of lust and love, ignoring logic. Reason. Behavior that defied explanation should have spiked his suspicions.

He curled the ring into his fist. He had one goal.

Finding Aimee de Miran.

*   *   *

In the palace's outdoor ballroom grove, the *menuet* filled the night.

The King's musicians were situated above the cascading waterfalls, their music carrying well beyond the oval ballroom and into the surrounding woods.

A number of giant torchères illuminated the magnificent amphitheatre.

Colorful gowns and justacorps twirled past as the dancers moved in time to the music.

Sitting on one of the grass-covered steps with the other spectators, Aimee looked about. She couldn't seem to locate Louise or Adam.

Both should have been here by now. Her nerves jangled. She'd spoken to Louise. She'd told her that she was going to tell Adam everything.

Then she'd spent the next hour calming Louise down. In no way did her cousin agree with her plan initially. It took some coaxing and convincing before she ceded.

Louise was supposed to be here well before Adam. Well before now. They were going to try to explain the matter together.

A tap on the shoulder made Aimee jump and twist around. Staring back at her was Laurent.

"Madame, Monsieur le Marquis wishes to speak with you in his personal apartments."

Adam? In his chambers? "Is everything all right?"

"Please follow me, madame." The servant turned and walked away. Aimee followed, unable to shake the anxiety tightening her entrails. Dread mounted by the moment during the long walk across the gardens and to the outbuildings his master's rooms were located in.

By the time they reached Adam's door, her insides were in a frenzy.

Laurent opened the door to the antechamber and she walked in. She found Adam seated at the ebony table in the room. No justacorps or vest on, he simply wore a white linen shirt and black breeches. He slumped slightly in his chair, one arm resting casually on the table, his expression difficult to decipher.

"Have a seat, Aimee," he said as Laurent quietly left, closing the door behind him.

Not his usual greeting. None of the warmth in his eyes or tone was there. She didn't know what to make of his mood.

Aimee sat down opposite him at the table.

He stretched out his long legs. "I've a question for you, *chère*. Actually, I have several. But we'll start with this one." He lifted his palm that was down on the table, to reveal the ring beneath it.

Aimee's heart sank, as she knew exactly whose ring that was.

Adam picked up the ring off the table and spun it. Silently, she watched the thing whirling on the wooden surface.

"Tell me, Aimee, have you been looking for this?"

She wasn't going to lie. Not a single falsehood would pass her lips. Whatever he asked, she was going to give him the truth. No matter the consequences, and she had a terrible feeling all was lost anyway.

"Yes. I've been looking for that."

"Why is Sard's ring in my pocket?"

"Because Louise dropped it there by accident in the Hall of Mirrors."

"And what was Louise doing with the ring in the first place?"

Aimee's gaze dropped to her lap.

"Look at me, Aimee." She lifted her gaze and met his dark eyes. "I want to hear the whole truth from you, and I want you to look me in the eye when you speak it. Understood?"

She nodded. She hated the situation she was in. She hated it that he hadn't put his arms around her this whole time.

"Good, now answer my question. What was Louise doing with the ring?"

"She . . . took it from Renault. She was quite distraught and wasn't thinking at the time. By the time she was in her right mind, she'd dropped the ring in your pocket. She begged me to help her. You know how Renault is, Adam. Or perhaps you don't know. He puts on a very different face with you than he does with Louise or me."

"So your reason for drawing near to me was the ring."

"Initially, yes, but—"

"And the day I first caught you in my room, you came not to give yourself to me but to search for the ring, is that correct?"

Dear God, that sounded so much worse coming from his mouth. "Yes, I will admit I didn't come here to give myself to you on that day, but I gave myself to you then and every day since because I wanted to."

There was a knock at the door. Adam rose, snatching the ring up off the table and taking it with him to the door. The moment he opened it, he stepped aside and muttered an oath. For the first time since she'd entered his rooms, she caught a glimpse of true ire in his eyes.

A somber man about her age stepped inside. He had two other men with him. She recognized one as being a lieutenant of Renault de Sard. She tensed.

"Monsieur le Marquis, the Lieutenant General of Police has sent us. He felt Madame de Gremont"—the man nodded toward her—"would be here. We're to escort her back to her apartments."

Aimee rose. Her stomach dropped. "Oh? Well, you may tell your superior that I am busy at the moment and whatever he wants will have to wait." Her heart pounded in her throat. Her mind spun. Her thoughts were of Louise.

Where was her cousin? What did Renault want?

Meeting Adam's gaze, she found once again he'd schooled his expression. She couldn't tell if he had something to do with the presence of these men or not.

"I'm afraid you don't have a choice, madame. It's an order," the young lieutenant said.

Fear iced through her body.

She glanced at Adam again. He said nothing. Did nothing.

He didn't believe her. Anything she'd said. No doubt including that she loved him.

How could she blame him?

Without further ado, but with shaky legs Aimee followed the three men sent for her. Afraid. And heartbroken.

* * *

Standing before the door to her apartments, Aimee watched as one of the men opened it for her and asked her to step inside.

Her stomach tightened when she saw Louise in her antechamber, seated on a chair, weeping into her hands, and Renault standing above her.

His usual cold glare was fixed on Aimee.

"Well, welcome, Madame de Gremont," the vermin said.

"What are you doing in my private apartments?" She managed to utter the question without her voice quavering.

"Let's not play any more games, madame. My ring is missing. And your cousin has confessed to stealing it."

Louise looked so utterly defeated, Aimee's heart went out to her. Crossing the room, Aimee sat down beside her and put an arm around her cousin. Louise immediately turned into her shoulder and wept some more.

"Your cousin says you are not involved in her thievery," Renault said. "That she acted alone. But I don't believe her."

It was Aimee's turn to glare. "She knows where the ring is. It can easily be retrieved and returned to you. There's been no harm done. You need not torment her this way!"

"I gave her proper warning of the consequences. She chose not to heed me. As usual." He threw a hateful glance at Louise. "I believe a *Lettre de Cachet* is not out of order here. Two, in fact, one for her and one for you."

That shot Louise to her feet. "Aimee did *not* steal the ring. I acted alone!"

"Yes, words from your mouth are ever so believable," Renault replied dryly. "I'll have the orders signed by the King in the morning." With that he turned and left, his men following him out. Leaving Aimee and Louise alone.

"I hate you!" Louise screamed at the closed door.

Aimee rose. "Louise, that's hardly helpful."

"I don't care. I do hate him. I can't believe I ever loved him. He isn't half the man Robert is!" Louise dropped onto the chair again, her face falling into her open palms. She cried anew. "I finally meet a decent man, one that's attentive and interested, and now I'm going to prison," Louise wailed.

Aimee moved to the door and opened it a crack. Just as she suspected. The three men were in the corridor, guarding them. She closed the door and slumped against it.

Aimee thought she, too, had finally met a decent man that was attentive and interested. Thanks to her multitude of errors and deceptions, his interest had waned. And she couldn't blame him for how he felt. She'd sufficiently earned his disdain and tainted their experience together. Sorrow surged inside her chest. She wrestled it back as best she could. Unlike Louise, she couldn't allow herself to succumb to the sadness.

Right now she needed to think of a way to untangle them from this mess.

She needed a miracle. Or three.

* * *

At dawn there was a knock at the door. Louise started awake from a light sleep, while Aimee simply rose from her chair, gripped by trepidation. They had spent the night in the antechamber, too unnerved to retire to bed. Louise had drifted in and out of sleep. Exhausted, her muscles taut, Aimee had been up the entire time. It was now morning and she still hadn't come up with a viable plan to escape the trouble they were in.

Aimee cleared her throat. "Come in," she said, without glancing at Louise, knowing she'd see fear in her cousin's eyes.

The young lieutenant from the night before stepped into her antechamber, offering a bow and brief greeting to both women. "Monsieur de Sard wishes to advise you both that you are free to leave your chambers. There will be no *Lettre de Cachet* drawn up against either of you."

Louise gasped, her mouth falling agape.

Aimee was stalk still. She couldn't believe her ears. "Why the change?" she felt compelled to ask.

"I don't know, madame. All I can say is that the Lieutenant General of Police had a discussion with the Marquis de Nattes before changing his decision. Perhaps you should speak to him?"

Adam spoke to Renault and got him to change his mind?

A surge of hope and a spurt of joy jolted her forward. She bolted from the room and raced out of her outbuilding, across the grounds all the way to the outbuilding where Adam's apartments were located.

By the time she reached his chambers, she was flushed and out of breath. Not bothering to knock, she burst into his antechamber. Finding it empty, she rushed through his bedchamber—also vacant—to his private cabinet room. There she heard a splash.

Without a moment's hesitation, she ran into the *salle de bain* and came to an abrupt halt when she found the Marquis de Nattes in his large copper tub.

Very naked.

Magnificent to behold.

She froze, her gaze sweeping over his stunning form, the sight of him inspiring an instant longing in her body and heart.

Adam fought to keep a straight face. Her expression was as amusing as it was arousing. "Good morning," he said.

"Good—Good morning . . ."

He lifted a brow. "Is there something I can do for you?"

She dragged her gaze from his body up to his face, her blush turning her pink cheeks a darker hue. Clearly realizing she'd been openly ogling him.

He sat up straighter, his chest rising out of the water.

"Oh, my," he heard her say softly, before she tore her gaze from his body once more and dropped it to an errant thread on her gown, plucking at it nervously. "Adam . . . I came to thank you for what you did. Whatever you said to Renault spared Louise and me an indefinite incarceration. I cannot express the depth of my gratitude."

Looking fatigued from a night of little sleep, her hair mussed, and her gown crinkled, she was still the most beautiful woman he'd ever seen. "You're welcome."

Still fidgeting with the thread, she said, "That's not all. I know you don't believe me, but I wish to say it again—from the heart—" She met his gaze. "I *never ever* once gave myself to you without desire as my motivation. It wasn't because of the ring. It was because I wanted you. I'm sorry that I lied and deceived you. I was in a difficult situation and"—she shook her head, self-disgust etched on her lovely features—"I made a mess of it all . . .

including the ridiculous way I told you I loved you. It was . . . *is* the truth, whether you wish to believe me or not. I do love you. Very much."

"I know."

Her eyes widened. "*Pardon?*"

"I said, I know. I know your affections are sincere."

"You believe me then?" she asked, incredulous.

"I believe you. When you told me you loved me in front of the King's apartments, you never tried to search my pockets as before. It was a pure utterance from the heart."

A smile lit up her face. "No, I never did! That's very true!" Tears glistened in her eyes.

"Come here, Aimee."

She approached, stopping beside the tub. Taking her hand, he pulled her down for a kiss. As she bent forward, her eager mouth met his. Adam grasped her shoulders and yanked her closer, purposely knocking her off balance and into the tub. She dropped in with a yelp and a splash.

Holding her tightly against his side, he cupped her cheek and gave her a deep, soul-quenching kiss, halting any words. Soft and languorous, he kissed her until her body yielded, her arms encircled him, until she grew hungrier, her kisses more urgent, no longer caring that she was in a tub full of water, fully clothed.

He grazed his lips along her jaw to her ear. "I know what you need."

Her hand slid down his chest, moving ever lower to his stiff prick. "What is it I need?" He heard the teasing in her tone. He caught her wrist, halting her eager hand. There were things he wanted to say first, without those delicious distractions.

Lightly he bit her earlobe. "New clothes."

She lifted her head. Her delicate brows drew together. "New clothes?"

"A new wardrobe, only the finest fabrics, for the Marquise de Nattes."

She pushed against his chest to get a better look at his face, obviously searching for sincerity behind his words. "The Marquise de Nattes? *Me?*"

He grinned. "Yes. You. I told Sard he wasn't going to imprison my future wife. Or her errant cousin. I pointed out that asking the King for orders of arrest for his former mistress would make him look weak. It wouldn't foster much confidence in His Majesty if his Lieutenant General of Police of Paris, a man in charge of maintaining order in a city of one hundred thousand souls, couldn't control this one woman."

She burst into laughing, and he loved the sound of it. Aimee rose up and straddled his hips. His cock jerked with delight, despite the clothing between them. "You're marvelous," she said. Cradling his face between her palms, she gave him one of her tender kisses that he felt down to the bottom of his heart.

"Since we are sharing truths," he said, opening the front of her sopping wet gown. "I have been in love with you for so very long, I couldn't even say when it began. You're mine. This was meant to be." He brushed a wet strand off her cheek.

"I am yours," she concurred. "Today and forever." Her lips met his again, and she anxiously aided in the removal of her wet clothes, tossing each article onto the white marble floor.

"You'll stay inside me this time?" she murmured against his mouth.

"You won't be able to stop me," he promised, slipping his hand behind her head, gently securing her soft lips more firmly to his.

Abruptly, she pulled away. "Wait, Adam. There is one more truth I want to share."

He frowned slightly. "What is it?"

"It's about your justacorps. They are indeed splendid, but to be quite honest . . ."

"Yes?"

"You look your best when you are wearing nothing at all."

He laughed and pulled her close. "I'll keep that in mind." Then he kissed his golden-eyed beauty with heated intensity and all the love he had in his heart for her.

Epilogue

In the city of Paris, there have been many weddings throughout time. But none, they say, was more beautiful or more enchanting than that of Adam de Vey, Marquis de Nattes, to his beloved Aimee.

What made this union so noteworthy was not the opulence and splendor of the nuptials, for there was definitely that. No, what brought spectators out in droves, lining the streets all the way to Notre Dame, was to see—love.

"True love" were the two words that rippled through the throng. A noble union not for political gain or advancement of power.

Just plain love.

A power unto itself.

It was said that the bride arrived wearing a magnificent golden-colored gown in a white and gold open carriage pulled by white horses. But it was her smile that people craned their necks to see. The smile of a woman in love. And she didn't disappoint the masses. Hers was as radiant as the sun.

In the spring a babe was born. A tiny boy with his father's dark hair and eyes, their little son added to the joy in the hearts of the Marquis and Marquise de Nattes.

Some say there was magic involved in the tale of Adam and Aimee; whispers of a magical ring abounded. Others believed a miracle brought them together at the palace. While many insist it was simply written in the stars.

Destiny may have caused their paths to cross that summer.

But it was their love that made their tale romantic, repeated throughout the realm.

And ensured their happily ever after . . .

The Lovely Duckling

1

*An "ugly duckling" is someone who blossoms
beautifully after an unpromising beginning.*
—Eric Donald Hirsch et al., *The New Dictionary
of Cultural Literacy,* 2002

"*Details,* Vincent. You cannot simply state you had two women last night without offering *details,*" Gilbert complained, sporting his usual lazy smile.

Joseph d'Alumbert rose from his plush chair and strode across the floral carpet over to the window in the antechamber—away from his twin brother Vincent and younger brother Gilbert. He knew full well Vincent wasn't about to withhold a single salacious detail of his evening of excess.

He simply wanted their younger brother to beg a little.

"Ah, the details . . ." Without turning around, Joseph knew his twin was grinning. He heard it in his tone. Though he and his brothers ordinarily shared the particulars of their carnal encounters, at the moment, Joseph didn't care a whit how Vincent's evening had unfolded.

He was on edge. Worse, since his arrival yesterday at the

Comtesse de Saint-Arnaud's country estate, he found himself looking out the window at the courtyard one too many times.

And here he was. Doing it *again*.

Joseph braced his hands on the window frame as he gazed
down at the empty cobblestone courtyard. It was late afternoon.
The Comtesse's week-long masqueraded affair was into its second day. Well under way. *She's not coming*, he mentally willed.

"*Well?*" Gilbert prompted Vincent, impatience in his tone.

"He had the d'Esseur sisters, Gilbert," Joseph responded for
his twin. "There's nothing new there. Everyone has fucked them."

"I haven't!" Gilbert said. "How were they, Vincent? How can
you be certain it was them? Everyone's identity is disguised."

Vincent chuckled. "Dear brother, you have been away in the
campaign too long. Marie and Jeanne d'Esseur are known for two
things. Their talented mouths. And their unfortunate, distinctive
laugh . . ."

The Comtesse's parties were never short on decadent diversions—to suit just about any taste. Yet last eve, instead of indulging in some debauchery of his own, Joseph had spent it in the
company of the Comtesse's fine brandy. Unable to focus on the
amusements at hand, he'd actually turned down women who
were eager to engage in just the sort of impersonal copulation he
preferred.

His thoughts were being pulled toward a female who wasn't
even in attendance.

"Fine. Wonderful. They had a distinctive laugh," Gilbert said.
"What else, Vincent? Out with it. Tell me before I stop asking
altogether."

At that, Vincent laughed. "We both know you won't," he needled Gilbert. "But since you *insist*, I shall tell you . . . I had them
in the gardens, behind the statue of Zeus . . ."

A black carriage pulled into the courtyard, capturing Joseph's attention. His brothers' voices immediately faded into the distance as he watched it halt before the main doors of the Comtesse's château. Sunshine glinted off its top.

He tensed.

Moments later, a figure alighted with the aid of the footman. She wore a mask. And a wig. But it didn't matter. It was *her*. He'd know her anywhere. The way she was dressed—the multiple layers of fabrics—made him certain.

Merde.

He'd hoped he'd convinced her to stay away. He knew exactly what she was after. Her letter had stated it plainly. She was here for the same reason everyone attended the Comtesse's gatherings.

For the carnal entertainment.

For anonymous sex.

Joseph tightened his jaw and held back the expletives thundering in his head. He wasn't about to let his brothers know how discomposed this woman had him. He'd never live it down. Women didn't normally stir him beyond the physical. Yet lately Emilie de Sarron had been affecting him on a number of disquieting levels.

Jésus-Christ, she didn't belong here. Not with this group. At hand were the very people who had driven her into seclusion ten years ago.

He was among the guilty.

He'd been a party to her humiliation the night Emilie had been introduced into society. As son of the Duc de Vernant, Joseph didn't make it a habit to take stock of his behavior. He did as he pleased. Behaved as he willed, without thought or concern. Without excuses or apologies. But the hurt he'd seen in her soft green eyes before she turned and left was still vivid in his mind. Still ate at his conscience. Even after a decade.

She'd withdrawn from society after that night.

She was never betrothed. Never married. He'd never seen her

again until last year when he spotted her at the theater. And she looked beautiful; her pale-colored hair and light-colored eyes had always been a stunning combination. Yet the many layers of clothing she wore were a sobering reminder of what made Emilie different from everyone else.

Driven by a need to know how she'd fared all these years, Joseph had sent her a letter the day after the theater. He never imagined she'd be so delightfully witty. Refreshingly frank. Surprisingly bold.

A year later he was still corresponding with her.

The more he got to know the real Emilie, the more he liked her. And the worse he felt for the impact he'd had on her life. A life that might have turned out very different had the incident ten years ago not occurred.

But he couldn't change the past no matter how much he wished it.

Emilie was the only one to affect his conscience when his conscience had never bothered him before. She was the only one to inspire a troubling sense of possessiveness. Or a level of interest he didn't normally offer women.

Limiting the women in his life to bed sport, the rapport he had with this particular female was novel. He'd never touched her, never tasted her, yet he knew her more intimately than any woman he'd ever bedded. Emilie was restless, looking for a reprieve from her staid existence. She longed for a bit of gaiety. She was starved for a taste of passion.

And she was intent on using the anonymity the masquerade offered to disguise her identity, in order to sample some.

Just imagine the stir it would cause if the Comtesse's guests were to learn Emilie de Sarron was back. After ten years of self-imposed exile.

"Are you listening to anything I'm saying?" Vincent's voice

cut through his thoughts. Joseph reluctantly pulled his attention away from the window.

His twin approached, stopped beside him, and looked down at the courtyard. "Well, well. A new lady has arrived. Do you know who she is?"

"No," Joseph lied.

Gilbert moved to the window and studied Emilie as she spoke to the footman. "What difference does it make who she is?" He grinned. "Someone new to play with."

An objection shot up Joseph's throat. He swallowed it back down.

He'd no right to object. Emilie was free to have sex with whomever she chose. This was something she wanted, and he wasn't going to interfere in any way. He'd offered his concerns about her intentions. Clearly, she'd chosen to proceed nonetheless. He had no idea how badly she'd been burned as an infant, but that fire had changed her life forever, scarring her body permanently. Scars she kept hidden beneath her clothing.

Just how easily a man would detect them during sex, he'd no clue. Her injuries were one of the few topics they had never touched upon in their letters.

The one thing he knew for certain was that *he* wasn't going to be the one deflowering her. No matter how stirring her latest letters—filled with sexual curiosity and sensual yearnings—had been.

He'd done enough to her already.

If she felt confident she could indulge in an amorous encounter without anyone identifying her or discovering her scars, then that should put an end to his disquiet.

But it didn't.

The idea of her giving herself to one or more of the men in attendance actually plagued him, and he had no idea why it should.

If that weren't bad enough, he had another problem. A sizable one.

Emilie had given him her trust, something he knew she didn't offer just anyone.

And he was lying to her.

Knowing she wouldn't correspond with him if he'd used his name, he'd misled her in his first letter. And in every letter since. Emilie de Sarron believed that the man she'd opened herself to, confided her most intimate thoughts and longings to—was his brother Vincent.

Joseph was too far into this now. To reveal his deception would only hurt her terribly and that was something he couldn't bring himself to do to her. Not again.

Somehow, some way he had to get through the rest of the masquerade without Emilie—or Vincent—discovering his lie.

Just how the bloody hell was he going to maintain the ruse *here*?

Emilie stepped around the footman and walked into the château. Joseph turned on his heel and snatched up his mask. "There is a party under way. I'm off." He marched out of the room without a look back.

Gilbert turned to Vincent. "Well? Shouldn't we join in?"

Vincent glanced down at the courtyard, noting the woman was gone. He smiled good-naturedly. "Absolutely. I believe the first thing I'm going to do is acquaint myself with the newly arrived lady."

* * *

"You're here!" Beaming, Pauline de Naylon, Comtesse de Saint-Arnaud, stepped around the desk in her library toward Emilie, her arms wide open.

Removing her demi-mask, Emilie smiled at her aunt, hoping

she didn't look as nervous as she felt. Her heart had pounded the entire trip from her town house in the city to the Comtesse's country estate. The closer she got to the Comtesse's château, the more she wrestled with her courage. What she was doing was daring. Risky. A tad foolhardy. She'd purposely distanced herself from many of the guests and their vicious tongue-wagging years ago.

It took everything she had not to turn and run back into hiding.

Pauline embraced her warmly and pressed her cheek to hers. "I'm delighted you came."

"Hrrmph." Twenty years Emilie's senior, her cousin Marthe d'Arbac, Marquise de Sere, scowled from the doorway. She'd all but dragged her feet from the Comtesse's main doors to the library. "Your invitation has drawn her into the Den of Iniquity. What is there to be delighted about?"

"Ah, Marthe." Pauline's smile faded. Her tone was flat. "You made the trip, too. It was lovely of you to accompany Emilie. Feel free to take your leave at any time." Pauline looped arms with Emilie. "She's in good hands now."

Marthe lifted her chin a notch and clasped her hands before her. Emilie sensed it was likely to keep herself from strangling Pauline. The two women had maintained an unwavering animosity, stemming from their court battle where Marthe and her husband, the late Marquis de Sere, had won guardianship of Emilie as a child and control over her vast fortune until she came of age—years ago. Pauline from her mother's side and Marthe from her father's side of the family, the only things they had in common were their age. And their widowhood.

Marthe's eyes narrowed. "I'll not abandon Emilie in this . . . *place*. It's utterly shocking what you allow in your home. Public fornication."

Emilie sighed. "Marthe, that will be quite en—"

"I allow private fornication as well," Pauline said. "Perhaps if you had a man more often, Marthe, you wouldn't be quite so shocked."

Emilie mentally cringed. A battle was afoot.

Just as expected, Marthe fired back. "Oh, you . . . ! You are utterly *brazen*! You see what I mean, Emilie? She is shameless. She always has been. We should get back in the carriage and return home immediately."

"She has been cloistered long enough!" Pauline countered, releasing Emilie's arm. She pointed an accusatory finger at Marthe. "You're to blame. You and that horrible late husband of yours—"

Emilie took a deep breath, striving for patience. The last thing she needed was bickering between her kin. Her nerves were far too frayed. She'd come looking for a break from the monotony in her life. But this wasn't the sort of entertainment she had in mind.

Both women meant the world to her.

If she hadn't wanted Marthe and Pauline to repair their rift, she'd have left Marthe behind, given her own carnal intent. Perhaps it was too ambitious to plan on enjoying a lover *and* bringing Marthe and Pauline together after all this time, hoping they'd finally make peace.

Emilie held up a hand to silence them and implored, "Enough. Both of you. *Please.* Darling Aunt Pauline, you simply must attempt to be nice to Marthe."

Pauline crossed her arms. "She doesn't make it easy. She's entirely too single-minded and obstinate."

Marthe sucked in a sharp breath, indignant. Emilie walked over and placed an arm around her. Giving her an affectionate squeeze, she quickly stemmed Marthe's flow of hot words. "Qualities you both share at times, no?" she asked, looking pointedly at both women.

Marthe clamped her mouth shut and looked away. Pauline simply studied the state of the nails on her left hand. Both refused to admit the truth.

Taking advantage of the silence, Emilie continued. "Now then, we've discussed this," she said to Marthe. "I'll not be dissuaded. I'm seeing this through. If you don't wish to stay, you may leave. I shall see you at home in a week."

"But Emilie . . ." Marthe said. "What you're planning to do . . . You're actually contemplating your own *ruin*. You don't belong here. You are not like these women."

Those words had bite, though Emilie knew they were innocently dealt.

She smoothed a hand down her cloak. It was summer. A cloak wasn't needed, but she wore one anyway. She owned several, various colors, various fabrics. Heavy to light. Ornate to plain. For every season. The more she covered her body, the more confidence she had. It was something she'd done since she was a child. It hadn't stopped the ridicule. Nothing ever had.

It gave her a certain comfort to envelop herself within the coverings of fabric. A barrier between her and the outside world.

But she was tired of the way she lived.

Tired of living vicariously through the characters in the books she read, the theater she frequented on occasion, and the precious few friends she corresponded with.

Tired of not really living at all.

Her discontent had become so deep, it had dragged her out of her safe solitary existence straight into one of the Comtesse's notorious masquerades. "You are correct. I am not like these women. Or any woman. Thanks to the scars," she said. "And no amorous encounter could bring about my ruin. My ruin happened long ago in a fire that took the lives of my parents and left me in this rather sorry—unmarriageable—state."

Marthe lowered her head.

"Love and marriage are beyond my reach. I've made my peace with that," Emilie said. "But I refuse to live out my life without ever knowing a taste of passion."

As long as it was real and as scintillating as the passion she'd read about.

"If passion is what you want, then that is exactly what you shall have, *ma chère*," Pauline said. "Besides, marriage is highly overrated. Trust me, I should know. I was married to the Comte de Saint-Arnaud. A lover is much more preferable than a husband. You can easily change a lover."

Marthe's head shot up. "Have you no decency?"

"Oh, hush, Marthe." Pauline walked up to Emilie and pulled her away from her older cousin. "You are going to enjoy yourself this week."

"But—But—what if they recognize her?" Marthe asked. "You know what they did years ago—"

"No one will recognize me," Emilie cut her off abruptly, not wanting to remember that night. Or talk about it. She knew Marthe meant well. Unlike her husband, the Marquis de Sere, who had been more interested in Emilie's inheritance than in her, Marthe's affections were genuine. "After such a lengthy absence, no one will think for a moment that I'd be in attendance. Besides, everyone wears masks at all times and even costumes. Isn't that so?" she asked Pauline. Her layered mode of dress wouldn't look odd here.

"Yes. The ladies especially. They make every effort to maintain their anonymity—with both elaborate masks and outfits. I find men don't make as much of an effort to conceal their identities, but they, too, wear the required mask. And no one, absolutely no one, is permitted to unmask anyone here. However, if during a carnal encounter, in a *private* setting, one chooses to reveal oneself, then that is between the lovers at play."

Marthe slapped her hands over her ears. "I can't listen to this."

Pauline's smile broadened at Marthe's discomfort. "There are plenty of men here to choose from, Emilie. Many of them were not there that horrible night."

Pauline's response made Emilie's heart flutter. There was a very special man somewhere in the Comtesse's home, one who wasn't part of that incident a decade ago.

Vincent d'Alumbert.

He'd mentioned in his letter that he, too, would be in attendance at the masquerade. She'd only ever seen him once, from afar, a long, long time ago. She was so eager to see him up close and in person. More than she could ever admit. Probably more than she should.

But she couldn't help having tender feelings for him. He and his letters were a source of joy. She felt so very close to him, having forged a connection with him she'd never had with anyone else. There was nothing she couldn't ask him. Or tell him. And she'd divulged plenty.

Given what she was attempting to do—indulge in debauchery—it settled her nerves just knowing he'd be present. On hand to offer advice if she needed it.

Pauline donned her silver-colored demi-mask with white plumes, then approached, placed her hands on Emilie's shoulders, and looked her firmly in the eye. "Are you absolutely certain you want to do this?" she asked.

Emilie tamped down her fears and self-doubt and steeled her courage. "Yes." Just once she wanted to be desired. For the next few days, she was going to step into the world of make-believe. With the aid of her masks, be transformed into someone else. For the first time ever, she wasn't going to be looked at as a misfit. Or damaged. She wouldn't be *Emilie Embers. Singed Emilie de Sarron.* Or equally as detestable, *The Ugly Little Duckling*— cruel names she'd endured all her life.

She deserved to be wanted. Kissed. Touched. Held. Every woman did, no matter her plight.

"Very well. Then let us begin." Pauline took Emilie's demi- mask of gold and red from her hand and tied it in place. "There's no time like the present." Looping her arm with Emilie's once again, she led her to the door. "You don't have to worry about approaching the men. They'll no doubt approach you."

2

The Comtesse opened the library door.

Sounds of chatter and gaiety rushed up to Emilie. Her pulse quickened. In the tapestry-lined hallway, groupings of people were clustered about, the throng in attendance having swelled into the corridor.

Be brave now. You are going to do this.

Nothing was going to ruin this for her. Certainly not the people who'd ruined what was to be a special night ten years ago. This time would be different. She'd made certain of it. She'd taken every precaution. Thought the plan through, contemplating every foreseeable scenario.

She had a strong feeling this was going to be a week she'd never forget.

The crowd shifted. A couple across the hallway caught Emilie's attention. A gentleman in a bright yellow justacorps had a woman pinned against the wall as she willingly, eagerly participated in a heated, most ravenous kiss. So engrossed in each other, they were completely unaware of anything else. Or anyone else.

Imagine having a man that hungry for you, Emilie . . . The wistful thought echoed in the empty chambers inside her heart.

She'd spent too many nights lying in her empty bed picturing it . . . wondering what it would be like with a very specific, potently appealing man.

But that man was a dear friend. And he'd never think of her in that way or desire her like that.

"Madame . . . Mademoiselle . . ." A male voice interrupted her thoughts. She dragged her gaze away from the lovers to the gentleman standing before her.

Her breath lodged in her throat. Though he wore a demi-mask, she recognized his tall, sculpted form immediately. And especially those blue eyes . . .

"Good afternoon." His voice was smooth, rich, masculine, as he addressed both her and her aunt with a slight bow. "Would you care to join me for a walk?" He held out his hand to Emilie.

"Wait!" Marthe's protest came from inside the library. Her rapid footsteps quickly approaching were met with the slam of the library door as Pauline swung her foot back and kicked it shut behind her. Closing Marthe inside the room.

"Of course she'd like to join you," Pauline said and gave Emilie a slight shove in the man's direction.

The next thing she knew, Emilie's hand was tucked into his arm, and he was leading her down the hallway. She was swallowed into the crowd. Emilie's mind raced. She had no idea where they were going. But one thing was certain—this was one of the Duc de Vernant's twin sons.

But which one? They were identical.

She'd told Vincent in her letter she'd have on a yellow silk cloak. In all likelihood this was him, but she couldn't blurt out his name. Worse, she couldn't shake the feeling that this wasn't her dear friend. Every fiber of her being screamed, *"It's Joseph!"* She began to quiver and quake, her ire mountaining by the moment as the very memory she'd fought for years to forget materialized in her mind. Joseph's vibrant blue eyes mocking her. His cruel laughter as he joined in with the others that horrid night echoed in her ears. The lash of their malicious tongues had cut deep.

And still stung after all this time no matter how hard she'd tried to forget it.

She loathed everything about the older twin.

A self-indulgent roué. Coldhearted. Arrogant and callous to the core. There was nothing appealing about Joseph d'Alumbert. He bore none of the fine qualities Vincent had. The mere thought of Joseph touching her filled her with rage. With outrage. With stomach-churning revulsion.

They'd reached the grand staircase, and he was beginning to lead her up the stairs. She'd gone no farther than the second step when she yanked her hand away as if it burned, surprising him with her action.

"I know it is against the rules, but I'll need your name before we proceed," she said, amazed her voice didn't quiver, alerting him to her discomposure. If this was Joseph, she'd feign a malady and remove herself from his distasteful presence. Posthaste.

He glanced past her and scanned the crowded vestibule, then returned his gaze to hers. A slow grin formed on his mouth and he leaned in. She tensed. "It is against the rules," he said softly in her ear. "And it is me, Vincent."

Joseph pulled back and was immediately bedazzled by the sheer radiance of Emilie's smile. Beguiling green eyes—a combination of innocent sensuality—stared back at him through her mask, mirroring her content.

"I was wrong . . ." she said, more to herself than him. Then

a sound of jubilation squeaked out her throat. She threw her arms around him, her soft body colliding against his, taking him off guard. With a grunt, he grabbed her waist and caught his balance just in time to keep them from tumbling down the stairs; his experienced hands instantly noted a delectable female shape.

"I'm so delighted it's you, Vincent," she said in his ear, seemingly unconcerned by their near fall. The soft scent of lavender emanated from her skin and tantalized his senses. She pulled away. "Come. I have something to show you." Grabbing hold of his hand, she raced up the stairs.

Accustomed to others ceding authority to him, Joseph found himself the one being led up the grand staircase. *Dieu, not your usual greeting.* A smile tugged at the corners of his mouth, amused by her antics despite himself. She was as delightfully unconventional in person as she was in her letters. This was, after all, "Vincent" and Emilie's first real meeting.

This was also Joseph and Emilie's first real meeting.

There hadn't been a real meeting ten years ago. Just a horrible fiasco.

Her warm hand securely holding his own, she briskly walked ahead of him down the upstairs corridor, the shapeless cloak enveloping her form ruffling with each rapid step she took.

He shouldn't be here with her. He shouldn't have attended the Comtesse's masquerade because of her. Most assuredly, he should have ceased his letters long ago. And he was bent on believing it was nothing more than guilt that motivated the heightened attention he gave her.

Looking back every so often, she flashed him a smile. His groin tightened. This was the closest he'd been to her in a decade, and her mouth grabbed his focus every time she glanced his way.

Dieu. There was no denying it. She had a pretty mouth. So lush. So perfect.

The kind of mouth that could give a man hours of carnal pleasure.

Emilie reached her door and pulled him inside her private rooms.

It was late afternoon and the sun shone from the tall windows in the antechamber, giving the motifs adorning the walls of white and gold a warm glow.

"I'm so pleased you found me." She stopped in the middle of the antechamber, and released his hand. Oddly, he had the urge to grab hold of it again. "I've only just arrived and I was hoping I'd see you sooner rather than later. I'm glad I mentioned I'd be wearing a yellow cloak in my letter. Clearly it made it easy for you to find me."

Yellow cloak? He'd forgotten. He'd been too stunned by her plan to remember the details of her intended wardrobe.

With her usual smile on her distracting mouth, she pulled off her mask, tossing it onto a nearby settee, then her wig.

A mass of flaxen-colored curls tumbled out, looking so soft he wanted to reach out and play with a silky lock. Joseph drank in her visage. It was less girlish, more womanly now. Big fathomless green eyes. Hair as pale as moonlight. She was ravishing.

She had the face of an angel.

Taking hold of both his hands, she gave them an affectionate squeeze.

"Your turn," she said. "Remove your mask, Vincent."

His brows shot up in surprise. That sounded a lot like a command, not something he would have responded to favorably had someone else dared. But no one else would dare to make demands of any of Richard d'Alumbert, Duc de Vernant's sons. One of the most powerful men in the realm.

For the life of him, Joseph had no idea why he found her non-conforming ways charming.

But he did.

Was this forwardness simply the way she was? Or had she been secluded for so long that she wasn't accustomed to the usual rules of etiquette?

Joseph pulled off his mask, tossed it carelessly at the settee, and returned her smile.

Instantly, Emilie's smile dissolved. She took a step back.

Her reaction astonished him. "Emilie?"

Her smile returned. Not as bright. Nor as natural. "I'm sorry . . . it's just that . . ." She shook her head and waved off the rest of her sentence.

He frowned. "It's just *what*?" he pressed.

"It's nothing really. It's just . . . well, when you removed your mask, it felt as though I was staring at Joseph."

Merde.

"I know that's silly. You're identical . . ."

Not identical. Not in her eyes. In her eyes, Joseph was loathsome. He didn't know which bothered him more, that she despised him—when he shouldn't care a whit what she thought. Or that deep down inside, he couldn't fault her for the way she felt.

At some point during the last year he'd connected with her, when he'd normally maintained a comfortable level of detachment in all his dealings with women. This was yet another example of how far he'd let matters veer off course with this particular female.

Something he needed to rectify where she was concerned.

He was too uncomfortably aware of her. Too in tune with her emotions for his liking.

He wanted to snap the disconcerting connection.

"Actually, I'm far better looking than my brother," he jested, trying to leaven the moment and take the stricken look from her face.

She burst into a laugh. A delicate sound he found appealing. "Well, now that we've established that, I have something I want you to see." She walked over to the writing desk.

He followed her, and tried to ignore her arousing scent.

"I asked my maid to unpack my books first," she said. "I wanted to show you a very special volume." Emilie leaned forward, searching through the books that were piled on the desk. Her cloak gaped open. Joseph got an instant view. Just above the décolletage of her gown he saw the top curves of her breasts. The sweetest, most tempting tits. And even more surprising, the expanse of lovely—unmarred—skin.

Lavender-scented skin.

His cock stiffened. Joseph yanked his gaze to the stacks of books on the desk, in need of a distraction. He'd be damned if he was going to think about what else he'd find appealing under all those clothes. He'd thought about her body too many times, her scars be damned, especially on those nights when her innocent—yet so stirringly sensual—letters had him on fire. Asking him unabashed questions about sex. Confiding in him how and where she wanted to be touched. Taken.

There was no way he would allow her to torment him any more than she already was.

"Really. And what volume might that be?" he asked. A discussion about books was good. A neutral subject. One that wouldn't drive him to distraction.

"Ah, here it is." Picking up a book, she opened it and held up an illustration for him to see.

Before him was a graphic depiction of a naked woman bent over the edge of a bed while a man took her from behind.

Jésus-Christ.

"It's an erotic text," she announced.

No argument there. His eager prick gave a hungry throb in full agreement, as it strained harder against his breeches.

She placed the book down on the desk, open to the inciting illustration. "I didn't realize there were so many positions to do this in." Her delicate brow furrowed. "I don't care for this one." She flipped a few pages forward. "I like pages five to twelve." Slowly she turned the pages, showing him her "favorites."

Heated illustration.

After heated illustration.

No doubt about it. Emilie would surely derive a measure of satisfaction if she knew the amount of torture she was presently inflicting on Joseph.

"Oh, and I like this one," she said, tapping the page. "This one" was a woman being taken while standing. Her back was against the wall as her lover drove his cock into her core. "Have you done this one, Vincent?"

All right. Enough was enough. Joseph closed the book, shutting out the stimulating images. The ones racing through his brain were another matter. He took a deep breath and let it out slowly.

"I'm not going to answer that." Thanks to Emilie, he hadn't had sex in nearly two weeks—if you added the travel time it took to arrive at the Comtesse's country estate and last night's baffling eve of abstinence. He was ready to climb out of his skin. The last thing he was going to do was engage in a sexual conversation with her. Not when images of Emilie's breasts and the damned depiction of the couple fucking against the wall were running rampant in his head. Only he was picturing taking this highly inquisitive virgin just the way she wanted. By God, he had the most powerful urge to sink his length into her, wondering just how tight her untried passage would be.

Her moss green eyes widened. "Oh? Why not? You've always answered my sexual questions before."

True. But that was through their correspondence. And not when she was standing in front of him looking like a sweet temptress, smelling better than any woman had a right to. His fingers itched to fist that silky blond hair, tilt her head back, and feast on that luscious mouth.

He resented her ability to so effortlessly inflame him the way she did.

He was changing the subject.

"Why are you showing me this volume, Emilie?" There had to be a reason, other than to drive him mad.

Her smile returned to her comely face. "Because I know you have misgivings about my plans here. And as much as I appreciate your concern, I have the matter well in hand. As you can see, I've studied everything thoroughly. I am well prepared."

"Well prepared? You're contemplating having sex. Not going into battle, *ma belle.*"

Emilie froze, his words unbalancing her.

Surely she hadn't heard correctly. Had he just called her . . . my *beauty*? No one had ever called her *that*. In fact, they'd called her just the opposite.

What could he possibly see that was beautiful?

There hadn't been a day in her life she'd felt pretty, much less beautiful . . . well, maybe just one time. One night. But it had turned from a dream to a nightmare.

You fool, he's simply being kind. Because that's what Vincent is. Kind. And he is—gracious God—pure male perfection . . .

Though she was trying, it was impossible to ignore his tall sculpted form. His dark hair and knee-weakening blue eyes. Or the heat he inspired low in her belly. Vincent d'Alumbert was as disarming in person as he was in his letters.

His appeal wasn't tainted—like his brother Joseph's—by poor character.

And she was drawn to him. Intensely so.

He's waiting for a response, Emilie. Answer him . . . She cleared her throat and collected her wits. "I'm quite aware I'm not going into battle. I'm simply trying to assure you that I am fully knowledgeable about the subject of sex and seduction. Thanks to your answers as to what a man likes in bed, and my books, I am prepared to proceed."

He sighed. "Emilie—"

She silenced him by pressing a finger against his sensuous mouth. So warm and firm. Emilie tamped down the regret that surged inside her heart, knowing full well she'd never experience a kiss from this man. No man would knowingly indulge in an amorous encounter with *Charred and Scarred Emilie de Sarron.* The only way for her to have some pleasure of her own was to be with a man who didn't know her. Didn't know she'd been in a fire. "I know what you're going to say. One needs to experience sex to be truly knowledge-able." Reluctantly, she removed her finger. She liked touching him. A little too much for her own good. "I agree wholeheartedly. That is why I'm going to have my first experience tonight."

He scrubbed a hand down his face. "Emilie, there is nothing wrong with anonymous sex. People do it all the time. But a man is going to want . . ." Vincent faltered.

"To have me naked," she supplied.

"Exactly. It's part of the pleasure. Skin against skin. Sex involves the senses, touch, taste, smell, sight. A man is going to want to see—"

"I'll manage." The words came out sharper than she'd intended. She didn't want to be abrupt, but his comments were undermining her confidence. And being in the presence of this beguiling man—whose letters oozed charm and had made her laugh, who'd impressed her with his intellect and honesty, and who'd given her the most tantalizing insight into a man's mind during sex—made it difficult to concentrate on her plan.

The allure of Vincent d'Alumbert was even stronger in person than she'd imagined. And she had to resist it. It was bad enough her feelings for him ran deeper than she'd like. She wasn't going to dwell on what she couldn't have in her life—a man of her own.

This delicious man.

Why long for something that was impossible? Instead, she was going to focus on what she could have.

And she could have some bliss in her life.

Nothing was going to stop her.

"You are a dear friend, Vincent," she said. "You've done a great deal for me already and . . . I loathe to ask for a favor. Or rather two favors . . ."

His eyes narrowed slightly. "What two favors?"

"I know you want me to succeed. But if I'm to concentrate on finding the right man to give myself to, I need you to keep Joseph away."

He stiffened slightly. *"And . . . ?"*

She smiled. "Oh, and I need you to help me choose a lover."

3

Merde! He must be mad, utterly insane, to have come here and made himself a party to this!

Joseph stalked down the corridor on his way to the dining hall. The "favors" she'd requested had echoed in his head since he left her. Hours later, his ire was full blown. White-hot. Prickling his skin.

Help me choose a lover. The hell he would! He didn't care how troubled his conscience was. He would not do her bidding. He didn't do anyone's bidding.

And he certainly did *not* find women their bed sport.

Dieu! She'd actually asked for his help in finding someone to bed her.

He could only imagine the amusement his brothers would derive from learning a woman had made that request of him.

Chatter and laughter emanated from the dining hall, violin music drifting through the din. Joseph secured his demi-mask in place just before he reached the threshold.

I need you to keep Joseph away . . .

Oh, he was going to stay away, all right. No problem there.

Once and for all he was going to stop voicing his concerns. In fact, he wasn't going to be concerned. He wasn't going to think about her attempts to be debauched tonight. Or how disastrously it might turn out.

For his involvement ten years ago, he owed her an apology— one he couldn't even offer because she wanted nothing to do with Joseph—but that was *all*. He didn't owe her a *lover*.

He wasn't getting involved with this plan of hers. No matter what.

She was a grown woman. She'd made her decision.

And he was making his: He'd decided Emilie de Sarron had occupied his thoughts long enough. She wasn't going to be a mental distraction anymore. Or a physical one. While she gave herself to God knows who and attempted God knows which sex act she'd chosen from her book, Joseph was going to do what he should have been doing at the Comtesse's masquerade from the start.

Delving into some much-needed sexual oblivion.

Joseph entered the grand dining hall. The mirrors on the walls reflected the candlelight from the wall sconces and the silver candelabras on the long linen-covered dining table that ran down the center of the room. The noise in the room was more boisterous than the usual noble gathering. No formalities or respectable social conduct on display here. Not when the purpose of the evening meal was to find a partner or partners for carnal entertainment afterward.

Open fondling and flirting were everywhere.

Joseph marched straight to his usual seat near the head of the table. His brothers and his friend, Georges, Marquis d'Attel, occupied the chairs near him.

"There you are. I was beginning to wonder if you were going to show up," Vincent said. "We still don't know where you disappeared to last night."

Into a brandy decanter. Fool that he was.

Joseph snatched the crystal goblet off the table and held it up. A servant was quick to appear and fill the vessel with wine. He downed it, and held it up again for more, eager to take the edge off his vexation. The sooner his irritation subsided, the sooner he could begin to enjoy himself. It surprised even him just how furious he was. And he refused to dwell on or attempt to decipher why her requests had made him *this* incensed. "I've been occupied. And last night is none of your concern."

Georges laughed. "Now that's evasive."

Seated on the other side of Vincent, Gilbert leaned toward Joseph, grinning from behind his gilded demi-mask. "An answer that begs the question: Just who were you 'occupied' with?" He elbowed Vincent. "Wouldn't you say, Vincent?"

Vincent was sporting the same foolish grin. "I would."

"In case it's escaped your notice, we are at a masquerade," Joseph stated sharply. "You're not supposed to know whom you're with." For his mental peace, he wished he didn't know Emilie was here. And he didn't want to know whom she'd be with tonight.

"Ah, my fine friends." Henri de Villeneuve strolled up and placed a hand on Joseph's shoulder. "Did any of you happen to notice our friend, Augustin de Coix?" Smiling, Henri gestured down the table with a motion of his chin. "He's actually found a woman who can tolerate him. She looks new."

That grabbed Joseph's attention. He shot his gaze down the table, spotting his friend Augustin, Comte de Coix, immediately. And the woman he was with. She was wearing a blue and gold demi-mask, dressed in a light blue cloak. His stomach plummeted.

Emilie.

His arm resting on the back of her chair, Augustin leaned into her, his mouth at her ear as he whispered to her, relaying an intimate message. Joseph's body went rigid.

"I don't believe I've ever seen her before," Henri said. "Have you?"

"Isn't that the woman who arrived this afternoon?" Vincent asked.

"No." Joseph mentally winced. The denial shot out of his mouth a little too abruptly.

Merde. Of all the men in the room, she'd picked Augustin? He was a self-proclaimed ass. He wouldn't satisfy her. He'd no skill or finesse in bed. Nor did he care to. He'd take his pleasure, then take his leave.

He was all wrong for her purposes. Damn it, he was wrong for her. Period.

Emilie smoothed a hand down the front of her cloak, bringing attention to it. *Dieu*, she was the only one wearing one. Of all the different costumes in the room, from moderate to outrageous, Emilie's cloak stood out. It all but screamed, "Emilie de Sarron." How much longer before his friends realized it was her?

"Look at the way she's dressed." The comment came from Gilbert's mouth, making Joseph want to throttle his youngest brother.

"I like the way she's dressed," Georges said.

"Hmmm, me, too," Henri concurred.

Joseph shot them a look, one that must have indicated just how stunned he was by their response.

Henri's brows shot up. "What? You don't agree? Look at her, Joseph. She's a comely little piece." A slow smile spread across his mouth. "When the ladies present are wearing low-cut décolletages, our clever little seductress wears a cloak, just to make her stand out."

"Absolutely," Vincent concurred. "She's made it a game. Just think of the fun it will be to peel away those layers and sample the tasty fruit within."

"She is clever," Georges said. "She's donned the cloak just to tantalize our imagination. Every man who looks at her is forced to wonder at the delicious form she's hidden under it."

Good Lord. Not at all the reaction he'd imagined.

Just then Augustin reached and yanked open Emilie's cloak. She started and, with a charming smile, gently closed the cloak again, rose, and left her seat. With nothing but elegance and grace.

Laughter burst out of Joseph's brothers and two friends.

"It doesn't look as though the lady is impressed with our Augustin," Henri said, still chuckling.

Joseph couldn't shake the sense of relief he felt as he watched her walk away from Augustin. Nor could he help but marvel at the way she'd handled herself. Despite her lack of experience, she hadn't let Augustin's brutish advances rattle her.

It occurred to him just then that her chances of succeeding with her plan were great. Aside from her intellect, she was even braver than he'd given her credit for.

Emilie wasn't going to be frightened away, like some faint-hearted ingénue.

One man in this room was going to be the first to enjoy this most exceptional woman. A woman who happened to have the sweetest face, and the softest green eyes he'd ever seen.

A foreign emotion rose inside him.

Joseph wrestled it down.

Feminine fingers brushed across his cheek. Looking up, he found an attractive dark-haired woman standing beside his chair, smiling down at him. Sporting a bright green demi-mask that matched the color of her gown, she wore a décolletage that was so very low, he wondered if she would spill out at any moment.

"Good evening, my handsome lord," she all but purred. "I have a dilemma. I wondered if you might assist me?"

"Oh? What is your dilemma?" he asked.

Her smile turned saucy as she twirled a lock of her hair around her finger. "It seems that all the seats are taken. I haven't anywhere to sit. I don't suppose you'd allow me to use your lap?"

He heard muted snickers from the fools he associated with.

"I never turn away a lady in distress." Taking her hand, Joseph pulled her down onto his lap. "Allow me to be of assistance."

"Why, thank you, kind sir." She snuggled against his groin, her ample bosom looking even more plentiful from his new vantage point. Right under his face.

She slipped an arm around his shoulders and brought them closer to him. "You may call me Juliette." A false name. Everyone used them. He loved the anonymity of it all.

She brought her mouth near his ear. "I am yours, my lord . . ." And began nibbling down his neck. Light little bites.

Now *this* was exactly what he should be focusing on. A sexual encounter with someone he didn't know. Someone who would never cross his mind afterward.

Joseph closed his eyes, eager to lose himself in the sensations, but the moment they were shut, words Emilie had written rushed into his mind.

I want to know what it feels like to have a man inside me. To know the sensations of each plunge and drag as he takes me to the ultimate fulfillment. Oh, I long to know firsthand how glorious it is to be in a lover's embrace, lost in passion, locked in the most intimate joining . . .

Joseph's eyes flew open. He cursed the mental diversion. *Don't think about her. Not now. Focus on the woman at hand.* He wasn't going to think about Emilie. Or if the man she chose would give her the pleasure she sought.

Juliette placed a hand on his chest, and slowly inched her way lower and lower.

"A bet, gentlemen," he heard Georges say. "A hundred *louis d'or* says I fuck the lovely lady with the cloak first."

"A hundred *louis d'or* says you fail and I succeed," Henri said.

Joseph arrested Juliette's hand and forgot all about the woman on his lap.

Her head shot up. "My lord?"

He ignored her, because the next thing he heard was, "I'll bet, too." Gilbert drained his goblet, his smile returning the moment he set the vessel back down on the table. "You gentlemen don't stand a chance when pitted against my charm."

Georges and Henri scoffed as they rose from their chairs.

"I go first," Georges said.

Jésus-Christ. Joseph rose with Juliette in his arms and handed her off to Georges. Georges grunted when she landed in his arms.

"There will be no bet!" Joseph decreed, accustomed to ruling his friends. "No one is having her." Words shot out of his mouth, without censor.

His friends and siblings exchanged curious glances. Joseph knew he sounded like a lunatic. Given the type of gathering they were at, he could hardly make such a statement. But he didn't care. Emilie was sexually untried. His corrupt friends wouldn't be gentle with her. Or take her with care, even if they knew it was her first time.

And the mere thought of them recognizing her in the throes of passion and saying something cruel to her tore at his very vitals.

He wasn't going to let them hurt her again, like he'd let them hurt her ten years ago.

"I'm having her," he added for good measure. "Go find someone else to amuse you."

Georges put Juliette down. "Ah, come now. You can't claim exclusivity here. We can all share her."

Joseph narrowed his eyes. "I'll claim whatever I want. Find. Someone. Else." He looked pointedly at each man before him.

That prompted Juliette to turn on a heel, miffed, and stalk away.

"I'd like a private word with Joseph." Vincent, who'd been silent until now, finally spoke up. The others walked away, grumbling.

"Brother, you lead and they follow. And for the most part, I don't mind going along, but"—he crossed his arms—"you don't dictate whom I bed. Now then, care to tell me who this woman is?"

"She's wearing a mask. How the hell should I know who she is?" He hated lying to Vincent, but the truth was far more complicated than his deceit. And more difficult to explain. There were things about what was going on that he couldn't explain to himself. And didn't want to try.

His twin sighed and shook his head. "Fine. Have it your way. You don't know her. She's got you intrigued, or some such nonsense. I'm still having her," Vincent said with finality.

Joseph's gut tightened. "Not until I'm done with her," was all he could respond. Pressing the matter any further would make him sound as though he'd gone completely mad. As it was, his behavior was absurd, bordering on irrational. He'd never cared who a woman was with before, during, or after he'd had her.

Vincent silently contemplated his words. Joseph's heart pounded away the seconds, wondering what he'd have to do to keep Vincent away if he didn't agree.

His brother's genial smile returned. "Agreed. You have her first. She's all yours tonight." He patted him on the back. "I get her tomorrow."

* * *

Their bodies touched.

He drew his arm around Emilie's waist and pulled her up tightly against him. Then he pressed his lips to hers. It was actually happening. Her first real kiss. An amorous encounter of her very own. His tongue snaked into her mouth and was presently swirling about. It felt, well . . . odd. But then she'd no experience in this area, and her masked gentleman was seemingly enjoying himself if the zealous sounds he emitted were any indication.

Emilie relaxed her shoulders and laced her arms around his neck, throwing herself eagerly into the kiss, anxiously waiting for the moment "it" would hit her. Passion. Hunger.

That all-consuming desire.

Just like the couple she saw in the corridor earlier. Just like the books she'd devoured again and again. *Just like you felt near Vincent . . .*

She'd purposely led her masked lover to the gardens. The perfect setting. They were under an indigo sky with a large luminescent moon and a thousand twinkling stars. What could be more perfect? All she had to do was let her lover take the lead, ignore the grunts from the couple who were mostly naked, rutting in the distance. And of course, resist the urge to pretend the man kissing her was Vincent d'Alumbert.

Just focus. Any moment now, she'd be swept up in "it."

Mimicking his tongue swirls, she angled her head farther to the right and hoped she was doing this correctly. He seemed to like it. He'd pulled her against him tighter, and groaned louder.

Minutes later, he was squeezing her right breast through her cloak and "it" was still nowhere to be found.

Worse, she was actually . . . bored.

This experience was of the blandest sort.

What was she doing wrong? He was handsome, or at least he appeared to be from what she could see of his face that wasn't covered with his demi-mask. There was nothing unpleasant about him. Not his smell or his taste. What was amiss here? Where was the heat? The exhilaration?

"Ah, there you are," Emilie heard just before a strong arm slid in between her and the man kissing her, and pulled her back, breaking their contact.

She jerked her head up and was surprised to find herself staring at Vincent, his arm still across her chest, holding her shoulder. He wore his mask, and the same attire he had on earlier. She knew it was him. He gripped her elbow. "Come with me."

"Just a moment, monsieur! Where do you think you're going with her?" her flavorless lover protested.

Vincent turned back around and shoved his mask off his face, a scowl etched across his handsome features.

"Oh, it's you . . . *Joseph* . . ." The gentleman's anger was immediately mollified.

"It's Vincent, you fool. The lady is coming with me. Any objections?" The question was weighty with authority, his elevated rank hanging in the air between the men. It was clear what was truly being asked: "Do you *dare* object?"

Her anonymous kisser glanced at her, his expression looking remarkably like regret, and then said a soft, "No."

With that, Vincent took her hand and stalked toward the château with her in tow, the tiny stones on the path crunching beneath her feet.

She was all but running to keep up, her free hand holding her cloak closed so it wouldn't fly open.

His comportment irked her. "Vincent, just what do you think you're doing?"

He didn't respond and kept on walking.

"Vincent, you just bullied that man." It bothered her to see it. He'd swooped in, without excuses or apologies. An arrogant display that was more in keeping with Joseph's character and not the Vincent she'd come to know. "Your conduct was rather poor, don't you think?"

Still no answer. Her ire spiked. She'd no idea what had gotten into him.

"Just because you're the son of the Duc de Vernant doesn't mean you're above reproach."

"You're wrong there. I'm afraid it does." His answer annoyed her further, as did the fact that he was affecting her. The simple touch of his hand was sending delicious tiny tingles reverberating up her arm to her breasts. Hardening her nipples. She'd spent long minutes kissing her masked gentleman with no reaction. Not a spark of heat. Yet some simple handholding with this man, and her body was aquiver.

It was exasperating. Vincent was a friend, albeit an annoying one at the moment. She didn't delude herself into believing he'd ever desire her. "I don't care a whit who your father is, you're not above reproach with me."

"Believe me, I'm very much aware of that."

His response surprised her. "Vincent, where are we going? What is all this about? I was in the middle of an amorous encounter when you so rudely interrupted." All right, perhaps she was a tad grateful that he'd put an end to the dull experience, but he didn't need to know that. What he needed to know was that she wouldn't tolerate any high-handedness from him.

"You were in the middle of an encounter, *chère*. It was hardly amorous. You looked ready to fall asleep. Trust me, I did you a favor."

Before she could offer up a hot retort, they entered the château's great room. There was a crush of people now. People who'd clearly consumed more drink, the laughter louder and the throng rowdier than before. Bawdy behavior was more evident and widespread. The light fondling she'd seen earlier around the table had been replaced by open groping. There were more than a few open bodices. Bare breasts. Open breeches. And in a few instances, open fornication.

Emilie was dragged past a giggling woman sitting on her lover's lap. Her masked man nibbled at the grapes nestled between her amble breasts, making her squirm and squeal with delight. Vincent continued through the crowd, maneuvering her out of the Grand Salon, through the grand vestibule, up the staircase, and down the corridor straight to her private rooms.

When she was finally standing in her antechamber, she pulled off her mask and wig and demanded, "Tell me what we're doing here."

"You're leaving. Now. This night." He tore off his mask and tossed it carelessly to the floor. "Where are your trunks?" Vincent turned and marched into her bedchambers.

She chased him in. "What do you mean, I'm leaving tonight? Why on earth would I do that?"

"I'll get someone to help you pack. Better yet, I'll help." He strode to the armoire and threw open the doors. "*Dieu*, you have a lot of clothes . . . Are there more in the cabinet?"

He, a d'Alumbert, privileged and pampered, was going to help her pack? Tackle the task of a *servant*?

"Vincent, what has gotten into you? Have you lost your mind?"

"I've asked myself that question many times since your recent arrival." He raked a hand through his dark hair. "Emilie, you can't stay. You must leave. The sooner the better."

She frowned. "Why?"

"Because this plan of yours isn't going to work."

"Really?" Emilie tilted her head to one side. "And why not?"

Joseph noted the stubborn look in her eyes. One that told him she wasn't about to leave without a good reason. *Think of one.*

"Fine. You force me to tell you," he said.

"Tell me what?"

"Joseph wants you." That wasn't a lie. Though he wished it was. "I can't keep him away." That wasn't a lie either. He couldn't seem to stay away from her no matter how he tried. And he couldn't keep Vincent away from her either.

His easy-mannered twin, who'd always done as Joseph asked, picked a fine time to be unyielding.

Her lips twitched as though she were holding back a smile. "That's it? That is the reason I must flee in the middle of the night?" She approached, the smile on her beautiful face growing larger with each step she took. "That's why you interrupted me in such haste?" She stopped before him. Lavender swirled around him, stirring his senses.

His blood warmed. "Ah . . . yes."

She gave him a radiant smile. "Vincent, you're a dear!" She threw herself against him, her arms entwining his neck.

Desire hit him in a hot wave on contact. His cock thickened as he took in the warm press of her body down the length of his and her silky flaxen hair against his cheek.

"I'm so moved by your concern. You're a wonderful, wonderful friend." She tightened her arms around him and snuggled in closer, inadvertently rubbing his engorged shaft with her belly. *Dieu . . .*

He didn't deserve the praise and he certainly couldn't take the physical contact, given his current celibate state.

Gently, Joseph pushed her away. Placing his hands on her

shoulders, he held her at arm's length and dipped his head, bringing him eye level to her. Big beautiful green eyes stared back at him, drawing him in. Just as distracting was that perfect pink mouth. Seeing another man sampling her drove him half mad. He was starved for those lips. Ludicrous as it was, he wanted them all to himself when he'd never cared much about exclusivity before. Thoughts of sliding his cock between those lush lips flitted through his mind. "So you see now why you must leave," he forced out, ignoring the mental images. "It's quite impossible to keep Joseph from you. He's told me he'll approach you tomorrow. And we both know how much you don't want that. Correct?"

"Correct."

"Wonderful. Then it's settled. You're leaving. Let's pack." Joseph released her shoulders and walked toward the cabinet where he was sure to find more of her wardrobe, then thought better of it. He'd no idea how to pack. And no interest in learning. Joseph turned back around to face her. "Better yet, I'll go see to your carriage and I'll have your personal effects packed and sent to you." Resting his hands on his hips, he smiled, feeling at ease for the first time since he'd arrived at the Comtesse's château, despite his stiff prick.

"I'm not leaving."

His smile died. As did his easy feeling.

"What do you mean, you're not leaving?" That stubborn look was back, her expression serious and uncompromising.

"I may not want Joseph to approach me. But I won't leave because of him."

Merde. "Emilie, we're talking about *Joseph*. Remember, horrible, terrible Joseph? You don't want him anywhere near you. You've said so. It's best you leave."

"Actually, since you put it that way, I've changed my mind."

His smile returned. "Excellent!"

"I want Joseph to approach me."

His smile died again. *Jésus-Christ.* There had to be something wrong with his hearing. "You *want* Joseph to approach you?" he repeated, incredulous.

"I do. In fact, I welcome his advances. I'll even encourage them. Then I'll do something he deserves. I'll rebuff him. He has it coming, don't you think?"

Joseph blinked. Speechless. Emilie de Sarron was torturing him. On every level imaginable.

She smiled. "The mighty Joseph d'Alumbert, contemptible and vile, whom society bends to, and placates at every turn . . . He has never been refused anything. Nor has he ever had a woman turn him down. I think I'll enjoy doing just that—refusing him. Turning him away."

Joseph rubbed his forehead, trying to knead away the dull ache that had just developed. Yet the discomfort was small in comparison to his throbbing cock. He couldn't believe it, but he was hard for a woman who'd just called him contemptible and vile. To his face.

Having mastered the art of seduction long ago, he'd fucked his way through the French court, and yet this one sexual novice had utterly seduced him—with the strokes of her quill, no less. A woman who didn't dress provocatively and had injuries to her body. And nothing—absolutely nothing—seemed to diminish his desire for her. His fever continued to mount to the point where it was influencing his behavior. His actions idiotic. Because no matter how hard he tried to ignore it or silence it, his every rakish instinct told him that a sexual experience with this unique woman would be nothing short of pure ecstasy. Clearly some otherworld forces were at play. How else could he explain being so ridiculously spellbound? Someone somewhere was making certain he was going to pay for all his misdeeds. Every one of them. This night. At the hands of this woman.

What poetic justice.

He took a deep breath and let it out slowly. "Emilie, don't toy with Joseph, or any man here. No man likes a cock tease. By your attendance at the masquerade, it is assumed you are willing to be taken. Playing the coquette here, with no intention of surrendering sexually, is most unwise. With anyone."

"Rape isn't permitted, if that's what you're suggesting," she countered.

"What I'm suggesting is that a man may not think you are seriously objecting if you lead him down the path too far. In a setting such as this, people play a variety of sex games and roles."

She was silent, and he could tell she was carefully considering his words. "I won't seek out Joseph, but if he approaches me, he will be played upon, and in the end, if he refuses to take no for an answer, he will be cast out of the masquerade. This is, after all, my aunt's home."

Joseph wanted to tell her that her aunt would never—could never—shut her doors to any member of the house of Alumbert, but he kept silent.

"As for the other men here, I don't intend to withhold myself. I want to surrender sexually, as long as they are not Joseph's friends. You don't understand, Vincent. I need this. I want a lover. I want to touch and be touched. To know the physical bliss that you and others have known."

"What if in the throes of passion, he tries to remove all your clothing?"

She tensed. An emotion he couldn't decipher crossed her features. The words had tumbled from his mouth. He hadn't meant to voice them, but the gnawing fear wouldn't relent.

"That isn't your concern," she responded tightly. "I'm staying. I'm proceeding as planned and that is final."

She turned on her heel, picked up her mask and wig, and headed for the door.

Joseph held back the profanities he wanted to bellow out of sheer frustration. Between his brother, Emilie, and this disastrous situation he'd created, he was sure to lose his mind.

Emilie was heading back out there, looking for a lover. Not a single man here deserved her. Least of all him. Joseph was the last person she'd want to touch her. To take her innocence. But when she placed a hand on the door handle, he shouted:

"I'll be your lover."

Her hand on the door handle, Emilie stared back at him. She didn't move. Nor say a word. Her sweet lips slightly parted, she looked frozen in shock.

He shouldn't have said he'd bed her. But he wouldn't take it back. There were numerous reasons why having her was wrong. And just as many reasons why this felt so right.

Maybe if he showed her just how desirable she really was, it would make amends for his transgressions against her. He hated it that she'd hidden herself away for years. That she hid inside all those layers of clothes. And most especially that she believed she couldn't stir a man's blood unless she masked that angelic face and her identity.

He wanted to prove her wrong.

By no means was he being selfless here. Selfishly, he wanted to be the one to touch her and be touched by her. To take this passionate, headstrong—untaught—female and initiate her into the sexual pleasures she so adamantly wanted to experience. By God, he wanted to fuck her so badly, it made his body ache and the crest of his cock wet with pre-come.

As it was, his sac was drawn up painfully tight. He was ready to explode.

He was going to have her. Tonight. Now.

And once he did, this incessant carnal craving for her would end. No?

4

He jests, Emilie told herself, her heart pounding hard. Scrutinizing his face, she looked for any sign that would confirm it.

His sensuous blue eyes gazed back at her, unflinching. Try as she might, she couldn't find any insincerity in his expression. Nothing that belied his words.

Dear God, he actually looked *serious*. He couldn't be. Why would he be?

"*Why . . . ?*" The word rushed out of her lungs on a breath, unable to muster more.

His brow furrowed. "Why what, *chère?*"

"Why would you want to be *my* lover?" The man could have any woman he wanted. With prominence, power, and fine looks, the d'Alumbert brothers were never short on female attention. They had their choice of mistresses. All of whom were beautiful and flawless.

She was neither.

The corner of his mouth lifted with a slight smile. He approached, all male grace and masculine beauty, his tall muscled form stopping before her. Her heart thundered so hard now, he was certain to hear it.

Vincent took her hand and, to her utter astonishment, lifted it to his mouth and pressed his lips to the sensitive spot on the inside of her wrist. A thrill shot up her arm. She felt a quickening in her belly.

He brought her hand to the bulge in his breeches and stroked her palm over his thick length. So large and solid. A feral need throbbed through her core and weakened her knees. "This is what you do to me, Emilie. You stiffen my cock anytime I'm near you. Anytime I think of you. Anytime I read one of your letters where you tell me, bold as can be, your sexual fantasies. I want you."

She was trembling all over, when she'd never trembled for anyone. This couldn't be real. It had to be a dream. One she'd had of him more times than she'd care to count.

He leaned in, his lips grazing across her cheek to stop at her ear. "There isn't a man here who knows you better than I do. I know what you want. How you want it. I can satisfy all your desires." Her breaths were ragged. Her head was spinning and her knees almost gave out when he whispered, "I'll take you, in every one of your favorite positions—pages five to twelve of your erotic book. Then I'll take you in some of my favorite ways. You'll enjoy every moment. All you have to do is say yes, *ma belle.*"

At his endearment, she jumped back, bumping against the wall. *My beauty* . . . Tears welled in her eyes. She blinked them back, embarrassed by them. She didn't allow herself to cry. Not for years. And never in front of others.

She reeled, trying to make sense of it all.

My beauty . . . It was the second time he'd said it, and with the same level of sincerity. How could he mean it?

"You . . . You want . . . *me?*" It seemed too incredible to conceive, despite the physical proof of his desire.

His half smile returned. "We both do."

"*Both?*"

"My prick and I." He crossed his arms, his smile broadening. "We are in complete accord on the matter. We both want me to bed you."

Oh God. Beautiful Vincent d'Alumbert desired *her*.

No man had ever desired her. Or ever would. Or so she'd come to believe after years of mean-spirited commentary and a night of abject humiliation where future suitors had indicated their scorn.

He took a step toward her. "Emilie . . ."

"I don't understand . . . You say you want me . . . but you know I have s—"

"Such a beautiful face?" he injected. "I know. You're rather breathtaking."

Breathtaking? She shook her head. "That's not what I was going to say. I have bur—"

"Breasts." He pressed his palms against the wall on either side of her head, hemming her in. "Very nice breasts, actually. I got a glimpse of them when your cloak opened."

He did? Nice breasts? "No . . . That's not it at all. What I'm trying to say . . . I have . . ." She forced the bitter words off her tongue. "Burns. And scars. I have scars and burns." At the moment, she hated them more than ever.

He leaned in, his mouth so close to her own, making her lips warm and tingle. "I'm still hard for you. I still want you."

Fresh unshed tears blurred her sight.

Gracious God. If this was a dream, she didn't want to wake up.

"What—What about our friendship, Vincent? I don't want to lose that . . ." She didn't have many dear friends. And none like him.

"A few days and nights of carnal diversions won't change anything. It's only while we're here. You've come to find a man to show you sexual pleasure. Let me be that man." He brushed his lips ever so lightly against hers. Her nerve endings quivered with life. She parted her lips for him, but he pulled away. "You won't be bored with me," he wickedly promised. "And you don't need to wear a mask with me either." He tugged it and the wig from her grip and dropped them to the floor.

"Let me give you what you want." Vincent slipped his hand inside her cloak and cupped her breast. She sucked in a breath. His thumb was drawing scintillating circles around the pebbled tip. Each circular caress making her feel weak and wet. Her sex, slick and needy. Her hardened nipple ached for his touch. "I'll make you come . . . hard . . . again and again." He grazed his thumb over her sensitized nipple, tearing a soft cry from her. "All you have to do is surrender to me. Say, ye—"

She shot up onto the balls of her feet, fisted his justacorps, and crushed her mouth against his.

Vincent pushed her up against the wall firmly. Cupping her face, he took command of the kiss, tilting her head to the side, sliding his tongue past her lips, possessing her mouth in a delicious, unhurried kiss. Unlike her masked lover in the gardens, Vincent gave her slow, luscious strokes with his tongue, sending waves of pleasure rippling through her. The light pulsing between her thighs intensified. He kissed even better than she'd imagined any man could. Emilie tightened her grip on his coat, a moan escaping her throat.

Her breaths erratic, she kissed him with urgency, unable to hold to his languorous pace. His taste was inebriating. She couldn't get enough, sucking and stroking his tongue with famished zeal. This was "it." The hunger and heat she sought. Her fever mounting by the moment.

Then his lips were gone. Her eyes flew open. Dazed and bereft, she stared back at him, unable to catch her breath.

He was smiling. "I just knew you were going to taste that good. And be that passionate. I can't wait to taste the rest of you. I'm going to savor every sweet drop."

His comment made her insides quiver. "That's odd . . . I was going to say the same thing."

His brows lifted, then he burst into a laugh. He pushed her back against the wall and gave her a fast fierce kiss she felt all the way down to her toes.

"I can't wait to have you, spirited and sensual Emilie de Sarron," he murmured, his mouth on the sensitive spot below her ear, slowly moving down her neck.

Emilie closed her eyes.

Oh my . . . No one had ever called her *that*. His words coiled around her heart. She cautioned herself. It would be too easy to fall wildly in love with him. And she couldn't.

This was only an affair. Of the temporary variety.

This is going to happen. Vincent is going to be your lover . . . She'd be pleasured by this gorgeous Aristo, reputed for his carnal skills. His sexual talents matched only by his twin's. Better still, her first amorous encounter would be with a man who actually mattered to her.

She was seizing the opportunity with eager hands.

Joseph slipped his arm around her waist and pulled her up against him, crushing his cock against her belly. His prick gave a hungry throb. He'd never taken a virgin. Never found the notion of having an inexperienced woman in bed enticing. Yet he wanted to sink his length inside her more than he wanted his next breath.

Grasping the fabric of her cloak with one hand, Joseph pulled it open, unveiling her. She stiffened and tried to pull away. He tightened his arm around her waist. "Easy. You're safe with me."

His gaze traveled down her slender neck, to the swells of her breasts above her décolletage. Luscious mounds rose and fell with her quickened breaths. The expanse of creamy skin beckoned and beguiled him. Lightly, he ran his fingertips over the curves of her breasts along the scooped neckline. She jerked in his arms. He could feel her racing heart. He knew her hardened nipples were pressing against the inside of her gown. And he could only imagine how good those distended nipples would taste on his tongue. When he met her gaze, he found her eyes were darker with passion. "The cloak has to go."

"My cloak?" There was a touch of alarm in her tone.

"We'll remove as much of your clothing as you're comfortable with, but the cloak goes." He wasn't going to relent on this. "You have a gown. You don't need it, and quite frankly, I hate it."

"Really?" She looked down at the thing. "I thought it was pretty."

Dieu, she'd worn them for so long, she actually did. No matter what color or expensive fabrics she chose, it was no more than a shapeless mantle that hung from shoulder to ankle. A different way to hide herself from society. He wasn't going to let her. He didn't want to see her hidden behind it any longer. She should never have been made to feel she needed to conceal herself in the first place. Joseph was determined to coax her clothing off her layer by layer. By the end of the week, she was going to be naked in his bed. Not for a moment did he believe she could repel him, no matter what her scars looked like.

And he had a strong suspicion he knew exactly where on her body they were located. In every illustration she favored in her erotic volume, the woman faced her lover. The marring had to be on her back. Something to keep in mind as he disrobed her.

"Sex is about mutual pleasure, and it pleases me to see more of you. Take it off, Emilie." He dipped his head and lightly bit her soft earlobe. He liked her little gasp. "Do it. I'll make it worth your while."

Reluctantly, he released her and stepped back. Like a curtain, the cloak closed again, cocooning her within. He waited. Impatiently. Fighting back the urge to rip the thing off for her.

A myriad of emotions crossed her face. She vacillated. *Merde.* It was a sobering sight. Seeing her struggle with the removal of a simple cloak pierced him to the core—proof of just how greatly the teasing and taunts she'd endured had affected her. Yet for all they'd put her through, incredibly she hadn't become caustic or bitter. As many would have in her place. She was quick to smile. Sweet and affectionate. Passionate and provocative. Engaging in every way.

She hadn't allowed anyone to break her true spirit.

She amazed him. He admired her. Something he couldn't say about any other female he knew.

Silently he willed her to discard the cloak. Wanting it more for her than for himself.

Slowly she raised her hands and grasped the fastenings. His heart soared. Averting her gaze, she loosened the ties, pulled the cloak off her shoulders.

She wore a light blue gown trimmed with yellow ribbons, and it accentuated her delectable feminine attributes—her body clearly defined before him for the first time. His mouth went dry. Even though he knew she had a luscious form, he was unprepared for the vision she'd be without the cloak.

"*Jésus-Christ*, you're ravishing," he breathed. By her expression, it was obvious his comment had unbalanced her. He'd noted the same reaction each time he complimented her. Damn it. He was going to keep giving them until she believed him.

"Come here, Emilie." He suddenly felt angry. All this loveliness senselessly shrouded. For years.

She stepped closer, her slight frown telling him she didn't care for the sharpness of his tone.

He captured her chin. "From now on, whenever we're alone, you'll not wear that cloak. Or any cloak. Do you understand?" She opened her mouth to respond, but he continued. "You'll not wear any caleçons for the rest of the week either."

"Not wear my cloak or my drawers?" Disbelief was in her voice.

He placed his hands on her shoulders and pressed her back against the wall. "That's correct. In fact, *ma belle*, it's an order. Your sweet little sex is all mine for the next few days. You're going to give me easy access to it, and I'll have you frequently and anytime I want." He smiled. "I catch you wearing either, I may just have to punish you in whatever wicked method I choose."

Curiosity flared in her green eyes. He loved it that his words didn't put her off. Instead they spiked her interest. Seeing this sent a shot of hot excitement through his body, causing his cock to seep more spunk. He had to have her. Soon. He couldn't take much more.

She tilted her head to one side, those magnificent eyes studying him. "I'm seeing a rather overbearing side of you tonight. For your information, I don't respond to orders." The mischief in her expression belied her stern tone. "I am, however, open to bargaining."

"Bargaining?"

"Yes, I'll cede if . . ."

"If?"

"You kiss me again." She was doing a poor job of hiding her smile.

He felt a smile tugging at his own mouth. Her response was novel, yet typical for Emilie, who did everything outside the norm. So unlike the women he cavorted with, who leapt at his commands in the boudoir, eager to remain in his favor. Emilie bargained. What she didn't know was just how much power she could wield. Truth be told, she had considerable leverage to bargain with. He'd agree to just about anything to have her.

"A kiss," he said. "That's all it's going to take, is it?"

"For now," was her saucy response.

Dieu, how he wanted to fuck her.

"Very well. Agreed," he said. "Open the front of your gown."

Her smile died. *"Pardon . . . ?"*

"You didn't say where you wanted to be kissed when we struck our bargain. And I'm going start with your lovely breasts."

She simply blinked and blushed, but didn't move.

Patience. This is monumental for her. But his cock was full, and heavy. He'd be able to proceed slower if he wasn't in such exquisite agony.

Joseph reached out and grasped the yellow ribbon resting so temptingly between her tits. Moving matters along, he pulled it loose. Her eyes widened. Her hand shot out and grabbed his wrist.

"It's all right. Let me. You came here for this . . ." Her hand still on his wrist, he opened the fastenings on her gown, his experienced fingers making quick work of it. She looked unsure, wanting to continue as much as she wanted to stop him. But thankfully, she didn't pull his hand away. "Let me give you the pleasure you seek."

She may be a virgin but she was no innocent. She was too well read on the subject of sex not to know exactly what his intentions were once the gown was opened. It kept her riveted. It stopped her from stopping him. Her breaths were quickening once more.

When at last he reached her chemise, she tensed. Joseph paused. Rumors he'd heard about her disfigured body raced through his mind. He shoved them aside, unconcerned, and gave the final article a quick downward yank.

No scarring or burns. Simply two perfect breasts and the prettiest pink nipples he'd ever seen.

Her gaze was fixed on his face, observing his reaction closely.

He took his time to take in the sight before him. With her pale blond curls sensuously mussed, the front of her gown open, and the neckline of her chemise tucked under her breasts, she was pure sexual allure.

The goddess of temptation—who could lure men to their misfortune.

He swore softly. "You look like every man's fantasy."

Her blush darkened, but her eyes softened and her delicate shoulders relaxed.

He caressed the outer curve of one soft mound. "I think it's time we started experiencing some fantasies together. Wouldn't you say?"

She shivered. Not from fear, or cold, but from anticipation and excitement. All this pent-up passion was his for the unleashing. How fortunate was he?

Her nipples protruded, so tempting and tantalizing, begging for his attention. He knew she thought he was going to go straight to kissing those luscious buds. Instead Joseph pinched one excited little tip. She cried out and grabbed his biceps, startled by the keen sensation. He held the sensitive teat firmly, letting the pressure build into scintillating throbs.

Her head fell back against the wall. For his efforts, she gave him a long hearty moan he felt down to the tip of his cock.

Leaning in, he brought his mouth to her ear. "In our carnal encounters, we'll only do what we both like." Gently, he pulled and rolled the tender bud with expert finesse, purposely giving her a steady stream of erotic sensations. He loved the sounds of her short sharp pants. "I know I'm enjoying this. Tell me, *ma belle*, how does this feel? You like this, don't you, Emilie." It was more of a statement than a question, given her ardent reactions.

He straightened and looked at her, his fingers never relenting on the captive bud. She leaned heavily against the wall, her breathing labored, her eyes closed. All she could do was nod. Her skin was flushed and a pretty blond curl had fallen onto her cheek. His heart raced as he watched her in her wanton state. He had to come so badly his sac hurt. But he couldn't stop what he was doing. Seeing the untamed desire on her face was rapture in itself.

He'd imagined her like this more times than he could count.

Releasing her nipple, he captured the other between his finger and thumb and pinched, giving it the same carnal treatment. She lurched and moaned louder, her fingers digging into his arms.

"Are you ready for your kiss, Emilie?"

"Oh God . . . Yes . . . *Please* . . ." Each word breathless.

A sweet plea no man could resist.

Still holding her nipple captive, Joseph cupped her other breast with his free hand and sucked the tip into his mouth. She gasped and arched, her fingers tangling in his hair.

The taste of the pebbled bud in his mouth spiked his hunger. He was ravenous for more. He wanted her complete surrender. No hesitations. No inhibitions. No will to deny him anything. Pure unbridled abandon. He licked and sucked at her breast, treating her other nipple to tender twists and tugs. The double stimulation had her writhing against the wall, tightening her fingers in his hair, the sensuous sounds she made inciting him further.

Famished, he turned and latched on to the other breast, his hands now holding her soft mounds up high, his greedy mouth laving and lightly biting the savory teat, feeding off her frenzy. He felt light-headed with lust. His body screamed for release.

Merde. He was *actually* shaking.

He tore his mouth away, swept her up in his arms, and stalked toward the bed. He deposited her on the mattress none too gently; she landed with a bounce and a squeak. His blood pounded in his veins. She had him so undone, all he could think about was driving his cock into her cunt.

She rose to her elbows, her tempting nipples erect and wet from his mouth. Joseph tore his justacorps off and threw the knee-length coat to the floor. His vest followed. Reaching for the fastenings on his breeches, he opened them, yanked his shirt free, and discarded it.

Slowly, her gaze moved down his bare chest to his engorged shaft straining out of the breeches. Her tactile perusal made him harder and bigger. He'd never been this painfully large, his cock feeling heavy as lead. Gripping the base tightly, he stroked his prick, trying to ease the discomfort.

Engrossed in his actions, she watched intently.

"You see what you do to my cock, Emilie? Does it excite you to see me aroused for you?"

She had a pretty blush to her cheeks. It made her blond hair look even paler and her green eyes more vibrant. "It amazes me . . . and thrills me and . . . Yes, it . . . arouses me."

God, she was as adorable as she was seductive. He doubted she knew just how soft and sultry her voice sounded.

"You want my cock inside you, don't you?"

She nodded. "Yes, I want it. I want it all . . . Every physical pleasure you can bestow. I want all of it."

Oh, he was going to give her all of it. She was going to take every inch of his aching shaft. He was going to ride her to what he knew was going to be an explosive release. For both of them. The carnal fire practically crackled in the air between them.

"Pull up your gown and remove your drawers for me. Show me your pretty cunt."

"You want me to—" She faltered. The concept of revealing herself for him was clearly still an obstacle.

"Pull up your skirts and bunch them up against your belly. Do it." He hadn't meant for his tone to be so sharp, but he was hanging on to his control by a thread. And it was quickly unraveling. He squeezed the swollen head of his cock to combat the throbbing.

She looked down at her gown and bit her lush bottom lip.

Joseph reached out and grasped her shoes. Pulling them off, he dropped them to the floor and said, "You want it all. That's what I wish to give you. To make the experience all it can be. I want to give you all the pleasure you deserve, *ma belle*." He'd told a lot of lies in the boudoir over the years, but he meant every word. "I know you were planning on being taken by a masked lover, doing no more than hiking up your skirts and having him fill you, sight unseen. You're not limited to encounters like that. You can have a much more intimate sexual experience. Allow yourself to experience it with me."

There would be no barriers when she was with him. He was going to level every one of them, and the misconceptions she had about her form and appeal. Even if it killed him. And given his state, it just might.

Her chest rose and fell with her rapid breaths. She made no other movement. And it didn't look as though she would.

She needs more coaxing. He'd try a different approach.

Joseph sank one knee into the mattress and then the other. "Very well. If you're not comfortable, we'll do it your way. I'll pull up your gown. I won't look. I'll take you through the slit in your drawers." He grabbed the hem of her skirts, praying she'd object to the suggestion. The thought of taking her that way sank his heart.

"No, wait." Her hand shot out.

Joseph released the hem immediately. She sat up, took a deep breath, then to his delight, grasped handfuls of fabric and began sliding the gown up her legs, pulling the voluminous layers up to her belly. Bunching the fabrics against her, she reached down for the ties on her caleçons.

Riveted, his gaze followed the actions of her nimble fingers as she loosened the ties, slipped the linen drawers off her bottom, and slid them down her legs. He grabbed hold of them when they reached her knees and pulled them off the rest of the way. She still had her stockings on, but he didn't care. He was transfixed by the lovely—unmarred—skin above her knees and the small patch of dark blond curls he could see between her legs, just below the fabrics of her skirts.

Wrapping his fingers around her ankles, he bent her knees, setting her feet down on the bed well apart. "Don't close your knees," he said when he saw them drifting together. "Lie back."

Clearly growing bolder, she only hesitated for a moment or two before acquiescing, though she watched his every move.

Her sex was open to him for his viewing pleasure. She was wet for him, her opening dripping with her essence, making her feminine flesh glisten and the light-colored curls between her legs damp with her juices.

Lightly, he grazed his fingers over the warm slick folds of her sex. With a cry, she all but lifted off the bed. She was so ripe for the taking. So primed, a few strokes over her clit would send her into orgasm.

And he refused to do it. She was going to come with him inside her first.

Leaning over her, he pressed his palm on the mattress near her head. His other hand gently massaged her soaked sex, not enough to make her come, just enough to keep her focus there and feed the fever. "You want to come, don't you, Emilie?" This little virgin knew exactly what he was talking about. In her letters, she'd boldly asked him a dozen questions about sexual climax.

Fisting the coverlet, she closed her eyes with a moan and arched into his hand. Her nipples were an appealing distraction. They were jutting out, needing to be kissed and sucked again.

"Answer me, Emilie."

"Yes! Yes, I want to . . . come."

He slid a finger inside her. She gasped and squirmed. He groaned.

A single digit was all he had in her and it was firmly clasped in her hot satiny sheath, the tight sensation mind-numbing. His cock twitched with anticipation. He couldn't wait to have her. If she hadn't been a virgin, he would have been buried to the hilt by now. Joseph eased his finger out and slid two back in. She squirmed a little harder as he gently stretched her. Sweat broke out on his brow.

"Please . . . I need . . ." Her words melted into a whimper when he withdrew his fingers.

He knew exactly what she needed. He needed a fucking release, too. He'd never needed any woman this badly, but her damned virginity couldn't be forgotten. Intent on stretching her tight little sheath beforehand, he wanted to minimize her discomfort, hurt her as little as possible when he entered her. "I'll let you come very soon. I swear it."

He lowered himself beside her and swooped in for a kiss, devouring her lush mouth. Penetrating her with his tongue. He feasted on her taste, forcing her mouth to open wider to accommodate his possession. His hand was back to caressing her sex, wet silky folds he couldn't stop touching, letting his palm lightly scrape over her clit on occasion, giving a constant spike of sensations. Throwing her arms around his neck, she mewed with each rhythmic stroke, her legs now sprawled open on the bed, no longer bent or tense.

Just the way he liked it.

He slid three fingers into her. With a lurch, she recoiled and tried to squirm away, but with his body half covering hers, and the material to her skirts caught under him, she didn't get far. Pushing and pulling his fingers in and out, he turned to her nipple and drew it into his mouth, instantly taking her focus from the intrusion of his hand to the sensations of his tongue. He continued to work her with his fingers, with his mouth, until he had her arching to him once more and moaning loudly. Three fingers didn't come close to how thick he was at the moment, but it was going to have to be enough, because he'd reached the end of his rope.

Pulling his hand out, he slid his slick fingers down his cock, coating it with her cream for easy penetration. He was so far gone, he wasn't certain how gentle he'd be.

He was on her in an instant, pinning her down, spreading her thighs with his knees.

"Say you want me to take you," he demanded, wedging his cock against her opening, his chest heaving with the exertion it took not to give in to the lure of her wet sex and drive into her.

"I want you, Vinc—" He crushed his mouth to hers, silencing her with a hot hard kiss. *Jésus-Christ.* His brother's name was the last thing he wanted to hear from her lips at the moment.

"Tell me you want the man you exchange letters with. The one who knows you better than any other man. Tell me you want that man. He's the one you want to surrender to." What the hell was he doing? Why did any of this matter a whit? Especially *now*. *She wants it. She's begging to be taken.* He should be fucking her. Forget the rest!

"Yes . . . you're the one I want," she said.

He had her mouth, his kiss a mix of savage hunger and alarming desperation.

Joseph plunged into her.

Hot pleasure roared through him; a cry erupted from her. He closed his eyes and clenched his teeth. The pressure around his cock was spine-melting, his thickened prick pulsing sharply inside the tight confines of her cunt. The sweetest torture.

Emilie's face was buried in his neck, her arms squeezing him fiercely.

"Are you all right?" he said in her ear, his voice more a rasp than a whisper. He felt her nod. Sweet little liar. Her body was rigid and tense. She wasn't all right.

"Try to relax. Almost there." He was halfway.

At that, her head jerked up. "Almost?"

He withdrew a little and drove back in, this time sinking his cock completely. She bit her lip and gave a strangled cry.

Pure pleasure exploded through his senses.

Nothing in heaven could be finer than this. He'd never been inside any woman who felt this good. Never experienced the intense sensations radiating up his cock. He reared then slowly tunneled back into the snug creamy heat. The friction along the sensitive underside of his cock was magnificent. He couldn't stop thrusting, celebrating in every stunning sensation. It took him several moments before he noted her body drawn up tight; he could tell she was holding her breath. "Look at me," he said.

She looked up at him, her eyes watery.

Joseph brushed an errant curl off her soft cheek. "It's done, *ma belle*. Breathe through it. The discomfort will pass. There's only pleasure from now on." He kissed her luscious mouth and gave her perfect sheath more strokes of his cock, fighting back his release, basking in the stunning pleasure of each plunge and drag.

She was beginning to relax, her body yielding. Returning his heated kiss, growing hungrier.

Shifting his body, he changed his angle and picked up the

tempo. "*Dieu*, that feels good. So good. You feel that?" She concurred with a whimper. Her hips jerked up and down until at last she found her rhythm. If he could have smiled, he would have. He knew it wouldn't take her long. She was too naturally, deliciously hot-blooded not to be swept up. She was made for a man's pleasure. For his pleasure.

You're mine . . .

Joseph hooked his arm under her knee and brought her leg up, his thrusts harder and faster now, making constant contact with her sensitive clit. "Page eight . . ." he murmured to her.

She was frantic now, driving her hips up to meet each solid thrust, her body reaching for him again and again.

"That's it. That's perfect," he growled. The most glorious tremors rippled along the feminine muscles, gripping his thrusting cock. A bead of sweat rolled down his back.

He could feel Emilie's fingers digging into his shoulders, her sweet sex creaming around his cock, bathing his shaft. She was so slick, her essence trickled onto his sac. The sensation drove him wild. *Seigneur Dieu.* She was the sweetest fuck he'd ever had. He loved how perfect the passion was. How deliciously she'd submitted to it. To him. Her every sensual reaction unpracticed, untamed, and beyond her control. It was inebriating. It made his mind spin.

She squeezed down around him, a groan erupting from his throat. She was on the edge of orgasm. He'd never emptied himself inside a woman, but with his sac so heavy with come and the need to let it go immense, he braced himself for her release.

It came immediately. Her hips shot up with her scream, throwing her head back. He rammed her for all he was worth, riding her as she contracted around his prick, milking him. Barely able to hold back his orgasm, he wouldn't pull out. Didn't want to. He was gluttonous for more. Intent on remaining inside her as long as he could, he held on by sheer iron will.

But then her body gave a squeeze and another final clench and his orgasm slammed into him, his semen bubbling up his sac and shooting down his cock. He barely pulled out in time, rearing onto his knees, just as hot blasts of come erupted out of him and onto her belly and thigh. Ecstasy flooded through him. He bellowed out his bliss as thick steady streams drained out of him in waves, melting his muscles with each powerful spurt of semen that shot from his prick.

His release went on and on. He floated in euphoria, until he'd emptied his cock, until the final shuddering drop.

On all fours, sucking in gulps of air, he looked down at her.

Hair mussed, her lovely flaxen curls were fanned out haphazardly around her head. With her gown open at the front, he could see that a soft pink blush had colored her skin from her cheeks to her breasts. Her beautiful nipples still erect.

She was a vision.

The most gorgeous one he'd ever seen.

She gazed back at him, a small smile on her face, and in her eyes he saw something akin to joy. Funny, but he was feeling much the same way. It had to be the incredible climax he'd just had that inspired the sentiment. In fact, he felt more than joy. He felt great. Better than ever. A unique sense of deep contentment he'd never known after sex seeped into his marrow.

Joseph leaned down and gave her lush mouth a soft kiss. "Don't move." He snagged her caleçons, and wiped her belly and thigh clean. "You're not going to need these anyway. Not for the rest of the week." He smiled.

It was only when he grabbed the base of his sex that he noticed it wasn't coated with just her juices and his come. There were traces of blood. Her virginity. A sobering sight and a reminder of what had just happened. He'd claimed her maidenhead. Quickly he wiped himself clean, rose off the bed on shaky legs, and tossed the garment to the floor for the servants, hoping Emilie hadn't seen the blood, concerned the sight might upset her.

He didn't want her to have any remorse over her lost innocence or regret over the tumble.

He cleaned himself at the water basin then returned to the bed with a damp clean cloth.

Stretching out beside her, he propped himself on one elbow and pressed the cool cloth to her sex. She flinched.

"Tender?" he asked. He'd been too rough for her first time, but he couldn't help it. She'd driven him wild.

She caressed his cheek and kissed him. "I'm fine. I don't care about the tenderness or the loss of innocence. Or for that matter, the blood you were trying to hide from me. I knew to expect it." Of course she did. His enlightened virgin. The only virgin he'd ever paid any attention to, much less bedded.

The only woman to hold his interest for a year. An unprecedented feat.

"I shall cherish this experience, in fact, everything we do together as lovers this week," she said. "I loved every moment of this night. And I've developed an immense fondness for page eight." Her smile drew one from him as well.

He lightly brushed the cloth over her clit, making her gasp. "There are other pages waiting to earn your regard."

She laughed. "And I look forward to them with great eagerness and anticipation." She pressed her mouth to his once more. He returned her kiss. A long, languorous, delicious kiss.

"Thank you," she whispered against his lips. "You made my first experience wonderful. I'm glad it was you, Vincent."

Joseph flinched, the reality of the situation hitting him hard. She'd never know the man she'd been with was him. He could never tell her any more than he could reveal his other deceptions.

And he hated it.

Hated it that he'd be her lover for the rest of the week and she'd never once scream his name in pleasure. And he'd no idea why the notion bothered him at all. He and his brother had been switching places all of their lives—the boudoir included. They looked so much alike that, since childhood, even their nurse had had trouble telling them apart.

This was the first time he'd ever pretended to be Vincent yet wanted to reveal the truth.

But the truth would devastate her. Worse, it would diminish the encounter for her. He couldn't stand that thought either.

Because of what had happened between them tonight, it was more important than ever to maintain his ruse.

Bedding her had complicated matters. And raised the stakes. The amount of pain he'd cause her if she learned the truth was even greater. Moreover, it had done nothing—absolutely nothing—to sate his lust for her. This sampling of Emilie had only increased his hunger.

She snuggled closer; the scent of lavender caressed his senses. Silky blond curls brushed his jaw as she trailed warm kisses down his neck, her soft breasts pressing against his bare chest. Joseph closed his eyes and pulled her tightly into his arms.

He wanted her again. Had to have her again.

There was no way he could resist her and walk away now.

There was no way he'd let Vincent or any man here have her until he'd had his fill.

And he had mere days to get it. He wouldn't continue the affair beyond the week.

5

"Good morning." Emilie walked into her aunt's private apartments the next day smiling and sat down at the table with Pauline and Marthe in the antechamber. Her presence in the room had effectively silenced the two older women's bickering. Arguing that could be heard from the hallway.

The subject of their argument was Emilie. As always. But she was in too fine a mood to be aggravated.

A servant stepped forward to pour her a goblet of water with orange slices. Reaching for the crystal vessel, Emilie brought it to her lips and stopped short when she saw the looks of shock on her mealtime companions' faces.

"Is there something amiss?" she asked and took a sip.

"Why, Emilie . . ." Marthe began. "You're not wearing a cloak."

"And it isn't morning. It's midday," her aunt was quick to point out.

Emilie motioned the servant to place two slices of ham on her plate as well as a hearty portion of mutton. Normally she didn't much care for mutton and gravy, but she was famished. She'd yet to break the fast.

"I'm afraid I slept in," she said to her aunt and to Marthe. "I don't believe I need a cloak today, dear Marthe. It's rather warm." As a habit, she'd placed one on earlier, but even the lightest of the lot felt heavy and cumbersome. She'd walked out of her rooms in simply her gown, feeling light and free and entirely different. Thanks to Vincent. She even felt . . . well, pretty.

He'd made her feel desirable. He'd made her feel desire, delicious and pure. He'd made her feel like a woman. Whole. Undamaged. Not for a moment in his arms did she feel in any way less than any other female. She hadn't had to hide her identity. He wanted her. Just as she was. And that alone made it impossible to deny what she'd been trying to suppress for many months. She was in love with him. Rather hopelessly, actually.

She wasn't naïve enough to think Vincent was going to propose marriage or that his affections ran as deeply as hers.

The prudent thing to do in this situation was to guard her vulnerable heart and leave promptly, sparing herself the anguish it was going to be to part with him at the end of the week. With certainty, the longer she stayed with him, the greater the heartache.

But she refused to leave—heartache be damned. She wouldn't deprive herself of the opportunity to be with him. That way, in her old age she couldn't bemoan how she'd missed out on an incredible week, on creating cherished memories—all because she'd lacked the courage to face the heartbreak and had run.

Vincent had kept her up until the early-morning hours making love. She wouldn't deny herself more of the same. Heated memories flitted through her mind. She felt her nipples harden and her heart dance. There was a delicious soreness to her private muscles that reminded her of the magical night she'd had—one that hadn't required any make-believe at all.

Cutting into the ham, Emilie looked up.

Pauline's surprise was turning into a large grin, Marthe's astonishment quickly becoming horror.

"You had a man last night," they said in chorus.

Emilie glanced over at the elderly servant. The man looked ancient and perhaps hard of hearing, but still . . . She was hesitant to speak.

Her aunt impatiently waved the servant away. Only when he'd gone did she place her hand on Emilie's arm. "It was the man outside in the corridor, wasn't it?"

Emilie couldn't suppress her smile. "It was."

"I want to hear everything!" Pauline beamed.

Marthe shook her head. "I want to hear none of it."

"Hush, Marthe." Her aunt patted Emilie's arm. "Did your lover please you, *chérie?*"

Emilie's smile broadened. "He did. Immensely." He did more than please her. Seeing herself through his eyes had bolstered the confidence she'd lost in herself. Had made her heart soar.

Jubilation erupted out of Pauline with a joyful squeak. "Ah, this is wonderful!"

"Wonderful? She gives herself to a nameless man, forfeiting her—"

"Not another word," Pauline cut off Marthe's rant. Her aunt's smile returned as she gazed at Emilie. "Look at her. She's lovely—all aglow after a night of passion. She has needs and longings, just like any woman—except you, Marthe. It isn't right or healthy for her to remain secluded. Or deprived of physical love. It's the most wonderful thing in the world. And yet women are too often denied, trapped in unsatisfying marriages. While men have their mistresses, most of them openly, without discretion, a woman must be discreet if she takes a lover or abstain all together. Society tries to discourage women from indulging our physical yearnings while men are encouraged to satisfy theirs. It is because of this terrible injustice I have these gatherings. Women know they can come here, regardless of their circumstance, and are safe to partake. Without judgment. And with complete anonymity."

"Yes, quite the charitable work you're doing," Marthe injected blandly.

Pauline ignored her and continued, her smile still in place. "I am delighted you tasted passion with a skilled lover, *chérie*."

"Thank you, Aunt." Emilie looked at Marthe. "He was not nameless, Marthe. I knew exactly who he was."

"Yes, we both do! I recognized him immediately, despite the mask. Some men are just so sinfully potent, they stand out of the crowd," Pauline said. "Marthe, I'll have you know that our darling Emilie was with none other than one of the Duc de Vernant's very handsome sons."

At that, Marthe's posture straightened, her eyes widening. "You were? A member of the house of Alumbert?"

"Yes, it's true." Emile confirmed. Her smile had yet to leave her face. She could hardly wait to see him again, her body famished for his touch. His mouth. His body inside hers.

She didn't know a man could give a woman so much joy and pleasure.

"I must say, I was rather surprised who you selected, *chérie*, but"—Pauline shrugged—"if he pleased you, then I am pleased."

"Who was it?" Marthe asked. "Which one? Gilbert?"

Emilie laughed. "No, not him. I was with—"

"Joseph," Pauline responded.

"Vincent," Emilie quickly corrected her aunt.

Pauline frowned. "*Vincent*? Really? Are you certain?"

"Of course I'm certain. Vincent and I have been corresponding for the last year. I know him quite well."

"She'd never be with Joseph d'Alumbert," Marthe added. "Or any of his equally unappealing friends—who hang on his every word and follow him about as if he were the King himself. He may be the heir to a duchy but he and his companions are a horrid lot."

Pauline still looked confused. "I was so certain that was Joseph . . ."

"Well, it wasn't, rest assured," Emilie said. "I couldn't agree with Marthe's opinion more."

"Yes, why do you permit such men here?" Marthe asked. "Especially after the way they treated Emilie."

Pauline stiffened. "I may not like the man or his friends, but you know as well as I do that one does not forbid a member of the Duc de Vernant's family from attending any gathering."

It was true. Doors were flung open for the Duc's heir and those he favored. It felt wonderfully empowering to turn down one of Joseph's friends last eve—his mask unable to conceal his boorish manners. He was easily recognized.

Just one of the many who had behaved so heartlessly that night years ago.

Imagine how delightful it would be to rebuff Joseph—just as she'd done to his friend?

While she was here, she wouldn't deny herself that experience either. It was time someone brought him down a notch. Or two. She wasn't going to run or hide from Joseph or anyone. Anymore. Given the sheer abundance of decadent behavior and enthusiasm as people roamed about looking for their next carnal diversion, she was sure to run into Joseph.

It was inevitable.

She'd look him in the eye. And give him the cut.

* * *

"Wake up." Gilbert gave Joseph a jarring shake.

Joseph sat bolt upright, startled out of a deep sleep. He'd been dreaming of a sweet seductress with flaxen hair, captivating moss green eyes, and the most divine lips—as enchanting as the princesses in the fables he'd been told as a child.

Only this princess was in his bed. She belonged to *him*. Gave herself to him, wanted only him, engulfed him in the most sublime passion he'd ever tasted.

But the fair princess had been torn from his sight only to be replaced by Gilbert's face.

Joseph frowned. "What the hell are you doing here?" He raked a hand through his hair.

"Well, good day to you, too, dear brother. I see you're in a good mood. You could show some gratitude, you know. I could have let you sleep and miss out on the afternoon and evening festivities. I've been at the Basset table all afternoon. Strip Basset." Gilbert grinned. "I won. Joseph, you should have been there. A woman with the finest tits you've ever seen sat—"

Joseph grabbed a fistful of Gilbert's justacorps and yanked him closer. "What do you mean 'miss out on the afternoon and evening festivities'? What time is it?"

Releasing Gilbert, Joseph glanced past his brother at the tall windows. By the low summer sun, he realized the day was old.

"It's almost supper time, but if you hurry, you can squeeze in some amusements beforehand—"

"*Merde.*" He'd been with Emilie until almost dawn. After their delicious night of ecstasy, of sexual excess, he'd slept so deeply, so soundly. And for so damned long. None of this would have happened if she'd let him stay. He was certain that with her by his side, he would have awakened once she stirred.

After sex, he normally left, and yet last eve he'd had no desire to leave her side. A first. She'd turned him away—albeit ever so sweetly. Another first. He usually departed the boudoir with the woman begging him to remain. But he knew why she'd refused.

It was too uncomfortable to sleep in her gown and she wasn't ready to remove it for him. He'd decided not to press her. He'd coax the gown and the rest of her clothing off her soon enough. Tremendous strides had already been made in the few short hours they'd been together. He'd seen her blossom sexually before his eyes, her inhibitions lower.

Adorable yet mouthwateringly sensuous Emilie de Sarron had matched his ardor throughout the night—inciting the sweetest heat no man could resist.

He was hard at the thought of being back in her silky sex, all warm and wet and fisted so tightly around him.

"Since you're up, I'll return to the amusements below. Why leave Vincent to have all the fun."

Joseph's heart lurched. "Vincent?" His brother's name tumbled from his lips on a breath.

Gilbert smoothed his justacorps. "Yes. Vincent. Your twin. Remember him? I haven't seen him in hours. No doubt he's found the lady with the cloak he's been looking for and is enjoying some rapturous delights as we speak." Gilbert smiled.

Joseph tore out of bed.

* * *

Emilie moved through the grand vestibule slowly, squeezing her way through the crush of people. Searching for Vincent.

It seemed as though there were even more guests in attendance this night than the night before. She held on to the train of her gown, lest someone stomp on it.

She'd bathed and primped that afternoon, anxiously preparing to see Vincent again. And after much consideration, she'd finally selected her masquerade attire for this eve from the various costumes she'd brought. A cream-colored demi-mask garnished with small to medium light brown plumes ensured her anonymity and matched her gown.

It, too, was cream-colored and had a light brown overskirt that was drawn back to encircle her hips and fell in long drapes behind her. The very end of her train was a soft red.

Her gown had large brown and cream bell-shaped sleeves that were very much like the wings of a bird.

Her attire representative of just that very thing—a bird.

One of her favorites.

A little bird that was rather plain. Upon first glance, it wouldn't likely garner a second. But what made this creature special came from within. And she liked that. As much as she liked the sound of the bird's nocturnal crescendos.

This eve, Emilie was a nightingale.

She finally made it into the long corridor that led to the dining room. That was when she spotted him. Vincent. Or perhaps it was Joseph.

He was just ahead, moving with the crowd. Wearing a brown justacorps and black breeches, his tall chiseled form, his strong shoulders were eye-catching; his masculine beauty made him stand out at any gathering.

Her pulse quickened. She quickened her pace.

Clutching her train tightly in her hand, she negotiated around the people who walked between her and the ever-nearing d'Alumbert ahead. Anticipation building with each rapid step that brought her closer to him.

Which one was he?

Her instincts told her—Vincent.

But it didn't matter, really. She had good reason to stop either.

The moment he got within arm's length, she reached out and caught his hand, arresting his steps.

He turned to face her. She noted the surprise that momentarily flashed in his eyes, despite his brown-and-black-checkered mask.

"Vincent?" she blurted out softly as people pressed past.

His sinfully tempting mouth lifted in a slow seductive smile. "Yes?"

Emilie felt a surge of joy. She clasped both his hands and backed up, pulling him with her away from the center of the hallway where they were being bumped by the boisterous lot streaming past. She stopped short when her back met the wall.

She couldn't contain her grin. "I've been looking for you."

Releasing her hands, he pressed his palms against the wall on either side of her head. "Have you, now. Well, then . . . I'm glad you found me, *chérie*."

There was something about the way he spoke, or perhaps it was in the way he looked at her . . . Something was not quite right.

Emilie dismissed it as absurd.

He was likely putting on a bit of a performance, given the very public place they stood in and all the ears that moved past. She knew he'd do whatever it took to protect her anonymity. She trusted him explicitly.

"I'm absolutely famished," she told him.

"Famished?" It wasn't what he was expecting her to say.

"Yes, for Vincent d'Alumbert's delectable kisses." Smiling, she tilted her chin up a notch, bringing her lips closer to his irresistible mouth. "Kiss me."

6

"With pleasure . . ." Vincent murmured just before his lips met her eager mouth.

Grasping her chin, he held her face captive, angled, as he slanted his mouth over hers. Impatient for more, she parted her lips for him.

He didn't hesitate to slide his tongue inside.

Something was . . . different. His kiss felt different. The way he kissed her . . . heated, yes, but with a certain detachment and distance she hadn't felt from him the night before.

And where was "it"? The bolt of hot excitement that rocked her every time he touched her, kissed her. Or even neared.

This was the man she'd surrendered her innocence to and had spent a night and morning of rapture in his arms. She'd shared intimacies with him—on many levels.

This kiss didn't feel at all intimate.

Suddenly his mouth and the press of his hard body were gone and a growled oath shot out of him.

She snapped her eyes open and gasped.

Vincent's twin brother, Joseph, stood beside them. The firm grip on Vincent's arm and the angry frown on Vincent's mouth told her instantly that Joseph had yanked him away.

"I need to speak to you," Joseph said to his twin, his jaw tight. Though half his face was covered by his dark blue mask, she could tell he was fuming.

"I'm busy at the moment, in case it isn't obvious." Vincent kept his tone light but his voice was strained, clearly struggling with his ire.

"*Now,*" Joseph said, the word sharply dealt.

For a moment the two large men stared at each other in muted fury. But then, Vincent took a deep breath and let it out slowly. "Very well. This had better be urgent."

Before Vincent could offer her a comment, Joseph pointed a finger at Emilie. "You, stay here. Don't move from this spot. Vincent will return shortly." It was an order. Rather an odd one coming from Joseph. She couldn't imagine why he'd care if a woman waited for Vincent or not.

Dumbstruck, she watched the brothers walk away.

* * *

On opening the fourth door in the long hallway, Joseph finally found a room that wasn't occupied by couples engaged in open copulation.

Stepping inside the library, he was livid. Seething. His very entrails twisting in his gut over an emotion he'd never felt in his life. One he didn't even believe he was capable of feeling—until Emilie came along. The ridiculous, possessive emotion had torn through him the moment he saw Vincent in a heated exchange with her.

Vincent stopped in the middle of the room, ripped off his mask, and turned to face Joseph. "What was so important you had to interrupt me just now?"

Joseph was just closing the door when Gilbert pushed his way inside, a typical grin on his face. He grabbed a chair, sat down, and pulled off his mask. "I saw what just happened in the corridor. I don't want to miss any of this," he said cheerfully.

Joseph held back the few choice words he had for his younger brother, shut the door, and locked it. His focus was his twin.

"So? Are you going to tell me what you want, Joseph?" Vincent asked.

Joseph pulled off his mask. "Yes. I want your clothes. Take them off."

"My clothes?"

"That's correct. Remove them."

Vincent crossed his arms. "When did it happen?"

"When did what happen?"

"When did you take complete leave of your senses?"

Gilbert laughed, but it instantly died when Joseph shot him a glare. Gilbert's gaze averting to the ceiling, he feigned sudden interest in its mural.

"Vincent . . ." Joseph strove for calm, trying to mask the extent of his discomposure over the incident in the hallway around his brothers. The ridicule would be endless if they had any idea how it had affected him. As it was, he was stunned by how strongly he wanted to slam his fist into his brother's belly for kissing Emilie. The image of Vincent's mouth on hers was still boiling his blood. He shouldn't be this riled. Not after all the women he and Vincent had shared. "Either you remove your attire or I will remove it for you."

Vincent raked a hand through his hair. "Clearly, by your request for my clothing, you want someone to believe you're me. Fine. I don't care. Let me finish with the woman in the hallway and then the clothing is all yours."

"No!" Joseph cringed at how strongly that came out. "You're not having the woman in the hallway." He'd managed to lower his voice and keep his tone quiet and even.

"*Dieu.* Joseph, what has gotten into you? First you lay claim to the lady in the cloak and now this wo—" His twin stopped mid-word. Then a wolfish smile formed on his face. "The lady in the cloak is this woman. Isn't she?"

Merde.

"Well, well . . ." Gilbert rose, snickering, walked over to stand beside Vincent, and casually propped his elbow on Vincent's shoulder. "Aside from the tantalizing tidbits of his evening with the fair lady, I think Joseph is keeping a great deal from his brothers, wouldn't you agree, Vincent?"

"I would indeed, Gilbert."

They were both smiling at him, thoroughly enjoying themselves.

He didn't want to punch Vincent anymore. He wanted to punch both his brothers.

"So, Joseph, are you going to tell us who the lady is, once and for all?" Vincent prompted.

"No."

"Very well. I have a lovely nightingale who is waiting for me. Warmed and wet." Vincent took a step toward the door.

Joseph stood in his path. "I'm not done with her yet. And she isn't warm and wet for you. Her stirrings are for me."

Vincent patted Joseph on the shoulder. "I'm fine with that. By the way, she did say she was *famished* for Vincent d'Alumbert's kisses. I'm happy to finish what you started."

Joseph pressed his hand firmly against Vincent's chest to discourage any progress. "You're not having her."

"Can I have her?" Gilbert asked.

Joseph's gaze jerked to his younger sibling. "Not another word from you."

Gilbert's eyes widened, affecting an innocent look. "I was only trying to help—you know, break the impasse?" His lips twitched. He was fighting back a smile.

Joseph turned to Vincent and caught him holding back his mirth as well. *Merde.* They were playing with him. Purposely trying to push him into showing his sorry state.

Both brothers burst out laughing. "Well, well, I never thought the day would come when Joseph had a *tendre* for a lady," Vincent said.

"You're mad." Something deep inside Joseph balked at the protest.

Chuckling, Gilbert said, "I've just got to know who she is now."

"Me, too. I've never seen you so possessive over any other female. We're your brothers. We've never kept any secrets from each other. Who is she? And why didn't you use your own name instead of mine?"

"I can't use my name. Leave it at that."

"Not enough of an answer," Vincent pressed. His brothers stared back, still sporting their foolish grins. Sensing his discomfort, they were reveling in it. Clearly, they weren't going to relent until they got their answers.

"Look, she's not like the other women here. She's never done this sort of thing," Joseph said.

"Never done what sort of thing? Attended one of the Comtesse's gatherings? Or—"

"Fucked?" Gilbert finished Vincent's sentence.

Joseph let out a sharp sigh. "Both. There. Is that enough for you?"

If he wasn't so frustrated, he might have laughed. The looks on his siblings' faces, wide eyes and gaping mouths, were comical.

"The woman in the cloak is . . . was a virgin? You had a . . . *virgin*?" Gilbert asked.

"Since when have you ever been interested in deflowering women?" Vincent was clearly incredulous.

Since he met Emilie. A woman who took his breath away at every turn. And had him behaving in ways he'd never conceived. All he wanted to do was to possess that snug wet heat once more and ride her in more sexual positions from her erotic volume. Last night he'd delighted in satisfying her sexual curiosity and basked in the mind-numbing pleasure it was to fuck her.

The mere thought of having her again made him rock hard.

But he first had to get his brothers under control.

He never wanted to have to peel one of them off Emilie again.

"I hadn't planned on having her initially. It just happened," was his weak explanation.

"Good Lord, you've been trapped!" Vincent's expression had turned to alarm. "She's going to tell her family and you, dear brother, are going to be hauled to the altar."

"That's not going to happen."

"Of course it's going to happen! You're the heir to a duchy." Vincent began to pace. "We'll say you were with us. That the lady is lying or mistaken and—"

"Well, actually, she thinks you deflowered her, *Vincent*. You're the one who would be hauled to the altar." Joseph's words arrested Vincent's steps. For the first time since entering the room, Joseph felt a smile coming on.

Vincent's expression was one of abject horror.

"Me?! That's why you used my name? So you wouldn't be trapped?"

Joseph chuckled. "Be at ease, Vincent. I assure you she has absolutely no such intentions."

"Was the tumble any good?" Gilbert asked.

Both his brothers shot him a look.

"What?" Gilbert said to Vincent. "You're not curious?"

Vincent turned to Joseph. "Actually, I am. Was it any good?" His greedy cock gave an instant hungry throb. "It was heaven." The best he ever had.

"A virgin? Really?" Gilbert pondered the notion.

"So why not take credit for the tumble?" Vincent asked. "Just who is this woman? Since you're using my name, you could at the very least tell me."

Joseph stared silently at his brothers. As much as they needled him—and it was going to be incessant over this—he knew they wouldn't relay any information he gave them to anyone else. Perhaps if he enlisted their help, it might make it easier to get through the week?

If he didn't count the nerve-grating, aggravating ribbing he was going to endure from them.

Joseph drew in a breath and let it out slowly. "The lady is Emilie . . . de Sarron."

Gilbert and Vincent exchanged curious looks until dawning changed their expressions to mouth-gaping astonishment.

"You fucked *Emilie Embers*?" Gilbert exclaimed.

Fury rocked Joseph. He grabbed a fistful of Gilbert's justacorps and yanked him forward. Their noses butted. "If you ever—*ever*—call her that again—or anything similar—you will rue the day, brother," he hissed out through clenched teeth.

Gilbert's dark brows rose. "All right. I'm sorry, Joseph . . .

It . . . It's just a shock . . . That you'd bed someone who has . . . er . . . who hasn't been seen in years." He quickly corrected himself.

Joseph released him.

Gilbert had the good grace to look contrite.

"Let me see if I have this correct." Vincent rubbed the back of his neck. "You had a woman no one has seen in a decade, who you knew was both a virgin and Emilie de Sarron? And you used my name. Why?"

"Because she doesn't much care for Joseph. And I don't blame her. If I were her, I wouldn't either. Neither of you were at that party that night at the Marquis de Sere's château. Sere and his wife raised Emilie. Since their daughter was of similar age, they were both introduced to society that night. It was a grand affair. One that eventually garnered the Marquis's daughter her future husband. It turned out wonderfully for her and disastrously for Emilie." Joseph raked a hand through his hair.

"Augustin and Henri were well into their cups when the nasty commentary began," he continued, his tone sharper. "Comments about Emilie's likelihood of finding a husband. About her always wearing cloaks. Comments that drew a crowd around her and those two fools." Joseph shook his head. "I'd had my share of merrymaking and drink. I'd laughed along with the others around her at some of the things Augustin said. In my brandy-soaked mind, I actually thought Augustin's comments were to her benefit. That maybe the laughter and comments would cause her to finally cease wearing the unflattering garb. I behaved like a colossal ass. She kept looking at me, glancing my way. She knew a word from me would have silenced Augustin, Henri, and the crowd. I did nothing."

Those three words were as bitter as bile on his tongue. As always, whenever he thought about that night, his stomach clenched. "That party changed everything for her," he said. "She'd finally had enough—and withdrew from everything and everyone. After having to tolerate names like Emilie Embers and worse all her life, who can fault her?"

"And you're making amends by lying to her and—despite being the last man she'd ever want, aside from Augustin and Henri—by claiming her maidenhead." It was Gilbert's turn to shake his head. "She isn't going to be very happy if she ever learns the truth."

No, she wouldn't be. She'd be deeply hurt. "That's why we're going to make certain she never learns the truth," Joseph countered and couldn't ignore the sharp pang of regret he felt. She'd cried out Vincent's name twice last night in ecstasy.

Joseph didn't know how much more of that he could take.

For the first time in his life, Joseph was caught in his own web of lies. He couldn't stop wanting her. Couldn't get her forgiveness. Couldn't find peace without it.

"Joseph is making amends—in his own way. He's pleasuring the lady." Vincent turned to him. "You are pleasuring the lady, aren't you? I do have a reputation to uphold, you know."

By the mischief in his twin's eyes, Joseph knew Vincent was trying to leaven the moment. And he loved him for it.

Gilbert threw up his hands. "All right. I must know. You're going to get angry, Joseph, but I simply must ask. It's driving me mad . . . her scars. Everyone has heard rumors about how disfigured she is. How badly is she injured?"

A smile tugged hard at the corners of Joseph's mouth. There was nothing wrong with Emilie. It was time his brothers knew that. Joseph moved between his two brothers, hooked his arms around their necks, and drew their heads closer to him.

"I've seen nothing but the softest, most perfect, lavender-scented skin."

"Really? You have?" Gilbert asked.

"I have. Her body is lovely, and so sensitive to my touch, Gilbert, I can melt her with the lightest caress."

"Oh?" Intrigue and excitement tinged Gilbert's tone. He was affecting him.

Joseph hid his amusement. "And you'll appreciate this, Gilbert, knowing how much you love women's breasts . . . Hers are perfect."

"Perfect?" Gilbert asked.

"Perfect. She has the most beautiful tits you've ever seen. Unmarred, soft plump mounds with delicious pink nipples, made for a man's mouth. The tastiest teats, a man can't help but savor . . ."

Gilbert shifted. "Th-They're that good?"

"Oh, yes. That good. And then there's the blinding pleasure of being inside an untried, passionate woman, like Emilie. All that snug silky heat squeezing you so tightly, it makes you throb."

Vincent cleared his throat. "Th-Throb? Really?"

"Yes, really. You never want to leave her honeyed sheath. The torture is sublime. One that you want to go on," he said to Vincent, then turned to Gilbert, "and on . . ."

Smiling smugly, Joseph removed his arms from around his brothers and walked away, knowing he'd accomplished what he'd intended.

"*Merde*, Joseph." Gilbert adjusted his stiff cock in his breeches.

Vincent shook his head, his prick just as stirred. "You did that on purpose."

Joseph grinned. "An eye for an eye—for playing me earlier." Talking about Emilie hadn't been without a personal price. It had served to heighten his hunger. Hot excitement was rushing through his veins straight to his already engorged sex. "Now then, your clothes," he said to his twin. Taking off his knee-length coat, he tossed it onto a nearby chair. "I have a beautiful woman waiting for me—whom I'm most anxious to enjoy."

He wished it was no more than lust motivating his eagerness to see her. But there was an undercurrent of softer sentiment beneath the untamed need.

One he hadn't yet mastered.

Or quieted.

7

Emilie waited. And wondered.

Uneasy.

She could make no sense of the kiss Vincent had given her. Crowds funneled through the corridor in both directions, and she was growing impatient for him to return.

Something was amiss. She wanted to know what. She had questions and wanted answers.

Glancing down the hall, she spotted him approaching through the throng. Or at least she thought it was him. He had on Vincent's clothing but Joseph's dark blue demi-mask.

It only added to her disquiet.

"Vincent, why are you wearing Joseph's mask?" she asked the moment he neared.

He halted his advance, touched the mask, and shrugged. "I must have picked up the wrong one after speaking to him."

It was the last thing he said before he shoved her hard against the wall and crushed his mouth to hers, snatching her breath from her lungs, his tongue possessing her mouth on her gasp. Her face trapped between his strong palms, he kissed her with dizzying intensity. Every nerve ending in her body leapt to life.

This was *it* . . .

The bud between her legs began to pulse, her questions dissolving as delicious raw hunger swamped her senses.

She laced her arms around his neck and held on to him during the maelstrom he caused with his powerful fiery kiss. Her nipples hardened and pressed against the inside of her chemise, eager for the carnal care he would bestow on them. She loved it when he touched them, what he did to them. What he did to her. She felt out of control, consumed by the yearning for him to fill that needy void between her legs. To feel that delicious stretching of her private muscles—bordering between pain and pleasure—as he fed her every delectable inch of his thick solid length.

"I need to fuck you," he growled against her mouth. His blunt statement practically buckling her knees. "I need to fuck you right *now*." In the hallway, with crowds of people moving about, he lifted her up against the wall, her toes barely touching the floor. She clung to his mouth, unwilling to relinquish it. She didn't care about anything except feeding her starved senses—with the only man who knew how to. He rolled his hips, pressing his solid shaft against her throbbing clit with the perfect pressure. Her cry was muffled against his lips.

"You have one moment, possibly two, to tell me whether you want me to take you right here or in private. Choose!" he rasped, and lowered her back down onto her feet, purposely brushing her sensitized clit down the bulge in his breeches. She lost her breath, the sensation stunning, despite the clothing between.

He had her mouth again, the heat and hunger of each kiss intoxicating her, inciting her further, obliterating everything but his mouth. His body. Him. His enlarged sex was up against her belly holding her focus, making her sex ache and leak.

Vincent tugged at her bodice, undressing her. She felt it loosen. Suddenly sounds around her rushed into her ears.

Her eyes snapped open and she saw that some people had stopped and were watching from across the corridor. It unsettled her down to the marrow.

She pulled her mouth away and grasped Vincent's hands, stilling them, her breathing quick and shallow.

"Private," she said in earnest.

His eyes were darkened with desire, his breathing as rapid as hers. "Pardon?"

"In private." She glanced over at those observing them from across the hall.

Vincent followed her gaze, tossing a look over his shoulder.

"Forget them." He pulled his hands free from her grasp, dipped his head, and reclaimed her mouth. His clever fingers were at her bodice once more.

Old insecurities rushed in on her. And a ten-year-old memory loomed—one where she'd been the center of attention in the crowd. One that threatened the wonderful sexual excitement she felt. Emilie may have found the courage to reveal some of her body to Vincent, but she couldn't do this in front of all of them.

She pulled back once more. "I can't." Not with those people watching.

He smiled. "*Ma belle*, you're at one of the Comtesse's gatherings. People do what they want wherever they want."

"I can't," was all she could say, a lump starting to form in her throat.

Thankfully he didn't argue or ask her to elaborate but simply took her hand and pressed a kiss to it. "Come with me."

Vincent led her through the throng in the hallway, away from the *voyeurs* who instantly protested their leaving, and through the crowded Grand Salon, passing a number of couples engaged in heavy copulation. Some against walls, others in chairs and on various other items of furniture. Chatter, laughter, and sounds of pleasure filled the air.

Vincent pushed open the doors leading to the gardens.

The night air was fresh and warm. Emilie filled her lungs with it as she rushed along behind him, trying to keep up with his purposeful strides.

He'd cut a sharp right, walking along the perimeter of the château away from the groupings of people in the gardens. He didn't stop until he'd rounded the corner of the grand abode.

The moonlight hardly reached this side of her aunt's home. It was darker and secluded by the row of shrubs and bushes they'd slipped through.

Vincent ripped off his mask and tossed it to the grass, a smile on his seductive mouth. He pulled his justacorps off his strong shoulders and tossed that to the ground as well.

A fresh wave of arousal flooded her body.

"You're not wearing your cloak, Emilie. That pleases me." His long skillful fingers were undoing his vest.

She pulled off her mask and wig and threw them to the ground, her eyes fixed on the male perfection before her—slowly disrobing.

He tossed off his vest and hooked his thumbs in the waistband of his breeches, his linen shirt still on.

"Are you wearing your caleçons?" The darkly seductive quality to his voice made her shiver.

"Perhaps."

He lifted a brow. "*Perhaps?* You'd better not be wearing your caleçons, Emilie. Or I'm going to have at that pert little derrière of yours before I have at your sweet sex."

A thrill tickled down her spine. That sounded more appealing than deterring.

He took a step toward her. She took a playful step back, keenly aware of the slickness between her legs. She loved how he made her heart race and her blood warm. Everything he said, every look he gave her, made her feel wild and wicked. And beautiful. It was almost inconceivable. His effect on her was so potent, she wondered if she could ever satisfy her desire for this man with just one lifetime.

"Lift up your skirts and show me if you have your drawers on," he said.

She felt so wonderful, it was difficult to keep a straight face. "That's an order. And as I've said before, I don't take orders."

He bolted for her. She squeaked in surprise, grabbed her train, and ran. Vincent caught her around the waist in short order, and brought her down with him onto the soft grass.

The next thing she knew, he had both her wrists in one strong hand pinned to the ground above her head, his body half covering hers.

Staring up at his handsome face, she panted, not from the exertion of her run, but from his tantalizing proximity.

He smiled, and with his other hand grabbed a fistful of her skirts. "Now we're going to see if you've been a good girl or a bad girl, Emilie." Slowly, he dragged her skirts up her legs, the fabrics lightly brushing against her bare skin. When he'd pulled them to her hips, his smile broadened. "Ah now, there's a pretty sight. No caleçons. Just soft blond curls . . . so very wet with your juices." He cupped her.

Softly, she moaned, spread her legs a little farther, and arched into his warm palm.

"You want me to take you, don't you, Emilie?" he said, caressing her sex with rhythmic strokes, but maddeningly they never reached as far as her throbbing bud.

"Oh, yes . . ."

She wiggled and arced, desperate for friction against her clit. With her wrists firmly pinned above her head in his hand, and his leg securely over hers, her movements were limited.

"I love it when you squirm," he said. "It's an arousing sight to behold, *ma belle*."

He lightly flicked her clit, then returned to his previous long luscious caresses over her erogenous flesh. Her frustration erupted from her throat. She writhed and twisted, still trying to rub against his elusive palm.

He chuckled. "You want your clit rubbed, Emilie?"

"Yes!" Dear God, she was dying for it. He was driving her to the brink of insanity.

"Well, you have been very good . . . no cloak . . . no caleçons. I suppose I should reward you."

"Good. Open your breeches and give me my reward."

He laughed. "My, my. Aren't we saucy." He lowered his head and whispered in her ear, "That sounded like an order. I should tell you, I don't take orders."

He thrust three fingers into her. She cried out, the pleasure of being filled quivering up to the tips of her breasts.

"I haven't been able to stop thinking about this perfect snug sex." He pumped his fingers in and out, each stroke sublime. "As eager as I am to ride you, I'm going to taste you first."

He pulled his fingers out. She whimpered at the loss.

Holding her gaze, he brushed his slick fingers over her bottom lip, applying her essence to it. Stunning her. Before she could react, he lowered his head and licked the juices off, then crushed his mouth to hers and drove his tongue inside. He kissed her hungry and hard. She tasted herself and him in her mouth, his intensity making her head spin.

His hand was at her bodice, finishing the job he'd commenced in the corridor. Pulling and tugging with practiced haste until he'd opened her bodice. Then his hand and mouth were gone. She opened her eyes to find him kneeling between her legs, pressing his palms against the grass on either side of her head. "I'm going to remove the gown and the stays."

Alarm shot through her.

He must have seen it. He brought his mouth down onto hers, his hand slipping inside her bodice, where he found her raised nipple and pinched it through her chemise. She cried out into his mouth, his perfect twists and tugs spiking her fever.

He broke the kiss. "You want to come, don't you, Emilie?"

She closed her eyes and let her head loll to one side, the sensations at her breast echoing in her clit. "Yes."

"The sooner we remove the gown and stays, the sooner that will happen." He pinched the nipple, drawing another cry from her throat. "I'm going to make you come with my mouth. Then again with my cock." Holding her nipple captive, he pulled her chemise down, tucked it under her other breast, and drew the excited tip into his hot mouth. The voluptuous sensations streaked from her breast down to her aching core. Her sex responded with a warm gush.

She was trembling with need, with uncertainty, her mind awhirl.

"*Dieu.* Every part of you tastes so good." He released her breasts and gazed into her eyes. "I'll leave you in your chemise, but this night the gown and the rest go. What say you, Emilie?"

"I . . . I don't think—"

He pressed his fingers against her lips, silencing her. "You trust me, don't you?"

She gave him a shaky nod.

"You don't have to think . . . All you have to do is lie there just as you are, on your back, and enjoy," he said, removing his fingers from her lips. "What say you, *ma belle*? The chemise remains. Will you let me remove the rest?" He cupped her breast and gently grazed his thumb across it. "Say yes . . ."

If she stayed on her back, he wouldn't have access to the ugly marring.

She swallowed, her desperation to have him giving her the fortitude to push the word off her tongue. "*Yes.*"

His pleasure at her response showed on his face. Vincent wasted no time removing her gown, pulling the article off with her aid and very little trouble, and tossing it aside.

"If it gets ruined, I'll buy you ten more," he said, attacking her stays and discarding them with as much ease. He tucked the loosened neckline of her chemise under her breasts and pushed the hem up to her navel, then sat back on his heels.

"Ah, Emilie . . . you are so very beautiful," he marveled.

Emotions tightened her throat. She couldn't respond. She was grateful for whatever miracle brought this man to her.

He spread her folds and lightly scored his thumbs up and down her slick sex. "You look utterly delicious. A treat no man would pass up." He lowered himself and nestled between her thighs.

Emilie braced for the thrill of his mouth.

Warm lips pressed against her inner thigh. She flinched on contact. He trailed light bites and hot kisses toward her sex, getting closer and closer. Her pulse racing, she tensed, knowing what he was about. This was something she'd told him she wanted in one of her letters. Had asked several questions about it after learning of it in one of her books, but never—ever—had she actually imagined it happening—with *him*.

He lowered his mouth onto her and gave her a luscious soft

lick from her opening up to her throbbing bud, sending her arching off the grass with a cry.

"Emilie—" He reached up and toyed with her nipple until she focused her eyes on him. Her breathing was labored. "As much as I like your heated reactions, and they are delicious, *ma belle*, you're going to stay very still for me and let me savor you."

"Savor quickly."

Amusement entered his eyes, despite the clear desire reflecting back at her. "Was that an order, Emilie, because I don't take—"

"*Please . . .*" she quickly added. Damn him. He was toying with her when she was on the verge of expiring on the spot with lust.

"A plea for pleasure . . . That I can't deny." He lowered his dark head, eased his tongue inside her, and slowly drew it out. Sucking her. Kissing her. Licking her. The light sensations over her ultrasensitive sex making her whimper. She fought not to squirm, not wanting to give him any reason to stop.

He licked around her clit. She fisted the grass and squeezed her eyes shut, sensing his next move. Waiting for it. Desperate for it. Her legs trembled near his shoulders.

He closed his mouth over her engorged bud. She bit back her wail of delight; her body jerked as he gave her soft steady sucks. Each pull of his mouth raced her closer to a powerful orgasm that was ever-nearing. Unstoppable. Barreling toward her. Then he lightly bit her.

Ecstasy exploded inside. She drove her hips up hard against his mouth, pleasure flooding her senses, her sex contracting in rhythm with her wild heart.

He continued to lap at her sex, her juices, cherishing her private flesh with an unfed hunger. Tirelessly enjoying her until she quieted, boneless, her legs leaden and sprawled apart.

She didn't care if she was lying on the grass, exposed to him. She felt no shame. Just an overwhelming sense of bliss.

Vincent rose to his feet between her legs. Holding her gaze, he wiped his chin with the back of his hand, and licked his bottom lip clean of her essence.

"I love the way you taste," he said with such raw hunger in his eyes, it sent a quiver through her womb. A surprising reaction given the magnitude of her climax.

She watched him strip off the remainder of his clothing, luxuriating in his strong chest, his rippled abdomen, her gaze moving all the way down to his large cock. It held her attention as he knelt down between her knees. Memories of his talents with that particular part of his male anatomy swirled through her system.

She sat up and reached for his shaft. Wrapping her fingers around its base, she stroked his sex up to the crest of his cock and back down—in the very way he'd described in his letter when she'd asked where and how men liked to be touched. He briefly closed his eyes.

"I want to taste you, Vincent." She felt him tense.

Gently, he pulled her hand away from his prick and leaned into her, forcing her onto her back once more, and lowered himself on top of her. "Two things, Emilie. First, I don't like the name 'Vincent' much. I don't want to hear it during sex."

Before she could comment on his rather absurd statement, he stroked his cock along her wet folds, grazing her clit and making her gasp.

"Second," he continued. "As much as I'd love to have my cock in that beautiful mouth—and I most definitely will next time—I have to get back inside that slick tight sheath of yours. Now." He lodged himself at her entrance and pushed.

She lost her breath the moment the crest of his shaft slipped inside her. A groan rumbled out of his chest, shimmering through her. He bore down on her, deliciously forcing her sex to stretch as

he fed her a glorious inch at a time. His slow and steady possession incited a fresh, fierce hunger.

"*Dieu*, I love how you're even tighter after an orgasm." His
voice was hoarse.

He withdrew, and just as he was sliding back in, she became
impatient and jerked her hips upward, forcing the head of his
cock to collide with her womb, making them both gasp.

He growled her name and buried his face in her hair, his
labored breaths matching her own, warming her neck. Softly he
said, "You feel so good . . . I'm throbbing so hard."

So was she. Her feminine walls pulsed around his large thick
cock.

Lightly, he bit her earlobe then the sensitive spot under her
ear. "Lovely Princess Emilie, you are an enchantress . . . and
more heaven than any mortal man has the right to." He began to
slide in and out of her.

She laced her arms around him.

She didn't know how he did it, but his words were like a balm.
Taking away years of pain. Transforming her. Had any other
man uttered those words, she would have dismissed them, convinced he was mocking her. But from Vincent's mouth, he made
her believe the unbelievable.

Because she trusted him.

Because she loved him.

She sought out his mouth and kissed him with a mix of love
and lust. Pulling her arms from around his neck, he pinned her
wrists to the ground, picking up the pace, giving her deep solid
thrusts. Pinned under him, all she could do was take each one,
sensations radiating out from her core to her entire body in dazzling waves with each downstroke. She reveled in his strength, in
every plunge and drag as he rammed her with unbridled abandon. Violently aroused, she was swept up in his sensual storm.

Light pulsing inside her sex signaled the beginnings of her climax. She strained against him, trembling on the edge. "I'm going to . . ."

Her orgasm slammed into her, ripping a scream from her throat, sending violent spasms through her core and around his thrusting cock.

He growled and grunted, driving into her unrelentingly until the spasms began to ebb. Then he jerked his cock out, crushed her to him, and groaned long and hard against her neck. His body shuddered, his muscles tense and taut as he spent himself on the grass between her legs.

Languid, Emilie caressed his back, holding him until his body relaxed and his breathing slowed.

Lifting his head, he gazed down at her. His blue eyes were soft, his smile moving her to one as well.

"I loved that," he said.

I love you . . . She caressed his cheek. "Me, too."

She couldn't reveal her feelings any more than she could reveal her scars. There were some walls she just couldn't scale. Despite the recent changes in her, she couldn't lay herself that bare. She hadn't survived this long by exposing herself completely. No doubt if she did, he'd run.

Holding her tightly, Joseph rolled, pulling her on top. She tensed. Smiling, he slipped his hand behind her head and pulled her mouth to his, kissing her sweet lips. Skimming his free hand under her chemise, he followed the lush curve of her bottom upward until he touched upon rough, thick, bumpy skin.

She shrieked against his mouth and jumped away so quickly it stunned him.

He snapped open his eyes to find her sitting several feet away, looking positively stricken and ready to bolt.

"You said you wouldn't!" Her beautiful eyes were full of hurt and panic.

Merde. If his brain hadn't been so foggy in the afterglow of a powerful orgasm, he wouldn't have made the blunder.

Joseph raised himself up onto one elbow. "I'm sorry, Emilie. I wasn't trying to remove the chemise. I like touching you. I got carried away. I didn't mean to upset you."

"I've got to go." She dropped to her knees and was about to stand.

"Wait!" He sat up. "Don't go. Come here, *ma belle*." He patted the spot beside him. "On your back, beside me." He reclined back onto his side. "The night is young still. Stay with me." Joseph held out his hand.

Silently he beseeched her.

She looked unsure, and he hated seeing the mistrust in her eyes.

"It won't happen again. I promise." Seeing the look on her face made him realize just what a daunting task it was going to be to have her discard the chemise. One that he was even more determined to take on. But it required a gentle hand. And a good deal of patience and understanding.

She rose. He held his breath.

Emilie walked over and lay down beside him. Joseph wanted to shout with joy.

She snuggled closer. "Never again," she warned.

He leaned over and lightly kissed her. "Emilie, I'm certain it's not as bad as you believe."

She stiffened. "It's very bad.

"Why not let me be the judge?"

"No! It would ruin everything between us." She lifted her head and tried to sit up, but he quickly claimed her mouth and eased her back down. Capturing her sweet face, he gave her a long unhurried kiss, cherishing her mouth, her taste, his tongue giving hers slow, swirling caresses.

When at last he ended the kiss, her body was no longer rigid, but soft and wonderfully yielding. She gazed up at him with touching tenderness in her eyes, the sight of which filled his heart with a deep sense of contentment.

"I didn't mean to get so upset with you earlier, Vincent. I'm sorry."

"No need to apologize. I understand."

A smile formed on her lovely mouth. "I'm so glad you're nothing like your brother."

Joseph's chest tightened. He hated the low opinion she had of him. Her disregard for him, though not unfounded, bothered him to the core of his being. "You know," he said, brushing an errant blond curl off her cheek, "Joseph is sorry for what he did or rather what he didn't do that night. He told me so himself."

Still smiling, she rose up onto her elbow, matching his pose. "No he didn't, Vincent. But I do adore you for wanting to offer an apology on his behalf. The mighty Joseph d'Alumbert would never admit to any wrongdoing against anyone."

She was right. He never would. Never had. Until tonight when his brothers had managed to do something rare—corner him.

"Men like Joseph don't change."

That was just the thing. He had changed. He hadn't wanted it, hadn't expected it, but it had happened. And it was all because of one flaxen-haired beauty—a woman who stirred soft sentiment during sex and all the time in between.

8

Joseph put on his gray justacorps and secured his black demi-mask. It was midafternoon, and he was anxious to see Emilie.

He still hadn't coaxed her out of the final article of clothing—her chemise. Still hadn't managed to convince her to let him stay the night, that she shouldn't worry if in her sleep he caught a glimpse of her scars.

Yet despite his failings, over the last four days they'd shared in the most soul-satisfying sex. It was the greatest bliss he'd ever known. Not to mention he'd taken her in every position she favored in her naughty book. At least twice.

She was the first person he sought out upon awakening and the last person he saw before retiring for bed—usually in the early hours of dawn. He'd taken up eating supper by her side—away from his brothers and friends, his brothers making a point to walk by every night to bid *"Vin-cent"*—stressing the name between chuckles—a bon appetite.

Joseph smoothed his vest and smiled. Emilie had told him she'd be wearing a very special costume this night. He couldn't wait to see it. Couldn't wait to take her out of it.

Dieu, she'd look comely in anything. Even barefoot wearing sackcloth.

He snatched open the door and was surprised to find a solemn-looking servant, a much older man, standing at his door ready to knock.

"My lord."

"Yes. What is it?" Instantly irked, he wanted no delays in seeing Emilie.

"Madame de Naylon, Comtesse de Saint-Arnaud, wishes to speak to you."

His hostess?

"Can this wait? I'm rather busy."

"She insists you join her immediately in the library. Please follow me."

The elderly man gave a short bow and, turning on a heel, made his way down the hall.

Merde. What on earth could Emilie's aunt want?

* * *

The Comtesse de Saint-Arnaud rose from behind her desk the moment Joseph entered the library.

The servant closed the doors behind him.

Joseph pulled off his mask. "Madame, you wished to see me?"

She walked around the desk in silence and stopped before him. "I presume I'm speaking with Monsieur Joseph d'Alumbert?"

"You are."

"Good, then let me be plain and to the point."

"I'd appreciate that, madame. What is this about?"

"My niece. I believe you are toying with her."

Joseph's heart gave a small lurch. He schooled his features, affecting a look of indifference. "Possibly. The ladies are wearing masks. I couldn't say exactly who I'm 'toying with.' Isn't that the point to your gatherings? Anonymity?"

"Don't try to be clever. My niece is very dear to me. Her experience with men has been sadly limited. She believes she's having an affair with Vincent d'Alumbert."

"Then you should speak with him." Joseph turned to leave.

"He has a scar on his shoulder, doesn't he?" the Comtesse called out.

That stopped Joseph dead in his tracks. He faced the older woman once more. "Pardon?"

"You heard me well enough. Apparently there aren't many ways to tell the two of you apart. But according to your very good friend, Augustin de Coix, who was well into his cups earlier, as boys he and Vincent climbed a tree. Vincent fell out and suffered a rather nasty gash to his shoulder. It left quite the mark apparently. What do you suppose my niece will answer if I ask her whether her lover has any markings on his shoulder?"

Joseph's stomach dropped. "I don't know which niece you speak of, since it is my understanding you have more than one. However, if my brother is truly fucking her, her answer will be, 'No.' I was the one who fell out of the tree. Not Vincent," he lied. "Augustin is a fool who can't recall what he did yesterday, much less an incident that occurred many years ago."

"You'll show me your scar, of course."

Joseph walked up to the Comtesse. "Madame, I suggest you remember whom you are speaking to. I'm going to ignore the insulting request you've just made. I'm going to pretend this conversation never happened, for your sake."

He marched out.

Merde. He had to find Vincent. He had to change clothes with him.

He had to speak to him. Fast.

* * *

Emilie's gown was white with tiny pearls embellishing the bodice. On her demi-mask, there were more pearls and soft white plumes. The square neckline was adorned with the finest, sheerest gauze. She felt beautiful in her costume.

As beautiful and elegant as a swan. And that was exactly what she'd chosen as her masquerade attire this eve. A swan. She hadn't even bothered with a wig. She felt so changed, she was certain no one would recognize her.

She couldn't wait to see Vincent. Couldn't wait to see his reaction to her lovely costume.

Walking along the corridor that led to the grand dining room, she spotted him stepping out of the library. He was wearing exactly what he said he'd wear—a black demi-mask and gray justacorps and breeches.

Rushing through the crowd, she walked right up to him, beaming. "Vincent."

He looked startled to see her, then he glanced over his shoulder. Her aunt stood in the doorway of the library, closely observing them.

"You have me mistaken for my brother," he said and stepped around her.

She laughed and caught his hand, halting his progress. "Vincent, what game are you playing?" She stepped in close and lightly ran her finger along the side of his neck. "You sport the love bite I gave you last night."

"Good evening, *Vincent*," his twin said, grinning as he approached with the youngest d'Alumbert, Gilbert.

Vincent lowered his head and squeezed her hand. She heard a very clear *"Merde"* slip past his lips.

"Good sirs, will you kindly step into the library," Pauline said to the three Alumberts before Emilie. "Darling, you come, too." Her aunt was looking straight at her.

Emilie was seized by an uneasy feeling. One she couldn't shake as she entered the room with the three men.

Joseph held Emilie's hand, refusing to let it go just yet. Knowing his lies were about to be revealed, he wanted her touch until the moment she'd likely rip it away from him.

"Do you have anything to say, Monsieur Joseph d'Alumbert?" the Comtesse said.

"Indeed I do," Vincent responded for him. "I'd like to know why I'm in here. There are festivities I'm missing out on."

Madame de Saint-Arnaud let out a sigh, clearly exasperated. "I'm speaking to Joseph d'Alumbert." She looked straight at him.

Vincent responded, "And I'm answering. I am Joseph."

"Are you still going to try to deceive her?" Madame de Saint-Arnaud asked him.

Joseph couldn't voice the words. He simply held Emilie's hand, his thumb gently caressing it.

"What is happening?" Emilie spoke, her soft green eyes on him.

Gilbert strolled up to the Comtesse, smiling. "Dear Madame de Saint-Arnaud, you are clearly confused. But don't be embarrassed by it. They look so much alike that I, their own brother, sometimes confuse them. A common mistake. Now, why don't we put our masks back on and enjoy the rest of the evening. What say you?" He spoke to the group before him.

"I say that this man"—the Comtesse pointed straight at Joseph—"just entered this very room moments ago and admitted to me he was Joseph d'Alumbert."

"Did you do that?" Emilie asked him, but before Joseph could respond, Vincent interjected with a laugh.

"Vincent does that all the time." Vincent shook his head. "He envies me, you see. I am, after all, the firstborn. The heir. Pay him no mind."

"Forget it, Vincent." At last he found his voice, simply because the lies had become too much to bear. Joseph looked at Emilie, cherishing the last moments her soft delicate hand rested in his. "I am Joseph. He is Vincent, a good brother, and a poor liar."

"Really? I thought I was a good liar."

"And I am Gilbert d'Alumbert." Smiling, Gilbert walked up to Emilie and gave a short bow. "Apparently, I'm the only one who hasn't kissed you, but I'm happy to accommodate—"

"You're not helping," Joseph cut him off sharply. This was no time for his brothers' usual foolery.

Her sweet lips parted, she stepped in front of him, her hand still absently in his, her eyes moving from Vincent back to him. She was a vision in her white gown. He hated it that he couldn't pull her to him. He hated the distress etched on her brow, her breasts rising and falling with her quickened breaths.

"The only one who hasn't kissed me?" she said softly. Incredulous. Shocked.

"Good Lord, you haven't shared her without her knowledge, have you? I've heard that you gentlemen have been known to do that, but—"

"No!" Joseph quickly silenced the Comtesse's rant. He squeezed Emilie's hand to gain her full attention. "It wasn't like that. You've been with me. Just me. Joseph."

"Except our kiss in the hallway . . . Which was quite delicious indeed," Vincent said. "I've never touched you."

"*Merde*, Vincent. That's not helpful," Joseph exploded.

Vincent held up his hands. "Sorry, Joseph."

Emilie pulled her hand from his grip. Tears glistened in her eyes. "This is all a game to you, isn't it? A cruel game."

"No, this is no game. The letters, what happened between us here, were real. Sincere." Joseph caressed her cheek. She jumped back.

"Don't touch me, Joseph."

Those words sliced him deeply.

"Do not speak to me about sincerity when you've done nothing but deceive me! What are you going to do now?" she asked him. "Run about and tell all your friends how you had Singed Emilie de Sarron?" She angrily swiped a tear that ran down her cheek. "Just think of all the laughs you will have. We all know how much you love to laugh at another's expense."

She turned and walked out of the room.

Joseph felt as if the air had been knocked out of his lungs. He placed his hands on his hips, trying to breathe.

"I hope you're pleased with yourself," the Comtesse said.

Joseph's gaze shot up to hers. Teeth clenched, he growled, "Madame, if you were a man, I'd lay you low for what you've just done."

"What I've just done? Sir, you blame me for your poor conduct?"

The commotion outside grabbed Joseph's attention. There was laughter. And he could hear Augustin's booming voice.

Joseph stalked from the room. Entering the hallway, he noticed a crowd had formed in the grand vestibule. He gravitated to it. His heart missed a beat when he saw Emilie in the middle of the crowd with Augustin beside her.

He was laughing along with the throng. Emilie was unmasked; the beautiful swan's mask lay on the floor.

She cracked her palm against Augustin's cheek. "You are vile and a fool."

The crowd roared.

Joseph pushed his way through the mass and entered the center.

Augustin rubbed his cheek, no longer looking as amused as before. "Ah, Joseph!" He pointed to Emilie. "Look who has been at the gathering. Some of the men may have actually fucked Singed de Sarron."

Joseph smashed his fist against Augustin's thick jaw, knocking the man to the floor. A gasp rippled in the crowd. Calmly, he placed his hands behind his back and slowly strolled the perimeter of the large circle, looking out at the crowd. "None of the men here have had this woman. None of you have been that fortunate. But I have. Joseph d'Alumbert. Anyone who finds amusement in that may step into the circle. I promise you, if you do, you will be joining the Comte de Coix on the floor."

He paused and took in the dead silence.

Joseph continued. "Let me correct everyone on her name. You may call her Mademoiselle de Sarron. Or if she permits it, Emilie. But I have different names for her."

Joseph stopped and faced her. Her gaze nervously darted to the crowd, and back to him.

"She is Emilie the Brave. Emilie the Beautiful. Emile Who-Has-Stolen-My-Heart de Sarron. And I want her to be mine for the rest of my life, more than words can say . . ."

A collective gasp rose from the onlookers, but no one was as stunned as the blond beauty before him.

"Will you marry me?" he asked from the heart.

Her chin dropped, and he saw the glistening paths of tears she was too proud to show.

"Out!" he commanded the crowd without removing his gaze from her. Reluctantly, people began to disburse, murmuring as they left.

Joseph approached her, cupped her face, and tilted her chin up. When her gaze met his, he gently wiped her tears with his thumbs. "I am sorry about what happened that night. I've wished a thousand times that I'd done something. Anything that would have spared you the pain of that eve. Initially I wrote to you a year ago out of guilt—a troubled conscience—but I fell in love with you a little more with each and every letter. I'm sorry for the deceptions, but I won't apologize for being with you. I'm not sorry about that. There's a connection between us and it's wonderful. You know it, Emilie. You feel it, too. Say you'll marry me. I love you, Emilie, and I know you love me. I can see it in the way you look at me. I can feel it in the way you touch me. Be mine, *ma belle.*"

Tears slid down her cheeks. She shook her head. "How can you want to marry me? You don't even know what I look like . . . what the scars look like."

He smiled tenderly at her. "I don't care."

"You say that because you've never seen them . . ."

"I say that because I've seen all I need to see to know unequivocally—you're what I want. Whom I love."

She closed her eyes and swallowed hard. He took advantage of the moment, dipped his head, and kissed her. A soft gentle kiss, praying all the while she wouldn't push him away.

The moment he felt her return his kiss, her lips parting for him, he slid his tongue inside, wanting to shout with jubilation. Tender yet ardent, it was filled with more emotion than any kiss he'd ever given or received.

It heated his blood and warmed his heart.

He needed her. They needed each other.

Impatient to have her, he broke the kiss and grabbed her hand. "Come with me."

Joseph briskly crossed the vestibule, climbed the stairs, and made it back to her private apartments in no time. The moment he closed her door, he pushed her up against it and feasted on her delectable mouth, his fingers immediately at the fastenings of her bodice, undoing them before she could protest.

But she didn't protest. She softly moaned into his mouth, her hands moving to his back, fisting his justacorps.

"Emilie . . . admit you love me. I can even feel it in your kiss. I'm the same man you corresponded with. Whom you wanted to share your most intimate thoughts and longings with. I'm the same man who's made love to you every night since your arrival. Your hurt and anger at me for my part in that night so long ago is not unjust. If I could change that night, I would. Let me make it up to you—by loving you, by cherishing you the rest of our lives. Say it, Emilie. Speak the truth. Say you love me. Say you'll marry me."

Emilie was trembling. It was the truth! She couldn't believe she was deeply in love with Joseph d'Alumbert. That she had been all this time. "I do love you. But I can't—"

He cut off her words with a brief, hard kiss, then he stepped back and removed his justacorps. Then his vest.

"What are you doing?"

"I'm going to have you. No gown, no stays, no chemise. Nothing between us."

"I can't do that. I can't expose myself that way."

"Yes you can, Emilie."

"No! It's—It's the reason I can't marry you. If you were to see how ugly the scars are, you'd understand. You'd be repulsed. And you wouldn't want me for a wife."

He smiled. "I could never be repulsed by you. But if you think you can drive me away with your scars, go ahead and try. It won't work." He opened his breeches and pulled off his linen shirt, discarding it. "Take your clothes off, Emilie." He took her hand and brought it to his cock. She couldn't stop herself from wrapping her fingers around his hard shaft. Arousal flared in her belly. He stroked her hand along his length. "You're mine. I'm going to come inside you. I'm going to stay inside you until the end."

Her sex clenched hard and moistened. Every fiber of her being screamed, *Yes! Do it!*

Suddenly she was sick of hiding. Concealing. Afraid of her scars being seen.

He said he couldn't be repelled. Could that miraculously be true?

She wanted to be with this man. She loved seeing herself through his eyes. She loved how happy she felt around him.

She loved him so very much. She wanted to hold on to the bliss he brought—for a lifetime. And her scars were the final obstacle in their paths.

Emilie pulled her hand away from his beautiful prick and began to strip. A slow grin formed on his handsome face. He helped her discard her clothing down to the final chemise.

Her beautiful swan costume lay scattered on the floor.

He picked her up in his arms and carried her to her bedchambers. Setting her down before the bed, he removed the last of his clothing.

He stood naked, unabashed. "Your turn, Emilie."

Her heart pounding, she drew in a shaky breath. *I can do this.* Grabbing handfuls of her chemise, she pulled it up over her head in one quick movement, fearing that with a slower progress she'd falter.

Standing naked, she met his gaze.

He was smiling. "I just see beauty."

That's because I haven't turned around and showed you my back yet. Emilie swallowed hard and forced herself to turn her back to him.

Facing him were her scars, covering her back, and down the backs of her arms to her elbows. Pink to dark red blotchy skin. Thick. And raised. And uneven.

And horrible to behold.

Not having the courage to turn back around to see his reaction, she waited for him to speak, her insides quivering.

She felt his lips against her shoulder first. She lurched. He slipped his arm around her waist and bent her forward, her palms bracing against the mattress. Kiss after kiss was pressed against her back as he slowly made his way down her spine. Tears welled in her eyes and fell onto the bed. She was so stunned, so moved, she couldn't believe what he was doing.

He straightened, leaned over her, and near her ear he repeated, "I just see beauty."

Shaking, she couldn't speak. Overwhelmed by emotion. Overwhelmed by him. Her only sounds were her ragged breaths.

He captured her nipple between his strong warm fingers and gave it luscious rolls and tugs, instantly swamping her with sensations. His other hand reached around and he began fingering her with devastating finesse. "I'm going to take you from behind— one of my favorite positions."

Already wet and feverish for him, she would have agreed to just about anything.

"You want my cock, Emilie?"

"Yes!"

"Yes, *Joseph.* I want to hear my name from your lips."

"*Joseph* . . . I want your . . . cock."

He slid his shaft along her slick folds, grazing the engorged head over her pulsing bud. She gasped.

"Joseph, I love you. Say it." He was smiling. She could hear it in his tone. The rhythmic strokes across her private flesh were sublime, flooding her body with pleasure, inciting an all-consuming hunger.

"Say it, Emilie," he insisted.

"I love you, Joseph."

"I will marry you, *Joseph*," he said.

"Yes! Yes, I will marry you, Joseph . . . Please . . . I want you inside me."

"There's a request I cannot refuse." Grabbing her hips firmly, he drove his cock into her.

She cried out and fisted the counterpane, deliciously stretched and full by his possession, which was exquisitely deep.

He thrust again. And again. Gliding his shaft over a sweet spot inside her slick walls, giving her a barrage of knee-weakening sensations. Making her moan and gasp.

"*Dieu*, I love your tight grip on me. How does it feel? You like being taken this way, don't you?"

"Yes!" She'd love anything as long as it was him doing the taking.

Pushing her bottom toward him, she was eager for more, reveling in the glorious friction of his driving sex. It was sheer rapture, and she was fast approaching a stunning release.

"You're going to come, aren't you? I can feel it," he rasped. "Your sweet sex is sucking me in with the most delicious tiny spasms."

Dear God, it was true. She couldn't help it. Couldn't stop it. Her inner muscles were milking his shaft greedily, ravenous for more.

"Come with me, Emilie. I want you to come when I do."

Oh, how she wanted that.

He slipped his hand between her legs, paying homage to that

tiny bud so sensitized with desire, sending torrents of scintillating sensations straight into her core. The strokes of his hand and the strokes of his sex were double the pleasure and shot her into ecstasy, his roar of pleasure joining her scream as he pulsed inside her and poured himself into her depths.

She sobbed with joy and rapture, her sex wildly contracting around his plunging shaft, milking him until he'd spent his final drop.

Her breathing and her thundering heart slowed; her legs and arms were lax.

Emilie's entire body hummed with satisfaction. And bliss.

He swept her up in his arms and deposited her tenderly on the bed.

Lying beside her, he pulled her to him. "You're going to let me stay the night."

She smiled. "Is that an order?"

Joseph returned her smile. "Take it any way you wish. I'm not leaving."

"I know. That's why I love you." Slipping her hand behind his head, she pulled him to her for a kiss. She was lying completely naked and comfortable in his arms—loved and in love.

The transformation was complete.

By the magic of this man, Emilie de Sarron had indeed changed from an ugly duckling to a most beautiful swan.

The Princess and the Diamonds

1

"Are you absolutely certain you want to do this, Montfort? You'll be turning on your peers," Renault de Sard asked from behind his desk.

Mathias Paul Thomas de Tesson, Marquis de Montfort, found himself seated in the home of the Lieutenant General of Police of Paris, sequestered in his private study—rather than at his public office.

This was no ordinary meeting. Its secrecy paramount. The mission at hand was to topple some of the highest-ranking nobles of the realm, aristocracy that considered themselves untouchable. Above the law.

Unfazed by the Lieutenant General's comment, Mathias sat back in the silk upholstered chair.

"You need a spy. The King wants his ban on Basset enforced. And I am at your disposal." He'd been eager since Sard approached him two days ago. In fact, this was the first time since Charles's death that he'd felt any fire at all. "Besides, you know as well as I do they turn on each other every time they sit at a Basset table." He couldn't keep the disdain from his tone. His disgust wasn't simply directed at those breaking the King's new law, but at himself.

He hadn't been any different from those who still gambled at the game. Lord knows he was no stranger to the gaming tables. Women and gambling had been his favorite forms of recreation. He'd enjoyed vice. And with his wealth and skill, the monetary losses had been minimal and without detriment.

Gambling had never really cost him. Until five months ago. Five months ago Basset had cost him the life of his closest friend.

"Yes, well, I have finally impressed upon His Majesty that if we don't make examples of men of high rank, his edict will continue to be ignored—and more prominent families will be brought to their ruin," Sard said.

Mathias didn't need anyone to explain to him the damage Basset caused. The card game wildly popular among those wealthy enough to play with high stakes, Basset could make or break fortunes in minutes. He'd seen both men and women lose staggering sums.

Lose everything.

He'd stopped playing when the King had issued his decree. He only wished Charles had done the same. He'd be alive now. His wife wouldn't be a widow, and his young daughter would still have her father.

Charles would never have lost all that he owned—or committed suicide.

"I quite agree," Mathias said. "Unless you bring to heel those involved who are of the highest rank, the wealthy will continue to pay the King's edict no mind." He stretched out his legs and crossed his arms over his chest. "What do you wish me to do, and how soon may I begin?"

"I like your enthusiasm, Montfort." Sard smiled. "I need you to gather names. Tell me who the regular players are, who the biggest players are. And of course, most importantly, who the dealer is—the one that minds the bank—and reaps the biggest rewards at the game."

Mathias gave the Lieutenant of Police a mirthless smile. "No problem."

"Do you have anyone in particular in mind we can focus on? If we're to make an example of him, he must be highly notable."

Mathias's smile broadened. "I've the perfect man to suggest. The Duc de Navers. Is that notable enough for you, Sard?"

Sard lifted his brows. "A duke?" His brown eyes danced with delight. "Oh, Navers will do just fine. Perfectly, in fact."

It was perfect. In so many ways. Charles lost his wealth to Navers. In his very own mansion in the city—Hôtel de Navers—the Duc was making a fortune from his biweekly private gaming den. Right under the nose of the Paris police. Without concern. Or regard for the royal edict.

Navers wasn't the only noble who hosted Basset games. But he was the one Mathias wanted to focus on.

"Navers's games are masked," Mathias added. "Only those with funds enough to play are permitted. That includes any wealthy merchants from the bourgeois. The mask allows for anonymity, and makes everyone equal while playing Basset, regardless of title. Money is the only thing that is held in esteem at the gaming table. If you lose everything, then and only then are you unmasked. Before you're permitted to leave the table, you are made to sign your ruin."

At that Sard frowned. "How will you know who is who?"

"I've played many years with the same people. It won't be difficult for me to determine who is in attendance. Mannerisms, expressions of speech are not covered by a mask. Neither is a man's or woman's style of play. No one will go unreported."

"And you've no conflict of conscience or qualms in advising me of each and every person there?" Sard pressed. Clearly the man wanted to be assured of his commitment to the mission.

"None," he said without hesitation. "The rule in Basset is that you have no friends." He didn't have any friends left. At least none like Charles.

For him and his family, for others who'd suffered the same fate, and for any further such tragedies, he was going to put an end to Basset once and for all.

Nothing and no one was going to stop him.

* * *

"Is there anything I can say that will stop you from doing this?" Bernadette asked, worried.

"Or I?" Caroline looked just as concerned.

"No." Gabrielle's response was unequivocal as she studied her attire in the mirror with a critical eye. "I think it looks perfect. The binding around my chest is a tad too tight." She squirmed, uncomfortable. "But overall, I think I'll pass for a man."

She was taller than most women. For once, her height was an asset.

Bernadette sighed. "I'll loosen it a bit, but you do have breasts, Gabrielle. You are a woman. For God's sake, you're a princess wearing men's clothing. This mad plan of yours has me worried sick."

"Everything will be fine." Gabrielle removed the blue satin justacorps she wore and handed it to Caroline. She fumbled with the closures on her breeches a bit before opening them and pulling out the shirttails.

Her plan had her more than a little anxious, too, but she refused to show her unease to her two closest confidantes, her ladies-in-waiting. Both distant cousins, they were a few years older than Gabrielle and the only ones she trusted to take with her on this secret trip from Versailles to Paris.

The only ones she'd divulged her true intentions to. There were only three people she trusted in the world, her half brother Daniel and the two women before her.

"Hold up your arms," Bernadette said, slipping her hands under the shirt and loosening the binding around Gabrielle's breasts. "There, is that better?"

Gabrielle took a deep breath. "Much better." She readjusted her clothing and accepted the justacorps Caroline handed to her.

"What if the King realizes you're not in the country with your uncle at his château?" Bernadette asked.

"Never mind that." Caroline waved off Bernadette's comment. "What if His Majesty learns you stole some of the royal diamonds and intend to gamble them at the *Basset* table? He's put a ban on the game." She shook her blond head. "I don't even want to think about what he would do!"

"The King has done nothing to enforce the ban. And as for the diamonds, I didn't steal them. I'm borrowing them. Stealing implies I intend to keep them. I don't," Gabrielle said. "They'll be returned once I win enough to cover Daniel's debt." Listening to Caroline carry on only spiked her fears. She knew what she was doing was risky, but what choice did she have? "I'll not abandon him. He is barely seventeen, and they took advantage of him."

Her half brother was not in the habit of gambling. He was coaxed and bamboozled into it, and it infuriated her.

"At seventeen, he is a man, has been a man for two years now. He should have known better than to gamble and lose a vast fortune—at an *illegal* game," Caroline argued.

"There are those twice his age, and older, who have been lured to the Basset tables," Gabrielle countered. She adored Daniel and was crushed when her mother, who had once been the King's mistress, passed away. She'd lost her mother and Daniel in the same week. He was removed from the palace—sent to live with his father's family. The King, having legitimized all his illegitimate children from his many mistresses, had lost interest in her mother once Gabrielle was born. She'd married the Baron de Leclerc, Daniel's father, shortly thereafter, but sadly he'd died within the first year of their marriage.

The King had permitted Daniel and her mother to remain at the palace, close to Gabrielle, but once her mother was gone, her beloved brother was torn from her. He was only eight.

They'd been inseparable until then.

She wrote to him constantly. Worried about him always. Missed him madly, for she rarely saw him.

When he came to her last week and told her what had happened at the Duc de Navers's Hôtel, Gabrielle was devastated for him.

He was in financial ruin. He couldn't pay his servants. Couldn't maintain his château.

She refused to see him financially destroyed. It was difficult enough seeing him so heartbroken and dispirited. Daniel would do anything for her. No matter what. She, in turn, would do anything for him. Including taking some of the Crown gems and using them to win back Daniel's fortune.

"I'll not see my brother destitute, Caroline." Gabrielle picked up the periwig off the bed and placed it over her hair. If she didn't help him, no one else would. No one in his father's family or on her mother's side would wish to cover his gambling debt. Especially one so sizable.

And the King had never cared in the least about Daniel.

Bernadette swiped an errant curl from her cheek, her dark hair a sharp contrast to Caroline's fair coloring. "We don't wish to see him destitute either. We're just . . . well, we're most concerned about your scheme."

"I know you are." Gabrielle placed her hand on Bernadette's shoulder. "But I am no novice at Basset. I've played many times at court with His Majesty and the courtiers—until the King banned the game. I'll do fine." She was far better than most. "I'm not without wit and luck," Gabrielle added.

One didn't survive the politics and intrigue at court without having a good dose of both.

Or without being resourceful and clever.

Gabrielle had fooled His Majesty into believing she was visiting with her uncle. Fooled her uncle into allowing her the use of his private town house in the city while he was at his château. With no funds at her disposal—for members of the royal family didn't carry coin—she'd thought of a solution and slipped away from the palace with a pouch of diamonds. She'd even managed to turn her entourage of musketeers back to the palace without raising suspicion.

Trickery and deception weren't things she liked. But they were part of her world and deeply entrenched in the royal palace.

Being a convincing liar was more than an essential asset at court.

Her skills in dupery were finely honed after her mother's death. Only then, when she found herself alone in the palace without her mother's protection, did she learn just how much her mother had shielded her from. Duplicity hadn't come easy to her at first. Her conscience had weighed on her in the beginning.

Now she was numb to it.

Besides, desperate situations required desperate measures.

She had two weeks.

Clearly, luck was on her side; she'd made it to her uncle's town house in Paris. From here she had easy access to the Duc de Navers's gaming den at his Hôtel—and what amounted to four nights of Basset.

If she was to succeed in recouping Daniel's losses and not lose the diamonds she'd gamble with, luck had to remain on her side.

She couldn't—wouldn't—fail. Nothing would get in her way.

2

"Ten wins. Seven loses," the banker said, placing four gold *louis* in front of Mathias. He was up four hundred *louis d'or* already.

It was night and a large torchère in each corner of the Duc de Navers's drawing room illuminated the three Basset tables.

And the masked players.

Mathias cast the occasional furtive glance about the room. One by one, he carefully studied each person, certain he knew the identity of at least seven in the small crowd. Including the banker at his table and the banker's assistant—the *croupière*.

The banker had all the advantage in Basset, and tonight the banker was the Duc de Navers's own nephew, the Marquis de Raigecourt. He'd know him anywhere. The tall, boney man's distinct features were easily recognizable, despite the black demi-mask. Navers himself was by his side—sans a mask—acting as the game's *croupière*. At times there were many cards in play. It was the *croupière's* responsibility to supervise, watching the cards so that nothing that was in the banker's favor would be missed.

Despite his winnings, despite his success in identifying a number of men in the room, Mathias felt edgy. His stomach was as tight as a fist. This was more difficult than he'd imagined. Being here playing Basset inspired thoughts of Charles.

He hated being in a gambling den again.

Hated it that he hadn't tried harder to convince Charles to stop playing when he saw his losses getting out of hand.

And he hated it that at one of the other tables was one of the Lieutenant General's sergeants. Valette, Sard had called him. He was to be his assistant on this mission. He didn't need an assistant and he didn't see how the somber sergeant added to or aided in the mission.

Mathias turned over three cards and placed a bet—ten *louis d'or* stacked on each. *Jésus-Christ*, he wanted to leave. *You're helping to put an end to this game that has brought many to ruin. It's the least you can do for Charles.* It was the only thing keeping him from walking out of the stifling situation.

Vaguely he heard the door open behind him, then a brief exchange of words between the doorman and another patron before a slender young man approached and sat down at his table, now making the players total six.

A young man Mathias didn't recognize.

The doorman approached and whispered in Navers's ear. Navers halted play and turned his attention to the newly arrived player.

"My doorman tells me you don't have any *louis d'or* to bet with," Navers said.

"That's correct. I don't," the young man admitted, the pitch of his voice slightly odd. Almost forced. His interest piqued, Mathias studied him closer. A youth like this wouldn't be someone Sard would be interested in. He wanted the names of much more important men.

But there was something almost . . . captivating about him.

Below the youth's brown demi-mask, there was a delicate jaw. And lips that were, well . . . *pretty.*

"No currency other than *louis d'or* is acceptable." Navers's annoyance laced his tone. "No Spanish *pistoles* are allowed."

"That's excellent, because I don't have any Spanish *pistoles* either." The young man smirked. *A cocky youth.*

Navers laughed, completely without mirth. "Then what the bloody hell do you intend to bet with?"

The youth pulled out a velvet pouch from the breast pocket inside his brown justacorps, loosened the silk ties, and spilled its contents onto the table. A number of pea-sized diamonds tumbled out and twinkled back at them.

Astounding everyone at the table. Including Mathias.

"Basset is a game of high stakes. That is part of the thrill," the youth said. "It isn't uncommon for people to play for lands . . . and jewelry. This one right here"—he flicked one of the diamonds— "is worth five hundred *louis d'or.* I'll start my bidding with it." He scooped up the other diamonds and placed them back in the pouch.

The Duc, like a dog about to be given a bone, was practically salivating. "Welcome to the game." He grinned.

Mathias, on the other hand, was far more gripped by the sight of the youth's hands. Delicate, slender fingers. Too refined to be male. Scrutinizing the new arrival closer, he noted the justacorps he wore was of quality and yet was ill-fitting. Too loose in the shoulders. Anyone who could afford a costly overcoat like that would have had the thing properly tailored.

And then there was the youth's cravat. He wore it oddly higher than was the norm, covering most of his throat, keeping Mathias from seeing the distinct masculine feature of an Adam's apple.

He couldn't shake the feeling that the concealment was done intentionally.

Much of the young man's face was hidden behind the mask and the periwig. Since they weren't at court, no man in the room—save for the Baron de Ragon at the other table—wore the itchy thing, and the Baron only did so because he was concealing his baldness—just like the King. It was the reason His Majesty had made it mandatory for all gentlemen of quality to sport the periwig.

Mathias himself detested them. He detested the court and all its pomp and circumstance and had only attended twice—briefly.

It wasn't common to see a periwig on someone this young— outside the palace.

Mathias's suspicions continued to mount as his gaze dropped to the youth's chest. His justacorps was open and beneath was the usual long vest one expected to find, but it was in shadow thanks to the chair he happened to inhabit and the positioning of the torchère. There was no way Mathias could see clearly if there was a hint of female breasts there.

Yet as he moved his focus back to the youth's mouth, mentally tracing the lush curve of his lips, the slender neck, the delicate movements of the hands, his every instinct told him this was no male youth.

He knew a woman when he saw one. He'd spent too many years indulging in debauchery not to be certain.

Why was she concealing her gender? Women were permitted to play. Perhaps she was afraid that if she lost and needed someone to cover her losings, she'd be beholden to the man who advanced her funds in ways she didn't want to be.

He'd known a few ladies of quality who'd paid off their debts with sexual favors—though none would ever admit to it. Perhaps this was the very thing this woman wanted to avoid. Numerous questions whirled through his mind.

Who was she? Didn't she have a husband or any male in her life who could have stopped her from donning her outrageous attire, traveling through Paris at night to an illegal gaming den to gamble at an illegal game?

If Mathias wasn't taken aback enough by her disguise and actions, he was completely leveled by the sheer daring of her play. She played with confidence. The very same confidence exuded from her speech and mannerisms.

Luck was with her, perched firmly on her shoulder, in fact. She obviously knew it. It made her dauntless. In his opinion, a tad reckless.

And yet he watched her win her *couch* and then proceed to make a *paroli*, clearly after a *sept-et-le-va*—a chance at winning seven times her sizable bet. But only if her winning card was dealt yet again by the banker.

And it was.

In stunned amazement, he watched her indicate she was going for a *quinze-et-le-va*—fifteen times her bet on that same card. The odds of it turning up again, slim. And yet, to the Duc's horror and the awe of every player at the table, her card turned up a third time.

He'd never seen such adventurous play rewarded so favorably so quickly. She'd only just started and had already won a sizable sum.

Then she did the most amazing thing of all. She gathered her diamonds, having not lost a one, and her stacks of *louis d'or*, dropped them into a pouch and into her pocket, rose, and quit the game.

When that amount of good fortune was on your side, he didn't know anyone who could have resisted the lure to play on for more winnings. Yet she'd stopped when she was ahead—well ahead.

Before her luck could run out.

He was more than a little intrigued by this intriguing woman.

The moment she rose, the Duc was on his feet. "You're not leaving already, are you?"

"Yes."

"Why don't you sit back down. I'll see that some of my finest brandy is brought out and some food—for everyone. The night is young. Come now, have a seat. Let's play another round or two while the servants attend to your needs." The Duc, like everyone else, knew the longer she stayed, the more likely it was that her luck would change, and the Duc could recoup the losses he'd suffered because of her.

"No. I'm interested in neither your brandy nor the food. I am, however, tired of playing." The way she spoke, with a certain elevated importance, told him she was of significant rank. A member of the house of Bourbon, maybe? Perhaps she was a part of the Prince of Condé's family? *Merde.* That was absurd. To think that she'd be related to the King's own cousin was ludicrous—as ludicrous as believing she was one of His Majesty's own issue.

As if a royal princess could or would slip away for this or any other nocturnal escapade.

What on earth was this woman about?

She moved around the table, but the Duc stepped in front of her. "Will you be here Saturday night?"

At that she smiled, an adorable dimple appearing near the corner of her mouth.

Mathias had the incredible urge to rip off her mask and wig for a better look at her appealing features. He couldn't pinpoint her age. Try as he might, he couldn't picture her face.

"You'll have me and my diamonds back?" she said in that odd voice she was using.

"Of course. Until Saturday, then." Navers personally escorted the mysterious woman to the door, giving no indication he'd noted her true gender.

Riveted by the way the woman had played, Mathias's concentration on his own game had gone awry. He'd lost half his winnings, and he used it as an excuse to leave. "My luck has turned on me," he said, rising, slipping his coin into his pouch and tucking it into his inner breast pocket. "I'm taking a break."

Valette, still playing at the other table, gave him a curious look.

Mathias responded with a look of his own. One that said, *stay put.*

He moved around the tables slowly, trying not to make it obvious that he was following the "youth" who had just left, forcing himself to keep to a stroll and not bolt from the room after her.

But once outside the drawing room, Mathias picked up his pace, his long legs eating the distance to the doors that would lead to the courtyard—where he'd likely find her and her carriage.

He pushed open the doors and stepped outside, a warm summer breeze wafting up to greet him. There were a number of carriages lined up in front of him. The sounds of crickets and nickering horses drifted through the night air. Glancing in both directions, he spotted her ahead in the distance and raced to her as she made her way steadily and swiftly up the cobblestone path.

"You there!" he called out, arresting her steps.

She turned, her mask still on her face, yet he could tell she wasn't pleased he'd stopped her.

Mathias walked up. It was the first time he noted just how tall she was. Normally he towered over women. She reached above

his shoulder. *The perfect height for a kiss* . . . Having no idea
where that errant thought came from, he shoved it aside.

"That was quite the game you played," he said.

"Thank you. I wish I could say the same about you." She
turned and walked away, dismissing him completely.

Mathias choked on a mirthless laugh, stunned. *Dieu.* She'd
just given him the cut. Not something he was used to receiving—
especially from a woman. Then again, she wasn't a typical female.
He didn't know any woman who would don a man's attire.

Watching her walk away, he glanced down her body, noting her long luscious legs clearly visible in her male clothing. He
loved shapely legs. She definitely had those.

Mathias arrested her steps with his next words. "I can't imagine why you need to dress like a man to play."

Gabrielle was fixed to the spot, her heart pounding so hard,
she feared he could hear it.

The man standing behind her was the very reason she'd
stopped playing. The weight of his regard had been on her the
entire time she was at the Basset table. He had the most piercing
light-colored eyes she'd ever seen. She felt as though his clever
eyes could read every thought in her head. Know her every secret.

Unsettled, she walked away from a winning streak, fearing
she'd lose her concentration, then her luck, the longer she sat
across from him.

Undeniably, he was observant.

No one else at Navers's Hôtel had noticed she was a woman.

Get away from this man. Fast. He was trouble. There weren't
many people who could rattle her. He had.

She turned and faced him, forcing herself to look him in the
eye. "Sir, I have some advice for you. If you wish to play better,
you might consider avoiding intoxication. It muddles the mind.

Clearly, drink has you thinking quite absurdly." Thankfully her tone didn't belie her inner distress.

Amusement flashed in his eyes and he shook his head. "*Dieu*, you are a spirited little piece, aren't you?"

"What I am is bored of this conversation." Did she sound convincing?

The meddling man didn't seem as put off by her impertinence as she'd hoped. He approached. Still smiling, he pulled off his mask and ran his fingers through his hair.

Her agitated heart gave a lurch. Gracious God . . . Against her will, she took in his cheekbones, his masculine jaw, and his alluring mouth. Even with his mask on, she could tell, seated across from him at the Basset table, that he was attractive, but without it, he took her breath away. She could better see his eyes, and they were a stunning contrast with his shoulder-length dark hair. The night's silver light was too dim to allow her to determine their true color, but those piercing eyes were mesmerizing. Disarming. Dangerous. Especially since nothing more than a simple gaze had warmed her blood and fluttered her insides.

His male beauty unbalanced her, and she couldn't imagine why.

There were plenty of handsome men at His Majesty's palace, but this man stood head and shoulders above them all—in more ways than one. He was deliciously tall. She'd always hated her height. It wasn't an asset for any woman to be at eye level with a man. Or taller in some cases. But standing near this man, she actually felt small and feminine. A first.

Leave now, her instincts screamed. "Good night, and good luck." Her response was purposely curt and dismissive. She turned toward her carriage, but he caught her arm, both surprising her and halting her progress.

Her head snapped toward him. "Unhand me!" she demanded, unnerved by the thrill that shot up her arm from his touch.

"Are you always this rude?" he asked.

"Oddly, I had the same question for you," she countered and yanked her arm free, as furious as she was frightened. "Is it your habit to follow strangers and make nonsensical accusations?"

The corner of his mouth lifted into what amounted to a smirk. Then he stunned her by stroking the back of his fingers along her jaw and down her cravat-covered throat.

She jumped back, his caress sending delicious tingles lancing into her womb.

"You are no man, or boy," he said. "I know a woman when I see one, and when I feel one. This game you are playing isn't without consequences. You've won yourself a sizable sum. Do not return here on Saturday. You don't want to become mixed up with this."

This man needed to be put in his place, so that he didn't become a problem. Her situation was complicated enough.

She didn't need more problems.

"I have the Duc's personal invitation to attend. And I shall attend on Saturday," she stated unequivocally. "You're the one who should stay away, since I'm sure you don't want to part with more of your *louis d'or.*"

She turned yet once again, intent on marching away, when she felt her mask and periwig yanked off her head.

She squeaked in surprise, looking just as astounded as he. Standing there, holding her mask in one hand and the periwig in the other, he had an expression of utter astonishment.

"*Jésus-Christ* . . . You're beautiful," she heard him whisper. "Who the bloody hell are you?" he asked forcefully.

Panic surged up inside her. Gabrielle bolted for her carriage, her knees wobbly. Her pulse racing. Not waiting for her footman, she yanked the door open herself and practically threw herself inside. "Go!" she shouted to her driver, slamming the door shut.

The carriage lurched forward, knocking her from the edge of her seat, where she'd just settled herself, onto the carriage floor, bashing her hands and knees against it with jarring force. Pain shot up her arms and thighs; she barely caught her cry.

Picking herself off the floor, Gabrielle settled back in her seat, her breaths sharp and shallow. An alarming thought ripped through her mind, and she grabbed her breast pockets. Relief flooded through her the moment she felt both pouches, the one with the diamonds and the other with her winnings.

Already she'd won back half her brother's debt. Another night like tonight and she'd have all she needed. But now there was an obstacle in her path. A tall dark stranger. One who inspired dread and inexplicable and unwanted feminine reactions. She simply had to return on Saturday.

There was no doubt in her mind; *he'd* be there.

What was she going to do?

There are only three days until Saturday. You'd better think of something, Gabrielle.

* * *

Still clutching the periwig and mask, Mathias craned his neck, watching the town houses thread by from inside his moving carriage. He'd raced to his driver, shouting out orders to follow the mysterious woman's carriage at a discreet distance.

He wanted her to think she got away from him.

Merde. A million questions were whirling in his head. He was no untried youth. He'd seen a pretty face before, but when the moon's silver light illuminated hers, a bolt of lust rocked him so hard, it shifted the ground beneath his feet. She was ravishing. He'd never seen a lovelier face. He'd never seen her at all. Anywhere.

And he'd never had such a stunning physical reaction to any woman, especially one who hadn't so much as touched him.

He was still hard. Mathias shifted in his seat, trying to alleviate his discomfort.

Though undoubtedly a full-grown woman, she was younger than he'd imagined by her comportment.

The carriage slowed down, then stopped. He recognized this street. Exclusive stately town houses for the social elite. His footman opened the door to the carriage. Dropping the mysterious woman's items he was still clutching in his hands onto the seat, Mathias stepped down.

If not for the full moon, he wouldn't have been able to make out much.

"There, my lord, the fourth one in." The footman pointed up the street. "That is the one the carriage turned into."

Mathias silently studied the town house from a distance. It had a rosy-white façade, just like the others near it. By tomorrow he'd know who owned the fourth town house.

He wasn't going to wait until Saturday to talk to her. She was determined to return to the Duc's gaming den. He'd seen it in her eyes.

Mathias wanted to know why.

Face it, you want to know who the hell she is. You want to know everything about her—including *just how good she'd taste.* She'd left him utterly seduced, with a pulsing prick, and the powerful urge to melt that icy façade. There was fire behind those big beautiful dark eyes. He'd seen an instant spark of desire in them when he'd caressed her. Though her tongue could be sharp, he knew down to his marrow that he could coax her to put it to better use.

There was no reason for her to become entangled in the mess that was about to occur with the Duc and those who frequented his private gaming den. He couldn't speak of his mission, but he could make sure she was steered away. And if she was looking for nocturnal amusements, he'd be happy to provide a new form of entertainment—one of a carnal nature—for her.

He couldn't remember the last time he'd been this captivated by a woman. And just as astonishing, in the five months since Charles's death, this was the first time he felt the gloom that had descended on him lift.

By tomorrow night he'd know the identity of the woman.

He'd know all the answers to his multitude of questions. Not only was he sure of it, he was looking forward to it.

The next time they'd meet, he wasn't about to let her run away.

3

"I still cannot believe how much gold coin you won!" Bernadette exclaimed, closing her book and resting it on her lap.

It was the third time in the last hour she'd repeated the same thing. Bringing the total to twenty times today.

Forming a smile, Gabrielle closed her own volume, settled back in her chair, and relaxed her shoulders. She hadn't realized she'd been sitting practically on the edge of her seat, her muscles tense.

She couldn't relax. She couldn't concentrate on the book of poetry. It wasn't simply because of Bernadette's or even Caroline's constant interruptions and carryings on about her winnings last eve.

It was because of a confrontation with a man outside her carriage whose physical appeal was far too potent for her liking.

Last eve, she'd shoved the pouch of diamonds under her mattress and had tossed and turned all night, worried about just how much of a problem he was going to be, about what would happen to Daniel if she didn't succeed in winning back the money he'd lost.

About losing the diamonds in the game if her luck turned on her.

Now, it was almost supper time, and she was exhausted.

Caroline closed her book as well. Setting it on her lap, she rested her hands on it. "Are you quite certain you still have all twenty diamonds?"

"Yes, I counted them before putting them in a safe place." Gabrielle tried to sound reassuring despite the numerous doubts assailing her and undermining her confidence. But she kept her doubts to herself. Though Caroline and Bernadette were her closest companions, there was much she didn't share with them. Truth be known, there wasn't anyone she completely opened up with.

After she lost her mother and Daniel, her heart broke. Left at the palace with no one to protect her, no one to trust until Caroline and Bernadette came along, she learned to cope by holding her tongue, distancing herself from everything. Detaching from everyone at court.

The backstabbing and jostling between her half sisters, between the courtiers—all for the sake of gaining the King's favor—no longer affected her. She'd taught herself not to react to it.

In a world where she had little control over her destiny, she could at the very least control how things impacted her.

No one at court could hurt her—because she simply didn't care. And there had been many who had tried to hurt her in the eyes of the King.

She, unlike her half sisters, didn't vie for her father's attention. She didn't waste a moment's thought about whom the King would select as her husband.

He wouldn't matter to her either.

Only Daniel and her two closest friends mattered, and even they were kept at an arm's length.

"You know, at first I was quite agitated over your plan," Bernadette said. "But now, I must say, I do believe you are going to succeed." She smiled.

Gabrielle maintained hers, hoping it looked genuine. "Thank you, Bernadette."

"And you didn't encounter any real problems?" Caroline asked.

How she wished Caroline would leave the matter alone. The questions about last night added to her fatigue. "I've already mentioned, Caroline, that I encountered a small problem. But it was nothing I couldn't handle."

"Yes, but you won't say how small or what the problem was," Caroline pressed.

"It was small. Nothing for you to worry about. Now then, let's return to our reading, shall we?" As she opened the volume to where she'd left off, hoping to lose herself in its prose, she stared blankly at the page, her anxieties about the Basset game on Saturday welling up inside her again.

She simply had to attend. There was no choice in the matter.

An argument drifted up the hallway and into the study, snatching Gabrielle from her thoughts. Glancing up from her book, she noted the dismayed expressions on her companions' faces as the voice of the majordomo eclipsed another male voice. Gabrielle rose and dropped her book on her chair, intent on investigating the disturbance, when the meddling man from last night strode bold as could be into the room.

Her stomach dropped.

She couldn't believe he was here. She couldn't believe how good he looked. She didn't think it was possible, but he looked even better than he did last eve. In the bright light of her uncle's study, with its many wall sconces and candelabras aglow, his striking male features were illuminated. And devastating.

His magnificent height, his broad shoulders, his . . . Oh God . . . gray eyes, no, they were more than gray. They were a stunning light silver that set her insides aquiver.

He stopped dead in his tracks the moment he made eye contact with her.

"Monsieur!" The majordomo came running into the room. "My orders are that no guests are permitted—"

Gabrielle cleared her throat, uncertain she could speak without her voice quavering while the darkly handsome stranger moved his gaze over her, his tactile perusal irking her as much as it was inflaming her. And that irked her further still.

"It's all right, Aubert," she said to the servant. With a nod, the majordomo bowed and left the study.

He found you! She cursed her luck. The entire ride home, she'd checked repeatedly to see if they were being followed.

There had been no sign of him.

He was far cleverer than she'd given him credit for. Damn him and his physical allure.

"You look better in this attire than the one you had on last night," he said with a hint of a smile on his lips.

Caroline and Bernadette moved close to her.

Placing a hand on her arm, Caroline asked sotto voce, "Is this the 'small problem' you mentioned earlier?"

"Good Lord, there's nothing small about the man," Bernadette whispered, eyeing him.

Gabrielle took a deep breath and let it out slowly, striving for a level of composure she didn't feel inside. "Enough. Not another word from either of you." Her voice was soft but firm. She didn't want them giving this man any information about her or them.

"Ladies, please excuse us. I have a word or two to say to our *visitor*," she remarked louder, holding his gaze firmly.

"Alone? In private?" Caroline asked, her unease tingeing her tone.

"Yes. Please leave now." Out of the corner of her eye, Gabrielle saw her two friends exchange concerned looks, but without further ado, they dropped their gazes as they passed the man standing in the room, and exited the study, closing the door quietly behind them.

"How did you find me?" She didn't waste a moment's time getting to the point.

He cocked his head, a lock of dark hair falling across his brow, looking ever so appealing. "I followed you."

"Why? What on earth are you doing here?"

"I've come for a visit."

Her brows shot up. "*A visit?* Are you entirely well in the mind? What about our encounter would have made you think I would want a visit from you?"

The smile that tugged at the corners of his mouth looked more like a smirk. He approached, stopping before her. Towering over her. Yet she refused to step back, or do anything to indicate in any way she was unsettled by him.

"You asked what I was doing here and I responded. You never asked if I thought you'd like a visit from me."

Her ire mounted by the moment—thanks to his unmitigated gall, the smug look in those light-colored eyes.

And his wonderful scent.

Though she couldn't quite describe it, it was tantalizing in the extreme. She actually had the urge to lean in and inhale deeply.

"The point to you being here is?" she pressed. Dear God, how she wanted him to leave. She didn't know what to make of his unprecedented effect on her. Or how to control it.

He was making her feel dread, and heaven help her . . . desire.

She wasn't at all like some of her half sisters. She wasn't the type of woman who became giddy over a handsome face.

"I want to know why you were there last night," he said.

She simply glared back at him.

He lifted a brow. "Not going to answer?"

"No. What I do and why I do it is none of your concern."

"Fine. Then I shall tell you what I know." He folded his hands behind his back and slowly strolled around her. "I know who owns this town house, the Marquis de Gaillard. I know he's got quite a reputation when it comes to keeping mistresses. He maintains a number of them at any given time. His favorite is with him at his château as we speak." He stopped behind her. His body was so close to hers. A luscious heat emanated from him and inspired a quickening in her belly. He leaned in, his mouth all but touching her ear. "This very town house is one he offered to a former mistress, one whom he's since tired of," he said softly, his warm breath caressing her skin, sending tiny tingles down her spine. "You have a wealthy benefactor. You don't need the coin. Why don't you tell me why you were there last night—dressed as a man?"

Gabrielle didn't respond. She was working too hard at keeping her breathing even. The information about her philandering uncle wasn't new. Her reactions to this man were. Her nipples were hard. Her senses were awakened and highly attuned to him. Reacting to any and every small thing he did.

"What is your name?" This time his lips brushed her ear. She jumped and spun around. His slight touch sent a bolt of startling sensations right down to her feminine core.

"You need to leave. *Now*," she ordered.

"You need to answer my questions."

"I owe you no explanations or answers," she tried saying

with finality, but wasn't sure she'd succeeded; the light throbbing between her legs was a horrible distraction.

Her treacherous body was behaving in the unruliest way.

"Are you going to be there on Saturday?" he asked.

"Yes."

"That's the wrong answer. Stay home."

"No." She uttered the word firmly. Could he tell the frenzy he'd incited inside her?

"I could tell the Duc about you, you know. That you are a woman."

The last thing she needed was to pique anyone else's interest, but she didn't cave in to threats. Others had tried to coerce her at court.

With no success.

Gabrielle collected herself and schooled her features. Affecting her usual blasé tone, she said, "Do you think he'd care? I don't. I got the distinct impression his only concern was recouping his losses and perhaps winning some coin from me."

She'd done it. She'd successfully countered his threat and taken the life out of it. It was visible on his face.

He sighed and rested his hands on his hips. "Look, believe it or not, I am trying to help you."

That inspired a laugh. "Help me? I won a considerable sum last night, while you lost half your winnings. What help do I need from *you*?" She didn't wait for him to respond. "You and I both know why you're here. Clearly you've nothing better to do with your time than to poke your nose where it doesn't belong. And when you learned who owned this home, you of course thought, 'poor lonely mistress, so neglected by her lover.' Naturally she would eagerly allow you a tumble. Isn't that so?"

She was livid—with herself for reacting so strongly to someone who was of no importance to her. And for not putting on a convincing enough performance last night. Though she didn't think she'd failed miserably at behaving like a male, having this man see through her disguise clearly suggested otherwise.

The only thing that gave her any pleasure was that he was so far off course with his belief that she was the Marquis de Gaillard's mistress.

He stepped close to her. She jumped back, something she hadn't meant to do, a knee-jerk reaction on her part that made her want to kick herself. It showed weakness.

He advanced another step. She couldn't back away this time, even if she wanted to. She'd backed up against the tall marble table in the room.

He slipped his fingers under her chin. "Do I want to fuck you? Yes. I won't deny that. What man wouldn't want you?" He leaned in, his solid body pressing against hers. She leaned back away from the lure of his mouth and gripped the edge of the table. "Can you feel how hard you make me? What you do to me?"

Her heart pounded. How could anyone possibly miss *that*? The stiff bulge inside his breeches pressed against her belly and made her sex throb harder.

"I see what I do to you, too, beautiful Snow Princess."

At the word "princess," she flinched.

He didn't seem to notice and continued. "So very alluring, yet with a cold and haughty veneer. I see through that icy exterior of yours," he said. "I see the way your body reacts to me. You know as well as I do any carnal encounter between us would be heated, intense, and delicious."

Other men had made comments about her physical appeal. She'd always dismissed them as empty compliments, as the flattery was only offered in front of the King. She should have done the same with what he was saying, but instead, the look in his eyes, the low timbre of his voice, and his hot hard body pressed against hers made it impossible.

And thrilling.

She swallowed twice before she could say, "Please . . . st-step back."

To her surprise, he complied. She suddenly found him a good two feet from her, his hands back on his hips.

For a man who was as sexually aggressive as he was, she hadn't expected immediate compliance. Though she didn't think he'd force himself on her, she thought she'd have to insist.

He was forever doing the unexpected.

To her chagrin, without the heat and press of his body against hers, she actually felt *bereft*.

"I believe some introductions are in order here," he said. "My name is Mathias de Tesson, Marquis de Montfort. And you are?"

Well, at least he hadn't been able to learn her name. But then again, who would, or could tell him? No one knew she was here, except her uncle, and he was presently a distance away. She was careful not to venture out into the city where she might be recognized, unless in disguise. And then there were the servants. Her uncle paid them well. They knew to hold their tongues or lose their employment.

Gabrielle decided to change tactics. Holding her silence was only fueling his curiosity about her. She'd toss him a bone.

"*Well?*" he prompted.

"Silvie," slipped past her lips. It was the first name that entered her mind and the very last one she should have offered *him*. She mentally chastised herself for choosing *that* name. Of her many given names, that was the one her mother, Daniel, and at times even Bernadette and Caroline called her. Only those closest to her used it.

But never in the presence of the King. His Majesty didn't care for it.

"Silvie?" He said her name with a weighty skepticism, as though he didn't believe her. "Silvie what?"

Fool, now that you've offered the name, you can't exactly change it, can you? "Just Silvie."

"All right, just Silvie, what were you doing at the gaming den, dressed as a man?"

"I was doing what everyone else was doing at the gaming den. Playing Basset. I like the thrill of the game. It's exciting. And I dressed the way I dressed because I didn't want anyone to recognize me, *obviously*." She sharpened her tone, hoping he'd tire of her coarseness and leave her be.

"I don't believe you, Silvie. There is much more to all this than you are saying." He stepped close and gently cupped her cheek. "There is more to you than you allow others to see. Behind the tall thick wall where you conceal yourself is the real woman. One I'd very much like to know."

No one had ever dared touched her like this. Or spoken to her the way he did. Worse, she liked the way he was touching her. Too much.

"Heed my warning, beautiful Silvie. Don't go to the Duc's gaming den on Saturday. For if you do, there will be consequences you don't wish to face."

He stepped back, kissed her hand, bade her a good night, and walked out of the room, leaving her body heated, trembling from the inside out, and her mind spinning from his ominous parting words.

* * *

"Where have you been?" Valette rose from his chair in Mathias's library. He'd just returned home, only to be informed by his

majordomo that the sergeant was here and had insisted on waiting for his return.

The man irked him. There was nothing he liked about the
single-minded civil servant.

"I don't believe I owe you a moment-by-moment accounting
of my time. Do remember your place." He didn't normally stand
on ceremony, but this man of inferior birth had the most boorish
manners.

Mathias's senior by at least five or ten years, Valette had small
dark eyes and a long nose that reminded him of a rodent.

"We are supposed to be working on the Duc's private gambling den together," Valette said.

"No, I'm supposed to be working on it. You're supposed to
be assisting."

"Yes, well, there were twenty men there last night. You've
only given me the names of seven. We'll need the rest."

There were nineteen men there last night—and one very beautiful, very sensuous, very obstinate woman.

"I'm to be reporting on the goings on," Mathias corrected
him. "I've already indicated how the Duc is advancing funds to
those whose luck has turned, keeping them in the game, driving
up their debt and taking land, horses, anything of value from
them, assisting them all the way to their ruin."

"Yes. True." Valette scratched his head. "That has already
been reported back to the Lieutenant General. However, as
pleased as he is with the information you've provided thus far, he
needs to know who attends the games."

"Not everyone. Just the regulars. That is my objective."

He wished he knew why Silvie, if that was even her real name,
showed up at the Duc's Basset table. The reason was much more
involved than she wanted to admit.

She was being secretive. *Merde.* The more she withheld, the more she spiked his interest. He could tell there were many layers to this fascinating woman. He wanted to peel them all away. He was too intrigued by her, and he wanted her too damned much. The Marquis de Gaillard was a colossal fool not to enjoy his mistress more.

He didn't deserve her.

Clearly, he didn't favor her, and Mathias had no qualms poaching. But Silvie would require a slow seduction. Something he was not used to.

He wasn't accustomed to having to work at landing a woman in his bed. Yet with this woman, every fiber of his being told him she'd be worth the effort and the wait.

In the meantime, Mathias prayed she'd heed his warning and remain home Saturday night.

The last thing he wanted was to have her become a regular at the Duc's Basset tables.

4

Gabrielle strode into the Duc de Navers's private gaming den, feeling confident. All day she'd sequestered herself in her private apartments away from Caroline and Bernadette, and worked on bolstering her confidence and courage.

She could do this. She could. She *would* win back the rest of Daniel's debt.

And she'd be damned if she was going to let Montfort scare her away. No one rattled her. Not even the King of the most powerful nation in all of Christendom.

No one was going to keep her from doing what she needed to do.

Montfort may be gorgeous, but he was also overbearing, pushy. And annoying beyond words.

It was bad enough he had followed her, showed up at her home, dictated to her, and aroused her body.

Now he'd even muscled his way into her dreams. She was

having carnal dreams about the man that were becoming more and more heated. Erotic dreams, in which he was doing more than just caressing her hand or cheek. He'd stroked her body, in places no man had ever touched. Gabrielle woke up each morning exhausted, her sex achy and mortifyingly wet.

As if she didn't have enough on her mind. Thanks to Montfort, her thoughts now wavered between the diamonds tucked under her mattress, and fantasizing about a certain Marquis on it.

She'd never had a lover. Never been with a man. Never found any at court particularly stirring. And yet, Montfort was beyond stirring. He was wreaking havoc on her mind and body.

There were fewer people in attendance in the Duc's drawing room.

The same three tables were set. She strode to the same chair she'd used last time. It had been lucky. She'd use it again. The last few days she'd observed men in a way she'd never done before, the male servants, and from her window, the men on the street. Their walk. Their mannerisms. She'd practiced mimicking them.

She wanted no one else guessing her gender.

Ignoring how itchy her periwig was, she glanced about. No Montfort. Could it be that the obnoxious man wasn't showing up tonight? Could she be that lucky?

The banker sat down, joining the other four players at the table. Gabrielle pulled out her pouch of *louis d'or*. She had two pouches on her. One with the diamonds and another with half the winnings from the previous night. Thankfully, she didn't need to risk the diamonds tonight. She'd brought them strictly for luck. Tucked in her pocket, they'd brought her great fortune last time.

She needed more of the same tonight.

Half her winnings from the previous game was still a handsome sum and more than enough to win back the balance of her brother's losings.

The banker began dealing out thirteen cards per player. It was then she heard the door open and close behind her. A figure approached the table and sat down in the vacant chair across from her.

She didn't need to look up. Her nerve endings tingled, already keenly aware of the identity of the newly arrived player. Dragging her gaze up, praying her senses were wrong, she was immediately captured in a pair of light gray eyes.

Montfort.

He didn't look as though he was happy to see her. Good. The feeling was mutual. *Liar*, her body screamed. It was atingle with glee. *And a traitor.* Gabrielle fought back the urge to gnash her teeth.

A strong hand gripped her shoulder, yanking her focus up. She found Navers smiling down at her. "Welcome back," he said, seating himself beside the banker. It was obvious he intended to assist him by being the game's croupière again.

She responded with a nod.

"Let us begin." Navers's comment was to the group. "Place your bets."

Gabrielle turned up four cards and placed three *louis d'or* on each, trying to ignore Montfort and her racing heart. She hadn't been this discomposed the last time.

Mathias was making her nervous—worse than before.

Forget him. Stay focused.

The banker dealt a ten and then a five.

She'd won her *couch*.

Joy and confidence shot through her system. Her nerves dissolved and she relaxed her shoulders. She couldn't help but glance up at Montfort and had to fight back her smile. He'd won his *couch* as well. It delighted her. Not because she cared whether he won or not. What made her happy was that the very same thing happened the last time when she'd had such enormous luck.

They'd both won their *couch* on the first deal.

It was a good sign. One that suggested luck was on her side—that a repeat of what happened the other night was about to happen again. Substantial winnings awaited her this night.

Not wanting to do anything to disrupt something as fickle and fleeting as luck, she echoed her pattern of play, doing everything exactly the same as she'd done before. Crooking the corner of her card, she indicated she was going on for a higher payout. She was going for a *sept-et-le-va*—a chance at winning seven times her bet. It was a daring play that had paid off the last time.

The banker turned up his card. However, this time her winning card didn't show up. She watched as he took her money.

Her gaze drifted to Montfort. His expression was unreadable but his winnings were clear. He'd played it safer and won another couch.

It's all right. It's a loss, but you'll win it back. The night was young and she still had plenty of money left.

Less than an hour later, she was down to her last few *louis d'or.* Her palms were sweaty. Her heart galloped and her head was horribly itchy from the cursed periwig.

She'd lost almost every coin she'd brought with her.

Montfort, on the other hand, was untroubled. Why should he be? He had a good-sized stack of gold coins before him.

Her luck would turn for the better. Good fortune had been missing all night and was due to show up. She wasn't going to panic. Nor dwell on how much she'd lost. Turning up two cards, she placed her final coins on them.

The banker dealt his cards. "King wins. Knave loses."

To her horror, her money was swept up by the Duc. *Oh God!* She could barely breathe. She'd lost it all. Half of what she'd previously won for Daniel.

"Sir, are you listening?" The Duc's voice jolted her out of her whirling thoughts. Quickly she realized he was speaking to her.

"Pardon?" she asked.

"I said, are you going to make another bet?"

All she had on her to bet with were her diamonds. She needed one good win to turn things around. Dare she try? One player at the table had already bet everything he owned and lost. She'd watched, sick to her stomach as he was forced to sign over his château and hôtel. The other players at the table rose and left, all considerably lighter in the purse, but at least they still owned their homes.

She and Montfort were the only players remaining at their table.

Knowing the odds were better with fewer players in the game, she made up her mind to play on.

Did she have a choice really?

Deciding she'd risk only one diamond, she reached inside her breast pocket and pulled out the pouch of diamonds, praying no one could see how her hands trembled. Somehow she got her fingers to work and not fumble while loosening the ties.

Gabrielle pulled out a diamond and set it down on her card.

"Not enough," Navers said.

Gabrielle frowned. "What do you mean? The diamond is worth at least six hundred *louis d'or.*"

"The stakes are higher than that. You bet at least two or you don't play."

A small voice whispered, *Walk away.* But she quashed the voice. She couldn't win if she didn't play.

Gabrielle pulled out a second diamond and set it down on her card.

Montfort placed his bet on his own cards.

With trepidation in her heart and her stomach queasy, she turned and watched the banker's hands as he flipped two cards over. "Ten wins. Eight loses."

As fast as that, her diamonds were taken away.

She was shaking and pulled her gaze up from the empty spot that once had her precious gems to Montfort. He'd won a *sept-et-le-va*.

"I'll take payment in diamonds as well as coin." Montfort astonished her with his request. "It will save you the trouble of having to deal with the gems, Navers," he added.

The Duc thought for a moment then waved someone over. A man about Navers's age had been standing in the corner of the room the entire time observing the goings-on. He approached. Like the Duc, he wasn't wearing a mask.

"Check the diamonds," the Duc ordered him. Pulling out an eyepiece from inside his justacorps, the man examined both gems.

"The bigger one is worth about six hundred *louis d'or*," he advised Navers. "And the smaller of the two, about four hundred."

With a nod from Navers to the banker, the banker pushed her diamonds and the balance of Montfort's winnings toward him. Frozen in disbelief, she watched helplessly as Montfort scooped up his winnings, dropped them into a pouch, and quit the game.

In moments, he was out the door with the King's precious gems.

On wobbly legs she rose, murmured she'd had enough, and walked across the drawing room, forcing herself to keep to a swift walk and not break into a full-out run after Montfort.

The instant she made it to the hallway, she tore after the man with her diamonds.

* * *

Mathias stopped short in front of his carriage and raked a hand through his hair. *Merde. Merde. Merde!* He hated seeing the Comte de Rochemore lose everything. This was the first time since Charles's death he'd seen a loss of that magnitude.

Jésus-Christ, the man had four daughters! He'd never come up with a dowry for them now. Tonight he'd sealed their fate. There would be no marriages. No children. For any of them. All four young women would have no choice but to enter a convent and live out the remainder of their days in the cloister.

Whether they wished it or not.

Curling his fingers, Mathias let loose a string of expletives. He was so overwrought, he wanted to slam his fist into something. Anything.

This game had to stop. He wanted it to stop. But he didn't want to be the one to bring Basset to an end anymore. He thought when Sard had approached him, this would be easy.

It was gut-wrenching.

He'd started all this for Charles, thinking this was the least he could do for him. After watching Rochemore sink farther and farther into debt at the Basset table tonight, he decided he'd done enough for his friend.

Charles could have done a million things differently, not the least of which was having the courage to deal with the aftermath of his financial losses.

Instead, he'd chosen to abandon his wife and child after he'd driven them into poverty.

Mathias was tired of torturing himself over his death. Tired of wondering if he could have done more. Seen more sooner. He'd spent months letting it eat at him. It was Charles who should be the one consoling his wife and child.

He should never have left his family to fend for themselves, destitute.

Mathias had stepped forward and purchased a town house in the city for Charles's wife, Marie, and the child, so they'd have a home to live in. He even gave Marie a monthly allowance.

He was sick to death of the weight he felt in his chest over Charles's untimely death.

The last thing he wanted to do was to enter another gaming den. Tomorrow he'd have another meeting with that weasel Valette, and would have to give up more names.

Which brought him to a different dilemma. Silvie. A willful woman who didn't have enough good sense to walk away from a losing table.

He'd had to watch that fiasco, too. Her tension and horror mounted with each hand she lost. He didn't want to sense it. Or notice it at all. Normally he didn't notice a woman beyond her physical attributes, and yet he was attuned to Silvie. And the carnal heat between them.

She had him utterly enthralled at every level. He wanted her so badly, his sac ached.

This attraction to her was the last thing he needed.

Especially when he was an informant for the King's Lieutenant General of Police on a mission to report the names of those who regularly frequented Navers's gaming den. He wanted to do just that—and be done with the matter.

But this mysterious woman was convoluting matters considerably.

Silvie was playing games—beyond Basset. He didn't know what to make of her secrets. He didn't know how to snap the fascination. Or how to ignore the sexual pull between them.

He couldn't tell her the details of his mission—especially to a woman he knew nothing about. And he certainly couldn't seem to impress it on her to stay away from Navers's Hôtel.

"Montfort!" A female voice grabbed his attention. He turned around and saw Silvie racing toward him. He knew it was only a matter of time before she came after him. He had her gems, after all. They were important to her. He'd seen the devastation in her eyes when she'd lost them.

She stopped before him, her breathing quick. "I need to speak to you," she said.

"Yes, well, I need to shake you for your fool-headed play. What did you think you were doing in there? I thought you had some experience in the game. You don't stay and continue to lose money when you've no luck on your side to speak of!"

She lowered her eyes. "Yes, you're right, of course." Her response was soft, her manner demure. And he was stunned. Since when did this woman become so docile?

"I really must speak to you," she repeated and looked around. They were alone in the courtyard, save for the horses and the drivers. "But not here. Come to my town house. Tonight. I'll meet you there."

With that she stalked away briskly.

Mathias was drained and angry and, now thanks to her, his cock was hard—for a woman in men's clothing. *Excellent.* Before Charles took his own life, Mathias had a normal existence. He attended the theater, was welcomed in all the best Salons in Paris, and actually had women who gave him their name as well as their bodies. And yet here he was, covertly working to topple a Duc and turn in his peers, all the while panting after another man's mistress who was cloaked in secrecy. If he had any good sense at all, he'd get in his carriage and go home, but wild horses couldn't keep him from Silvie's town house or from hearing what she had to tell him.

He was going to demystify this mystifying beauty and get her out of his system.

This wasn't going to get any more involved than it already was.

5

The moment Mathias arrived at Silvie's town house, he was asked by the majordomo to follow him.

As the man led him across the grand vestibule, Mathias tried his level best to learn the name of the lady of the house from the servant. To learn how long she'd been living in the town house. Hell, to learn anything about her at all. Although no one else seemed to know anything about the Marquis de Gaillard's new mistress, surely the majordomo did.

It proved to be a futile exercise. The somber servant was tight-lipped.

They began climbing the stairs. Mathias realized he wasn't heading to a drawing room. He was being led to her private apartments.

His greedy cock thickened further and strained harder against the inside of his breeches. Easy now. He never knew what to expect with this woman. She wasn't the most predictable of females. He wasn't about to make any assumptions.

Reaching one of the doors in the corridor, the servant knocked and opened it upon hearing his mistress's bidding.

Mathias stepped in. The servant closed the door behind him, leaving Mathias standing in an antechamber, with chairs of light blue damask. He looked around. The room was empty.

"In here, please," he heard her say from the bedchamber.

His heart began to race. *Merde.* He was acting as if he was some nervous youth about to fuck his first woman.

Entering the bedchamber, he found her standing near the large four-poster bed. In a rich red and white gown, her hair in long dark curls cascading onto her creamy shoulders, she was breathtaking to behold.

Dressed in feminine attire that showed off her fine female attributes, she was utterly entrancing. What was conspicuously absent was her jewelry. She wore none.

She'd had on a few fine pieces the other day, so he knew she owned some. In no way was he going to presume it was omitted on purpose because she anticipated sex and didn't want it getting in the way.

Mathias was going to let her take the initial lead, then take over, moving one slow seductive step at a time.

In her bedchamber, alone with her, mere feet from her bed, he'd do absolutely nothing that would jeopardize this moment.

She had her hands folded before her. He watched as she smoothed her skirts and refolded them. *She's nervous. All the more reason to take it slow.*

"Thank you for coming," she said.

"You're welcome." He offered nothing more, but simply waited for her next words. Her next move.

She smoothed her skirts again and paused, almost as though

she was grappling with her next words. Finally she said, "I find myself in a bit of a situation."

"Oh? And what situation is that?"

She bit her lush bottom lip and dropped her gaze to the floor briefly before she lifted her chin, looked him straight in the eye, and said, "I need my diamonds back."

Mathias held his tongue. Any response and she likely wouldn't elaborate. He wanted her as much as he wanted to know about her.

For the life of him, he couldn't understand what all the secrecy was about.

Moreover, he doubted Gaillard cared a whit if his mistress played some Basset—illegal or not. So why the desire to disguise herself?

His silence worked. She continued. "The diamonds are . . . very important to me, you see. I cannot lose them. I am willing to compensate you for them."

His groin tightened. Every fiber in his being anticipated exactly what compensation she was offering. Still he kept silent.

His gaze dropped to her hands. He noted she was clutching them tightly. *Dieu*, he knew the diamonds were important to her, but he hadn't anticipated her being in such distress over them. It was palpable.

"If . . ." She stopped and started anew. "You give me back my diamonds, and I'll . . . rather . . ."

Out with it, Gabrielle, she told herself and pushed the rest of the words off her tongue. "I'll be . . . yours for the night."

The flare of hot interest in his eyes made her sex clench. All right. She'd admit it. She was hardly the sacrificial lamb here.

You know as well as I do any carnal encounter between us would be heated, intense, and delicious. His words had been haunting her for days and even more so at night.

The King would select her husband soon. She'd heard that copulation with a husband for the purposes of procreation was entirely different from sex with a lover. Before she was married to a man who would likely ship her off to some isolated château, she wanted to know what it would be like to couple with a man who heated her blood the way this man did.

The more she'd contemplated the proposition on the way home, the more it held appeal. She'd enjoy an amorous encounter, experience firsthand some of the physical pleasure she'd heard about, and gain back her diamonds.

The benefit to her was twofold.

Slowly, he approached, all that tall strong masculine beauty coming her way. Gripped by anticipation, her insides quivered.

Mathias stopped before her, forcing her to lift her chin in order to look him in the eye. Dear God, how she loved his height. No, more than just his height. There was so much about him that she found physically appealing. His gaze dipped briefly down to her décolletage, her nipples hardening at the mere glance.

Mathias slipped his warm fingers under her chin, leaned in, and slowly grazed his lips up the side of her neck. She closed her eyes, her breathing instantly quickening. The sensations felt so good, so decadent.

"You're going to let me have you any way I want?" he murmured in her ear.

There were different ways? "Yes . . ."

"And you want two diamonds for your body . . . for one night?" His hot mouth retraced its tantalizing path, ever so lightly back down her neck to the curve of her shoulder.

"Hmm? Oh, yes . . . two . . ." She licked her lips. "Both diamonds." This was so much better than anything anyone described.

Lifting his head, he hauled her up against him and claimed her mouth, his tongue slipping past her lips on her gasp. She fisted his justacorps and held on as his tongue swirled and stroked hers with mind-spinning intensity. He tasted so good. No, he tasted better than good. Better than anything she'd ever known. Hungry for more, she matched him stroke for stroke with the same famished zeal. She'd never been kissed before, never knew a man this exhilarating. She rubbed herself against the hard bulge pushing against her belly. His groan spiked her need and moistened her sex, the light pulsing between her legs growing stronger with each skillful sweep of his tongue. She'd no idea how this man had the ability to awaken her long-dormant body, to set every nerve ending quivering with excitement.

He broke the kiss sooner than she wanted. A protest escaped her throat. She snapped her eyes open, her breathing sharp and shallow, and there, in those sensual light-colored eyes, was the very same hot need scorching through her blood.

The sight weakened her knees.

"Wh-What say you, Mathias? Do we have a bargain?" She was dying to touch his skin. To explore every inch of his powerfully sculpted physique.

No, more than that. She was dying to know the feel of him inside her, their bodies joined in a lovers' embrace, a connection she'd never craved before.

He cupped her breast and rubbed his thumb across her distended nipple through her clothing. His rhythmic strokes over the sensitized peak made her shiver, the sensations lancing into her core.

"Ah yes, the bargain . . ." The sweet torment on her nipple was driving her to distraction.

"Yes?" she prompted, desperate to get on with it. "What's your answer? What do you say?"

"I say . . . I don't pay for sex." He dropped his hand away. "Ever." With a turn of his heel, he started toward the door.

In her heated haze, it took a moment for his words to register in her mind. Her heart lurched. She raced up and jumped into his path, stopping his progress.

"Surely you jest! You're not actually leaving?"

She sensed his anger and struggled with what to do. What words would convince him to stay? He couldn't leave her like this. She wanted him so badly, it hurt.

"When a woman gives herself to me, it's for one reason. *Only* one reason. Because she wants to." He reached inside his dark gray justacorps, pulled out a small pouch, and tossed it onto the side table beside them. Next thing she knew, he was lifting her off the floor as if she weighed nothing at all and set her bottom down on the side table, too.

Gripping her knees through her gown, he spread them apart and stepped between them, his actions taking her by surprise. A thrill shot up her spine.

With her legs apart, she was all too aware of his proximity to her slick sex, aching to be filled.

"You want your diamonds, here are your diamonds." He picked up the pouch beside her and shoved it into her hand. "Open it. They're both in there."

She loosened the ties to the dark blue velvet pouch and peered in. Just as he'd said; the King's diamonds were indeed both there. She closed up the pouch and met his gaze, perplexed.

"You're going to just give them back to me? Without any compensation of any kind?" Her body screamed, *No! Take me!*

"They are yours. No conditions attached."

"But . . . But you could have used these as leverage, to force me to—"

"Give me sex as well as information about you? I'm quite aware of that. I won't use coercion. What you give me is going to be of your own free will."

She was astounded and moved beyond words. She didn't know any man who wouldn't have used the situation to his advantage. No man she knew would have returned the diamonds without making some sort of demand for some kind of gain. His gesture was generous and touching and for the first time she saw him in a totally different light.

It made her want him more.

He pulled the pouch from her hands and dropped it beside her on the wooden surface. His hips still between her legs, he gripped her bottom and pulled her tightly against him, her sex coming in contact with the bulge in his breeches. She gasped, their clothing muting none of the delicious sensation. He rolled his hips. She lost her breath and grabbed his sleeves, the bud between her legs now throbbing fiercely.

"You don't have the diamonds to hide behind any longer," he said, his mouth so temptingly close to her own. "So if you want me to take you, you're going to have to be honest about it. You're going to have to admit to it. Ask for it. What is it going to be, Silvie? Are you going to give yourself to me?"

Her sex answered with a warm gush. She wanted him to be the one to introduce her to carnal delights.

In her life she'd never wanted anything more.

Her hands flew to the front of her gown. Feeling his heated gaze on her all the while, she quickly opened the fastenings and slipped off her sleeves. She attacked the stays next, spreading and pulling, her breaths ragged, her fingers fumbling, eager to free herself from the confines of her clothing for him.

She wasn't in the least bit embarrassed by having him see her in a state of undress. Not when she was burning for him, her clothes feeling hot and suffocating.

Not when she had to have him or die.

Seeing her struggling, he lent an expert hand here and there until finally he pulled off her gown and tossed it to the floor, then stepped back in between her opened thighs.

He slipped his hand under her knee-length chemise and grasped the ties of her drawers, purposely brushing the heel of his palm against her mound. She jerked at the decadent sensation.

His smile broadened as he loosened the ties to her caleçons and massaged her slick sex through the fabric. Gripping his shoulders tighter, she bit her lip, trying to keep down her whimpers and soft moans, without success, her mewls punctuating the silence in the room.

"Your drawers are wet," he said, seemingly pleased by it.

It wasn't something she could control. It was what he did to her.

He slid the drawers off her, too, followed quickly by her garters, stockings, and shoes.

By the time she was down to just her chemise, her fever had reached an unbearable pitch. Always guarded and reserved, it felt wonderful to be this unbridled. Unrestrained. Her life a stifling existence, she'd found a new freedom—all due to a man who incited her senses like no other.

He pulled off the last article of clothing and let it drop to the floor. There was something wicked and thrilling about being naked before him while he was still fully dressed. She watched his gaze move over her form with male appreciation. It fluttered her stomach.

"You're beautiful," he said, caressing the back of his fingers between her breasts, down her quivering belly. Dipping his fingers into her sex, past her soaked curls, he captured her clitoris between his index and middle finger and gave it a light pinch. She practically shot up off the side table as a cry left her throat, the sensations sending her rushing headlong toward a precipice. She was about to hurl over it when he released his hold on the throbbing bud and removed his hand. By the smile on his face, she could tell he'd purposely stopped her from falling over the edge. She squeaked out in frustration.

"I knew you'd be as fiery in the boudoir as you are out of it. Beautiful Snow Princess, I like how you melt for me." He rested his hands on the tops of her thighs, his thumbs so close to her needy sex. "Ask for it, Silvie. Let me hear the words from that pretty mouth. Ask for it and I'll give you what you want."

She was quaking both inside and out. "I want you to . . . Will you . . . Take me." She couldn't catch her breath.

Still with a devilish smile, he removed his justacorps, his vest, and opened up his breeches. "With pleasure." His voice was low and sinfully sensual as he pulled out his shirttails and yanked the linen shirt off, too, sending it to the floor to join the rest of the clothing.

His solid chest was bare. She drank in its chiseled perfection, moving her gaze down over his muscled belly all the way to his sex boldly jutting out of his breeches. Once, not long ago, she'd had a glimpse of an erotic illustration, but had never seen the male anatomy up close.

Gabrielle reached out, her hands trembling slightly, and ran them over the dips and ripples, his skin warm beneath her touch, under her hand his heart beating quickly, racing her own.

Taking her hand, he brought it to his shaft. Immediately, she curled her fingers around his rigid length, reveling in his groan. She luxuriated over the feel of him in her hand, like velvet over steel, riveted by the pleasure etched across his handsome features as he moved her fist up to the engorged head and down to the base with long unhurried strokes. The proportions of his sex were as impressive as the rest of him. It was inebriating to watch him, to stroke him. To pleasure him.

"I've been fantasizing about you since we met. Dreaming of

all the ways I'm going to fuck you." Dipping his head, he brushed his mouth against her lips. "How do you like being taken, Silvie?" he whispered. "Fast, or slow?"

She couldn't stop stroking him.

"Yes." She parted her lips for him, eager to have him in her mouth.

"Yes to which?" His mouth teasingly hovered over hers.

"Yes to all of it. Both. However you want. Just do it now."

Softly, he chuckled. Removing her hand from his sex, he stripped off the remainder of his clothing.

This time he spread her legs a little wider when he stepped in between.

"The bed is over there," she said, stating the obvious, her senses in a frenzy, desperately trying to move things along.

He pulled her up against him, her sex kissing his shaft, the slightest smile playing on his beautiful mouth.

"I've been hard for you for days," he said, stroking his erection against her sleek folds. "You're going to take my cock right here, Silvie." He kissed her mouth, her jaw, the sensitive spot below her ear. "We'll use the bed next time." With that, he lowered his head and sucked her sensitive nipple into his hot mouth. She cried out and thrust her hips hard against him, a completely reflexive response. Unfazed by her eruptive reaction, he leaned her back, the back of her head pressing against the wall while his mouth sucked and savored her nipple. Alternating between breasts, he gave each sensitive tip its due carnal care until he had her writhing and panting. A fresh rush of warm wetness flowed from her core onto his hard shaft pressed firmly against her folds.

He groaned. "I love that . . ." He lightly bit her nipple; she held his head to her and whimpered. "I love how you're creaming on my cock." Raising his head, he wrapped her legs around his waist and possessed her mouth with a kiss. It was demanding, hot and delectably fierce.

He gripped her hips. Then his cock was wedged firmly at her opening. Her heart hammered. Her body celebrated. At last! Joy and pleasure swamping her senses. She wiggled and squirmed, gluttonous for more.

"Easy, *chère*," he rasped against her mouth. "I know you're eager. Allow me."

She gripped his shoulders, just as he drove forward. A sudden sharp pain made her recoil and cry out.

"*Jésus-Christ!*" exploded from his lips, his shock evident on his face. He'd only penetrated her partway, her body shaking with a mixture of pain and pleasure.

Her need was still a strong undercurrent through it all.

He started to pull out.

"No!" She tightened her legs around his waist, the sudden movement causing him to sink an inch deeper. His growl eclipsed her moan. No pain this time. Just a delicious stretching. She drew her arms around him. "Don't stop." She rained kisses on his mouth, his face, his neck, famished for his taste. For him. "Please ... give me more ..." Already the discomfort had receded, overshadowed by the agony of her unfulfilled desire. Her core was pulsing hungrily, his partial possession maddening. She wanted all of him. Tentatively, she moved her hips, trying to take him in.

"*Merde* ..." He tightened his grip on her hips, stilling her. The muscles in his shoulders tight and tense beneath her hands, he rested his forehead against hers, his breathing as labored as her own.

"I want you, Mathias ... Please, don't stop. Not now. It doesn't hurt anymore ... Take me ... I want more ..." She couldn't believe what was tumbling from her mouth. She never spoke of her needs and wants. Not ever.

Impatient, she tightened her arms and legs and tried to move her hips again, an awkward, unpracticed movement that garnered her only a small measure of success. Frustration erupted out of her.

He swore softly. "All right, Silvie . . . Loosen your legs. Let me give you more." He slipped his hands under her bottom the moment she complied and lifted her into his plunge, burying his cock into her with a single luscious glide.

Her head fell back, a soft sound of pleasure leaving her lungs. Oh God . . . He was so deep. She felt so full. There was no pain, just pure pleasure. It felt better than anything she could have imagined. It felt incredible.

"How's that? You like that, Silvie?" he asked, his voice gruff with desire. "You want more, don't you?"

She couldn't speak, her body shaking, her sex throbbing. All she could do was nod.

He reared and, hauling her to the edge of the side table, lifted her into his solid thrust, penetrating a fraction deeper. Her sob of bliss mingled with his grunt. He began to move, fast and hard. His powerful plunges should have hurt, but instead his thick hard shaft sent her into delirium, his strokes so deep they were making her wild.

"I love how tightly you're clasping my cock."

She had no response. She was beyond words and burning with fever for this man. His palm was pressed to the wall, his free hand to the small of her back holding her in place as he drove his cock into her with bedeviling skill. Gabrielle simply held on, his mouth tantalizing that sensitive spot below her ear, her neck, her shoulder. She was overwhelmed with sensations.

"You're on the edge, Silvie," he rasped in her ear. "You're

about to come for me, aren't you? I can feel your sweet little clenches."

Dear God. She couldn't control that either. Tiny contractions were rippling through her core, around his ramming cock. The physical reactions he could elicit from her body astounded her. Physical reactions she'd no idea how to curb or quell. Her release was imminent. She could feel it coming on. Fast. Sensed it was going to be shattering, and that immediately frightened her. He frightened her. His power over her was so intense. So strong. She was terrified to be that vulnerable to him. She'd struggled against men who wielded power over her all her life.

Wavering on the edge of orgasm, Gabrielle fought it back, suddenly afraid of what would become of her if she completely surrendered.

Afraid to let go.

He had her mouth, possessing it with his tongue, his taste intoxicating. His thrusts, sublime. "Let go, Silvie. Don't fight it, *chère*. Give yourself over to the pleasure." But still she fought back her orgasm, violently shaking with effort, her body rioting for release. Trying to outlast him.

"Why don't we give that pretty clit of yours some attention?" she heard him say.

Oh, no . . . Before she could react, he'd pulled his hand from the wall, slipped it between their bodies, and without missing a stroke, he captured her clit between his fingers and pinched it— applying the most perfect pressure.

Her senses exploded with blinding ecstasy. She surged up hard against him, screaming into his mouth. He didn't relent, not with his force of thrusts or his hold on the pulsating bud, ramming her with his cock through the stunning untamable spasms contracting her slick walls. Her body was awash with waves of spine-melting sensations. Then she felt it—the ripples of another hot wave of rapture. Right on the heels of the first. This time she didn't fight it. This time she let it crash over her, abandoning herself to it, her body shuddering from the force.

Gabrielle willingly let herself drown in the soul-satisfying pleasure flooding her system. Vaguely, she was aware of his hand slipping out from between their bodies, his fingers gripping her hips and his body stiffening. He reared, jerking his cock from her sheath and crushed her to him. Burying his face in her hair, he roared out his pleasure against the curve of her neck, his strong body racked with its own rapture as his warm semen shot onto her thigh and hip.

She tightened her arms around him, and held him, their labored breaths the only sound in the room.

She felt euphoric. She couldn't believe it. *She* actually felt . . . *happy*. It was the first time in a long time.

Mathias's muscles were heavy as lead. His legs weak. He couldn't recall the last time he came that hard. But the wonderful languidness quickly dissipated as questions began to crowd his mind and clear the sexual fog.

Questions he was going to bloody well have answers to.

He forced himself to pull away from her warm soft form and break from her embrace.

The moment their gazes locked, his heart squeezed tightly. Her cheeks pink, her hair mussed, she looked adorable, sweet, and so beautiful—very much like the innocent she was.

For the first time since he'd met her, her eyes were unguarded. Open and honest.

They told him she was a little shaken, a little wary, out of sorts, and unsure what he was about to do, how he was about to react, now that he knew she'd been a virgin. *Dieu*. Quelling the raw emotions swirling through him, Mathias scooped up the first article of clothing he touched from the pile on the floor, and grabbed the base of his prick, noticing the telltale signs of her lost innocence in the red streaks on it. She looked away, her eyes downcast, her blush coloring her cheeks.

He wiped himself clean, then quickly wiped off her soft thigh and silky hip. Crumpling the caleçons in his hand, he tossed them away and slipped his hand under her chin, capturing her undivided attention.

"We're going to talk."

He saw disappointment flash in her dark eyes. *Jésus-Christ.* Did she think he was simply going to let this go? He'd just taken her virginity. He'd thought she was sexually experienced. She was supposed to be Gaillard's mistress.

He never would have said the things he'd said to her, done the things he'd done, had he known she'd been a virgin.

He felt his ire mounting just thinking about the entire damned mess, a million questions spinning in his head.

"Would it be all right if I used the *salle de bain* to . . . wash up a little first?" Her voice was soft. Gone was that hard edge she usually had. And the wall that was always up—the one she hid behind—was conspicuously missing.

Merde. You just took her innocence. At least let her refresh herself before you make demands of her. Curbing his anger, his frustration, his impatience, he helped her down off the side table.

"Of course," he said.

She thanked him. Sliding out from between him and the table, she bent and picked up her chemise. He watched her raise her arms and slip it on, admiring her lush curves, her pretty breasts— not too big or small—and then there were those gorgeous legs. God, how he loved women's legs, and hers went on forever. He could still feel their silky strength wrapped around his hips.

As she left the room, he was sure of one thing. She was never Gaillard's mistress. The man would have fucked her before setting her up in his town house, providing her with a full staff.

Mathias braced his hands on the edge of the side table and blew out a breath. Damn it. What was going on here?

You didn't want things to get more involved. Well, things just got a hell of a lot more complicated.

A virgin.

He took a *virgin.*

Of all the different kinds of women he'd bedded, this was a bloody first.

He shoved himself away from the table and began to pace. He wasn't just angry at her. He was livid with himself. He'd noticed signs of her inexperience. In her kiss, in the way she touched him. In the look of surprise when he'd played with her clit. As if it were novel. A decadent new discovery. The look of wonder and delight in her eyes.

And he'd ignored them all. Purposely closing a blind eye just so that he could sink his cock in her.

From the beginning she hadn't wanted to tell him a thing about herself. She hadn't wanted to confide in him a single truth.

And it bothered him more than he could ever say.

He'd just had sex with a woman he didn't know a thing about, and it was torturing him. He was no stranger to anonymous sexual encounters. He'd no idea why he should give her secrecy a second thought. She didn't seem bothered that he'd just claimed her maidenhead.

Why should he be?

Lord knows he had enough to deal with. Navers and his mission for the Lieutenant General of Police were where his focus should be.

Not on this one woman who was at every turn up to no good.

Mathias stopped pacing, raked a hand through his hair, and let out a sharp breath. He walked over to the wash basin in the room, poured water into the bowl, and sluiced it onto his face. He washed, wishing that he could purge her from his thoughts by simply washing her wonderful scent from his skin.

He couldn't let this rest. He simply had to know who she was. What she was all about. And he was finding out as soon as his little secretive seductress reentered the room.

6

The moment she reentered the room, her dark eyes swept the bed-chamber, surprise flashing in their dark depths when she spotted him lying casually on his side, naked in her bed.

Propped up on his elbow, Mathias patted the spot beside him. "Come here."

He saw her take a deep breath and let it out slowly before she complied and slipped in bed beside him.

Rolling onto her side, she mimicked his pose, and Mathias could tell that while she'd been in the other room, she'd managed to erect her usual wall.

The barrier was firmly in place between them, solid and true.

And he was going to knock the fucking thing down.

"Take off your chemise," he said.

That took her off balance. By her expression, it was obvious that wasn't what she expected him to say. "Pardon?"

"You heard me. Take it off. You don't need it." His tone was firm. As was his gaze.

She hesitated for a moment, then sat up, pulled the article off, and tossed it onto the floor. She returned to her pose on her side, looking a little more self-conscious than before.

Her bravado was a little askew. He hoped that would work in his favor.

"What is your name?" he asked, trying to ignore her many female attributes, especially those pretty nipples, trying not to think about how good they tasted.

"Silvie."

"Your full name."

"What difference does that make?"

He tilted her chin up a notch. "The difference is I just fucked you. Now answer me."

"And do you know the name of every woman you tumble?"

"No, but I think it's a good idea I learn the identity of all those who pretend to be a nobleman's mistress, but turn out to be a virgin."

"I didn't say I was Gaillard's mistress. It's something you assumed."

"And you did nothing to acquit me of the notion. Now let's start again. What is your name?" His voice was a bit louder, sharper.

"I'm not going to answer that," she stated.

He clenched his jaw, holding back the expletives bellowing in his head. This woman was beyond maddening. "Why the hell not? Is it because you can't or you won't."

"Both."

"Who is Gaillard to you?"

She bit her lip, clearly considering whether or not to answer. Finally she said, "He's a member of my family."

Wonderful. The man's family was huge. It was going to take considerable effort, not to mention time, to eliminate them one by one until he figured out the identity of this particular woman.

A weary sigh escaped her. "Mathias." She placed a hand on his chest. His unruly cock immediately jerked in response. "If you are worried you are going to be dragged to the altar because of what happened tonight, rest easy. That isn't going to happen. No one is going to force you to marry me. I am not seeking a husband . . . although . . ."

He removed her hand from his chest, her touch a serious distraction. "Although?" he prompted.

She lowered her eyes. "One is being selected for me by my father."

He'd no idea why her words felt like a blow to the belly. He felt . . . winded. "Do you know who your husband will be?" Why in the world did he ask that? Why on earth would he care to know?

"No."

Just talking about her getting married was tightening his vitals. He changed the subject. "Why are you here? Why aren't you at home? Why are you playing Basset? Is this some sort of thrill or are you doing it because you have to?"

"Because I have to."

"To cover a debt? You're trying to win back money?"

"Yes."

"Your debt?"

She shook her head. "No, someone else's."

"*Merde.* If your father is looking for a husband for you, there must be some sort of dowry. Your father has means." Someone prominent if he was part of Gaillard's family. Thus the need for her to hide her identity with a disguise. "Get him to pay the debt and stop going to Navers's gaming den."

"I can't ask my father to help. He'd never do it. I've got to do this myself. On my own. And I can't lose the diamonds either." She suddenly looked tired. Lowering her head onto the pillow, she tucked her hands under her cheek. "Not a single diamond."

He brushed an errant curl off her cheek. "Why?'

"Because I took them from him, and he doesn't know."

Jésus-Christ. "Who is it you're helping?"

"Another family member."

"Why not get Gaillard to help you?"

"Because he doesn't know about it and he wouldn't help if he did. No one in the family will help—not to clear a gambling debt. Just me. I had to trick Gaillard just to let me stay here."

"Where does your father think you are?"

"A sojourn . . . with Gaillard at his country estate. I have to return home next week. I have until then to win back the money to cover the debt."

That left only two more nights of Basset before she'd have to leave. He admired her loyalty. Her strength. He didn't know any woman who would have had the courage to do what she'd done.

And he knew, behind that hardened exterior, she was scared.

Mathias caressed her soft cheek with the back of his fingers. "Why don't you let me give you the money and we can put an end to the Basset games."

At that, she jerked her head up off the mattress and frowned. "No. I do things on my own. I won't be beholden. Not to anyone. I can do this—by myself."

He shook his head and muttered a curse. "Silvie, it's a game of chance. There are no guarantees."

"I *can* do this," she repeated a little stronger. "And I will do it, by next week." She rolled onto her other side, once again tucking her hands under her cheek, her delicate back now facing him.

"You know," he said, placing a hand on her shoulder, "you can lean on people for help when you need it. You can trust people."

"No, you can't. You can't trust anyone."

Mathias realized then the magnitude of her gift to him tonight. She'd never trusted anyone, yet she'd trusted him. She'd surrendered herself to him, and it hadn't been easy for her. In the throes of passion, he'd noted how she'd struggled with it.

He reached out and tucked her up against his body, pleased she didn't pull away. He was hard, but he wasn't going to make any sexual advances. Taking a woman's virginity on a side table was bad enough, but he'd done something he'd never done before during sex.

He'd lost control.

The way he'd ridden her had been too aggressive for an innocent. His conduct shocked him. For a man with his vast experience, his actions were always controlled and measured in any sexual encounter. The motions too well practiced for anyone, much less a sexual novice, to unravel him.

Mathias dipped his head, bringing his mouth near her ear. "You're making it easy for me to learn who you are, Silvie. A few well-put questions to Gaillard and I will know your name."

She shrugged with a gentle rise and fall of her shoulder. "I doubt he'll be forthcoming, but if he is, it doesn't matter. By the time you learn anything, I will be home and married off."

Again that tightness gripped him, only this time it was all the way up to his chest.

"And what are you going to do about your lack of innocence?" he asked. "Your future husband will expect a virgin bride."

"That's what he'll get. I have half sisters who have managed to fool their husbands on their wedding night into believing their maidenhead was still intact. I'll do the same."

His brows shot up. "You're going to *trick* him?"

She turned and met his gaze over her shoulder. "What difference does it make if I'm not a virgin on the night of the wedding? All he's after is an heir. As long I provide him with a legitimate heir, the rest isn't any of his concern. And the child will be his. That much I'll do. Then he'll leave me alone, and I won't matter beyond that—which suits me just fine."

He couldn't help but wonder what had hardened her so. She wasn't as cold and calculating as she wanted the world to believe. Clearly, she had compassion. She was going to great lengths to help someone she loved. Whom others refused to aid. "I don't believe you, Silvie. You make it sound as though you want very little in life."

"What more is there for a woman to want? A marriage to a highborn noble. Children." Her tone was flat, just as before. He got the distinct impression that at some point in her life, she'd stopped wishing for things altogether.

"And what matters to you?" he asked. "Surely, there's got to be something you want."

There was a lengthy silence, and for a moment, Mathias thought she wasn't going to answer.

She rested her head back down onto the pillow and tucked her hands beneath her cheek once more. "I want to leave my father's home. I don't like it there," she said at last.

His brow furrowed with concern. "Have they hurt you?"

She didn't turn around, but this time there was no hesitation with her response. "Don't be ridiculous. No one hurts me. I don't let them."

* * *

"Dear Lord, this only gets worse!" Bernadette fretted.

"Shhhh! Keep your voice down." Gabrielle frowned and glanced at the closed double doors to her bedchamber. Mathias was asleep inside and voices easily carried through from the antechamber of her private apartments.

As ladies-in-waiting, it was her friends' duty to help her dress each day. It was considered an honor to be that close to a member of the royal family, and thus, the positions were given only to women born into the nobility. Bernadette and Caroline had arrived mere moments before. Upon hearing their voices in her antechamber, Gabrielle awoke, threw on her chemise, and dashed out of her room before they walked in to find Mathias in her bed.

She'd been forced to tell them he was here.

They surmised the rest.

Caroline was pacing in front of the hearth, wringing her hands, wearing out a path in the wooden floor. "First you steal some royal gems, then you lie about your whereabouts. Now you've . . . you've . . ."

"Been bedded," Gabrielle supplied.

Caroline stopped dead in her tracks. "Yes . . . *bedded*. You're no longer a virgin, and you're to be married."

Bernadette slapped her palms against her cheeks and shook her head. "If the King finds out any of this," she said in a loud whisper, "I don't want to think about what he'll do. To all of us!"

Gabrielle marched over to her friends and, grasping each by an arm, dragged them over to the farthest corner from her bedchamber door. "You'll not mention the King again," she said, sotto voce, then paused to cast a glance at her bedchamber door and listened, thankful of the silence. "You'll call me Silvie. Nothing else. Mathias knows nothing about who I am, and I intend to keep it that way. You'll do nothing—absolutely nothing—to give me away. Understood?"

They nodded.

"You said he is the Marquis de Tesson. He's a man of means, no? Couldn't he advance you some funds to cover your brother's debt?" Caroline asked, hopeful. "He clearly likes you."

"That's an excellent idea!" Bernadette smiled. "Then we can return home with the diamonds and all will be well, as if we'd never left . . . except for the part about a missing maidenhead."

Gabrielle let out an exasperated sigh. "It is not an excellent idea. It is a bad one."

Caroline nodded glumly. "I suppose it would be rather inappropriate to ask the man bedding you for funds. It would be as though he's paying for . . . well, you know." She blushed.

Gabrielle released her hold on their arms. "I don't have to ask him. He's already offered to pay Daniel's debt, and I turned him down."

Bernadette's mouth fell agape. She clamped it shut. "You told him about Daniel?"

"Never mind that!" Caroline waved her hand. "*You turned him down?*"

She had. And she'd been struggling with the soft sentiment his offer had inspired ever since. Again she found herself comparing Mathias to the men she knew. None of the men at court would have offered to help her unless there was political gain in it for them. Unless doing so would elevate them in the eyes of the King.

And since Gabrielle wasn't one of His Majesty's favorite daughters, men didn't waste their time and effort on her. All forms of generosity and assistance were for those who had the King's esteem.

She hadn't expected Mathias to offer to help.

Not since her mother had anyone extended a hand to her for no other reason than to aid her. She'd stopped expecting people to help her a long time ago.

He'd unbalanced her in the worst way with his offer and his return of her diamonds. And though it would be easier to believe the worst of him, her instincts told her he was sincere. That these weren't merely ploys to gain her trust.

She believed him, despite her comments about not trusting anyone. It was an unprecedented first. Utterly uncharacteristic and astonishing, actually.

She wouldn't accept his touching offer or divulge her identity, but she couldn't deny how moved she was by him.

"I'll not be beholden to him. Or anyone." She had to force the words off her tongue.

Words that normally came second nature to her.

The urge to lean on him—when she'd always stood strongly on her own—was fierce.

And unsettling. She couldn't allow Mathias to affect her any more than he already had.

Once she returned home next week, she wanted no ties with him, or to feel obligated in any way. No sense of gratitude. No attachment of any kind. She'd decided this morning she'd continue a physical involvement with him, but only until she returned to the palace.

That was as far as she was willing to go.

"I don't need his money," she continued. "I am going to win what I need. I have a good feeling my luck has changed." Gabrielle glanced at Bernadette. "As for Daniel, Mathias doesn't know the particulars. He's simply aware I'm playing to win enough funds to cover a debt for a member of my family."

Just then she heard stirrings from inside her bedchamber.

"You must go." She pushed them toward the door, but they didn't make it in time. Mathias opened the door to the bedchamber.

Her head snapped in his direction, her breath lodging in her throat at the sight that greeted her.

On the threshold of her antechamber, with nothing more than a sheet of fine bed linen around his waist, Mathias stood—in all his muscled glory.

"*Oh my . . .*" Bernadette breathed. "Will you look at those arms? Solid and hard like sculpted marble . . . and then there's the rest of him . . . I completely understand why you are sans a maidenhead today."

Caroline slapped Bernadette's arm. "Bernadette!" she whispered sharply.

Gabrielle ignored their comments, too captivated by the inciting masculine beauty before her, her blood already heating for him without so much as a touch, her mind conjuring hot memories of those strong arms around her, that muscled body against her, and heaven help her, that delicious part of his male anatomy stroking inside her sheath.

"Good morning, ladies," he said, his voice rich and inflaming, his light-colored eyes sweeping past Bernadette and Caroline before they locked on to her. A tiny shiver quivered through her.

Gabrielle cleared her throat as her friends returned his greeting. "Good morning, Mathias. My friends"—she gestured behind her—"were leaving. Weren't you?" she said to the two women standing in a trance beside her, openly gawking at the man. Gabrielle elbowed Bernadette, simply because she was the closest.

Bernadette jumped. "Hmm? Oh, yes. We were just leaving. Come, Caroline."

"Oh . . .Yes, of course." Caroline smiled. It was actually more of a grin. One that made her look quite daft.

Both women bade him good day and had proceeded to the door when Bernadette abruptly stopped, turned, and out of habit, despite Gabrielle's order not to curtsy to her during their stay at her uncle's town house, she began to sink low. Gabrielle rushed forward, threw an arm around her shoulders.

"Oh, Bernadette, don't tell me your knee is acting up again?" Gabrielle said, giving her friend a stern look, one that was a silent reprimand for her blunder.

It took a moment for understanding to appear in Bernadette's eyes. "Ah yes, my *knee* . . ." She glanced at Mathias. "My knee acts up every so often, you see." Bernadette bent forward and rubbed it through her gown.

A rather poor performance. The woman was definitely not meant for the stage.

Gabrielle noted Mathias's frown but, to her relief, saw no sign of suspicion. "Caroline, why don't you take Bernadette to her rooms."

Caroline moved forward and supported her friend as Bernadette pretended to limp.

"Do you need assistance?" Mathias asked.

"No." Gabrielle answered for her with a smile. "She's fine. She has Caroline. Isn't that so, Bernadette?"

"Yes, I'm quite capable of returning on my own . . . with Caroline's help, that is," Bernadette quickly added.

A slight smile lifted the corner of his mouth. "All right then." He moved his gaze to Gabrielle. "I'll wait for you inside," he said, setting her pulse racing with heated excitement. With that, he reentered her bedchamber, closing the door behind him.

She turned to her friends, who were once again in a trancelike state, still staring at the spot where Mathias had been standing.

Smiling, Gabrielle couldn't wait to join him.

"I've decided to keep him for a few days. Do be careful around him." She couldn't muster a stern tone, not when she felt so light.

Not when pure bliss was waiting for her on her bed.

Gabrielle walked out of the antechamber and into her bedchamber. Sure enough, lying across the width of her bed was solid male allure.

Perhaps it was because she'd finally had some sleep last night, the first time since she'd arrived in Paris. Or perhaps it was because of the Marquis on her bed who'd brought her more joy in one eve than she'd had in years, but she couldn't remove the smile from her face.

She stopped at the end of her bed.

Propped up on his elbow, Mathias returned her smile.

Dieu, she had a beautiful smile. It lit up her face and caused the most adorable, tiniest dimples to form on either side of her luscious mouth. He held out a hand, pleased by how quickly she stepped forward and took it.

He brought her hand to his mouth and pressed a soft kiss to her knuckle. "Take off your chemise, Silvie." He felt a tremor of excitement quiver through her, and that pleased him further still. Beneath the bed linen wrapped around his waist, he was at a full cock stand. In fact, he was hard from the moment he laid eyes on her in the antechamber in that knee-length undergarment.

He watched as she slid the hem up her thighs, her belly, to finally sweep it up over her erect nipples and off, the linen garment falling to the floor.

Soft curves and satiny skin, she looked so good, she took his breath away. With her standing this close to him, he could detect the soft scent of her arousal, an aphrodisiac to his senses, his every muscle tightening with hunger.

"You are a vision, Silvie."

It was easy to forget she'd been an innocent last eve—that is, until he noticed her averted gaze, and the pretty blush coloring her cheeks.

She wasn't quite used to being naked before him. He didn't want her being embarrassed or inhibited around him in any way. He wanted her unrestrained. Unabashed. Without hesitation of any kind.

And without the wall she erected between them.

Most of all, he wanted her to learn to open up to him. In and out of bed.

Starting in the boudoir, he was going to make certain she never held back from him again—the way she'd attempted to last eve in the throes of passion.

And there was no time like the present to start working on it. Mathias sat up.

He took her hand and pulled, bending her forward for a kiss, his fingers threading in her hair as he savored her taste. She softly moaned against his mouth. Normally, he wouldn't still be in a woman's bed in the morning. He'd made it a habit to leave after sex.

Staying any longer, in his experience, gave the mistaken impression that the amorous encounter was something more than just recreational.

Yet he couldn't bring himself to leave her sleeping form last night.

He was so inexplicably drawn to this woman, it was mind-numbing.

"Come here," he said giving her arm a sharp pull, purposely making her lose her balance. She fell across his lap with a surprised yelp, her hips resting on his linen-covered thighs.

Rising up onto her elbows, she tossed him a questioning look over her shoulder. "Mathias, what are you doing?"

"It isn't fair to pay tribute to just the front part of your delectable form, *chère*. I think equal adoration should be given to your backside, especially . . ." He ran a light hand over the gorgeous curve of her bottom, making her squirm. "When you have such a beautiful derrière."

He caressed her bottom once more, luxuriating over its sweet curve and delighting in the feel of her skin. She gave him a little wiggle.

"Mathias . . ." There was a tinge of breathlessness to her tone. Planting her palms onto the mattress, she started to rise. Gently, he gently pressed her down onto the bed with a firm hand against her back. She was deliciously draped over his lap, inspiring a number of salacious ideas, and he wasn't anywhere close to being done.

"Not yet, Silvie. Just relax. I'm not going to hurt you."

She looked unsure, almost leery about what his intentions were while he had her across his lap, but she didn't protest further and she didn't try to rise.

That she was putting trust in him at the moment made him happier than he'd ever admit.

He slipped his hands between her thighs and spread her legs apart, feeling her stiffen, a mixture of innocent apprehension and arousal. The way her body was angled, her bottom tilting up, he had a perfect view of her glistening pink softness. *Dieu*, she had the prettiest sex he'd ever seen. Lovely nether lips. And the sweetest little clit. A man could spend hours with his head buried between these long silky thighs in oral worship.

At the first stroke of his fingers over her sleek folds, she lost her breath.

"You're wet for me." He smiled at her deepening blush, and tenderly massaged her soaked sex. She was resting on her forearms, her head turned and her dark eyes watching him. Her breaths were already becoming choppy and quick. Closely watching her reactions, he stroked her, keeping the pressure consistent, gliding his slick fingers up over her clit from time to time, purposely giving her little jolts of heightened sensation to build her hunger, keep her keen.

"You like this, Silvie?" He brushed her clit again, enjoying her soft cry.

"Yes . . ." She panted and pushed up against his hand, trying to rub her engorged little bud against his evasive fingers. "I want . . . *oh!* . . . I . . . want . . ."

He loved how she was becoming less coherent, more feverish. His strong, spirited Silvie was unraveling, and watching it happen before his eyes hardened his cock to painful proportions.

"What do you want?" He was stroking the slit of her sex,

milking more heated responses. He liked the sound of her moans, her occasional little wiggle and lifting of her bottom.

"I . . . I want . . . you . . . inside me."

"As you wish." He thrust two fingers into her tight warm core. She let out a sound, a mixture of a cry and a sob, her hips jerking hard. Holding her firmly, he immediately went to work on that sweet hot spot inside her feminine walls, giving it short quick strokes that made her buck, her legs shake. She whimpered and tried to squirm away. Knowing the sensations over that sensitive gland were deliciously intense, Mathias tightened his hold, keeping her in place, letting her get used to the erotic sensation, without playing with her clit, all the while plying steady skillful strokes.

His name rushed past her lips on a pant. She was wiggling harder, unable to hold still. He soothed her with words, coaxed her along, encouraging her to give herself over to the pleasure, telling her how good she felt around his fingers, how hard a release he was going to give her.

Within moments, she was widening her legs, giving him easier access, and rocking her hips with mouthwatering allure. She'd dropped her chin, her hair hiding her face, her trembling now stronger than before. Her breathing was choppy and her sex had soaked his busy fingers with more juices.

Mathias drove her straight to the edge. "You're going to come for me, without holding back in any way." It wasn't a question.

"Y-Yes!" She confirmed what he could feel around his fingers. If he wasn't so hard, his cock so unbearably full, he might have smiled.

No hesitation there. Just sweet surrender.

Her orgasm hit her hard, wrenching a scream from her. Silvie stiffened.

With lightning movements, Mathias pulled his hand out of

her contracting sheath, yanked off the sheet around his waist, and stuffed a pillow under her hips to keep her bottom angled.

He filled her quivering core with one fluid stroke, pushing his whole length into her, knowing she liked it deep. She mewed a welcome, followed by a shiver of delight, accepting his possession, taking his deep long thrusts, her slick walls decadently pulsing around him.

He basked in those wild uncontrollable clenches, holding back his climax, shaking with the effort. Her body sucking him in with each glorious spasm, she was hot and soft and exquisitely snug; she had the most incredible cunt he'd ever known.

Just as her contractions began to ebb, his control snapped. Ecstasy slammed into him. He pulled out, his semen shooting from his cock with stunning force, pouring himself onto her sweet bottom, until he was completely drained.

Collapsing onto his back beside her, he was as boneless as she. It took him several moments before he could calm his breathing and move his muscles. Grabbing her chemise, he cleaned them both, tossed the thing to the floor, and gently eased the pillow from under her hips.

Her breathing almost normal, she rolled onto her side facing him, her hands tucked under her cheek. Propped up on his elbow, he gazed into her eyes, noting the softness in the look she was giving him—the very same softness he'd seen last eve. They lay there in silence, but it wasn't awkward. In fact, there was a deep serenity to it, the likes of which he'd never experienced before.

He caressed her cheek, allowing himself to enjoy the features of her lovely face. She had no exotic coloring, but she was a classic beauty. A dangerous beauty. The kind that could bring a man to his knees, if he wasn't careful. And *Dieu*, he loved her height. He never had to stoop to kiss her. She fit perfectly with his body, as though she were made for him.

In the quiet of the moment, he didn't sense a wall between them, that barrier she kept between her and the rest of the world. The look in her eyes was far from detached and he fully expected her to erect a barrier posthaste.

Taking advantage of her amenable state, he said, "You've given me your innocence, but you won't tell me about you. You can trust me with your secrets, just as you've trusted me with your body. I won't hurt you, Silvie. I won't betray your confidence or turn your secrets against you." He cradled her cheek in his palm. She lowered her gaze. Mathias placed a soft kiss on her lips, wishing he knew her thoughts. Wishing he knew how to silence this incessant desire to know more about her. "Tell me something, anything about yourself. Something I don't already know."

She lifted her gaze to his. "I've never met anyone like you," she responded with as much sincerity in her eyes as in her tone.

He was taken aback by the endearing comment.

Tenderly, he stroked his thumb across her cheek. "Tell me something you've never told anyone else."

She put her arms around him, snuggled up against him. "I'm glad I met you," she whispered in his ear. "That's something I've never told anyone else."

Her words took him by surprise and melted his heart.

He pulled her tightly against him, his arms acting on their own volition, returning her embrace, unable to dispel the notion that this was so right. Unable to silence the tender emotions welling inside him.

Merde. Two powerful orgasms with this woman had him undone.

Once the sexual haze dissipated, he fully expected to return to his old self. The last woman he should involve himself with was one with as many secrets as Silvie had.

Gabrielle closed her eyes, relishing the simple pleasure of being in the circle of his strong arms. She felt safe and, God help her, protected. She swallowed hard against the lump in her throat. The temptation to reveal all to him was so great.

She couldn't.

She was going to hold on to this last level of detachment. This final bit of distance. Why open herself up totally? She'd have to leave him soon and it would only hurt more if she did. It was clear the longer she spent with him, the more she fell under his spell. She'd already opened herself up to him more than anyone else.

There were a thousand reasons why she should end this now. Why she should send him home. And only one reason why he should remain.

Contentment.

Near him, she felt content. It was novel. It was wonderful. And oh so irresistible.

Married or not, there were many more empty years ahead of her. Did she have the strength to deny herself more of this man?

Lifting her head, she met his beautiful light-colored eyes, and then the words she'd been grappling with tumbled from her lips. "Will you stay?"

7

"Ten wins. Six loses."

Mathias couldn't believe it. She had won another *sept-et-le-va*. How fortunate could one person be in a game that was mathematically stacked against the player, in favor of the banker?

Her winnings tonight had more than covered the losses from the last game.

Though he knew she was pleased, she did an excellent job schooling her features. Not acting exuberant in any way. No one who gambled at Basset celebrated each win.

Not when luck was a fickle mistress. At times she loved you. More often, she left you.

Especially in Basset.

He hated this game with a passion. Too many tragedies had occurred because of it.

Not an hour ago, another prominent family had come to ruin.

At the table next to him, the Baron de Tremblay had lost his entire fortune. Mathias's very entrails twisted in his gut watching the man leave Navers's drawing room sobbing.

Silvie was just as grief-stricken for the man. Mathias had seen it flash in her eyes before she masked the emotion.

He wasn't experiencing any of Silvie's good fortune.

He couldn't concentrate. Not just because of Tremblay's loss. It was Valette. The police sergeant's eyes had been on him the entire night. Valette was at the next table over and he could actually feel the weasel's stare.

Casting a glance in Valette's direction, he locked eyes with the man.

Mathias looked back at his cards, fighting the urge to gnash his teeth.

Something wasn't right. Ever since yesterday when Valette had paid him another visit, he couldn't shake his feeling of unease. Valette told him that Sard wanted more names.

Twenty players were in attendance. So far, he'd managed to decipher the identities of a total of seventeen of them.

But there was something else going on. He had a gnawing feeling that something was going to happen.

Something was being hatched by Sard and his sergeant that Mathias wasn't privy to. In the pit of his belly, he feared there might be a raid on the Duc's home.

Every time the door opened, Mathias lost his focus and tensed.

Valette had said he wanted the names of *all* in attendance. He kept insisting that everyone had to be made accountable. That it was important that the arrests would be numerous.

There was one name he couldn't give.

Mathias pulled his gaze to Silvie. Even if he knew her name, he'd never tell Sard or Valette. Short of telling her about his mission, he'd done his damnedest over the last few days to convince her to stay away from Navers's gaming table.

To no avail.

She'd donned her male attire and here she was, winning a small fortune, just as she'd predicted. *Merde*, her breasts were bound, her head covered with that ridiculous periwig, and her feminine form completely concealed, and he was hard just looking at her, knowing under all that was Silvie.

He'd spent the last four glorious days with his beautiful Snow Princess sitting in the courtyard of her town house, under the sun's warm rays, listening to her read him her favorite poems. He'd developed an appreciation for poetry he'd never had before. Poetry didn't mix with his previous life of vice.

And then there were the magnificent nights sharing carnal delights with Silvie. He only pulled himself away from her a few hours a day to change his clothes and attend to matters at home.

There was no finer bliss than time with this complex, fascinating woman. But their time was running out.

There were only a few days more until the next Basset game at Navers's home. Then she'd be gone. He tried his hardest to ignore the ache that thought left in his chest. It was even harder to push away gut-wrenching thoughts of her married to another man, and his claiming his conjugal rights.

This wasn't his normal reaction to the imminent end of an affair.

Every day that brought him closer to the date of her departure increased his emotional turmoil. He was riddled with tender feelings for a woman who was still a mystery, his ceaseless desire to know everything about her adding to his inner torment. As was his mission—one he couldn't tell her a damned thing about.

And he hated, loathed all the secrets between them.

"Queen wins. Seven loses."

Mathias's body went rigid. *Merde.* She'd just lost her wager. A tidy sum.

Silvie rose, surprising him. "I've had enough," she announced, and scooped up her winnings. Mathias couldn't have been more relieved to see her go. The sooner she got out of here, the better. At least she'd heeded his advice about leaving the table once her luck had turned. She was still walking out with a sizable win.

Navers rose. "Why leave so soon? Stay for another game."

Never one to be told what to do, his Snow Princess icily remarked, "I'll see you at the next game." Then she walked around the Duc and left the room.

Mathias wanted nothing more than to leave with her, but Valette was watching and he decided he'd play another hour.

* * *

Gabrielle tucked her pouch of diamonds and winnings back under her mattress.

She wasn't sleeping much at night. Mathias and his delicious kisses and decadent lovemaking were the new cause for her sleeplessness.

But she didn't mind. She gloried in it, grateful for knowing him, for having created memories to cherish.

Removing her periwig, she let down her hair and sat on the edge of her bed in her men's attire. The hour was late and she wasn't going to bother changing.

Mathias would be leaving the gaming den and arriving soon. Before he intoxicated her with his touch, she was going to have a talk with him.

The devastating loss by one of the players tonight had shaken her.

Seeing the abject horror in Mathias's eyes as the man left sobbing had astounded her.

The reaction seemed out of place—too strong for a seasoned gambler like Mathias. He had to have seen losses of that magnitude before. More often than she had.

Equally baffling was the way he kept looking around, as though he was expecting someone.

Footsteps in the corridor yanked her from her thoughts. She rose in anticipation. Within moments Mathias walked into her bedchamber. He smiled when he saw her.

A smile that didn't reach his eyes.

"Congratulations on your win," he said, taking off his justacorps and tossing it on a nearby chair. "You're thrilled, no doubt." He started on the buttons on his vest.

Her insides danced as she watched him undress.

"Yes. I am thrilled. Mathias, there is something I'd like to know."

He tossed off the vest and raked a hand through his long dark hair. "Do you have any brandy?" he asked, completely ignoring her statement.

She frowned, but walked over to a wooden cabinet in her bedchamber and opened the doors. Her uncle had a crystal decanter filled with his favorite brandy and crystal glasses there.

The moment Mathias saw the decanter, he marched over. "Allow me," he said.

She stepped away and watched him pour himself an ample amount and drain the crystal vessel just as quickly. To her astonishment, she saw the tremor in his hand as he lifted a fresh goblet to his lips.

"Mathias." She stepped forward, took the goblet from his grip, and set it back down in the cabinet. "What is amiss?"

It was his turn to frown. "What are you taking about?" He walked away undoing his cravat.

"You are in distress. It's rather obvious. What's wrong?"

"Nothing." He tossed the cravat onto the chair and held out a hand. "Come here." She knew that tone. It was carnal in nature. The moment she took his hand, he'd pull her close, kiss her, and scramble her senses.

"No. We need to talk."

"*Merde*, Silvie. The last thing I feel like doing tonight is talking."

"Mathias, why won't you answer me? Why won't you tell me why you are so upset?"

"*Jésus-Christ!*" The words exploded from his mouth, making her jump. "Woman, do you jest? You are actually making demands of me when you won't answer the most basic question?" He was all but hollering at her.

She'd never seen him like this and she refused to let this escalate into a heated argument by raising her tone in return. Not when he was so overwrought. "I am simply concerned about you," she responded softly.

It was clear her gentle voice had impact. He let out a sharp sigh and placed his hands on his hips. "Silvie, I don't want to argue with you, *chère*. *Dieu*, I just plain want you. I just want to hold you and make love to you and forget about everything, including your imminent departure."

At the mention of her leaving, her heart constricted painfully. She walked up to him, laced her arms around his neck, and buried her face in his shoulder. His strong arms encircled her, holding her tightly. Tears stung her eyes and threatened to spill. She blinked them back and composed herself.

The moment she met his gaze, he cupped her face and lowered his mouth onto hers. His kiss was soft and tender and made her ache. Heart and body.

"I wish I didn't have to go," slipped past her lips when he broke the kiss.

He rested his forehead against hers. "So do I."

Lovingly, she caressed his cheek. "Are you all right?"

"Seeing someone lose everything bothers me," he responded, surprising her.

"It was evident on your face."

"I lost a close friend a few months ago. He took his life after losing all that he owned in a Basset game."

She cupped his face and gave him a gentle kiss. "I'm so sorry, Mathias. Why do you still play if seeing losses upsets you so?"

At that he pulled away from her. "I just do." His tone was tight.

"Is there something you're not telling me about Navers's gaming den? You were always looking at the door."

He cocked his head slightly. "Did you win enough to cover the debt?"

Changing the subject wasn't a good sign. "No. I had almost enough, but then I lost some."

"Does that mean you'll be returning in a few days to play a final game?"

"Yes."

"Silvie, why don't you let me give you the rest?"

Taking his hands, she pulled him toward the bed. Her mind and heart were in wild conflict and she was afraid to answer questions in such a vulnerable state. "I believe you said something about wanting me?" She stopped when the back of her legs bumped the bed. Releasing his hands, she began to open her breeches.

He had the remainder of his clothing off by the time she had the breeches undone and stripped off. He removed her cravat, then her linen shirt, and finally the binding around her chest. Picking her up, he deposited her gently on the bed and stretched out on top of her.

The hot press of his solid body against her set her blood on fire, made her sex tighten.

He dipped his head and grazed his mouth along her neck, a slow fiery path that ignited her senses. "Who is this woman I kiss?" he whispered in her ear. "The one who gave her innocence to me." He spread her legs with his knees and stroked his cock along her slick folds. A soft moan slipped past her lips. "She's wet for me," he groaned. "She gives herself to me . . . comes for me . . . She's given me such pleasure and yet I may never know who she is . . ."

"Please, Mathias. Don't do this. Not now." She was in extreme emotional tumult.

"Tell me something about you." He brushed his mouth over hers. "Tell me anything. Tell me something you've never told anyone else."

"I'll miss you with all my heart."

* * *

"We're going to talk," Mathias said the moment he entered Sard's study. The Lieutenant General of Police rose from his chair.

"Have a seat." He gestured to one of the two silk damask chairs in front of his desk.

"No, I prefer to stand. I'll get right to the point. I want to know when you intend to make arrests. I've given Valette a number of names."

Sard sighed and sat down. "I'm afraid I can't discuss that with you, Montfort."

"Why not?"

"Because the King decides when the arrests will take place and that information remains between His Majesty and me."

"Look, tell the King you have names. You have details. Make your damn arrests and be done with it."

"If only it were that easy."

Mathias narrowed his eyes and planted his palms down on Sard's desk. "What is going on here? What is it you're planning?"

"What I'm planning is to please the King. That is always my plan. He wants to see his ban enforced. Do what is required of you and give me the names of all the players at Navers's gaming den."

"I've given you all the names I know. The players are masked. There isn't a lot of talking. Those are all the names I can come up with. And since I'm no longer of any use to you or the King, I'm done." Mathias pushed himself off the desk.

The corner of Sard's mouth lifted, stopping short of a smile. "You don't get to decide when you're done. His Majesty decides. He's been made aware of your involvement. If this matter takes much longer, he will get impatient. His Majesty wants a large arrest."

"Are you planning on a raid on Navers's gaming den?"

"Again, that is none of your concern."

"Damn it! I'm involved here. It is my concern. I did not need to help. I agreed to assist. I have every right to know what is going on."

"Who's the young man?"

Mathias rested his hands on his hips, lest he strangle Sard's thin neck. "What young man?"

"Valette tells me that a young man shows up every time. He sits at your table always and he gambles with diamonds."

Mathias's stomach fisted. "Yes, I know who you mean. I don't know him."

"Really? Valette said he saw you talking to the young man outside near the carriages. He felt you knew him. He said you *touched him*."

Every muscle in his body slowly tightened. *Merde.* "What the hell are you suggesting, Sard?"

The King's Lieutenant General of Police rose. "Before I approached you, Montfort, I thoroughly investigated you. I felt from what I learned about you, you'd be the perfect man to aid His Majesty and me in this matter. I knew you'd be sympathetic, given the death of your friend. From all accounts, you've not exactly led the life of a saint. Vice was your choice of entertainment. Everything I learned about you suggests you have a penchant for beautiful women."

"So?" His heart was beating in slow hard thuds.

"So if you have secrets, they need to remain that way. I personally selected you and I'll not be embarrassed before the King. Be discreet and I'll not arrest you for your conduct."

"Arrest me for what conduct?"

"Sodomy is a crime."

Mathias reached out across Sard's desk, grabbed his vest, and yanked him forward, their noses all but butting. "I'm going to pretend you didn't say that, Sard."

He'd hardly led a monkish life, but he'd never had any sexual interest in men. As for the law, it was a joke. Everyone in the entire realm knew the King's only brother, Philippe, Duc d'Orléans, preferred men in his bed. The younger the better. It was an open secret no one discussed.

Mathias released Sard. Unfazed, the Lieutenant General held his gaze. "If the young man means nothing to you, get me his name—and conduct yourself in a manner that would please the King."

Holding back the profanity burning up his throat, Mathias turned on his heel and stalked out.

Moments later Valette was permitted back into Sard's study.

"Well?" Valette asked.

Sard smoothed his vest and sat back down at his desk. "We're going to go ahead with the raid at the next Basset game Navers hosts in his home."

8

The afternoon sun was warm and pleasant in the courtyard of Gaillard's town house. Seated in the shade of a walnut tree, Gabrielle had a book on her lap. She'd yet to read a single word. Her mind crowded with thoughts, it was difficult to focus on the sonnets.

She was leaving tonight.

Everything was packed. Right after the Basset game, she'd be on her way to her uncle's château, where members of the King's Guard would find her two days hence to escort her back to the palace.

The last few nights with Mathias had been bittersweet.

She didn't want to leave him. But what choice did she have? She was the King's daughter. A princess trapped in a gilded prison, she had to return to Versailles. Return to her role and accept the husband her father selected for her.

Around Mathias she was a different person than she was at court. With him, it was easy to be light. To laugh. It was difficult to be distant with him when all she wanted was to draw near.

She'd never lacked strength in her life. She'd relied on her strength to make it through all these years. But she didn't possess enough to say good-bye. Not to his beloved face. For that reason, she hadn't told him she was leaving tonight instead of tomorrow, as he believed. She'd already completed her note and would leave it with the majordomo for him.

"There you are." Mathias's voice grabbed her attention.

Joy welled up inside her the moment she saw him walking down the cobblestone path toward her. The light breeze caressed his long dark hair, and his light gray justacorps not only accentuated his broad shoulders, but was a perfect match with those knee-weakening, beautiful eyes.

Her nerve endings sparked to life.

Smiling, he sat down beside her on the stone bench, slipped a hand onto the nape of her neck, and pulled her close for a kiss. Long and luscious and languorous. It was heaven.

He was heaven. Behind her closed eyes, she felt the sting of tears. In the years to come, would he remember her still and think of her from time to time? Or would she fade in his memory?

"I brought you something," he said, smiling.

His smile was contagious. "Oh?"

Reaching inside his justacorps, Mathias pulled out a pink satin box, a little smaller than his palm.

Surprised, she took it from his hands, placed it on her lap, and lifted the pretty lid.

Her eyes immediately filled with fresh tears. She fought them back.

Inside was a small leather-bound volume with the name SILVIE on the cover. Pulling the small book out of the box, she held it in her hands. She was so moved, she couldn't speak.

"It's a book of poetry. I saw it at the bookseller and had the cover custom made," he explained. "Do you like it?"

She nodded, and put her arms around him, her throat tight with emotion. "I'll cherish it always. I'll think of you each time I read it," she said near his ear.

Grasping her wrists, he removed her arms from around his neck and held her hands. "I've been thinking, Silvie. I'd like to speak to your father."

Her brows shot up. "Speak to *my* father? Why?"

He gently squeezed her hands. "Since he is looking for potential husbands for you, I'd like him to consider me."

Her heart lost a beat. Hope surged inside her. She had to tamp it down. "My father isn't exactly an easy man to speak to. He—He may have made his decision. If that is so, he isn't one to change his mind." Dear God, this was the first time Mathias had ever discussed the future—with her in it.

"I can be persuasive, Silvie."

Her mind was spinning. Could it work? Might it actually happen?

Dare she wish for it? No, she wasn't going to wish for it. Her father was unpredictable. With the brood of children His Majesty had sired, he usually gave his daughters in marriage to those he favored at court. Like gifts. The probability of the King being amiable to the idea of marrying her to a man who had a reputation for vice was slim. It mattered little that the King himself was vice-ridden. His Majesty rarely saw the irony in things.

"I have to think . . ." she said. "My father isn't easily dealt with . . ."

"I want to marry you, Silvie."

"Why? You don't know me."

"Yes, I do. I know that beneath that hard exterior is a woman who is tender and kind and beautiful from the inside out. She makes me smile. She makes me happy." He nuzzled her neck. "She makes me so damned hard." His warm breath tickled her neck and sent a delightful shiver through her. He lifted his head and looked into her eyes.

"I love you, Silvie."

She grabbed his justacorps and kissed him hard, afraid the same words would slip past her lips. Words she couldn't say. It would shatter her, knowing he couldn't be hers. Knowing her father wouldn't agree. Why pick Mathias when there were scores of men who followed the King around each and every day at the palace whom he knew and liked and wanted to reward?

Mathias's words only weighted her heart more.

"I have to go," he said when he broke the kiss. "We'll discuss this matter later." He rose. "There is one more thing, Silvie. Under no circumstances are you going to Navers's Hôtel tonight. I've left a purse with your majordomo. It is the balance of the debt. You are going to take it and forget Basset. There is going to be trouble, and you're not getting involved in it."

Gabrielle set down the items on her lap on the bench and stood. "What do you mean, 'trouble'?" When he paused, she added, "Either you tell me what you mean, or I am going."

He sighed. "Silvie, if I trust you enough to be my wife, and that is what you are going to be regardless, then you need to know there is a chance that there may be a raid tonight by the Paris Police. The King wants his ban on Basset taken seriously."

Gabrielle's pulse began to race. "You're involved? You are helping the Police?"

"Yes, and as committed to it as I am, I'll not hold my tongue about the raid and place you in harm's way."

A most extraordinary plan took shape in her mind. The best one she'd ever devised.

A life-altering plan.

* * *

Mathias smiled on his way from Navers's Hôtel to Silvie's town house. Slumped back in the moving carriage, he felt weary, but happy, and most of all, relieved.

It was over.

And he'd been right.

Two hours into the evening, thirty men from the Paris police, including Sard, burst into Navers's home and arrested the Duc, his nephew, and all the players in attendance.

But not Silvie. For once she'd actually heeded his advice. And he was thrilled she wasn't caught. He couldn't wait to see her. To make love to her.

To make plans on broaching her father. Just how difficult could the man be? Whatever he was like, whoever he was, Mathias would get his way.

Silvie would be his. She loved him. He knew it. He knew in time, she'd come to verbally express the emotion that was in her eyes each time she looked at him.

The carriage pulled up to the town house. He alighted with a bounce in his step. His heart raced, now that he was so close to her.

He couldn't wait to share the details of the night. Describe the look of outrage on the Duc's face. There were enough men of quality there that the sweeping arrest, with a *Lettre de Cachet* for each man Mathias had named, would rock the aristocracy and make them take heed.

The King was deadly serious.

There would be no more Basset.

Mathias stopped before the door to the town house. He looked up at the night sky. It was punctured with a million twinkling lights. "Rest in peace, Charles," he said, then knocked on the door.

As usual, the majordomo answered. "Good evening, my lord."

Mathias stepped inside. "Good evening." He proceeded to cross the vestibule. Because he was there every day, he simply showed himself to Silvie's private apartments.

"My lord, the mademoiselle is not here."

Mathias arrested his steps. "What do you mean, not here?" Silvie never left the town house, except in disguise to play Basset.

"She left, my lord. She took her party and her trunks and departed this afternoon."

Mathias's stomach plummeted. He turned and raced up the stairs, down the hall, and burst into Silvie's rooms. He stopped short in Silvie's bedchamber.

It was empty.

He threw open the doors of the armoires. They were empty, too. He slid his hand beneath her mattress. No diamonds there.

No anything.

Jésus-Christ, she was truly gone! He looked around the empty chamber, incredulous and in shock.

Mathias returned to the vestibule, moving slower down the stairs than he'd ascended them. His legs felt leaden, his insides cold and numb.

The majordomo waited patiently at the bottom.

"Did she leave me a note?" he asked. He hated the desperation in his voice, but at the moment, he didn't care.

"No, my lord."

"A message of some kind with you or perhaps another member of the staff?"

"Any message or note would be given to me, one way or the other. I'm afraid there is nothing, my lord."

"Where did she go?" he demanded, his frustration showing.

"I'm afraid I couldn't say, my lord."

"What is her name? How is she related to your master?"

"My apologies, my lord, but again, I couldn't say."

Wouldn't say was more accurate. But he couldn't blame the servant. Giving out information about one's employer or his houseguest would surely result in the man's dismissal.

Mathias felt as though someone had punched him in the stomach. He couldn't believe she'd left without saying good-bye. Or leaving a note.

He couldn't believe he'd misread her affections. *Fool. You proposed marriage and declared your love.* She neither accepted the former nor claimed the latter. She said she was leaving and she'd left.

Mathias moved to the door. The servant was there promptly to open it for him.

"One last question," Mathias said.

"Of course, my lord."

"The purse I gave you, the coin . . . Did you give that to the mademoiselle?"

"Yes, my lord. I handed it to her personally, just as you requested. She took the purse with her when she left."

Mathias stepped outside, reeling. The door closed softly behind him.

His love was rejected. But apparently his money was acceptable.

9

"You know, you should look happier, Montfort," Sard said, stepping down from the carriage after him. "You are at Versailles." He placed a hand on Mathias's shoulder. "Look at it. It's magnificent, beyond opulent. It is a fitting palace for the most powerful monarch in all of Christendom."

Mathias, having shared a carriage with the man from Paris to Versailles, thought nothing could be more annoying than his snoring. He thought wrong. Sard was annoying awake or asleep.

He followed the Lieutenant General of Police into the palace. The servants and guards knew him well, and Sard was left to walk through the corridors unchallenged.

"Can you tell me again why the hell we're here?" Mathias asked. He hated court, with all its ludicrous rules. It was hotter than Hades, and yet he was being forced to wear a periwig. It was the King's command that every man of quality wear one at court.

"The King wishes to speak to you. Probably about your

assistance with the arrests at Navers's gaming den. We caught nineteen that night. The only one we didn't get was the young man with the diamonds."

At the mention of Silvie, his insides tightened. It had been two weeks since he'd discovered her gone. Thanks to her, agony and anger accompanied him wherever he went. The last thing he felt like doing was having an audience with the King.

They stepped into the Hall of Mirrors, overcrowded with hundreds of courtiers. Curious looks were cast their way as he and Sard walked up the middle of the long corridor. His Majesty was easily spotted. Several carpeted steps higher than the throng before him, he stood in front of his solid silver throne.

Mathias and Sard bowed deeply before him.

"Your Majesty, this is the Marquis de Montfort," Sard said as he and Mathias straightened.

"Your Majesty," Mathias bowed again, unsure what else to do. The King surprised him by climbing down a few steps and stopping before him.

"Sard tells me you were invaluable in the arrests at Navers's home. He has sung your praises, and his own." King Louis gave his Lieutenant General a brief sidelong glance. "He has reminded me on more than a few occasions that he was the one to select you for the mission."

Sard simply smiled.

"I was quite impressed with what you did, Montfort," the King continued. "Sard tells me you didn't require any persuasion, and that you were eager to aid in enforcing my ban and worked diligently, demonstrating the utmost commitment to your mission."

Dieu, Sard had really played this up—for his benefit, so *he'd* look good.

"It was an honor to be of assistance, Your Majesty," Mathias said, hoping the audience with the King would end soon. There was no doubt about it; he had an intimidating quality about him. And Mathias was never one to be intimidated easily.

"Your efforts have abounded at the palace, Montfort. You even managed to impress one of my daughters. She thinks quite highly of your character. I find I share her opinion." The King smiled. "In light of that, I've decided to give you a reward."

"A reward, Your Majesty?"

"Yes, an honor bestowed upon you, by me."

"No reward is necessary, Sire."

"I disagree," the King announced with finality.

Clearly, there would be no debate over it. He was going to keep quiet, take his "reward," and leave. Soon, he hoped.

"I've decided to give you the hand of the very daughter you've impressed so much."

Mathias froze, as did his breathing. There was no way he had heard that correctly.

"You . . . wish me to marry your daughter, Your Majesty?" Praying there was some sort of misunderstanding.

"Yes, you're not married and it is *an honor*," the King stressed again, sounding irked that Mathias was not ecstatic over this madness. *Merde.*

He felt as though he'd stepped into some sort of bad dream. He was being strong-armed into a marriage.

Sard placed a hand on Mathias's shoulder again. "Of course, the Marquis de Montfort knows that, Sire. He's simply over-whelmed by your generosity, aren't you?" Sard squeezed his shoulder.

Mathias cleared his throat. "Yes, this is definitely a surprise, Sire."

King Louis gave a nod. "It is understandable that you are astounded. It isn't every day a man is offered a princess as a bride. I feel your marriage to my daughter would further demonstrate my disdain and intolerance for Basset. I have awarded the man who helped in enforcing the ban one of my own daughters."

Merde.

"I'm sure you're eager to meet your future bride, Montfort." The King glanced about.

About as eager as he would be to sever a limb. He'd been a devoted bachelor. He'd only ever met one woman whom he'd wanted to marry, and she had disappeared.

"Where is Princess Gabrielle?" the King snapped at those around him. Perfect. The man wasn't in one of his more genial moods today.

Mathias simply had to get out of this ludicrous situation. Under no circumstances was he marrying "Princess Gabrielle."

"Here I am, Sire." A too-familiar voice snagged his attention.

There was Silvie, elegantly curtsying before the King. Holding her gown, she ascended the steps, and stopped beside him.

Mathias stood there, mouth agape, barely breathing. *Mother of God, she's a princess.*

Sard slapped his arm. He shot him a look. It was then he noticed Sard and the entire throng in the Hall of Mirrors were in a deep curtsy or bow.

Quickly, Mathias bowed before the King's daughter. *Merde.* He'd deflowered the King's daughter. A princess. Princess Gabrielle. He'd deflowered a princess. The King's own daughter. He'd had her numerous times in various ways. He'd thoroughly debauched her.

And seeing her again, his eyes drinking in her beauty, he felt his cock stir.

Excellent, Mathias. If the King finds out what you did with his daughter, you are a dead man.

"You may rise, sir," she said to him.

He straightened. Her expression schooled, she was standing two steps above him, her hands folded in front of her.

She'd put him through two weeks of hell, thinking she'd not had any affection for him. Clearly, she'd been behind this "reward" of his.

He couldn't be more overjoyed.

Just being this close to her made his heart ache. He wanted nothing more than to touch her, pull her into his arms, but the King and his entire court were watching.

"It is a pleasure to meet you, sir." She held out her hand.

Eager, he took it and pressed a kiss to her knuckle. "The pleasure is all mine, Princess." Mathias turned to the King. "Your daughter is beautiful, Sire. I am delighted to have her hand in marriage."

He gave a nod then descended the steps. "It's too warm in here," he complained and headed to the gardens, the court following behind.

When the crowd had moved away, his princess spoke again. Her eyes softened, the love he'd seen on oh so many days and nights reflected in their depths. "I know you are angry with me, Mathias. Please understand, I couldn't leave you a note telling you how much I love you. How much I wanted to accept your marriage proposal—until I made certain I was able to convince the King that he should reward you with me. It is something my father often does—gives his daughters away in marriage as gifts or rewards. I swear that from now on, there will be no more secrets between us."

Mischief twinkled in her dark eyes. "You know, I've been told I should be honest with my future husband. That I shouldn't try to trick him on our wedding night. I think it's only right that I inform you, I'm not a virgin."

His lips twitched as he fought back a smile. "We have something in common. Neither am I."

"I also want you to know I have a difficult time sleeping at night. Especially if there is something hard in my bed."

Mathias couldn't hold back his smile. "That's understandable. I've heard that beautiful princesses are very sensitive that way. I fear I may exacerbate the problem, Princess."

"Princess of snow?" she gently teased.

"Princess of my heart. Princess that I love. The only Princess for me."

"And will you ride off with her, taking her from this palace, and bring her to your castle?"

"Indeed." He took her hand and placed it over his heart. "I will bring her to my kingdom, the one we create with our very own magic, where I shall cherish and love her—ever after."

A promise Mathias sealed with a searing kiss.

Glossary

Antechamber—The sitting room in a lord's or lady's private apartments (chambers).

Basset—A card game banned by the King and played by the wealthy. It brought about the ruin of many people of quality.

Caleçons—Drawers/underwear.

Chambers—Another word for private apartments. A lord or lady's chambers consisted of a bedroom, a sitting room, a bathroom, and a cabinet (office). Some chambers were bigger and more elaborate than others. Some cabinets were so large, they were used for private meetings.

Chère—Dear one. A term of endearment for a woman (*cher* for a man).

Chérie—Darling or cherished one. A term of endearment for a woman (*chéri* for a man).

Couch—A term in the card game Basset. It's the first bet placed on any given card. Once a player wins his or her *couch*, they can either accept payment or let their money lie and go for a greater stakes, like a *sept-et-le-va*—seven times the original bet.

Dieu—God.

Justacorps—A man's fitted knee-length coat, worn over his vest and breeches.

Hôtel—A mansion located in the city. Members of the upper class and the wealthy bourgeois (middle class) often had a hôtel in Paris in addition to a palatial country estate (*château*).

Lettre de Cachet—Orders/letters of confinement—without trial—signed by the King with the royal seal (*cachet*).

Ma belle—My beauty. Endearment for a woman.

Merde—Shit.

Salle—Room.

Salle de Bain—Bathroom. A small room located in one's private apartments in either a château or hôtel. The room usually had a fireplace, a tub, and a toilet (that looked like a chair with a chamber pot). The room was small on purpose so that the fire from the fireplace would keep the space warm while one bathed.

Seigneur Dieu—Lord God.